P9-BIV-410

FICTION

LAND WITHOUT EVIL

To My Cuz, With love —
This book reminds us
that no matter what, we
always have our dreams — and
our dreams — and
we're even more fortunate —
we have each other!
Love,
Barbara

LAND WITHOUT EVIL

A Novel by
MATTHEW J. PALLAMARY

CHARLES PUBLISHING • LOS ANGELES

Land Without Evil

© 1999 by Matthew J. Pallamary

First Edition January 1, 2000

All rights reserved. No part of this book may be reproduced in any manner whatsoever without written permission except in the case of brief quotations embodied in critical articles and reviews.

Send all inquiries to:
CHARLES PUBLISHING COMPANY, INC.
1302 STEWART STREET
OCEANSIDE, CA 92054

Library of Congress Cataloging-in-Publication Data
  Pallamary, Matthew J.
  Land without evil / by Matthew J. Pallamary—1st ed.
       p.   cm.
  ISBN 0-912880-09-0 (hardcover: alk. paper)
  1. Guarani Indians—Missions—Paraguay—History—18th century
  Fiction. 2. Jesuits—Missions—Paraguay—History—18th century
  Fiction. 3. Shamanism—Paraguay—History—18th century
  Fiction. I. Title
  PS3566.A4635L36   2000
  813'.54—dc21   99-33503

Book Jacket and Page Design: Kara Meredith/Oceanside, CA
Author's Photograph: Gerry Williams/San Diego, CA

Printed in the United States of America on acid-free paper

This book is dedicated to Ashley Butler Geist,
Gene Warren, Paul Lazarus, Audrey Bartram, Joseph
Pallamary, Alfonso Perez, Jan Stebel, Maurice Smiddy,
and Terence McKenna.

Thank you for enriching my life with your presence.
Looking forward to dancing with you again in the next one.

Author's Note

This work of fiction is based on true events, extensively researched. Every effort was made to keep the narrative within the proper cultural context. Any of the author's omissions, mistakes, historical or cultural inaccuracies, or errors are in no way a reflection on the professionals whose work inspired the story.

The situations referred to herein dramatize timeless human truths that cross social, racial, cultural, and historical lines. The fears, concerns, injustices, and patterns of human behavior that we acted out a quarter of a millennium ago carry the same immediacy and consequences today.

Forest Names (re'ra kaa'güy)

Avá-Katú-Eté	The true men, what the Guarani call themselves
Avá-Tapé	Man who is the messenger bird of Tupá
Avá-Nembiará	Avá-Tapé's father, paí of the people—Man who plays or jokes
Kuñá-Mainó	Avá-Tapé's love—Woman who is the sacred hummingbird, messenger of the sun
Kuñá-Ywy Verá	Avá-Tapé's mother—Woman of the shining earth
Pindé	Avá-Tapé's little sister
Avá-Guiracambí	Kuñá-Mainó's father
Avá-Canindé	Big man saved by Avá-Nembiará who becomes chief
Santo	Avá-Canindé's oldest son
Rico	Avá-Canindé's youngest son
Avá-Karaí	Avá-Tapé's best friend—Man who is a master
Avá-Takuá	Man who is bamboo, the weakest in character

Jesuits

Father Antonio	Head priest
Father Lorenzo	Priest
Father Rodrigo	Priest
Bishop Cristobal	Jesuit bishop

Glossary

añag	Jaguar, mythical and otherwise, usually malign
ará-kañí	The fleeing of the light
chicha	Ceremonial drink
kandire	When a man is becoming kandire, flames spring from his chest as evidence that his heart is illuminated by divine wisdom
kuruzú	Feathered cross
mbaraká	Dance rattles
nanderú	Our Father
paí	The solitary one who lives on the threshold between the world above and the world below, midway between man and the gods
paí guazú	Great shamans—Christ was identified with this
takuapú	Rhythm sticks, used only by women
techó achy	The base passions and evil appetites of humans; imperfections; animal soul
yasaa	A sacred feathered sash presented at a shaman's initiation
yoasá	A dance that crosses one thing with another
Ywy Mará Ey	Land Without Evil

*T*hroughout the world there is certainly no people or tribe to whom the biblical phrase: "My kingdom is not of this world" is more applicable. The entire mental universe of the Guarani revolves round the concept of the beyond. — Egon Schaden

Your Holiness,

*I am writing to you with great urgency, in this year
of Our Lord, seventeen hundred and fifty-eight, from the
southern continent of the Americas, somewhere in the province
of La Plata, two weeks' march from the great Mission of San
Miguel. I fear that matters here at the far reaches of your
light on earth are in danger of slipping out of control.*

*It was from the San Miguel Mission that we set forth with
open hearts to carry God's Word to these savages. But as
Your Holiness has doubtless heard, we encountered resistance
to the teachings of Our Lord from a shaman by the name of
Avá-Nembiará, whom I fear is possessed by minions of Satan.*

*Most of the Indians here are content to participate in
ritual dances while listening to the exhortations of this man
who abandons himself to fits of demonic possession. He is the
only one who has not, and will not, come to the mission to
learn and witness the Word of God. He is the only one who
has rejected the Word of Our Lord Jesus outright.*

*His resistance to the Word carries the force of his conviction
that the fate of his people is bound to the promise of their
old gods; that they will receive signs pointing the way to an*

eternal land beyond the terror of the sea, a place that they call the Land Without Evil.

My only hope for their salvation lies in saving the soul of the possessed man's only son, Avá-Tapé. Though he is only sixteen, his people look to him out of respect for his father's position. He has a quick mind that questions everything, and he learns faster than any man I have ever seen in the seminary. Such a thirst for knowledge!

If I can gather him into the fold of the priesthood, I may ensure the safety of his people. If I cannot, I fear for the loss of his pagan soul, and his degeneracy back to the animal and demonic ways from which I have worked so hard to rescue him. If I win his heart, I am confident I will also win the hearts of his people, and in winning their hearts, I will save their souls.

To date, the missions have provided a refuge for the Indians against the worst depredations of the Spanish and Portuguese settlers, but I fear that the settlers may enslave the Guarani. For weeks I have heard rumors of hostile tribes in this part of your dominion and have great fear that they may be led by mercenaries working in the interests of the settlers. Many lives and souls will be lost if the Guarani are not under the protection of the Church and the mission.

Please advise me, Your Holiness. I fear I am losing my grasp on their wild and untamed souls.

Your humble servant,
Father Antonio Rodriguez Escobar

ONE

Avá-Tapé gazed up at the crescent moon looming high above. He felt the weight of the humid rain forest air hanging thick and still, and the presence of the trees pressing in on him. Firelight flickered at the edge of the clearing, darkened from time to time by the formless shadows of the dancers, led by his father.

Rattles shook and a new round of chants rose into the starlit sky as each syllable took wing and fluttered through the darkness like the cry of night birds.

Like Avá-Tapé, most of the tribe huddled around the fire watching the men dressed in feathered headdresses, armbands, and anklets dance as one. Their movements kept a rhythm that gave meaning to the unseen forces between the beats of time.

Avá-Tapé's round face made him look younger than his sixteen harvests, but his dark, almond-shaped eyes missed nothing. He sat straight and alert, his long arms and legs coiled, ready to spring into the dance with the others.

While watching the pageantry unfold, Avá-Tapé pondered what his father had taught him.

Chaos.

Order.

Destruction.

Concepts that brought fear to the white man's view of life, but were beautiful, wondrous, and harmonious in his father's world.

He sighed, remembering how important he had felt helping the Christian priests with their sacraments. His chest grew tight, hurting him, as the two realities fought for possession of his heart.

By the force of his visions, his father, Avá-Nembiará, had become the most powerful holy man of their people. Most of them now called him Nandérú, "our father." In front of the whites they called him *paí*, the solitary one who lives between man and the gods. Some whispered that Tupá, the son of gods, spoke through Avá-Nembiará.

Two men tossed another log on the fire, showering the night in a flurry of shimmering sparks. The tempo of the chants increased and the dancers quickened their pace. Flames jumped higher.

Avá-Nembiará's voice rose above the rest, its tone full of yearning. Avá-Tapé shivered and watched his father's dance become erratic. Avá-Nembiará's movements grew larger and wider, until he threw his whole being open like the wings of a butterfly embracing the sky. A moment later, his steps grew fitful and jerky as he dance-staggered out of step with the others, keeping a rhythm only he could hear.

The chants and dances of the others faded until Avá-Nembiará remained alone clutching a feathered rattle, swaying before the fire, his handsome angular face impassive, short black hair flattened against his sweaty forehead.

Fire glow highlighted the brilliant colored feathers of his headband, reminding Avá-Tapé of the lights above the heads of the Christian saints in the pictures the whites had shown him. Light from the orange flames caressed the sweaty sheen of his father's muscled form as if infusing it with new life. Swirling patterns washed over Avá-Nembiará's dark features, illuminating his glazed eyes and changing expression.

Avá-Nembiará sank to the ground and tilted sideways, then straightened as though pulled upright by the head. His normally sharp eyes became unreadable hollows that glinted in the flickering light. Other than the fire's crackle, the clearing remained silent and still. No wind. No bird or animal cries. No sound from the awestruck tribe.

Avá-Tapé held his breath, expecting flames to burst from his father's chest, until Avá-Nembiará spoke. His words and voice were those of another.

"The time of destruction has returned. The Earth is old. Your tribe is no longer growing. Your world is bloated with death and decay. I have heard the Earth cry out to our Creator Father. 'Father,' it says, 'I have devoured too many bodies; I am stuffed and tired; put an end to my suffering.'"

"Tupá," someone whispered.

"The weight of your faults has made your souls heavy and holds you from magic flight. You eat the food of the whites and live their ways, not the ways of your ancestors. The growing weight of your faults has brought you to the end of the world through the fleeing of the light. The bulk of your errors will soon block it. The sun will disappear and there will be nothing for you to do on this Earth. This will be the moment of the *ará-kañí*. This will be your last day. The last time that you shall see this world."

Spiraling patterns from the fire accented Avá-Nembiará's features as he spoke. Sometimes the calm face of Tupá and the sweep of his grand language dominated; other times the tenseness of an all too human expression came back amidst strange words. Avá-Tapé looked around at the faces of the people. Some showed the same intensity, some fear, others concern. The older men's expressions revealed acceptance.

"You do not have to fall to the crushing weight of *techó-achy*," Avá-Nembiará continued. "You can free yourself from the weight of your faults, lighten your bodies, and reach perfection by abandoning the food and the ways of the whites. You must journey to where you can dance until your bodies rise above the earth and fly across the great primeval sea to the Land Without Evil."

A murmur rose from the crowd.

"*Ywy Mará Ey*, a paradise of abundance and wealth. True immortality awaits you there. You do not have to die to enter. It is a real world that lies in the place where the sun rises. Only dancing believers dwell there. To find paradise you must..."

The clearing came alive with the soft rustling of robes fluttering like the wings of bats as Father Antonio rushed forward brandishing a cross, followed by a mob of black-robed Jesuits. "I exorcise you, Most Unclean Spirit!" he bellowed, dark eyes blazing. "Invading enemy! In the name of Our Lord Jesus Christ."

He made the sign of the cross, causing the people to scatter into the forest. Avá-Nembiará looked up at the priests, his expression dazed and unfocused.

"Be uprooted and expelled from this creature of God." Father Antonio's hands moved deftly as he made the sign of the cross again. "He who commands you is He who ordered you to be thrown down from the highest Heaven into the depths of Hell. He who commands you is He who dominated the sea, the wind, and the storms. Hear, therefore, and fear, Satan! Enemy of faith! Enemy of the human race! Source of death! Robber of life! Root of evil and seducer of men!"

Satan? Confusion swept through Avá-Tapé. Tupá spoke through his father. Not Satan!

Avá-Nembiará shook his head and glared at the Jesuits. His features hardened. He rose, standing tall in the firelight, his headdress backlit by flames. His shiny skin glowed orange as if holding a life of its own, in stark contrast to the dark formless robes of the priests that seemed to swallow light. His father looked every part the Holy Man. Avá-Tapé felt a surge of pride swell in his chest.

One of the priests looked over, his glare pinning Avá-Tapé. "Begone!" the man shouted.

Avá-Tapé didn't move. Father Antonio started speaking Latin and making elaborate movements around Avá-Nembiará while Father Lorenzo sprinkled him with holy water. Avá-Tapé stood on trembling legs, wanting to run, but willing himself to stay.

When the priest started toward him, Avá-Tapé ran to his father's side. Father Antonio continued his rituals and Latin chants while thrusting the cross at Avá-Tapé and his father. Avá-Nembiará put his arm around his son, grunted, and pushed his way through the black robes. The priests let out astonished gasps, and Father Antonio stopped his invocations.

Avá-Tapé walked into the darkened forest at his father's side, leaving the muttering priests alone in the clearing.

TWO

Avá-Tapé lay on his jaguar skin in the darkness of the adobe house, envious of the soft breathing of his mother and sister that spoke of deep sleep. Unable to still his thoughts, he closed his eyes and let them drift back to the day he had first seen Father Antonio eight harvests ago.

After many days of rain, this one had dawned warm and lazy. The moist air smelled fresh. Most of the men had gone hunting, leaving behind the old men, women not busy with gardening, children, and Avá-Takuá—a man as fit and strong as their best hunter, but who often complained of sickness before a hunt. The only reason the men allowed this was because Avá-Takuá was a poor hunter whose loud mouth and foul temper scared off more game than the roar of a jaguar. His health always improved when the men came back with fresh game.

After sleeping half the day, Avá-Takuá would come from his house and order the women to bring him food and drink while yelling at the children to get out of a warrior's way, or he would show them how a deer felt when a jaguar brought it down. Avá-Tapé always kept far away, never giving Avá-Takuá an opportunity to yell at him.

Today, some of the older boys decided they wouldn't let Avá-Takuá sleep the morning away. Not wanting to miss the fun, Avá-Tapé hid in the bushes with his best friend, Avá-Karaí, who was a few harvests older. Neither of them took part in the mischief, but they couldn't keep themselves from watching the fun from a hiding place.

The older boys had gone on a hunt of their own, catching two spider monkeys and four macaws. Holding mouths and beaks shut, they crept up to Avá-Takuá's *maloca* and tossed the animals through the door. A flurry of beating wings, cries, and screeches filled the house as the boys scattered into the jungle.

After a cacophony of screams, both human and animal, the monkeys scampered out the door, followed by fluttering birds and a scowling Avá-Takuá, who stumbled outside, blinking in the daylight. He stood short and wiry, hair sticking up in tufts, a bewildered expression on his face. His too-close eyes narrowed and scanned the clearing.

Avá-Takuá rubbed his eyes with the balls of his fists and frowned, blinking like a monkey. No sounds came from the trees except the calling of birds. He half-turned back toward his house when a voice called out.

"His eyes are too close together."

Avá-Takuá whirled, rage tightening his already angry features. "Who's there?"

"He looks like a monkey's face on a man's head," another said from behind the *maloca*. Avá-Takuá turned again.

"Monkey face," the first voice said.

Avá-Takuá's shoulders hunched as he paced back and forth in front of his house like an angry cat. "I know who you are," he bellowed, shaking his fist. "If I get my hands on you, I'll whip your bottom with a wet hide!"

"Monkey face!" a third voice called, then the others joined in the chorus. "Monkey face! Monkey face!"

Avá-Takuá stormed toward the *maloca* until a giggle slipped from Avá-Karaí. Avá-Tapé held his breath when Avá-Takuá's head swiveled and his glare came to rest on their hiding spot.

"Run!" Avá-Tapé screamed, stumbling from the bush and sprinting for the trees. He heard what sounded like a growl, but didn't look back. Something crashed in the bushes behind him, followed by his friend Avá-Karaí's terrified yelp.

Looking back, he saw Avá-Takuá drag his best friend from the brush, kicking and screaming. Turning forward, Avá-Tapé ran into something soft and black that sent him sprawling to the ground.

"Whoa, slow down there, little one," a voice with a strange accent said. Avá-Tapé recognized the language as Guaraní, but it sounded different from any speaker he had ever heard. He looked down at strange foot coverings, then at black cloth that went up to a face so white, his heart jumped. A spirit! He scrambled backward, almost bumping into Avá-Takuá.

"I won't hurt you," the black cloth said, his voice soothing, then deeper as he stood taller and squared his wide shoulders. "And I won't see anyone else harmed, either."

Avá-Takuá let Avá-Karaí go and stepped back, mouth open, eyes wide. Avá-Karaí scrambled into the jungle, taking safety behind a tree.

"I am Father Antonio and I come in peace," the man in the black cloth said, bowing his head and holding his palms out. "I am a priest and a humble servant of Our Lord Jesus."

Avá-Tapé sat up breathing deeply, trying to slow his racing heart. The white man had soft brown eyes, short dark curly hair, and a flat nose. The warmth in his eyes and the softness of his voice diminished the shock of his white face, but still...

"Who are you and what do you want?" Avá-Takuá growled. "How do you know our tongue?"

"There are many of your people all over this part of the world," Father Antonio said. "Most speak as you do." He held up what looked like a thick animal hide. "I have come to share the Good Book with you and the Gospel of Our Lord Jesus Christ, with the hope that you will accept Him into your heart."

Avá-Tapé inched backward. He remembered watching hunters take out a deer's heart and eat it. He had never heard of a book, a Gospel, or a Jesus Christ, but the thought of a man getting inside his heart made him squeamish. Maybe the white man was a spirit. He put his hand over his chest. He wasn't letting any man get inside his heart.

Avá-Takuá backed away. "These words have no meaning to me."

"I understand that," Father Antonio said. "It will take time. For now, know that I bring only good will." He reached into a bag at his side and pulled out a handful of shiny colored beads. "Take these." He held them out.

Avá-Takuá stopped his retreat. His eyes narrowed to slits. "I have nothing to trade," he said quickly.

"They are a gift."

"You want nothing?"

"Only that you listen to what I have to say."

A gamut of expressions passed over Avá-Takuá's face before he tentatively stepped forward to accept the proffered beads. "I only have to listen and you will give me this gift?" he asked as if not believing what he had heard.

Father Antonio winked at Avá-Tapé. "And a promise that you will leave the little ones alone."

Avá-Takuá smiled sheepishly. "It was only a game." He took the beads.

Only a game, Avá-Tapé thought, opening his eyes to the darkness of the adobe house. His mother and sister still slept soundly. No sound came from outside. He rolled onto his back, remembering Father Antonio's big brown eyes and the kindness he had shown that day. So different from the harsh voice and angry glares of this past night. How could so many things have changed?

He closed his eyes again. From those first frightening moments when he heard those terrifying words, Avá-Tapé never thought he would open his heart to Jesus, but Father Antonio's soft-spoken patience and the conviction behind his soft brown eyes had been reassuring.

The far-off cry of a monkey made Ava-Tapé open his eyes again. He wanted to sleep, but his mind would not slow down. How had things come to this? His thoughts went to a long-ago day when he had been sitting with Avá-Karaí and the other children in a circle in Father Antonio's house, learning to read from the New Testament.

"How will I know I have accepted Him in my heart?" Avá-Tapé asked. "Will He speak to me? Show me?"

"Know the truth and it will set you free," Avá-Karaí said.

Father Antonio smiled. "Very good, Avá-Karaí!"

Avá-Tapé scowled at his friend when the priest turned away.

"You are a special child in the eyes of the Lord," Father Antonio said, patting Avá-Tapé on the head. "If you study the Good Book the way Avá-Karaí has, you will know soon and you will know without a doubt."

"The words in the book will bring Jesus to me?"

"That is correct," Father Antonio said. "That is why you must all study the Bible. It is the Word of God."

Avá-Tapé spent every spare moment trying to read and understand chapter and verse, all the while watching, hoping, and waiting for Jesus to come into his heart. More than anything he wanted to be the first of his people to accept Jesus as his Lord and Savior.

The few times he tried to share this new knowledge with his father, Avá-Nembiará held his hand up and shook his head. "I have heard this all before. And still I do not believe. Jesus is a foreign god. Not a god of my fathers."

Now, after all his studying, Avá-Tapé felt more confused than ever. He had lived half his life learning the ways of his grandfathers and half learning the ways of the white man. Before the Jesuits came, the village had been small. The people hadn't gardened as much. The forest gave them everything they needed. The men hunted and fished while the women gathered fruits, nuts, berries, and roots. Life had been simple. The people had lived and worked together, all sharing the same beliefs.

Now they believed one way, then another. The only one who never changed was his father. At first Avá-Nembiará had listened in silence to the stories of Jesus that Father Antonio told. While most of the tribe embraced Father Antonio's teachings, Avá-Nembiará returned after much time alone in the forest, saying that he didn't believe what the Jesuits taught. He would continue living the old ways, worshipping the old gods, the ones his father and his father's father had known. By this time the people had left the village, built the earth houses, and had begun work on the huge house of God in which they sang. He remembered his father's scorn at the undertaking.

"Fools," Avá-Nembiará said. "So quick to throw away the only world we have ever known for a handful of beads. Now they break their backs to build a house for a god who does not speak. They only have to go to the forest to hear the voice of the Creator in the cries of the animals, the wind in the trees, and the song of the water. They only have to open their eyes to see His power in the flight of a bird and the strength and swiftness of a jaguar. The Creator does not live in houses built by man, He is in all things that live."

From the beginning, Avá-Nembiará refused to stay among the Jesuits. He lived in the forest the way he had before the whites changed the world. He allowed his family to live at the mission only because the rest of the tribe had moved there. For now it was safe for them, but more and more he spoke of the day when the people would return to their rightful place in the forest, while Father Antonio spoke more and more of the dangers of doing so.

"Father," Avá-Tapé said when he was alone with Avá-Nembiará one day. "Are you angry that I live with my mother in the mission?"

"I am angry with no one, my little man. We cannot be told what to believe. Each of us has to make our own choice and believe what is right for us. One day when you are becoming a man you will choose for yourself." Avá-Nembiará smiled and stroked his son's head. "I long for the time when your mother and I can pass the nights together again." He sighed. "Kuñá-Ywy Verá, my woman of the shining earth."

Avá-Tapé opened his eyes again to the darkness of the adobe house. He didn't want to think of these things anymore. He closed his eyes for the last time, letting his father's words follow him down into sleep.

He thought he had chosen when he accepted Father Antonio's teachings, but this past night had shown him differently. He had not yet made a choice, but the time to make one would be coming soon.

THREE

Avá-Tapé awoke blinking at the brightness. The shaft of sunlight coming through the tiny window in the adobe wall
hurt his eyes. He rubbed them, sat up, and stared at the softer
patch of yellow that shone on a small square of the hard dirt
floor. Even that hurt. He closed his eyes and felt a trickle of
sweat run down his bare back, soaking into his loincloth at his
waist. His headband was wet and his hair hung damp over his
ears. His skin felt warm.

Propping himself up on one hand, he looked around and
saw that his mother and sister had let him sleep. Without them
the house looked vacant. A few skins on the floor, two pots by
the hearth, a couple of scooped-out pumpkins they used for
mugs, and a small chest for clothes. Nothing more.

Reduction. Another name for the mission. That's what had
happened to his life and his world. The Jesuits taught him the
meaning of the word. He remembered the way the voice of
Tupá boomed through his father, adding to its meaning. "The
Earth is old; our tribe is no longer growing. Our world is
bloated with death and weary with decay."

Since the white men appeared, his people had been re-
duced by half. His father said that death had come to so many
because of the spirits of sicknesses that the white men had
brought to them.

Avá-Tapé rose from his jaguar skin and looked out the front
door to see more proof that Tupá's words were true. A line of
low, white-washed houses with sagging walls lined the dusty
street with roofs supported by wooden posts forming a continu-

ous veranda. Some houses had small windows shut with wooden grates. The rest had a single opening for a door. Their insides were as sparsely furnished as the one he shared with his mother and sister.

The air felt thick and hard to breathe. Though his skin felt hot, Avá-Tapé could feel the moisture. A wave of dizziness washed over him. He widened his stance, closed his eyes, and waited for the spell to pass.

After last night's spectacle he didn't know what to do. His mother and sister had already gone to work in the fields. He had lived through sixteen harvests and was too old to work with the women and children. He had to decide how best to benefit his people.

His father, Avá-Nembiará, stayed in the forest where he could purify himself through fasting and dancing. Away from the white men. He only came to the mission to heal the sick and visit his family. Avá-Tapé's mother, Kuñá-Ywy Verá, didn't like being apart from her husband, but she had resigned herself for now.

The rest of the people clung to life in the mission, torn between their devotion to their Lord Jesus and the mystical ways of the *paí*. None had believed that the end of the world was upon them until hearing the spirit of Tupá speak through his father. Avá-Tapé suspected that more of them, particularly the older ones, would soon abandon the mission and move back to the forest, closer to Avá-Nembiará.

He stepped out into the hot sun and headed toward the forest on the other side of the mission. Except for a few small children and older women, the streets looked empty. More of the now familiar anthills had appeared. Another house tottered on the edge of collapse from the water-filled burrows left by ants. Avá-Nembiará said that the nature spirits had come to take back the land stolen from the forest.

Passing rows of houses, Avá-Tapé peered in at their darkened interiors, seeing different versions of the same scant furnishings and various degrees of dilapidation.

He turned a corner, stumbled, and wiped sweat from his brow. His skin felt hot, his throat dry. He needed water. He looked up at the sun. Well past morning. Why had he slept so late? He waved away a large flying black ant that buzzed by his ear, then heard the familiar voices of the people rising up in song. He recognized the words.

Ave Maria.

He stopped and listened, picking out the sopranos of the younger children. Their voices never failed to move him. It seemed odd that they'd be singing on this day. A Mass? Were the Jesuits performing their rituals because they didn't want the people to stray from Jesus?

He tried to fathom the actions of Father Antonio and the other priests. Did they fear Tupá? The stories he'd been taught about Jesus the Son of God told of a kind man. The priests often asked for His help in the mission church that the people had built. They said the building helped them get closer to their God. Inside, they performed ritual after complex ritual, but their God remained silent.

When his father, Avá-Nembiará, fasted and danced to be nearer to his Creator, the spirit of Tupá, the son of gods answered, speaking through him, but the priests drove Tupá away, calling him Satan, an unclean spirit and invading enemy. Why did these men of God, spiritual men, fear the world of spirits?

He thought of the Bible story that told of the chosen ones who allowed their Savior to be nailed to a cross. Were they afraid that the spirit of Jesus would seek its revenge on the living?

He made his way along another row of houses, turned a corner, and saw the church in the square at the center of the mission. The singing drifted toward him on the thick midday air. From the sound of the voices, most of the people were there.

Sweat rolled down his forehead and burned his eyes as he drew closer. The rain-filled holes that the ants had made around the foundation had grown deeper. More ants swarmed by the corner, and the walls had new cracks that made them slant outward as if a strong wind had tried to blow them down. Both sides were propped up with rough-hewn cedar logs.

Avá-Tapé's breath came hard, feeling heavy in his chest. He stopped at the front of the church and gazed up at its facade. His people had sculpted Jesus and His disciples on the front and sides, but they had also concealed small details and symbols from the spirit world of their own ancestors. He smiled when he spotted the images of Nanderú Guazú and Nandé Cy peering out of the sky above Jesus.

Even here the two worlds collided.

The singing stopped and the voice of Father Antonio began droning in the strange tongue he called Latin. Avá-Tapé went to the massive wooden doors, pulled one open, and stepped into the shade of the interior. Most of the tribe crowded the pews. A life-sized wooden carving of the Lord Jesus hung at the back of the church, His hands and feet impaled on a cross.

Below it, Father Antonio stood behind the altar holding a gold chalice aloft in the air. Flickering candles behind him and to his sides glinted off the sacred gold utensils on the altar. The priest's dark curly hair had been cut short. His broad face and wide shoulders stood a head above most of the people. He looked even more imposing in the glow of the candles, his purple and gold robes flashing silk and gold filigree.

Out of habit, Avá-Tapé made the sign of the cross. He didn't want to risk offending any gods. Father Antonio's fiery eyes glared at him, then went back to the chalice. Avá-Tapé felt lightheaded again. His vision grew hazy. He thought of his father alone in the forest and felt a sudden urge to run, but something made him stay.

"In the name of the Father, the Son, and the Holy Ghost."

Father Antonio's voice boomed, jolting Avá-Tapé back to the moment. He heard a faint buzzing that grew louder. He looked behind him, then glanced up and saw ants swarming through the doors, windows, and cracks in the floor and walls. A low murmur passed among the people as flying ants filled the church.

Father Antonio raised his voice higher. "Holy Mary, Mother of God, pray for us sinners..."

The ants seemed attracted to candles and the altar in the same way that moths sacrificed themselves to fire. Father Antonio waved his arms as the swarm fell upon him, the sacred utensils, and the altar. He brushed at his face and beat at his arms and the altar. His robes flapped like some huge demented bird. The ants kept landing on his face, hair, and robes.

Screams cut through the air and the people ran for the doors. Father Antonio continued to flail, knocking the gold chalice from the altar, spilling red wine onto the floor. Avá-Tapé saw ants crawling on his own arms. He brushed them off as people rushed past him, out into the square. Watching Father Antonio thrash around at the altar brought sadness to his heart. He turned and let the flood of people carry him out of the church.

He made it to the street before his knees started to wobble. His legs felt as if they no longer connected to his body. He stumbled and fell. In his mind he heard the voices of the people buzzing like thousands of ants. He clamped his hands to his head and the sound rose in pitch until the words of the Ave Maria thundered through his mind.

Pulling himself up, Avá-Tapé staggered a few steps more and slowed. Dizziness rushed through him like a powerful wind, its vortex swallowing him in a haze of gray. His stomach writhed. He closed his eyes as his thoughts took flight, then leaned forward and lowered himself to the ground, listening to the final strains of the Ave Maria.

FOUR

The sound of his heartbeat pulsed through Avá-Tapé as he floated. Snatches of the Ave Maria flitted through his mind, mixed with cries both human and animal. He tried to focus on one sound, one thing, but his thoughts would not remain still. Instead they danced. Father Antonio. Tupá speaking through his father. Ants swarming in the church. His father dancing in the firelight, shaking his rattle...

The sound of the rattle rasped, first to the beat of his heart, then slower, languishing on each moment like the flight of a bee from flower to flower. The rhythm became a non-rhythm that splintered off on its own dissonant pulse, drawn out in longer echoes, blurring the pause between the beats until the sound became a oneness that held both unity and chaos.

No heat.

No cold.

No sensation.

Being and not being.

His heart swelled and his essence blossomed, rushing into the expanse like a flurry of sparks rising up to the heavens. He embraced blackness for an eternal moment outside of time, then had an awareness of his feet growing into the earth. His arms turned into branches, his fingers leaves, and the top of his head sprouted into a tree-top in full leaf. The voice of Tupá rose from the place where the sun sank below the edge of the earth.

"You are the chosen one among chosen people. These visions are the sign of the *paí*. You must abandon the evil land that you live in."

Images of the sickness and decay that came with the white men played across his mind. A horde of rats feasted on an infant's corpse. A man vomited worms. Maggots sprouted from the glazed eyes of a dead woman. Cries and anguished moans filled darkened nights as Avá-Tapé saw the deaths of many. Tupá's voice continued.

"Abandon this darkened land so your people can inherit the Land Without Evil and live in happiness. The old ways tremble at the roots of their beginnings and balance on the edge of destruction. The world must change. You must change worlds. Leave the imperfect world of men for that of the gods."

Tupá began to chant using words Avá-Tapé had never heard, yet their tone and content felt familiar. As the chant filled his mind, Avá-Tapé's visions changed from death to life.

Healthy children played in fields of *maize* and *manioc*. Brightly feathered men and women sang and danced amidst a great feast of beans, sweet potatoes, peppers, pineapples, game, and fish.

The wondrous scene brought joy to Avá-Tapé until his vision faded and the roar of jaguars rose from the place of the rising sun. The *añag*. Dread rushed through him like water over falls.

As if in answer to the challenge, Tupá's voice came to him from the place of the falling sun. A pack of jaguars charged from the horizon to his left. Tupá appeared from the right, tall and majestic, eyes clear like those of Jesus. A magnificent glowing headdress adorned his head. He held a bow in one hand and a spear in the other. Fierce yet wise. Warrior and hunter.

"Tupá," Avá-Tapé whispered.

The opposing forces hurtled toward each other, colliding in a shower of light, leaving the image of a feathered cross—the meeting place of time and space. The cross shook and danced to the rhythm of a chant which Avá-Tapé thought belonged to Tupá until he recognized the voice of his father. He stared at the moving cross and his father's face came into focus, full and shining like the moon. "You spoke the name of Tupá," his father said quietly. "When you return you must speak of your visions."

Avá-Nembiará wore a cotton sash plaited with feather ornaments, a bracelet made of the same materials, and a tiara of multicolored feathers. Holding the feathered cross in one hand and his rattle in the other, he gazed upward with outstretched arms and uttered something unintelligible, then he knelt next to Avá-Tapé and blew on his head, singing a gentle chant.

A chill rippled through Avá-Tapé and he became aware of his hot, sweat-soaked body. His stomach felt hollow, his joints ached, and his throat hurt. He licked dry lips, wanting something cool to drink. His words came in a scratchy whisper. "Water."

Avá-Nembiará propped his son's head in the crook of his arm and brought a gourd of cool water to his mouth. Avá-Tapé drank, letting the wetness trickle down his throat.

"Rest, my son. The spirits of darkness have crept into your body and tried to steal your soul. Stay with me and hear my voice. I will travel with you to the places near the land of the dead and guide you back to your body."

Where had he been? How long had he gone? How had he come here?

His eyes burned and his father's face blurred. Too much to think about. He closed his eyes, letting darkness swallow him.

He drifted like a leaf on the breeze, finally settling on the dark, dusty streets of the mission. A pair of glowing amber orbs blinked back at him from the darkness of a blackened doorway followed by a low growl. A jaguar trotted out carrying the limp form of a bloody infant in its massive jaws. A woman screamed and the jaguar ran *through* him, loping down the street where it met with dozens of other glowing orbs. Avá-Tapé heard hisses, growls, and a series of thumps followed by the sound of tearing flesh and crunching bone.

He turned to run and heard voices, and then the sun climbed from behind the forest. Looking back, he saw that the jaguars had vanished. He walked slowly toward the voices and the sunlight turned brighter, then smoke poured from the forest, washing out his sight.

He awoke to the smell of tobacco smoke. His heart fluttered like a hummingbird. His father leaned over him, blowing smoke across his body from a big cigar, moving from head to foot. Shaking his rattle, he chanted, blowing more smoke. Avá-Tapé felt stronger. Not so much pain. He tried to sit up and tell his father of the *añag*, but Avá-Nembiará silenced him with a gesture.

"Not yet, my son." He gently pushed Avá-Tapé down. "Wait until your strength is full before giving me your visions." He continued blowing smoke up and down the length of his son's body, then blew on the top of his head. Avá-Tapé drifted...

He saw the people gathered in the light of day at the fire circle where his father had danced. Women held babies in slings. Children ran freely. Men carried bows, spears, and blowguns. Pottery, digging sticks, tools, food, and other implements were piled high on top of a square of branches lashed together with long poles. Excitement filled the air.

"*Paí guazú*," someone whispered. "The great Holy Man."

A tall man appeared before the people wearing dazzling feathered bands on his head and arms. He held a huge feathered cross high above his head. The backs of his hands had scars. Avá-Tapé recognized his eyes from the pictures in the Christian Bible. Jesus now stood at the head of the people in the form of *Paí guazú*, making an expansive gesture with the cross before turning and walking into the forest. An excited murmur passed among the crowd, then they followed *Paí guazú*.

A cool breeze blew and the people disappeared. Avá-Tapé floated up out of the clearing until he found himself at his father's house lying in a hammock. Avá-Nembiará leaned over him making sucking noises near his chest and throat, then turned away and spit something onto the ground.

He faced his son again and smiled. "I have sucked out the evil. Be still and let your spirit become one with your body. After you have eaten and are stronger, you can tell me of your visions." Avá-Nembiará went to the other end of the house and knelt by the fireplace.

Avá-Tapé gazed around in wonder, recognizing the house his father had built. So different from the dreary earth houses of the mission. This roof had sloping sides held up by wood supports. The roof was made of straw, the frame of reeds.

He rubbed his hands on his chest and arms. His body no longer felt hot. The chills and sweats had passed. He felt hungry. Easing himself out of the hammock, Avá-Tapé stood on trembling legs. Fearing he might fall, he took a few steps and sat by the fireplace. Avá-Nembiará gave him some *cassava* bread, a gourd full of juice, and a tiny bowl of *maize* mash mixed with herbs.

Avá-Tapé could only eat a little, but what he did eat made him feel stronger. He felt Avá-Nembiará gaze upon him, looked up and saw a sparkle in his eyes, but his father didn't speak until his son finished eating and started asking questions.

"How long have I wandered through the land of spirits?"

"Since your spirit went away the moon has gone and come again. Another one of the white man's spirits of sickness has fallen on the people." Avá-Nembiará's eyes darkened. His voice sounded tired. "Many are sick and many have died. It tried to take you from this world, but I flew to the other world and brought your soul back. I heard you call the name of Tupá. Tell me what you saw."

Avá-Tapé closed his eyes and let his thoughts travel back, telling his father how he had scattered into the wind like ashes. Avá-Nembiará's eyes widened at the description, but he said nothing. Avá-Tapé told of becoming a tree and of how the voice of Tupá came to him from where the sun sank below the edge of the earth.

"What did Tupá say?" his father said. A faraway look filled his eyes.

"That my visions were a sign of the *paí* and that I was the chosen one among the chosen. He showed me the darkness that has come to our people and told me to leave this place and travel to the Land Without Evil. When he chanted I saw happy visions."

"Tupá chanted?"

Avá-Tapé tried to recall the song, remembering its tone and familiarity, but its content hovered just beyond his thoughts. "I'm sorry, Father, but I can't remember."

Disappointment showed on Avá-Nembiará's face.

"Then the *añag* came and battled with Tupá," Avá-Tapé continued, "leaving behind a vision of you and the cross. I flew again and saw the jaguars in the mission stealing and eating a baby. I came back and flew to the place where Tupá spoke through you and saw the people gathered. *Paí guazú* was there wearing a beautiful headband. He held a huge cross high above his head and led the people into the forest. His eyes reminded me of Jesus in the Christian Bible."

Avá-Nembiará's eyes glazed over. His features never changed, but a succession of emotions passed behind his eyes before his gaze came back into focus, clear and piercing. A slow smile filled his usually serious features. Avá-Tapé had never seen his father act so strange.

"What is it, *paí*? What makes you act this way?"

Avá-Nembiará's face became serious again. "Did you not hear the words of Tupá?"

"The words of Tupá?"

He smiled again. "It has been many seasons since I have heard of such powerful visions. I never would have thought that my son—many would die to see what you have seen. You are a chosen one among a chosen people. The visions he has given you are the sign of a *paí*."

"A *paí*?"

"With visions as powerful as these, you might be the one spoken of who is to become the *Paí guazú* of the people. The great Holy Man."

FIVE

Outside the forest had turned black. The cheep of crickets and the sporadic bellows of howler monkeys filled the night air. Avá-Nembiará crouched in front of the fireplace adding herbs and vegetables to a pot. After putting more wood on the fire, he sat cross-legged in front of it. Avá-Tapé sat beside him gazing into the flames.

His father stared straight ahead, the light from the fire illuminating his face. "In the time of *inypyrú,* the beginning," he said, sounding far away, "the Creator Nánderuvusú lived alone in the middle of darkness where he kept vigil. Bats fought in the blackness. The Creator bore a light in his breast."

Avá-Tapé smiled. He had heard this story countless times, but never tired of it. His father never tired of telling it.

Avá-Nembiará picked up his cross and held it up. "He set in place a beam of wood running from where the sun climbs into the sky to the place where it falls when darkness comes." He ran his finger along the width of the cross, then down its length. "He placed another beam across the first, pointing toward the bright star of the night and made the eternal cross that supports the world." He waved his hand in circles. "Standing at its center, he made the Earth on top of it.

"The Creator had a companion named Nanderú Mbaekuaá, 'our great father who knows all things.' He suggested that they find a woman, so the Creator fashioned a clay pot and sealed it, then sent our Father to fetch the woman from the pot. The Creator made his home in the center of the cross. Both he and Nanderú Mbaekuaá brought children into the world. One child each. In the womb of the woman. This transformed her into our Mother, Nandé Cy.

"Nandé Cy took her basket and went to the garden of *maize* that had been newly made by the Creator. He grew angry because she wouldn't believe that He made food grow so quickly. In the heat of His anger He abandoned her, taking our Father with him." Avá-Nembiará made a sweeping gesture. "They left the earth and flew beyond the sky, climbing along the trail of the Eternal Jaguar."

A howler monkey bellowed in the night, making Avá-Tapé think of how Nandé Cy must have cried at being left alone. He remembered the white man's cross and the story of how they nailed Jesus to it. Could it be the same cross? He wanted to ask, but didn't dare. Avá-Nembiará would scoff at the Christian Savior. He believed that the myths of the whites polluted the beliefs of his people.

Avá-Tapé couldn't understand how the white men could crucify the son of a god, just as he puzzled over their reaction to the presence of Tupá in his father. If Tupá walked among the people, would the whites nail him to a cross? He shuddered. It was unimaginable that any of the Guarani could treat the son of the gods that way. Strange how the whites said one thing and did another. "Love each man as your brother," they preached, yet they crucified the son of their god. No wonder they came to the land of the people bringing spirits of death.

"I must sleep," Avá-Nembiará said, breaking his reverie. "And travel to the world of spirits. Too many souls wander there. I cannot find them all, but I have to save as many as I can."

"Are mother and Pindé safe?"

"The spirits of death have not come for them. They have been safe in their house of mud at the mission." He gestured around himself. "My house is ready. The time is coming to bring them out of the white man's world to live with me again here in mine. I can build another house. A dance house to teach my young *paí* the ways of the great ones." He rose and ruffled Avá-Tapé's hair. "Sleep well and have great visions. We will speak more when the light comes back to the world."

His father went to his hammock, leaving Avá-Tapé to ponder his words. Avá-Nembiará wanted to take his family from the mission, and build a dance house. If he did this, many of the older men would join him. Father Antonio would be unhappy.

"My father speaks of taking us away from the mission," Avá-Tapé remembered telling Father Antonio two harvests ago. He looked from Avá-Karaí to Father Antonio and back again. The three sat in an awkward silence where they had been doing extra study after the other children left Bible class. Avá-Karaí had grown taller since the day Father Antonio came. His face had gone from round to long and his square jaw worked from side to side whenever he was deep in thought, like now. His eyes had a way of looking at people that made them uncomfortable if they didn't know him, as if he saw too much.

Father Antonio's thick eyebrows knitted together. He set down his Bible and looked first to Avá-Karaí, then to Avá-Tapé.

"It's not safe to live outside the protection of the mission," he finally said.

"But my father has been doing it all this time and we lived safely before the mission was built."

Father Antonio nodded. "Your father has been lucky. Before the mission was built the jaguars did not run in packs..."

"My father says the mission made them do this," Avá-Karaí said.

Father Antonio waved his hand. "You don't understand, my sons. The dangers of the world outside here are too great to count and they are changing every day. We have come to you bringing the gift of love from Our Lord Jesus Christ." He made the sign of the cross, then lowered his voice. "Other men come from different parts of the world, but they do not bring gifts and love. Only greed and hunger."

"How do you know?" Avá-Karaí asked.

"I have lived in many places among many different people before I came to this part of the world. I have seen the best and the worst of men. Some would think nothing of taking all you have and making slaves of you."

The idea of strange men taking what little they had both angered and frightened Avá-Tapé. He opened his mouth to speak, but once more it was Avá-Karaí.

"I wouldn't fear these men. Jesus will protect me."

"That's right," Avá-Tapé said nodding. "We could leave the mission. Jesus would protect us."

A slow smile spread across Father Antonio's face. "That's why the mission was built. To protect you."

And who protects my father? Avá-Tapé thought. The gods of the forest? Tupá? Now his father said he was chosen to be a *paí*. Would the Christian God be angered? If he didn't become a *paí*, would he anger the gods of his people? Which gods were right, or were they all wrong? What would happen if they left the mission? They were dying now by staying. What could be worse? He stared into the flames, trying to reconcile the world of the whites and the world of his people.

Nothing fit.

He stayed in his father's house drinking herb mixtures and eating more with each passing day. His strength returned slowly. Avá-Nembiará spent most of his time at the mission healing those stricken by the white man's sickness. The Jesuits, busy with their own healings, didn't interfere. Father Antonio even accepted some of Avá-Nembiará's concoctions which helped overcome the disease. Still, many people died, including one of the priests.

Avá-Tapé wanted to go with his father to take care of the people, but Avá-Nembiará made him stay at the house in the forest, away from the mission and its rampant sickness. Each night after the sun left the sky, Avá-Nembiará returned to ask his son about his visions, then he would tell another story about his ancestors and their beginnings.

"You called to Tupá in your visions," his father said one night. "You said he chanted. Can you remember his chant?"

Avá-Tapé closed his eyes and tried to recall the moment in

his dream. He remembered the joy he felt when he saw the children playing in the fields and the singing and dancing of the people. He could almost hear Tupá's chant, but it stayed beyond the reach of his thoughts, flitting in and out of the light like the beautiful butterflies he had tried so hard to catch as a child. The harder he tried, the more elusive it became, until he gave up, shaking his head in frustration.

IIis father sighed. "Maybe Tupá will return and sing again. If he does, you must grasp his chant and hold it to your heart. It is his gift to you. It is the thing that will carry you to the other worlds. Now tell me of your vision of the *añag*."

"I heard their roar from the place where the sun climbs into the sky. Tupá came from the place where it falls. They fought and disappeared, leaving behind the cross of the Creator. Then I saw the *añag* in another vision, roaming the streets of the mission. Eating children."

Avá-Nembiará put fresh wood on the fire and sat across from his son. "After the Creator and our father left Nandé Cy on the Earth," he began, "she gave birth to their children, the twins; Kuarahy, the sun, and Yacy, the moon. The jaguars of the future devoured her. Kuarahy and Yacy had many adventures fighting the *añag* who killed their mother. Because of their adventures we now have plants, fire, our bows, and animals to eat."

"I saw the *añag* at the mission eating children. There is danger. Can I go with you tomorrow?"

"The death spirits who took you are stealing the souls of our people. Some I have brought back. Some I have lost. You have gone and returned. You are stronger now. Your spirit is safe. Tomorrow we will go to the mission."

Avá-Tapé lay awake most of the night, puzzling over how much time had passed since he'd been there. When he and his father first entered its streets the next day, nothing seemed different. Walls still leaned and roofs sagged. The hills and water-filled burrows of the ants had shifted and changed, but they had not gone.

It wasn't until their visit to the first house that Avá-Tapé saw how seriously the spirits of the white man's sickness had taken possession of his people. He wrinkled his nose at the sour and bitter smell of the small darkened house. The scent of death. The blackened hearth told him that no cooking fire had been lit for some time.

Avá-Canindé, one of the biggest and strongest men of the tribe, lay on his back on a jaguar skin. His normally dark complexion looked pale and washed out, his broad face expressionless. Matted hair lay flat against his forehead, his big nose the only recognizable feature. Avá-Canindé's eyes reminded Avá-Tapé of the cold hearth; dark and hollow. His body shook.

His two sons, both younger than Avá-Tapé, lay in a corner, their bodies thin as *maize* stalks. Their usually round faces and wide eyes were drawn and empty like shrunken leather. Avá-Tapé saw the gaunt face of their mother looking toward the door, her mouth open as if crying out. He knelt beside her and touched her face. Cold. He touched her arm. Stiff and lifeless. Her clear, glazed eyes stared into nothingness. Avá-Tapé felt a flush of shame as if he had somehow violated her. He quickly rolled her in the skin she'd been lying on and went to his father's side to help comfort the living.

Avá-Nembiará spoke softly, sometimes breaking into a low chant, sometimes shaking his rattle as he blew smoke from his cigar, first over Avá-Canindé, then his sons. Before leaving, he forced each to sip some of an herb drink, then he and Avá-Tapé carried Avá-Canindé's woman out to the street.

"We'll take care of burying her."

Avá-Tapé recognized the soft, quiet voice of Father Lorenzo. Turning, he saw the balding priest sitting by the corner of the house, his head hung as if perpetually bowing to his God. His sad blue eyes looked even sadder under his jutting brow. His jowls had thinned. The stubble on his usually shaved face looked more white than black.

"The woman needs a Christian burial," Father Lorenzo said. "So her soul can find peace with the Lord Jesus." He made the sign of the cross and kissed his rosary.

Avá-Nembiará grunted. "Her spirit has gone to the land of the dead because of the white man's sickness. She did not want to come back. If not for her children, her man would have gone with her." He reached into his net bag and pulled out a small leaf-wrapped bundle. "Boil these in water and make the sick drink. It will help their spirits find their way back to their bodies."

Father Lorenzo bowed to Avá-Nembiará and accepted the bundle. "God bless you, my son."

Though they had opposing views, in times of great sickness, Avá-Nembiará and the priests had an unspoken agreement to work together, sharing each other's medicines and treatments. The priests knew enough to accept his father's medicines, though they frowned on his chants and treatments.

Avá-Nembiará walked on without speaking. Avá-Tapé followed, stealing a glance over his shoulder to see Father Lorenzo crouch next to the wrapped corpse and make a benediction. How different the stooped priest looked from the smiling man who had taught him as a child. Much had changed since they talked of making him one of them.

"My star pupil," Father Antonio had said a few moons ago. He had put his arm around Avá-Tapé's shoulders.

Father Lorenzo smiled. "He's our best reader. He will make an excellent teacher."

Avá-Tapé held a Bible to his chest and smiled up at the two priests. Their words made his heart happy. He had just read aloud a story of Jesus healing a leper. He wanted to be like Jesus. A healer. The same as his father.

"More than a teacher, he will be a man of God," Father Antonio said. "He and Avá-Karaí have the makings of Jesuits. I hope to make them the first members of our order from among these people."

Father Lorenzo made the sign of the cross and patted Avá-Tapé on the head. "I have great faith in your abilities, my son. The Church needs you."

Avá-Tapé closed his eyes and pictured himself in magnificent robes standing at the head of the church, healing his people with the magic of the white man's God. He had been learning all the words and all the rituals, hoping that the magic would come to him soon, but it hadn't.

Now he helped his father heal while the Jesuits grew further and further away.

They stopped at many houses. At every second or third one, they found the sickness. Avá-Nembiará went through the same motions with his smoke and rattle, ending each treatment with the herb drink. When they came upon the Jesuits administering their own treatments, Avá-Nembiará left them a leaf bundle and moved on, returning after the priests had gone to perform his own healing. By late afternoon they found three more of the tribe dead.

As the sun sank below the trees, they came to the church at the center of the mission. Avá-Tapé didn't see ants in the air the way he had the last time, but their presence was evident. The church walls still leaned outward. A large group of healthy men threw shovelful after shovelful of dirt into the now gaping holes beneath the church foundation.

What had happened to the gloriousness of the house of God? It seemed only days since Avá-Tapé had stood at its head wearing a white robe with black trim. Father Antonio and Father Lorenzo had given him the honor of lighting the sacred candles at the altar.

"You are the future of the church," Father Antonio had whispered.

Avá-Tapé remembered looking up into the Father's soft eyes. He had learned the magic chants and could say them as well as the priest, but they held no meaning. He hoped that if he continued to say them, their meaning might come.

Father Antonio hugged him and turned to the people. The whole church began singing the Ave Maria. Though Avá-Tapé didn't understand the meaning of the words, he joined the others, letting his voice rise with the swell of his heart. Today

he would cry out his yearning to the God of the white man
once again, hoping with all of his being that this day might be
different from the others. He hoped that on this day their God
would answer his cry.

No answer came.

Now God's house seemed to be crumbling back into the
earth.

While his father watched from a distance, Avá-Tapé cautiously ascended the front steps and peered inside. He saw
Father Antonio up to his shoulders in a pit where the high altar had stood. Two men of the tribe shoveled frantically, trying
to refill the hole, but the ants dug it out faster than the men
could shovel it in.

SIX

Thin shafts of sunlight pierced the canopy of leaves, dappling the ground and low hanging branches with tiny puddles of gold. Wisps of mist floated up from the earth. A steady cleansing rain had filled the night. Avá-Tapé breathed in the fresh, humid air and felt his heart rise. The new day brought hope after the long dark time of sickness and death.

He stood in the doorway of his father's house savoring the moment. He hadn't been to the mission in weeks. Many had passed on to the country of the dead, but more had battled the death spirits and won. Word of his father's healing spread. Much to Avá-Tapé's embarrassment, his father lavished praise on him for his part in the healing and boasted of how his son had the visions of a great *paí*. Each time Avá-Nembiará mentioned it, Avá-Tapé felt unworthy. He only wanted to stop the sickness. He felt nothing special, let alone the wondrous qualities that his father said made him a *paí*, yet he couldn't deny the reality of his visions.

In all the teachings of the Jesuits, and all the stories of their God and his son, Jesus, Avá-Tapé had never had direct experience with the world of their God. Only the words on paper and the words of the priests.

Though he never saw proof of His existence, Avá-Tapé feared the Christian God, especially after the stories of His wrath—but he had only tried to do good. How could he anger a God by helping? The only ones he could have angered were the spirits of the dead, and he would have to battle with them in the end anyway.

He heard chattering and looked up to see a group of spider monkeys swinging through the trees, scattering like leaves before the wind, then he heard something crashing through the undergrowth. His heartbeat quickened.

A man's head poked above the ferns. Avá-Tapé felt his tension drain when he recognized the huge form of Avá-Canindé lumbering up the trail dragging two poles hung with a net filled with his possessions. His two sons followed, each carrying a smaller version of their father's load. Avá-Canindé looked haggard, but his massive size still made him an imposing figure. Some of his weight and color had returned and his big nose still stood out on his broad face. The hollowness had gone from his eyes, giving them back their familiar, heavy-lidded look. His sleepy expression, thick lips and slow speech made him appear dull-witted, but when he spoke, his words carried great import. Avá-Canindé was a man to be listened to. He dropped his load when he came to the edge of the clearing, eyes brightening when he saw Avá-Tapé.

"I have left the evil and sickness of the white man's world to live with the great *paí* of my people," he said. "I want to return to the old ways and purify my spirit."

"Come in." Avá-Tapé turned away, embarrassed. "I'll make something to eat." He busied himself preparing a pot of boiled *maize* and beans so he wouldn't have to face his visitor.

Avá-Canindé came in followed by his sons, who sat behind him. "We will build a *maloca* near here, but not too close. The *paí* must have their solitude. Your father will show us the right place."

Avá-Tapé took a deep breath and willed himself to relax. "Until he comes, you can stay here."

"We will start building as soon as we have his blessing and then we will build a great dance house."

"I haven't heard talk of a dance house since the time of the old ones," Avá-Tapé said.

"We built them when I was a boy, but the white man's magic has almost washed them from our thoughts. The dance house is a place of great ceremony where a strong new *paí* could be initiated into the other world."

"A new *paí?*" Avá-Tape glanced over his shoulder at Avá-Canindé. The older man nodded and smiled knowingly. His two sons had matching expressions. Though they didn't say it, Avá-Tapé knew they meant him. More and more, the people had been talking about his visions and his part in his father's healings.

Avá-Canindé's older son spoke. "My father says we need to build a dance house so we can celebrate the prayer of the forest and bring our people back to the old ways."

Avá-Tapé studied Santo. He had his father's features and his mother's stature. Long skinny limbs, a full round face, wide smoldering brown eyes and the same short dark hair as his father. Santo had never had a sacred name of the forest. The Jesuits had given him and his brother Christian names, Santo and Rico. It bothered Santo that he had been named different from the others. Always anxious to please and be part of what was going on, he would do anything asked of him with no complaint.

His younger brother looked more like his mother. A small nose, delicate lips, and dark inquisitive eyes. Anything Santo did to be included in what was happening, Rico tried to do harder. When you saw Santo, Rico was never far behind. Looking at him, Avá-Tapé couldn't get the face of the boy's mother out of his mind. Her silent cry haunted him.

He looked back at Avá-Canindé. "Do you not fear the wrath of the Jesuit God? Their sacred book says 'Thou shalt have no Gods before me...'"

"Fear of Him does not matter. He is a silent and unspeaking God who has brought sickness and death. He is already angry. I prayed to Him and He did not answer. He has taken the mother of my sons. Now I must bow to Tupá, the son of the gods of our people. Gods who speak."

Avá-Tapé filled three gourd bowls with hot mash and served his guests before filling one for himself.

"Your father is the only one who has kept the magic alive," Avá-Canindé continued. "The rest of us accepted the Christian words and abandoned the ways of our fathers. We have given our children names picked by white men and have followed their empty words like monkeys. *Techó-achy* lies heavy on our spirits. We are slow, but the spirits of death are swift."

Avá-Tapé, Santo, and Rico listened while the older man spoke of his disappointment with the whites and his hope of dancing his way back to the old gods and the old ways.

"My dream is to follow Avá-Nembiará and the visions of the new *paí* that the people speak of." He paused and gazed at Avá-Tapé for a long uncomfortable moment.

Avá-Tapé looked down when he could no longer bear the weight of the older man's stare.

"I will follow the great *paí* to the place where the sun comes out of the earth," Avá-Canindé said, his voice rising.

"Together we will dance our way to paradise."

"But there is much work to be done before we make our journey."

Avá-Tapé jumped at his father's voice. Only Avá-Nembiará could come in silence and appear as if out of nowhere. He stood in the doorway, arms crossed. Avá-Tapé willed his heart to slow. He couldn't have stood Avá-Canindé's intensity much longer.

Avá-Canindé bowed his head. His boys followed suit. "My sons and I are ready to do whatever work needs to be done. Tell us where to begin."

"I see that my son has been a good host."

"He has the grace of a *paí*."

Avá-Tapé stiffened at the words. Why would the gods of his father want someone taught as a white man?

The two younger boys stood and ran to Avá-Nembiará's side. "Teach us how to be *paí*, Nanderú. We want to be magic like you."

His father smiled and put his arms around the boys' shoulders. "Maybe when you get older you will have great visions like Avá-Tapé." He ruffled their hair and stepped inside, filling the *maloca* with his presence.

Squatting by the fire, he filled a gourd from the pot and sat beside his son. Santo and Rico took their seats behind their father. "You will sleep under my roof tonight," Avá-Nembiará said to Avá-Canindé. "Tomorrow we will build a house for you and your sons. When it is finished we will build a dance house."

"We want to help," Santo said.

Avá-Canindé nodded. "We will have help with the dance house. Others will be coming."

Avá-Nembiará turned to Avá-Tapé. "Go to the mission. It is time to bring your mother and sister to live with us in the forest away from the sickness of the white man. You can make it before the sun falls. Stay there for the night and bring them tomorrow."

Father Antonio's admonitions filled Avá-Tapé's mind, but he stifled them. He couldn't disobey his father.

By the time he left the *maloca* the sun had begun to fall. Lengthening shadows fell across his path. The hum of insects and the calls of day animals gave way to the soft rhythms of night insects and the haunting cries of night dwellers. The long rays of the fading sun grayed and a warm rain started to fall. The patter of drops sounded like the dance of spider monkeys.

He took a few more steps, heard another sound, and stopped. The loamy smell of earth and the warm drops on his skin filled his senses, yet in spite of the rain's warmth, he shivered. Scanning the surrounding vegetation, he strained for a clearer view, but the lines and angles of the forest grew more indistinct with each passing moment.

Rain continued falling.

He started again, anxious to make good time, the only sound the beat of the rain and the slap of his feet. Two rhythms, then a third, barely audible beneath the other two. Quicker and quieter. He stopped again.

Looking ahead, he saw the first lights of the mission fires winking through the undergrowth. Warmth. Looking back, he saw two sets of smaller amber lights low to the ground. Cold. *Añag.* Off to his side two more. They blinked. A low growl made his heart leap into his throat. He tried to swallow, but the dryness of his mouth made it impossible. He walked faster, aware of stealthy movement behind and to his side.

When he reached the clearing, he bolted, arms and legs pumping wildly, his breath clawing into his chest. Darting around the corner of a building, he stopped and looked back. The shadowy forms of three jaguars emerged from the trees across the clearing.

Remembering his vision, he turned to run, slipped, and fell in the muddy street. Picking himself up, he ran through the dark streets of the mission to his mother's house and stumbled through the door. "The *añag!*" he said, fighting for breath. Kuñá-Ywy Verá jumped at his appearance, spilling the pot she'd been stirring, dousing the fire. His little sister Pindé ran to her side.

"Stay quiet." He pulled the pot from the hearth, but the fire had gone out. He took their hands and guided them to the corner farthest from the door. "Don't move," he whispered, crouching beside them. "Hopefully they'll pass into the night."

The rain fell harder.

A scream cut through the night, followed by hisses and growls. Another cry stopped mid-scream, then a series of thumps that he knew to be the sounds of tearing flesh and bone. He huddled closer and felt his sister trembling beside him, whimpering. He put a finger to her lips. His mother remained tense and silent.

By now the streets had sunk into complete darkness. No more sounds but the steady hiss of the pouring rain.

Avá-Tapé waited.

Listened.

Nothing.

Moments passed. He motioned for his mother and Pindé to stay where they were, rose slowly and crept toward the doorway, his senses poised for any sound or movement.

Halfway across the tiny room he saw a pair of glowing amber eyes blinking back at him from the blackened doorway.

SEVEN

Avá-Tapé's heart thrashed like a grounded fish. He dared not breathe. Move.

The cat's eyes widened and sank lower. Crouching. Avá-Tapé saw the jaguar in his mind, chest touching the ground, haunches up, tail twitching. How long until it pounced? He closed his eyes, wanting to pray for help, not knowing which gods to pray to. Hopelessness engulfed him until he remembered something his father had taught him.

He opened his eyes. The jaguar glared, unblinking, close enough to touch. Pulling his loincloth aside, Avá-Tapé grabbed his man part and let his water fly into the cat's eyes.

The jaguar bounded away hissing and yowling, leaving Avá-Tapé pissing all over the doorway. Suddenly, he broke into hysterical laughter. Each time he thought of the cat's shock, a new wave of laughter engulfed him. He clutched at his stomach and fell to the ground.

When his giggles subsided he calmed himself, letting the realization of what happened fill his mind, until he started to tremble. He had to do something before another cat appeared. Quickly, he built a fire, heaping wood upon it until a small inferno blazed in the hearth.

His mother and Pindé crept out from a darkened corner. "How much wood do we have?" Avá-Tapé asked, trying to force the tremor from his voice. He couldn't let them know his fear. "We have to keep the fire high to keep the *añag* away."

"You laughed at them," Kuñá-Ywy Verá said. "You laughed in death's face. Your father was right. Your visions must have been powerful." Her gaze met his with unspoken questions which she already seemed to know the answers to. Twin fires flickered in her dark eyes. Slender fingers brushed her silky black hair over her shoulder with a grace seen more in the animal world than the human one. The firelight accented the striking features of her oval face and the delicate hollow of her throat.

Avá-Tapé studied her quizzical expression. How could he explain? He had been lucky, nothing more.

Pindé ran from behind her and hugged him. "You saved us from the jaguars."

He put an arm around his sister. "I only remembered what father taught me."

Kuñá-Ywy Verá joined them, drawing both her children close. "I would have nothing to live for if I lost my loves," she whispered. "It is hard enough spending so much time without your father. If it weren't for you…"

Avá-Tapé pulled back. "Don't speak that way, Mother."

His little sister Pindé looked up with eyes that were smaller versions of his mother's. After eleven harvests she looked and acted more like her mother every day. She dressed the same, had identical mannerisms, and the same questioning eyes. Her posture, straight shoulders, and silky black hair all mimicked her mother. It wouldn't be long before he would be chasing away the older boys.

"There's plenty of wood," his mother said, picking up the spilled pot. "I can make us more to eat."

"I'm hungrier than those jaguars," Avá-Tapé said. He took a deep breath. His heart had finally slowed. "I will eat and watch the fire while you and Pindé sleep. Tomorrow we leave the mission and go to live back in the forest with Father."

Kuñá-Ywy Verá's face brightened, her joyful expression intensified by the glow from the hearth. Woman of the shining earth, Avá-Tapé thought, feeling a surge of warmth in his heart for her. Pindé jumped up and down clapping her hands until her mother silenced her with a finger to her lips.

Avá-Tapé stood by the door and listened while his mother and sister worked by the fire. Other than the steady beat of the rain, no more sounds came from the streets, but jaguars could be silent. He'd been lucky in the forest. If it had been a lone cat, he never would have seen it. From the cries he heard earlier, he knew that the hungry pack had killed or maimed at least one person, maybe others. He wanted to get a torch to go and investigate, but thought better of it. His place was to stay and watch over his family.

"Avá-Tapé," his mother said, "come and eat."

He sat with his back to the fire so he could watch the door. Kuñá-Ywy Verá gave him a gourd bowl filled with *manioc*, pumpkin, and beans. He and his mother ate in silence while Pindé jabbered about the boys in the tribe and some of the tricks they played on the girls. Avá-Tapé half-listened, grunting responses where he thought appropriate. Every so often, he caught his mother studying him, but when their gazes met she looked away.

"Why do you look at me like that?" he asked when he could bear it no longer.

"You look more like your father every day," she said softly, then sighed. "My little one is no more. You are no longer my son." She looked down at her food. "You are *paí*. One to be respected."

He started to protest until she silenced him with a gesture. "You cannot escape what is meant to be."

He could tell by her expression that her mind couldn't be changed.

"I will tend the fire and keep watch," he said. "You and Pindé sleep. Tomorrow we join Father."

Pindé looked to their mother. "Can I stay with Avá-Tapé?"

Her mother stroked her hair. "You need your sleep, my little one. You have a lot of hard work ahead of you."

"Avá-Tapé needs to sleep, too."

"Your brother is a man now. He will pass the night watching over us. He can sleep when it is safe."

While his mother and sister prepared for sleep, Avá-Tapé piled wood closer to the hearth, stoked the fire, and settled down beside it to wait out the night.

The rain fell in a steady hiss. Avá-Tapé kept his gaze intent on the blackened doorway, his back to the fire to keep his vision keen in the darkness. When sleep threatened to take him, he poured water over his head to keep his senses poised.

Why had the *añag* followed him? Was it a message from the God of the Christians or the gods of his grandfathers? Had another spirit stepped into his thoughts and given him the knowledge to act that had saved him and his family?

Where had the knowledge... His father! A *paí* of the Guarani. When the white man's sickness had stolen Avá-Tapé's soul, a spirit had given him an omen. A forest spirit? Were the other visions omens, too? He shuddered. Too much to think about.

He threw more wood on the fire, careful not to look at it too long, for fear of dulling his night vision, then he sat cross-legged, the fire's heat on his back, his eyes probing the darkness for signs of movement. The rain slowed, then stopped. Silence and darkness shrouded him. He needed the quiet to think.

He envisioned Father Antonio in his ceremonial robes crawling with ants. The altar of the Christians swallowed by the earth. The house of the Christian God ready to crumble back into the ground. The white sickness cutting his people down like *machetes* on *maize* stalks. The jaguars picking at the remains. The voice of Tupá speaking through his father. His visions.

It seemed as if the many spirits of nature were rebelling against the God of the Jesuits. Could the Jesuit God have brought the spirits of sickness? If so, why were the people victims of His anger? Were the spirits of the forest taking those who were weighted with the white man's imperfections?

The jaguars didn't run in packs when the people lived by themselves in the village. Not until the white men brought cattle. His father and Avá-Canindé both said that bringing animals foreign to the forest had upset the balance and angered the gods. The jaguars ran together to hunt and eat the cattle to restore the lost balance. Cows had no place in the forest. Without the protection of the mission, they wouldn't live.

He remembered sneaking down to the corral with Avá-Karaí the day he'd first heard of the strange animals. When the boys climbed the fence, the cows all stood and stared. Both boys jumped back behind the fence, uneasy with so many eyes scrutinizing them.

"Do you not think they are living *techó-achy*?" Avá-Karaí said. "They have sleepy eyes. Look how slow they are. They do nothing but chew. They are always hungry."

"Always hungry and they do not hunt," Avá-Tapé added.

Avá-Karaí giggled. "Sounds like Avá-Takuá."

Avá-Tapé shared the laughter, then Avá-Karaí grew serious again, nodding toward the cows. "My father says they walk straight to their death when they are slaughtered."

"They are too stupid to run."

"No forest animal would go to its death so easily."

"Its meat is soft and flabby like Father Rodrigo's stomach," Avá-Tapé said, laughing at his own joke.

Avá-Karaí chuckled, then his face grew solemn. "My father said that eating their meat will make our people soft, flabby, and stupid until they walk around with sleepy eyes like the cows. We will all walk straight to our deaths, slaughtered by the white men."

Avá-Tapé shook off a chill at the memory of Avá-Karaí's words. The people had grown slower and fatter living at the mission and, like the cows, most were always hungry, but didn't hunt. How many had gone to their deaths since the white men had come?

He peered deeper into the blackness and thought he saw the beginnings of a gray haze forming above the darkness outside. He glanced over at what remained of the wood next to the hearth. Nearly gone. How much time had passed since the attacks? He put more wood on the fire and kept his gaze steady as gray turned to silver, then indigo and crimson, finally blossoming into the first glimmer of the coming day. Blackness turned into shadow and formlessness into substance.

When the first cries of morning birds filled the air Avá-Tapé rose and stretched. His eyes burned and his limbs felt heavy. Tonight sleep would come quickly, but he had a long day ahead. He crossed the small room and stood in the doorway, looking out onto the muddy street. How many had died in the night?

Careful not to wake his mother and sister, he put a pot of *maize* mash on the fire and gathered his family's cooking pots, pottery, and gourds, piling them on top of carrying nets. When his mother awoke, he ate a gourdful of mash, then went to the forest to find two large cedar limbs so he could drag his family's belongings to his father's *maloca*.

When he returned, Pindé and Kuñá-Ywy Verá had most of their things packed into the chest. The rest they rolled into their sleeping skins. Avá-Tapé lashed the limbs and netting together. By the time they set out for his father's *maloca*, the sun had climbed above the surrounding buildings and the mud in the street had begun to dry.

Avá-Tapé led them past rows of quiet darkened houses wondering which had been visited by death and which had escaped. He pictured frightened families cowering by their fires. His stomach tightened at the remembrance of last night's screams and the sounds that followed. Tearing flesh. Part of him wanted to investigate, possibly help. Part of him dreaded what he'd find. His first duty was to get his family away from the dangers of the mission, to the safety of his father's *maloca*.

With the help of his mother and sister, Avá-Tapé dragged everything they owned through the drying mud of the mission streets. The hot sun beat down on them until they reached the forest. The shade and wet leaves on the path let the load slide more easily, but now they had to contend with low-hanging vines and branches.

Pindé stayed close by his side while his mother pushed from behind. No one spoke. Even Pindé, who usually chattered more than the squirrel monkeys and macaws combined, remained quiet.

Mist rose in wisps from the ground, floating toward the sky like spirits. Birds cried and monkeys chittered. Avá-Tapé kept his senses alert. If predators threatened, any changes in the sounds of the forest would warn him. He felt safer among the trees than at the mission. The farther they journeyed from it the more he felt the threat diminish.

Even though he feared all the gods, he didn't think he had offended any, yet he felt caught in an inexplicable struggle. Should he believe in a Christian God, the myths of his people, or both?

To survive, Avá-Tapé thought only one question needed an answer.

Which did he fear the most?

EIGHT

The sun passed mid-point in the sky and the shadows began to lengthen when they reached his father's house. Avá-Tapé's arms and legs hung limp and heavy like wet rope, his feet ached, and his body felt worn and brittle.

Dropping his burden, he made a circuit of the clearing surrounding his father's house, but saw no sign of Avá-Nembiará or Avá-Canindé. Pindé and his mother went inside and busied themselves at his father's fire.

He knew Avá-Nembiará would be close by building another *maloca* for Avá-Canindé and his sons. They would return by dark. He ate a healthy serving of vegetables and wild pig his mother had prepared, then stretched out on a hammock and fell asleep.

Some time later he became aware of the voices of his father and Avá-Canindé. His little sister Pindé whispered to Santo and Rico while his mother told of how Avá-Tapé had defeated the jaguar and laughed at death. Part of him wanted to awaken and correct them so they would know how the fear had taken him, but the need for sleep outweighed all else. He let the sound of their voices go and drifted back into deep sleep.

He became aware of himself back at the mission watching the doorway for jaguars. He had no fire to help him; only the feeble light of a pale, gibbous moon. If the jaguars came to the door he would be helpless unless he could force himself to piss again. Even that didn't guarantee safety.

A low growl came from the street. He held his breath as eight points of cold fire appeared.

The *añag* meant death. He had seen it countless times. Few survived. Those who did were lucky to escape with all their parts. In spite of what his mother and sister thought, he had been lucky the first time.

A jaguar poked its head into the room and crept in. Avá-Tapé backed into a corner. The cat circled and another came through the door, creeping toward his other side. Two more followed.

First one advanced, then another, each inching forward, testing their prey, each movement bolder than the one preceding it. Avá-Tapé remained immobile, nothing behind him but a wall.

The jaguar to his right leaped. Avá-Tapé screamed and fell backward. The cat came down on top of him, its breath hot and moist on his face.

"Wake up!" Pindé screamed.

It felt like a snare had jerked him through space. His arms flailed, his eyes flew open and he looked into the wide-eyed gaze of his little sister, who backed away.

He took deep breaths and sat up. "A dream." Daylight spilled through the door of the *maloca*. The cooking fire had burned down to smoking coals. The others had gone. "Where are they?"

"Helping Avá-Canindé build his house. Are you hungry?" She went to the fire and spooned something into a gourd bowl, chattering as though nothing had happened.

"When they finish Avá-Canindé's *maloca* they are going to build one for us," she said. "Father says he needs to stay here. He said you will stay here, too, because you are becoming a *paí*."

"What if I do not want to be a *paí*?" Avá-Tapé swung his feet over the edge of the hammock and stepped to the ground.

"Father said that Tupá chose you the same way he was chosen, only your visions had more power. Did they make you scream in your sleep?"

So many questions, he thought. So much talk. Did her

mouth ever tire? He felt sorry for the man who would take her as his woman. "I am not sure." He took the bowl she held out and sat cross-legged beside the remains of the fire. "I don't know what to believe. I'm not sure of anything anymore."

"Father knows." Pindé nodded. "Talk to him. He'll tell you what is true and what is not."

Avá-Tapé started to argue, then stopped. No sense fighting with his sister. Her mind was made up. If he didn't agree with her his ears would never get a rest. Her loose tongue could do more damage than any jaguar. "You're right," he said with as much finality as he could. "I'll talk about it with Father."

To his surprise she didn't say anything more.

He finished eating, then had Pindé take him to the others.

More than half the structure had been built. His father worked on the last section of a reed frame while Santo and Rico scurried back and forth gathering armloads of reeds and straw, which his mother tied into bundles. Avá-Canindé used these to thatch a roof.

Avá-Nembiará looked up from his work. "The warrior has risen from the world of spirits and returned to walk among men. I only hope he hasn't lost the ability for hard work and sweat." He and Avá-Canindé chuckled.

Avá-Tapé felt his face flush. He didn't think himself brave, just lucky. He could work as hard as anyone.

"When I was with him last, he worked more than two men," his mother cut in. "After a night of no sleep. I wonder if two ancient ones could do as well."

The chuckles stopped. Avá-Nembiará and Avá-Canindé looked at each other in mock indignation, then burst into laughter. His mother smiled. "Come help me tie these bundles, my son. Pindé, you help Santo and Rico gather straw. Much of the day is still left. If we work hard we can finish before the sun falls."

"And I would be honored to have you as guests to share the first meal with me and my sons in our new house," Avá-Canindé said. "As long as you are not offended eating with an ancient one."

"As long as he still has all his teeth," Avá-Tapé said.

They all laughed, including Avá-Tapé. His first laugh in days. It felt wonderful.

When the falling sun had turned the sky crimson, Avá-Canindé packed the last bundle of straw tightly in place, stood back, folded his arms and admired the finished structure. "Like the *maloca* I grew up in." He smiled. "Big enough for four families. My father would be proud."

Avá-Tapé circled the long rectangular structure. It had a thatched roof with sloping sides held up by hardwood supports. Inside, rafters and a beam of palm wood formed a junction between the roof and the end of the wall. Avá-Canindé called it the cock's foot. A fireplace had been built at one end. Their hammocks would go at the other.

"Santo, Rico," the boys' father called. "Quickly, gather wood before darkness comes. I will start a fire and prepare our first meal." He turned to Avá-Nembiará. "Nanderú, you and your family must sleep here this night."

They feasted on wild pheasant, beans, *manioc* and pumpkin. Avá-Nembiará blessed the house and food, but ate no meat so he could lighten his body.

If his father insisted that he become a *paí*, Avá-Tapé would have to lighten his spirit, too, but for now he didn't care. The succulent, salty meat of the roasted pheasant made his mouth water. He ate two servings.

When they finished, his mother made hot drinks while they gathered around the fire.

"Tell us how you overcame the jaguar and laughed at death," Avá-Canindé said in his slow deliberate way.

Avá-Tapé looked around, feeling the pressure from everyone. His mother's eyes full of unspoken questions; Pindé's a smaller version of her mother's. His father's sharp eyes silently urging him on while Santo and Rico looked at him in wide-eyed anticipation. Avá-Canindé waited patiently with his own heavy-lidded expectation.

Avá-Tapé's first impulse was to please them with a grand

tale, but people were talking about his visions already. He took a deep breath. "When I saw the *añag* ready to pounce, I remembered the words of a very wise man." He looked at his father. "So I did what this great warrior taught me." He paused, letting his words hang in the air.

When he didn't continue, Rico spoke up. "What magic did you use?"

"I pissed in his eyes."

Rico looked confused. The rest wore stunned expressions. Avá-Nembiará's eyes widened, then he choked on his drink and burst into laughter. Avá-Canindé clutched his stomach and rolled on the ground. Avá-Tapé felt his own body spasm as laughter consumed him. "You should have heard it hiss," he said between breaths. "I never saw a jaguar move so fast."

His words caused a new wave of mirth. Avá-Nembiará wiped tears from his cheeks. Avá-Canindé clutched his stomach tighter. Even his mother and Pindé giggled.

"Weren't you scared?" Santo asked.

"More than I can ever remember."

"And still you could do that."

"I was going to die anyway."

"Death is a great teacher," Avá-Nembiará said solemnly.

"One who pisses in the face of death is a great warrior," Avá-Canindé added.

Santo and Rico laughed. Avá-Tapé started to, but stopped. Avá-Canindé's words carried profound truth. He had never thought of his act in those terms.

"The *añag* have killed many great hunters," Avá-Nembiará said, nodding slowly. "One day when I was visiting another mission I saw a jaguar attack two horses tied together. It killed one and dragged it away, pulling the live horse with it."

Avá-Tapé looked from Santo to Rico to Pindé and saw terror in their faces.

"If a jaguar catches an ox alone," Avá-Nembiará continued, "it can leap on the ox's back, bite into its neck, and claw it open. They are attracted to the smell of the animal flesh that the white man cooks so often. That is why they hunt near the missions."

"It is a message from the spirits of the forest," Avá-Canindé said with eyes narrowed. "Telling the people that the heaviness of the white man's meat is an imperfection that weighs down their spirits."

They talked long into the night. Santo, Rico, and Pindé soon fell asleep. Kuñá-Ÿwy Verá helped them into hammocks and fell into one herself, leaving the men to talk among themselves. Avá-Canindé stoked the fire, poured fresh gourds of a sweet-tasting herb infusion, and sat down beside Avá-Nembiará.

"One who pisses in the face of death is a great warrior," Avá-Tapé repeated. "Funny words to the ears of a young boy. To me, great words of wisdom."

A slow smile spread across Avá-Canindé's face. "Wisdom that only a man can hear."

Avá-Tapé stared at the ground. "I was no man in front of that jaguar. I was like a little one who wet himself." He gestured toward his mother and Pindé, then looked back at the ground. "I am not as brave as they think. Fear held me in its hand. It could have crushed me."

He looked up and saw that his father and Avá-Canindé both stared at the ground as he did, then his father's head rose. Avá-Nembiará's usually sharp gaze looked softer, as if his eyes had an inner light. Though he couldn't see it, Avá-Tapé felt Avá-Canindé's stare on him, too. Finally his father spoke.

"What warrior wouldn't be so full of fear that he might piss all over himself?"

NINE

They built a second *maloca* next to the first for Avá-Tapé and his family, keeping it a fair distance from Avá-Nembiará's, so his father's *maloca* would stay separate, as a *paí's* house should be. Avá-Tapé and his father spent many nights sleeping with their family, making plans with Avá-Canindé to build a dance house, but they spent most of their time at his father's smaller *maloca*.

Word of their new community spread. One morning three more families appeared. More were rumored to be coming. A delighted Avá-Canindé put aside the dance house plans and helped build two larger *malocas* next to his in a semi-circle, leaving the open space free for the dance house.

Most days Avá-Tapé helped build the new *malocas* and stayed with his mother and sister. He spent nights with his father. As more of the people came to live, Avá-Canindé organized them and oversaw the building of new *malocas*.

Avá-Canindé took Avá-Tapé aside one morning when he came to help. "We have many hands for the work of men," he said quietly. "And not enough for the work of spirits. Stay with your father and follow him to the country of the spirits. Your work there is more important than any you could do here."

"What if I do not want to work with the spirits?"

"They have already chosen you."

Avá-Tapé's stomach tightened. "How can you know this?"

Avá-Canindé smiled. "This is how they said it would be. All of the people see. You are the only one who does not."

Uneasy about the notion of living away from the people,

Avá-Tapé walked the short distance to his father's house, thinking about how much his life had changed from the packed church and close living of the mission. He felt a pang of loss and wondered about Father Antonio and the Jesuits. Where had they been? Surely, they wouldn't sit and do nothing while people left the mission. He remembered the Masses he had attended and could almost hear the younger children's voices. He closed his eyes, letting the Ave Maria fill his mind. Why couldn't he live in both worlds?

He found Avá-Nembiará behind his *maloca* sitting in a small patch of sunlight with his eyes closed. "My son has come to join me," he said without opening them. "He brings a troubled spirit."

How did his father know it was him without seeing? How did he know what bothered him? "My heart is torn between the world of men, the gods of our people, and the God of the Christians. They all want a piece of it."

"That is the yearning of your soul."

Avá-Tapé sat beside his father. "I don't understand this talk of my soul. Father Antonio speaks of saving it from being damned to hell, and you speak of it dancing in the heavens. Feelings crash inside me like rushing water, first this way, then another. What of your soul, Father? What does it say to you?"

"That is why we sing and dance. *Ang* is the shadow, the trail of a man. His echo. Our word is the expression of our divine soul which does not die. Our human voice is the sound of the vital word—the first work of the Creator sent by the true Father."

Avá-Tapé thought of the Ave Maria again. "Like when we sing?"

"And dance. Dancing is how we express the divine within ourselves."

"And when we speak. These are words of the divine?"

"Everything we say. Singing and speaking. Especially our forest names. A man's vital word and his name are tied together. His name is more than a sound that tells who he is. His name is what he is."

Avá-Tapé thought of the meaning of his own name. Man who is the messenger bird of Tupá. Could this be why his father was so excited about his visions and the chant of Tupá? Was this why they said he should become a *paí?*

"As men, another soul is added to the vital word," Avá-Nembiará said. "This second soul grows as a man grows. It is *techó achy kué*, the animal soul responsible for the lowest appetites. It remains all his life and directs him toward animal behavior."

"We have two souls?"

"Day and night, light and dark, waking and sleep, planting and harvesting. All separate, but one. The first is the vital word of heavenly origin, the second the Earth soul. A *paí's* divine soul guides him to carry out holy acts by mystical rules. He does not eat the flesh of animals. He concentrates on the sacred, and practices the peace of his spirit. His animal soul drives him to eat meat and wallow in too much sex. It is a monkey he carries on his shoulders."

Avá-Tapé watched a pair of scarlet macaws flitting from tree to tree. Closing his eyes, he felt the warm sun on his head. The songs of birds filled the air. He heard a group of squirrel monkeys chattering at the edge of the clearing and imagined one riding on his shoulders. He could almost feel it pressing down on him.

"A *paí* changes his diet and dances to shake the monkey from his shoulders."

Avá-Tapé looked at his father and saw him smile.

"He cannot make a magical flight with the monkey's weight on him. He must lighten himself so his spirit can fly to the other worlds the way his voice rises into the air in song. Only in dancing can he free it.

"It can escape in sickness and in sleep, but if it travels too far it will not return," Avá-Nembiará continued. "That was the danger of your sickness. Your soul must be the messenger bird of Tupá. He came to you and gave you the gift of his word. You have to try to remember."

"And if my divine soul had not returned?"

"If your passing soul awakens the *añag* they will devour your spirit. If it makes it past the sleeping *añag*, it will arrive at the place where Urukera and Owl live. On seeing your spirit Owl will screech and summon the souls of the dead, who will receive you with a great show of affection, but they will want you to live with them. The only souls that pass freely are those of children, since they have no *techó-achy* to slow their flight. The more imperfections a soul gains in its earthly life, the more difficult it is to pass these obstacles."

"And what of the second soul? What happens to the monkey that rides on a man's shoulders?"

"The Earth soul changes into the spirit of death, which roams the world disturbing the living, causing sickness, madness, and death. It torments the living, trying to make a man's divine soul flee from its presence. I have seen many of them wandering near the burial places."

A cloud passed in front of the sun. The drawn face of Avá-Canindé's woman with its vacant stare and silent scream floated through Avá-Tapé's mind. He shuddered, thinking of her Earth soul coming to torment him. He shook his head to clear the vision.

His father's world fascinated him, but he feared it as much as he feared the wrath of the Jesuit God. He wanted to believe in one world or the other. It didn't seem as if both could exist. His father's world had given him signs and visions, the Christian world…

Part of him still yearned for a sign from the Jesuit God, but He remained silent. If only He would give him some idea of what to do.

A flock of birds took flight, then the monkeys scattered, leaving silence in their wake. He saw his father sitting straight, his head turned to the side.

Avá-Tapé strained to listen. Were the Earth spirits coming for their souls? Branches cracked and leaves slapped. Something big moved through the forest. He thought of the *añag*, but they didn't make that much noise. What kind of animal…

"Nanderú!"

Heavy breathing. He recognized the voice.

"Here," his father said.

Avá-Canindé rounded the corner of the *maloca*, chest heaving. He had obviously been running. "The Jesuits," he said between breaths. "Father Antonio. They have come to our village speaking of evil. They want to bring our people back to the mission."

Avá-Nembiará rose. "Take me to them," he said.

Avá-Tapé followed. The Jesuits. He had been sitting here thinking of their God and now they had come to the village. Could this be a sign?

TEN

Avá-Tapé followed his father and Avá-Canindé through the forest, hurrying toward the new village. When they neared it, they heard Father Antonio's voice, strong and forceful; the same voice he used to preach sermons about hell, damnation and the wrath of God.

They came into the clearing out of Father Antonio's line of sight, stopping when they saw him pacing in the spot they had saved for the dance house as though he were before the altar of the Christian God. His arms waved, his fingers pointed, and his robes fluttered like angry birds. Father Lorenzo, Father Rodrigo, and another priest stood behind him. The people surrounded him in a semi-circle, some with angry frowns, others with heads bowed, most with hurt expressions like children scolded for bad behavior.

"In the name of the Father, the Son, and the Holy Spirit, forgive them, Father, for they know not what they do. They have abandoned You and Your blessed works, led aside by the hand of Satan…"

"Your devil means nothing here," Avá-Nembiara said angrily. "Your evil spirits of white death live with you and your God at the mission. Here we are people of the forest like our fathers' fathers."

Father Antonio spun to face Avá-Nembiará, his robes flying like predatory wings. His face hardened when his gaze came to rest on his rival. Avá-Tapé stayed close to his father as they strode to confront the priest. Avá-Canindé followed a few steps behind. On seeing them advance, the other priests arrayed

themselves behind Father Antonio. Father Rodrigo handed him
a crucifix.

"Holy Father, forgive him his savage demons." Father Antonio brandished the cross. "Deliver his soul. Save us from this
minion of Satan."

"Your magic has no meaning here," Avá-Nembiará said,
brushing aside the crucifix. "Your Christian God works his evil
in the mission. He does not live in the forest. His dark spirits
of *techó-achy* bring the jaguars to the mission. Sickness and death
are his brothers." Scattered gasps rose from the people as he
stopped inches from Father Antonio's face.

The two men glared at each other, neither speaking; sinew
and feather against robe and cross. Father Antonio's eyes
shrank as if any fire they contained had dimmed. His shoulders
slumped. He drew back with a bewildered expression. "You
know not of what you speak." His voice shook at first, then grew
firmer. "The demons possess you in your frenzy. These are not
your words. These are the words of Satan's minions." He waved
the cross again and started speaking in Latin.

Avá-Tapé felt puzzled listening to Father Antonio, whose
words raged with great authority. The fire that faded from his
eyes told another story.

"My body dances with the spirit of my gods," Avá-Nembiará
growled. The muscles of his neck bulged like ropes. "They
speak through me and come to me in my visions. How does
your God speak? Why does He not show himself? Tupá has
shown Himself. Where is your God?"

Father Antonio opened his mouth but no words came.

"He is nothing more than a church, a cross of wood, and
an altar of stone," Avá-Nembiará said. "Like wood and stone, he
does not speak."

"May God have mercy on your soul," Father Antonio whispered. The three priests crossed themselves. "Evil has consumed you."

"My magic was not evil when you wanted it for curing the
sickness."

Father Antonio stared at the ground, then looked up, his gaze fixed on Avá-Tapé. Any spirit that might have filled the priest's eyes had now gone. "I implore you, my son." He stared at Avá-Tapé as if accusing him. "We have taught you our words and given you an education. Your soul is not lost yet. Save yourself from these savage ways. Save your people. Come back to us. Back to the Church. God will forgive you."

Avá-Tapé looked down, heart heavy, his thoughts muddled.

"My people have their own minds," Avá-Nembiará said quietly. "Let them think with their hearts. We allow you to live in peace at your mission. Let us live in peace in the forest the way our grandfathers did."

Father Antonio looked around. The people stood, their features hardening with resolve.

"May God forgive," Father Antonio said, walking past Avá-Tapé and his father, the three priests trailing behind him.

"The Bishop will not be happy when he hears about this," Father Lorenzo muttered.

Father Antonio looked over his shoulder at Avá-Tapé one more time before leaving. The fire that once blazed in his eyes smoldered like coals.

Avá-Tapé, his father, and Avá-Canindé stood in the center of the people. No one spoke. No one moved. All eyes looked to Avá-Nembiará.

"Anyone who fears the Christian God can go back to the mission," he said. "I will have no anger toward you if you follow the white God of fear. The Jesuits believe in him. I do not have dark thoughts toward them because of what they believe. It is their right as men." His head moved slowly, his eyes scanning each man, woman, and child. All eyes stayed on him.

"They have forced their Christian God on us, taught our young their ways and ignored the gods of our fathers. They frown on the old ways and force our people to believe that their God is the one almighty God. Our people moved to the mission as they asked, and now we are dying faster than we are born."

Is it the one God of the white man who is destroying our people? Avá-Tapé wondered, or are the old gods angry because we have turned our backs on the old ways?

"Sickness hangs heavy in the air at the mission," his father continued. "Many of you have lost families to these spirits. The *añag* have attacked others. Only one without eyes cannot see the signs."

"He speaks truth!" Avá-Canindé shook his fist. "The sickness took the mother of my sons."

"And tried to take my son," Avá-Nembiará added. "Tupá kept him from the country of the dead and helped me bring him back to the living."

Avá-Tapé felt the crowd's attention shift to him, its force pressing on him as if he should speak, but he sensed only confusion. His heart remained with his father, but his mind had gone with the Jesuits. He could still see Father Antonio's smoldering look. Had he been damned to Christian hell? Had the appearance of the Jesuits been a sign? Why did the Christian God remain silent? If there *were* a sign, how would it come?

If the Christian God wanted to give him a sign it would be in His house. A place of power. The church. He had to go there, to be alone in His presence and pray for a sign. Then he would know...

"The life we have known has been destroyed like a tree that falls from sickness in its roots," Avá-Nembiará said.

Avá-Tapé felt relief as the attention shifted back to his father.

"Our numbers grow smaller with each season. The white brothers of the Jesuits have conquered the land and made slaves of our brothers. The world that we have known is coming to an end. *Techó-achy* makes our spirits heavy. We have to fast and lighten our souls so we can leave this world before it consumes us."

"And dance," Avá-Canindé said. "We have to build a dance house so we can dance our lighter spirits to the Land Without Evil and live in paradise without the darkness of *techó-achy*."

"The dance house!" a voice yelled from the crowd. Avá-Karaí pushed his way to the front. Tall and wiry, his dark eyes blazed from his long face with the fire that had once been in Father Antonio's eyes. "The gods of my grandfathers are not gods of fear, they are gods of the forest." He held his muscular arms wide. "Gods of nature who follow the Great Father. His son Tupá has spoken to us with the voice of our *paí*. I have heard no words from the God of the Jesuits. Only the words of our people raised up in song to him. He has not answered. Tupá has."

"Enough of this talk of gods and men," Avá-Canindé said. "Let us build our dance house as our grandfathers did. Let us dance our way to paradise."

Avá-Tapé looked over and saw Avá-Nembiará's eyes fill with tears. He looked away, not wanting his father to know he had seen. Avá-Canindé went to Avá-Karaí and the two hugged. They came to the center of the circle with their arms over each other's shoulders and took Avá-Tapé and his father into their embrace. A murmur rose from the crowd, then they converged on the four men. Avá-Tapé felt warmth in his heart, but his mind still grappled with thoughts of the Christian God.

As the sun sank lower, children ran for firewood, women stoked cooking fires, and the men gathered in Avá-Canindé's *maloca* to talk of the dance house. Avá-Tapé sat beside the door half listening to their plans. When the sun turned orange he stepped outside and knelt beside the door, checking the clearing to be sure no one saw him, then he slipped into the forest and trotted down the path to the mission.

ELEVEN

The streets of the mission looked empty, but Avá-Tapé could hear the sounds of people inside their houses. The smell of cooking fires drifted to him on the warm, still air. A red sun hung on the edge of the horizon, bathing the church in a rose-colored glow. Avá-Tapé wiped sweat from his brow and gazed up at the sculpted facade, smiling when he saw Nandé Cy and Tupá mingling with the saints of the Christians—Avá-Canindé's work.

The walls stood straight, but the cedar supports had been reinforced. Fresh holes from burrowing ants lay at the base of the foundation. He heard voices, then saw Father Rodrigo rounding the corner, talking to two of his people, who carried shovels.

"Avá-Tapé!" Father Rodrigo ran toward him, arms wide. "You've come back to us." He looked up. "Thank God!"

Avá-Tapé could neither move nor speak in his confusion, then Father Rodrigo hugged him. "My prayers have been answered." He stepped back, clasping Avá-Tapé's shoulder, his eyes fixed on Avá-Tapé's. "Come see me after you speak to Father Antonio. We'll have tea and talk. I'll go put the kettle on." He hurried off, leaving Avá-Tapé speechless. "I'll be waiting," he called back. Father Rodrigo's discussion with the workers faded into the night, leaving an oppressive silence in its wake.

Avá-Tapé looked up at the looming church front, then climbed the steps to the massive front doors. Easing one open, he peered inside. The stained-glass window behind the altar shone faintly with the dying sun, giving the face of Jesus a flush of radiance. Light flickered on the walls from the racks of offered candles. Two large candles illuminated the altar. The rest of the church remained in darkness.

No sound came from within.

Avá-Tapé stood by the door, torn between the urge to go inside and the impulse to flee. As he turned to leave, a familiar voice echoed from the priest's chambers.

"Father Lorenzo," Father Antonio said, "would you be kind enough to take a letter to Bishop Cristobal?"

"As soon as I get the quill and parchment I will be ready."

After the sound of closing doors and shuffling parchments, Father Antonio began. "Your Holiness. Once more, I find I must write to you from the southern continent of the Americas. I fear that matters here are slipping out of control.

"We have encountered increased resistance to the teachings of Jesus from Avá-Nembiará, the shaman I spoke of in my earlier correspondence. The majority of the Indians now participate in ritual dances while listening to his exhortations. These discourses deal with themes that obsess the Guarani: their lot on Earth, the necessity to heed the norms laid down by their old gods, and their hopes of gaining the state of perfection which allows them to see the road to the Land Without Evil.

"The present state of dissension among these Guarani make them more than vulnerable to enslavement. I pray that you can still come as soon as God's will allows. I sincerely hope that your presence in this exotic land will still the uneasiness that troubles my soul.

"Please advise me, Your Holiness. I am losing my grasp on their wild and untamed souls. Your Humble Servant, Father Antonio Rodriguez Escobar."

More shuffling echoed through the church followed by the sound of opening doors and footsteps. Avá-Tapé slipped back out the door and hid by the base of the steps, stunned by Father Antonio's words.

Wild and untamed souls? His father possessed by minions of Satan? Enslavement by settlers? And the bishop—God's representative coming...

The church doors creaked open. Avá-Tapé ducked lower, watching the priests pass and disappear down the darkened street.

Father Antonio fears that my father will take their souls, Avá-Tapé thought. Who is the best one to guide them? My father? Father Antonio? Who do their souls belong to? The Christian God or the gods of my father?

Maybe now the time had come for him to find answers. He crept up the steps, slipped inside the church, and closed the door behind him, giving his eyes a moment to adjust. Fresh dirt had been packed in the hole which the ants had dug. The altar sat in its place of honor at the head of the church. The priest's chalice and other magic objects lay on a purple velvet tapestry covering the altar. Avá-Tapé went to the front of the church, knelt before the altar and crossed himself.

"Our Father who art in heaven," he began. The sound of his voice echoed in the emptiness, making him feel small and exposed. He decided to talk to God in his head in silent prayer the way Father Antonio had taught him.

"Hallowed be thy name," he continued silently. He repeated the words as he had countless times before, trying to give himself to them so he could sense their meaning, but they didn't feel like they had any power. He thought of the books, the writings, and the rituals the Jesuits had taught him. Was it all meaningless?

Where had the dark wind come from? Had the gods of the forest brought sickness, ants, and jaguars as a sign against the white man's ways, or had the Christian God brought these dark spirits to show the forest people that their ways were wrong? Did both Gods live? If so, which had more power?

"Our Father who art in heaven," he began again. "Your dark-robed children have taught me Your message and brought Your words to me from Your Bible. I have learned the rituals and spoken Your magic. I have shared Your body and blood with my brothers, but I have not seen or heard You speak. If You are too great for words, then all I ask for is a sign. Show me so I may know what is right. I only wish to do what is best for my people."

He stopped his thoughts, his senses alert, watching, waiting, listening with all his being.

Silence and darkness answered.

The candles burned lower and the church grew darker. All light from outside had gone, leaving the stained-glass window blackened, with only a few pinpoints of candlelight reflecting from its surface.

He prayed fervently. Hail Marys. Our Fathers. Prayers he had been given for penance. The repetition began to sound like chants, so he tried to put feeling into them.

Please, he thought, putting all his emotion into his request. *A sign.*

The doors behind him opened, followed by a gust of wind. His heart soared. He scrunched his eyes shut and silently thanked God, then opened them, rose, and turned to face Father Antonio's scowl. His heart jumped.

"What are you doing here defiling my altar!" the priest bellowed.

Avá-Tapé couldn't speak.

"Your Father sent you, didn't he?" Anger burned in Father Antonio's voice. Sadness filled his eyes. "In the name of the Father, Son, and Holy Spirit," the priest said weakly. He made the sign of the cross, pulled a crucifix from his robes and came forward holding it in front of him. Avá-Tapé stepped back and tripped, sprawling over the steps to the altar.

"Begone, minion of Satan! In the name and by the power of Our Lord Jesus Christ!" Father Antonio made the sign of the cross, almost touching Avá-Tapé with the crucifix. "Be uprooted and put to flight from the Church of God, from the soul made in the image of God and redeemed with the blood of the Divine Lamb." He made the sign of the cross again.

Avá-Tapé scrambled to his feet and backed away. Father Antonio pressed forward, thrusting the cross in his face. Shouts filled the church. Father Lorenzo and two other priests rushed in. One came up the center aisle, the others came up each side.

"You don't understand," Avá-Tapé cried out. His trembling voice came as little more than a whisper. His heart raged and his throat stayed tight. "I have come to pray. I have come for a sign from your God."

"How dare you blaspheme the house of the Lord." Spittle flew from Father Antonio's mouth. His eyes looked wild and accusing. Whatever sadness had smoldered there earlier now burst into wildfire. Avá-Tapé knew that his words had not been heard.

The other priests moved closer, reminding him of his dream of the *añag.* Cold panic rushed through him. His legs felt like water. He looked from Father Antonio to Father Lorenzo and the other priests, then bolted forward, knocking Father Antonio down.

Angry shouts echoed through the church as he ran for the doors. A hand grazed his shoulder as he pulled one door open and darted into the night.

TWELVE

Avá-Tapé ran through the darkened streets of the mission, wishing he was back in the safety of his father's *maloca*, but he couldn't go through the forest until daylight. The recent jaguar attacks made the streets and the surrounding forest more dangerous than usual.

He saw cooking fires through the windows of the adobe houses he passed. Fire would bring safety. He thought of stopping, but decided against it after the way Father Antonio acted. He had no way of knowing what might have been said to the people still living here in fear of the Christian God.

He stopped to catch his breath. All the firewood at his old house had been used the night of the jaguar attacks. Even if he found some, he had no way to start a fire. The smell of roast tapir and pumpkin came to him from a corner house at the end of the street. His stomach growled. When had he last eaten?

Creeping toward the door, he peered inside. In the light from the hearth he saw the lithe profile of a girl turning a spit over a fire. Long, silken black hair hung to her small waist, hiding her face until she turned toward him. In the half light, he saw a delicate nose and slender arms and legs. His heart beat faster. Her graceful movements reminded him of a butterfly flitting from flower to flower. How could he say something without scaring her?

A meaty hand grasped his shoulder, making him yelp. The girl looked up, surprised. Avá-Tapé stumbled sideways and fell. Two large feet appeared in front of his face. His eyes traveled up two tree trunk legs to a thick torso before meeting the round, massive face of a Guarani. Big ears and a pug nose. The man remained expressionless, then his thick lips spread into a gap-toothed smile.

"Avá-Tapé, man of visions, son of Avá-Nembiará, *paí* of our people. What brings you to my door?" He took Avá-Tapé's wrist and pulled him to his feet as though he weighed nothing.

Avá-Tapé saw the outline of the girl standing in the doorway. He felt awkward and exposed. He looked up at the man again. "I - I didn't mean..."

"This is a wondrous sign. Tomorrow my daughter and I go to the new village to live among our people, and on this night one who has heard the chant of Tupá comes to my house."

Avá-Tapé recognized the man, but couldn't remember his name.

"I am Avá-Guiracambí," the giant said as if reading his thoughts. He bowed his head and spoke softer. "You must bless our meal. Share food with us."

"I cannot bless your food," Avá-Tapé said. "I am not a *paí*, only the son of one."

"If you cannot bless my food, I am sure you can eat it."

The girl giggled. Avá-Tapé felt his face grow hot.

"You have come to my door on my last night at the *reduccioné*," Avá-Guiracambí said. "That is blessing enough. Come."

Avá-Tapé followed the limping man into the house and saw their few belongings packed in a corner near the door. The girl hurried to the fire. Close up, she looked more beautiful than he had imagined. Full lips. White teeth. A tiny nose. He tried not to stare, but couldn't keep his gaze from her. How different from her giant father.

Her eyes seemed to swallow him. They looked big and trusting yet questioning while seeming to have answers of their own—like his mother's.

"This is my daughter," Avá-Guiracambí said. She looked down. "Kuná-Mainó."

Hummingbird, Avá-Tapé thought. How she moves. He has named her well.

While Kuná-Mainó fed them pheasant and *maize*, Avá-Guiracambí spoke of his disillusionment with the Jesuits. Avá-Tapé stole glances at Kuná-Mainó, who turned away when his eyes met hers.

"You must stay until the sun returns," Avá-Guiracambí said. "When it comes, you can lead us to the new village."

"Three new *malocas* have been built," Avá-Tapé said, trying to keep his mind in the moment. "There is room for you and your daughter. But what of her mother?"

"She passed on to the country of the dead two harvests ago. I almost lost my Kuná-Mainó, but her spirit is young and strong. Her soul flew past the *añag* and came back to the world of the living, the same as yours. It is said that Tupá guided you. Now there is talk of you laughing at death and defeating the *añag* when they came for you and your family."

Avá-Tapé felt the expectant gazes of his hosts weighing on him. Why did people expect so much? Because of his father? The tongues of the people moved faster than jaguars. He wanted to be left alone to figure things out for himself, but the changing world around him wouldn't wait.

"Tupá sang and chanted when the evil wind of the white man's sickness tried to take my soul," he said, "but I cannot remember his words. Only his visions."

Avá-Guiracambí grunted. "His words will come when the time is right. Tell me of the *añag* you defeated."

Avá-Tapé wanted to tell of pissing in the jaguar's face, but couldn't speak of it in front of this beautiful girl. The way she looked at him made it hard for him to show his heart. "The wisdom of a wise man came to me in my time of danger."

Avá-Guiracambí's jutting brow furrowed in concentration and he seemed to come to a decision. "We should sleep," he said, rising suddenly. "Tomorrow we go to the village." He pulled out two ox skins and a jaguar skin, giving the cat skin to Avá-Tapé. "It is appropriate for a man of visions," he said.

After stoking the fire, he rolled up in his ox skin and quickly fell into a snoring sleep. Kuná-Mainó went to another corner without speaking. Avá-Tapé lay down near the fire.

As Avá-Guiracambí snored and the gentle breathing of his daughter filled the house, Avá-Tapé lay awake thinking about his plea to the Christian God and the answer he had received. Father Antonio, who once treated him like a son, had taught him the ways of the white men. When Avá-Tapé pleaded for a sign from their God, Father Antonio had been the messenger. The sign had not been one of love, but of sadness and anger.

He rolled onto his side with his back to the fire, watching the door, puzzling over all that had happened. He didn't feel welcome in the house of the Christian God. Father Antonio, a man who preached love and forgiveness, saw him as an enemy because of his father's beliefs.

He spent all night trying to make sense of everything that had happened, but nothing fit. By the time the first shimmer of silver lit the horizon he still had no sleep and no answers, only strong feelings. He tried to force sleep, but felt tense, as if preparing for some unseen ordeal—and now these new feelings for Kuná-Mainó had come to him. Something he hadn't planned for.

As the darkness outside turned to gray, he found himself studying the gentle curve of Kuná-Mainó's sleeping form. He closed his eyes, feeling their heaviness, wondering what it would be like sleeping next to her, feeling her warmth and soft skin...

He sensed a presence and thought of Father Antonio and the jaguars, not knowing which he feared more. He opened his eyes to daylight and saw two large brown eyes, long eyelashes and high cheekbones. She moved away. He sat up and looked around. Her father had gone. His heart raced as he felt her still scrutinizing him.

"You speak more with your eyes than with your mouth. My sister speaks much with her eyes, but her tongue rushes ahead of her thoughts. Her chatter can tire the strongest man."

Kuná-Mainó smiled. "It sounds as if your tongue has grown strong from its battles with hers. She has taught you well."

"Why do you watch me sleep?"

"They say you are a *paí*, but I remember watching Father Antonio teach you and Avá-Karaí his words and the ways of his people. They spoke of you being a Holy Man of the Jesuit God. Now they say you are a messenger of Tupá."

"I don't remember seeing you at church."

"I was there, but you didn't see me. I was a giggling little girl who waited for every chance to see you, but your eyes never came to mine. They were always buried in books and words."

"And now you are a giggling bigger girl."

Her expression darkened momentarily, then brightened. "There is talk of your visions, battles with jaguars, how you laughed at death, and how you and your father defied Father Antonio and his God in front of the people. That is what made my father decide to join you. Many families are leaving the mission to live with your father and Avá-Canindé."

Her eyes held him the way his mother's had so many times before. Expectant, demanding, hungry for truth. Yes, he had seen things when the white sickness took his soul and he had laughed after facing death. His father had stood up to Father Antonio. He had only been at his side. Last night at the church, he had stood alone. "The only vision I am sure of is the one of beauty that is in front of me."

She blushed and turned away.

"I don't know what happened," he continued. "I only tried to do what is right. I don't know which god has more power. I prayed to the God of the Christians, but He wouldn't answer. His priest became angry with me." He stopped, feeling as if he had spoken too much, but it felt good to have the words flowing out of him.

"I don't want to be a *paí*. I'm not sure of which gods to worship, but I think Tupá's magic saved me from the jaws of a hungry jaguar—and when it ran from me, I did laugh, but I don't know if all of this means as much as they say."

"They are signs," Avá-Guiracambí said, his huge frame filling the doorway. "Signs from the gods of our people, just as the silence of the Christian God is a sign."

"How can silence be a sign?"

"Sometimes what is not said means more than what is said."

Kuná-Mainó went to the hearth while her father limped in and began stacking things by the door. "A group of our families wish to join your father's village. As I speak, they gather what they want to bring to the village. Will you lead us there?"

Avá-Tapé stood and stretched. "Not only will I lead you, but I will help to carry your burden." He looked over in time to catch Kuná-Mainó's smile before she turned away.

THIRTEEN

Avá-Tapé brought twelve more families to the new village. Aside from all who had died from sickness and jaguar attacks, close to one-third of the Guarani had abandoned the mission to join Avá-Nembiará in his dream of reaching the Land Without Evil. Word of his visions spread quickly among those still living at the mission. More families would soon follow.

Avá-Tapé struggled up the path carrying a large part of Avá-Guiracambí's load. The rest of the people followed in single file, dragging their possessions. His father, Avá-Canindé, Santo, and Rico met him at the edge of the village.

"Get some of the men to help our brothers," Avá-Canindé said to his sons.

"What gift is this that my son brings?" Avá-Nembiará asked.

"Those who have heard the voice of Tupá and wish to follow his wisdom."

Avá-Nembiará looked past Avá-Tapé to Avá-Guiracambí. "It makes my heart warm to see you with us." He turned back to Avá-Tapé. "Your words carry strength. I feel your spirit strong in this. Has the war in your heart ended?"

Avá-Tapé pondered his father's words. The Christian God had answered with silence and an angry priest. Nanderú had sent His son Tupá, who had spoken through Avá-Nembiará and come to Avá-Tapé in his visions. "The war you speak of has ended," he said, drawing himself up. He looked over at Kuná-Mainó. "But a new war rages in my heart. One that I cannot win."

Avá-Nembiará looked from his son to Kuná-Mainó and back again. One eyebrow arched and a slow smile filled his face. "Help our brothers," Avá-Nembiará said to a group of men coming up the path. "Take them to your *malocas*, feed them and give them a place for their hammocks. Tonight we dance. Tomorrow we build new *malocas*. Avá-Tapé, bring Avá-Guiracambí and his young flower to the house of our family. Tell your mother to prepare for a celebration."

Other than a sliver of moon and a few flickering stars dotting the horizon, darkness filled the forest that night. Under Avá-Canindé's direction, the tribe built a bonfire in the clearing where the dance house was to be built. Huge flames licked at the darkened sky while the people gathered, circling the fire.

Avá-Canindé and the older men flanked Avá-Nembiará as he danced in front of the blaze. Each man shadowed his movements. Though they all had their own feathers and air of authority, no one matched the splendor or grace of Avá-Nembiará as he sang and danced.

His head blazed with its own fire as the radiant feathers of his headdress bobbed and weaved. Light seemed to fly off the prominent scarlet plumes of crested woodpeckers. Bright tail feathers of parrots and macaws with special powers hung from both sides, representing the souls of birds who were his spirit helpers.

A sash of cotton plaited with feather ornaments graced his chest. Bracelets of the same materials hung from his wrists. In one hand, he shook a cross, full with scarlet macaw feathers. In his other, he held a gourd pierced with an arrow: his sacred rattle, which carried its own spirits within. Parrot feathers decorated its top.

The other men held no rattles or crosses, yet they danced with equal fervor. None came close to Avá-Nembiará's perfection as he danced, seemingly oblivious to his surroundings. Each step, each gesture, he executed with deft precision, imbuing every nuance with meaning. Each beat alternated between the two poles of reality.

Chaos. The moments between the beats of time. Moments of destruction and the violence of change.

Order. The world in each beat of awareness. Fleeting moments of lucidity in an elusive world.

Chaos.

Order.

Chaos.

The divine dance of the universe.

Avá-Tapé watched his father in the halo of firelight and thought of the unseen intelligence that ruled men. The Jesuits tried to capture its glory in books, pictures, buildings and altars. All static, meaningless, and silent.

His father's dance had life, motion, and passion. His boundless energy came forth as an earnest expression of life and belief.

"Why don't you dance?"

A chill sprinted down Avá-Tapé's spine as Kuná-Mainó's warm breath caressed his ear. He turned and saw her face suffused with a gentle orange glow. Twin fires of gold danced in her eyes.

"The time is not right," he said, although part of him wanted to.

"How do you know unless you try?"

"My heart tells me," he said without hesitation. "I have been taught by the Jesuits how to worship their God and my father has taught me the ways of our grandfathers. I tried, but could not walk on both paths. My father's path has chosen me, but my feet have not been long on it. I have to learn to walk before I can dance."

She nodded, her eyes telling him she accepted his words. She looked back toward the bonfire. The singing and dancing had stopped. Avá-Canindé and the others sat among the people, leaving Avá-Nembiará alone before the fire, his face glistening, sweat dripping from his body. Would Tupá speak through him?

"The white man's evil wind has come again," Avá-Nembiará said, "sweeping our brothers and sisters away to the country of the dead."

Avá-Tapé could tell by his father's mannerisms that Tupá had not come. Avá-Nembiará spoke his own words.

"The whites have changed the thoughts of our children. Taught them to speak on paper using white words and books to worship their silent God. Our people and our old ways have dwindled to nothing more than smoking coals from a once great fire." He made an expansive gesture.

"The spirits of the forest have gone to the mission to take back what belongs to the forest. Ants have toppled their buildings and filled their streets and houses. The *añag* have crept upon them in the darkness, and still the white God remains silent." He paused, eyes scanning the crowd, challenging any who might speak. Silence and rapt attention answered.

"These are the signs of the end times," he continued. "We must go back to the old ways. We must dance. Rid ourselves of *techó-achy*. Purify our bodies and lighten our spirits so we can dance our way to the Land Without Evil."

He walked along the edge of the crowd, studying the faces of the people before going back to the center of the circle.

"Go now," he said. "Let sleep take you, so you can wake strong. The plan for our dance house is ready, but we have to build *malocas* for our brothers first."

The gathering broke up and the people drifted back to their *malocas.*

"They say his son has had visions, healed the sick, and defeated jaguars," Avá-Tapé heard someone whisper in the darkness.

"And he is not even trained as a *paí*," another answered.

Avá-Tapé knew they talked of him. He didn't like the attention. He looked over and saw Kuná-Mainó studying him, a faraway look in her eyes.

The people walked past, their eyes searching his. Some looked away when he returned their gazes. Others stared at the ground. More whispers. Pointing fingers.

"He will be as great as his father."

"Greater, they say."

"Father Antonio fears him."

Avá-Nembiará stared after the people as the last of them left the clearing, then his gaze came to rest on Avá-Tapé. Though his father didn't speak, Avá-Tapé sensed that he wanted to talk. He also felt a need. Things he felt but didn't understand. His father would have answers.

"Walk with me to the *maloca?*" Kuná-Mainó's voice caught his attention. He looked from his father to her. When he looked back, Avá-Nembiará had disappeared.

Torn between the urges to follow his father or stay with Kuná-Mainó, he took her to the *maloca.*

"Tell me of the dance," she said as they left the firelight.

Avá-Tapé gave one last glance over his shoulder, then looked ahead.

"What can you tell me?" she said. "I have never seen the Jesuits dance; only the older men of the tribe and your father. What meaning does it have?"

He tried to articulate his thoughts and faltered, then his father's words came to him.

"In dance a man is transformed into a tool of time. His body is a set of places that move in time. Its parts are moved through space to form patterns that show time. The movements, their order, the songs, how long the dance lasts, where it happens, the feathers and ornaments, all have meaning. The symbols come from deep in our lives. The dance acts out the stories of our gods and ancestors. It makes the end time move faster and paradise come sooner."

When they reached the door of the *maloca,* Kuná-Mainó studied him. "Tupá tells of what has happened and what is to happen," she said. "He wants us to sing and dance our way to the Land Without Evil."

Avá-Tapé smiled. In her own way Kuná-Mainó understood. "I have something I have to do," he said, stepping backward.

Mild surprise showed on her face. "You are not staying here?"

"My mother and sister will take care of anything you need."

"What is it that takes you from the fire of your home into the darkness of the night?"

"My father," he said, fading back into the shadows. "We have many things to talk about. I will stay the night in his *maloca*."

"Watch yourself," she called out softly.

"I will." He trotted by the feeble light of the moon and paused at the edge of the clearing, hoping no jaguars were in the forest, then he sprinted down the path, anxious for the comfort of his father's house.

When he saw the glow of Avá-Nembiará's fire, he slowed, letting himself catch his breath. The forest pressed in. No night birds cried, no howler monkeys called, and there were no signs of game foraging in the undergrowth. No sound, except the rasp of his own breathing.

When his breath returned to normal he went to the door and looked in. His father sat motionless before the fire with his back to him. "Come in, my son," Avá-Nembiará said before Avá-Tapé could open his mouth.

"Father," Avá-Tapé said, grasping for the words. "I want to become a *paí*."

Avá-Nembiará remained immobile, but his words came without hesitation. "I know."

FOURTEEN

"Your journey has already begun," Avá-Nembiará said without turning around. "I saw signs when you were little, but still I was not sure. When the dark wind of the white sickness carried you to the country of the dead, Tupá gave you visions. His magic brought you back to the land of the living."

What his father called visions, the Jesuits passed off as dreams with no substance. To Avá-Tapé, they were as real as the world of waking—and some of them had come true.

He seated himself across from his father. "You will teach me?"

Avá-Nembiará continued looking into the fire as though gazing into another world. "Fire is the teacher."

"Fire?"

"Fire is hungry. It eats but never has enough. This is life. This is what a *paí* must learn—to be a master of fire."

Avá-Tapé stared into the flames as they licked at the wood and thought of how the intensity of his father's dance had grown with each day. Were days passing faster? For him, each harvest came quicker than the one before. Was this a sign of the end times? "Are we beings of fire who burn with life?"

"Spirits do not have fire like men. They crave it as we crave life. When a *paí* heals with tobacco it is eaten by fire. To get helper spirits, a man must know the meaning of this burning. It is how spirits eat."

"Is it the same with animals—when they eat plants and eat each other?"

Avá-Nembiará smiled. "A *paí* must learn how the desire to

consume lives in the spirits who rule the universe. Spirit helpers not only need food. They are like food. They enter and live in a *paí's* body the same way food is eaten and stored in a man's body. When a *paí* learns the meaning of spirit helpers he understands his own hunger and how spirits connect him to all creation. He consumes the visible and invisible worlds.

"Not only animals, but the trees and plants have secret lives too. Secret worlds. Visible and invisible. All life consumes. To master passage from one world to another a *paí* must master the passages of his own body. He purifies himself by fasting and learns how food moves through him, the way his breath goes out during song, and how his soul travels to other worlds."

A log collapsed in the fire sending a shower of embers floating up to disappear into the darkness. Avá-Tapé thought of the world he could see and the worlds he could not.

Avá-Nembiará clasped his hands together. "When a man's spirit and body are one, it is like tobacco eaten by fire. As master of fire a *paí* knows this as the meeting of the world and spirit in time."

"Like the fish who is eaten by his bigger brother, who gets eaten by a bigger fish who gets eaten by a man or a jaguar." The words flew from Avá-Tapé's mouth the same way his thoughts rushed through his mind. "As we consume life, life consumes us. We are hunter and hunted. The spirit of fire."

Avá-Nembiará held his arms wide. "As a keeper of souls, a *paí* must master the fire that makes spirit change its form, then he can change his form and travel between the worlds." He shook his fists, emphasizing a world with each one.

Avá-Tapé watched flames lick at wood in their never ending quest that could be fed but never satisfied. He saw fire, felt its heat and saw what it left behind, but he could never touch or hold it. So it was with the spirits of the forest, the animals, and the spirits of men.

"How we move through the world," Avá-Tapé said hesitantly. "In time. We are born. The sun comes and goes from the sky.

The moon grows fat, then fades like an ancient one. Plants grow and give fruit, then die and are born again. We are here now, and then now is no more. Each time passes, solid, but moving like each step of the dance. Order and disorder. Fire."

Avá-Nembiará held his hand out, slowly clenching it into a fist. "And in the places between time where being becomes not being, spirit meets the world. Here is the fire."

Outside, the darkness swallowed everything. The soft chirrup of crickets filled the night, mixed with the calls of night birds. Being here, now, with his father, made Avá-Tapé feel as if the moment belonged to the time of another world. One that until this night he had only glimpsed. Now he looked through its doorway of fire into a place where the lines separating his body and spirit blurred.

"Tupá's chant," Avá-Nembiará said tentatively. "Has it come to you?"

Avá-Tapé had almost forgotten his desire for the chant, but his father's mention gave him a renewed sense of it. He strained to remember, but the memory slipped from his mind like the morning mists floating up from the floor of the forest. "It lives inside me," he said, "but flies through my head like a frightened parrot. I cannot catch it."

"If you live the way of a *pai*, eat how he eats, clean your body and quiet your thoughts, your fire will burn clean and bright. Such a parrot will not be able to turn away from the beauty of your flame. If your spirit is calm, it will come to you in a vision while you sleep."

Could he live the same way as his father? Eat as he ate? Not eat for days and dance with the same fervor? The Christian way had shown him the white man's magic of speaking on paper, but it brought him no closer to understanding the forces that moved his life.

His father's world of fire and spirits had touched his heart. He would never be happy unless he explored their mysteries and discovered what secrets they told about his life and that of his people—a life that seemed to be rapidly coming to an end.

FIFTEEN

Avá-Tapé worked hard helping to build the new *malocas,* taking every opportunity he found to be near Kuná-Mainó. Each time he saw her, she smiled and he would forget what he had been doing. Avá-Canindé caught him twice and teased him, telling him that the jaguars were sure to make a meal of him when the hummingbird flew near.

Keeping Kuná-Mainó and Pindé close to her, his mother assumed the role of directing the women and children in the cooking and gathering of food. Though the people looked to Avá-Nembiará as their spiritual leader, Avá-Canindé became their chief, making decisions for all of them while organizing the building of houses. He always deferred to Avá-Nembiará, often asking for guidance, but he took control of the growing village with a firm hand, freeing Avá-Nembiará to pursue spiritual matters relating to the health and well-being of the people.

Avá-Tapé spent most nights with his father, but made every excuse he could to sleep in his mother's house, close to Kuná-Mainó. In those rare times when they found themselves alone, she shared her thoughts. When others were around she acted as if he weren't there; but when none could see, she gave him secret smiles.

Avá-Tapé spent his days scheming about ways to be alone with her, but more often than not Pindé stayed close, making a nuisance of herself. He couldn't bear the thought of Kuná-Mainó seeing him angry with his sister.

Late one warm humid day, Avá-Tapé sat in front of his father's *maloca* with his back to the door. The air hung still, as if time had stopped, and the forest remained quiet, except for the scattered cries of birds.

Voices broke the stillness. Santo and Rico trotted up the path and plopped down beside him, their eyes wide and expectant.

"Tell us how you pissed in the face of the jaguar," Santo said, uncoiling his skinny arms and legs. His round face and wide brown eyes looked to Avá-Tapé in open admiration. Now that most of his weight had returned he looked more like his father.

Beside him Rico nodded, excitement flashing in his inquisitive eyes. His small nose and delicate lips remained a painful reminder of the boy's dead mother.

Avá-Tapé groaned inwardly, tiring of telling the tale, but secretly enjoying the younger boys' attention.

"I was not brave," he said. "If I did not piss in the eyes of the jaguar, I would have turned my loincloth brown."

"The smell would have gotten him," Santo added.

Rico giggled, and Santo's eyes brightened as his brother's laughter caught him. Avá-Tapé felt his own chuckle rising.

"A brown mark on a loincloth is the sign of a man," said a stern voice from behind the boys.

Santo's and Rico's laughter halted.

"Part of the manhood ritual," Avá-Tapé added, his voice suddenly serious when he saw his friend Avá-Karaí coming up the path.

"If a man does not have a brown stain on his loincloth he has failed the ritual." Avá-Karaí stopped behind the boys and folded his arms. Santo and Rico turned and looked up to see him rocking back and forth on his heels, his square jaw working from side to side. His piercing eyes held the younger boys.

No one moved until Avá-Tapé spoke with the same tone and authority. "Avá-Karaí passed the brown stain part of his manhood ritual when he was nine harvests and Monkey Face caught him in the bushes."

Confusion swept over the faces of the younger boys until
Avá-Karaí burst into laughter, followed by Avá-Tapé. Rico
giggled, while Santo leaned forward clutching his stomach.

"If I remember right," Avá-Karaí said between breaths, "you
made a brown stain on your loincloth when you ran like a
monkey from Avá-Takuá."

Another round of laughter swept through them until Avá-
Karaí dropped to his knees. "Your father is looking for the two
of you," he said, catching his breath. "Go before darkness
comes. Avá-Tapé and I have important things to speak of."

The boys' smiles faded. They looked to Avá-Tapé in a silent
plea for permission to stay. He shook his head and pointed to
the trail. He would share time with them later. Now he needed
to talk with his friend.

"Do you see the way they look at me?" Avá-Tapé said as the
boys disappeared among the trees.

"Not only them." Avá-Karaí lowered his voice. "Most of the
others, too."

Avá-Tapé stared at the ground. "They ask so much of me
with their eyes, as if I am one who knows. Old and young. They
make me something I am not…"

"You are no different in your heart," Avá-Karaí said. "I see
you as I always saw you, only now I see a boy who runs from
Avá-Takuá carrying the weight of the souls of his people on his
shoulders. The little boy spark is almost gone. You carry much
for one so young. You are starting to look like Monkey Face."

Avá-Tapé smiled, wondering if he should tell Avá-Karaí of the
letter to the bishop and the way the priests chased him from the
church. He decided to keep it to himself. No sense making anyone else carry the burden of his knowledge. "There is even
more that troubles me," he said, thinking of Kuná-Mainó, "but
I am not the only one who needs to talk. What is so important
that it brings you to the door of my father's *maloca?*"

"Something has happened," Avá-Karaí said, a faraway look
in his eyes. "It is always in my thoughts when I sleep and when
I am alone."

"A spirit?"

"No." He sighed. "A creature of such beauty that my heart soars."

"Beauty?"

"She has been in the village less than a moon. Her name is Kuná-Mainó."

Avá-Tapé flinched as if he'd been punched in the stomach. "Kuná-Mainó?"

"She used to be a skinny little girl when we were smaller. I had not seen her for many harvests. Now she is—she is…"

Avá-Tapé's heart rose in his throat. "Have you told her this?"

"No, but I will." A dreamy smile filled Avá-Karaí's face. "I will tell her when the time is right."

SIXTEEN

The men of the village no longer treated Avá-Tapé like the other boys. Many of them asked for his thoughts and listened to every word he uttered. He sensed them watching him as if expecting something. When he felt eyes on him, he turned quickly to catch someone staring before they looked away.

One day he felt the stares more than usual. When he couldn't stand the scrutiny any longer, he confronted Avá-Canindé behind one of the *malocas*.

"Why does everyone look at me with so much attention?"

Avá-Canindé looked everywhere but at him. "Don't you know?"

"Kuná-Mainó?"

Avá-Canindé smirked. "You have eyes for the hummingbird?" He shook his head. "That is not why the people look to you."

"Then why do they stare?"

"Don't you feel it?"

"Feel what?"

He laughed, then his eyes met Avá-Tapé's. "You are the only one who doesn't know, but you will soon enough."

"Know what?"

Avá-Canindé smiled and walked past Avá-Tapé, leaving him more perplexed than ever. What was happening? Had Avá-Karaí spoken to Kuná-Mainó?

He saw Avá-Canindé laughing and joking with the other men. Though he couldn't hear their words, he knew they talked of him. He wanted to go to his father, but Avá-Nembiará had been gone for two nights.

As the sun fell below the trees he went back to his mother's house, anxious to catch Kuná-Mainó alone. Tonight, he thought, if I am both brave and gentle, I will take her hand. I cannot sit and watch while Avá-Karaí takes her. She will see the way of my heart and I will learn of hers.

"You must go to your father," his mother said as he entered the *maloca*. "He waits."

"He has been gone for two days."

"Avá-Canindé came to me just now. Hurry before darkness comes."

Avá-Tapé trotted down the path to his father's *maloca*. As the light faded, so did his hopes of being with Kuná-Mainó.

He reached Avá-Nembiará's house in the gray of dusk when the crickets and other night insects began their songs. He heard the voices of men and saw the glow of a fire. His heart beat faster.

Stepping into the *maloca*, he found himself in the middle of Avá-Canindé, Avá-Guiracambí, Avá-Takuá and others, all dressed in feathers, as if readying themselves for dance. His father sat at the head of the circle closest to the fire, arrayed in his finest feather headband, sash, and armbands. Beside him sat a stool made of wood and deerskin strips.

Avá-Nembiará gestured toward it. "Sit."

Avá-Tapé looked around. All eyes were on him, expectant expressions on each face. He lowered himself to the stool, focusing his attention on his father, who spoke solemnly.

"Tupá has given you visions and the gift of his chant." Avá-Nembiará looked to each man, ensuring the importance of his words, then directed his attention back to Avá-Tapé. "Though you cannot hear his chant in your thoughts, you hold it in your heart. You must seek him again and ask him to touch your heart so you can remember."

Avá-Nembiará breathed on Avá-Tapé's chest and began singing one of his sacred songs. His words floated out of him in a breathy fashion. He bowed low as if picking a flower which he passed through the flow of his breath toward Avá-Tapé's chest.

With great ceremony, he spread out a sash and attached a small bundle of parrot feathers, all the while continuing his litany. After breathing on it, he put the sash on Avá-Tapé while tracing circles above his head with both hands. "You must never part from this," Avá-Nembiará said, his voice heavy with emotion. "It is one with you. Never allow yourself to enter a woman's body while wearing it."

Kuná-Mainó filled Avá-Tapé's thoughts. He looked to Avá-Guiracambí, whose eyes were on him. His face grew hot. Did the older man know his thoughts?

"You have traveled in the other world," his father said. "Your soul has passed the sleeping *añag* and returned to the country of the living with a gift from the gods. When the sun comes back to the world you must go on a sacred hunt. When you return I will teach you the ways of fire, healing, and traveling to the other worlds. If you learn well, you will have a true initiation and become a *paí* in your own right."

Avá-Tapé studied his father's stern face and saw a smile in his eyes. Avá-Nembiará turned and faced the others. "My brothers," he said, extending both arms. "I give you Avá-Tapé, messenger bird of Tupá, son of Avá-Nembiará, *paí* of the Guarani."

The other men stood, each coming to Avá-Tapé and hugging him, then Avá-Canindé and Avá-Guiracambí stepped outside and returned with a hollowed cedar log full of *chicha*. They all sat in a circle and drank, telling stories of the days before the white men.

Avá-Tapé had never drank *chicha* with the men. He felt nervous until his second gourd, then felt lightheaded. The other men treated him as one of them. Words flowed easily from his tongue. After his third gourd his mind spoke the words, but his mouth slurred them. Each man told the story of his first hunt, gesturing dramatically while enduring heckling and teasing from the others. When all had taken a turn, silence fell over the group.

"Tell us of the *añag*," Avá-Guiracambí said, raising his gourd to Avá-Tapé. The others all looked to him.

Any inhibition he felt earlier had been washed away by his fourth gourd of *chicha*. "I came through the forest at the time between the worlds," he said, rising unsteadily. "The sun did not light my way, but the night had not come yet. The rain came. Because of its chatter, the sound of my feet became part of its song. I couldn't tell if the spirits traveled with me or if the monkeys danced in the trees." He looked into the face of each man the same way his father had so many times before.

"I thought I heard another sound and stopped. Only the rain sang, so I started again. So did the other sound. I stopped and looked hard into the fading world. Like the brown river waters that come with heavy rains, the rain of that night washed out my sight. I saw nothing, but felt danger—and then I saw two eyes of cold fire gazing at me. Then two more. I smelled the cooking fires of the mission so I started to run, knowing I would be the *añags'* next meal."

His heart raced at the memory, and his throat became dry. He took a long draft of *chicha* to fortify himself.

"Tupá must have been watching, because I made it to the mission before they attacked, but in my fear I caused my mother's cooking pot to fall into the fire, bringing darkness. The rain still sang. I went to the door and found a jaguar crouching." He paused, letting his words hang, then continued. "Inside, my body jumped, but my feet and arms would not move. Everything I had eaten wanted to rush out of me. I knew my death had come." He looked over at Avá-Nembiará and caught his father's smile. "Then I remembered the words of my father and pulled aside my loin cloth. Water leaped from my body to battle with the cold fire burning in the eyes of the *añag*."

"What happened then?" Avá-Canindé said.

"Like our best bow hunters, my aim was true. The jaguar hissed and ran off into the night. The next thing I knew, I was on the ground seized by the spirit of laughter."

No one reacted in the quiet that followed. Avá-Tapé thought his storytelling had been a failure, then a chuckle burst forth from Avá-Canindé, followed by Avá-Guiracambí and the others. Avá-Tapé's own laughter engulfed him. He had never seen these men behave so comically.

"Then it is true," Avá-Canindé said through his laughter. "You did piss in the face of death."

Another boisterous round passed among them, then they drank more *chicha*. Avá-Tapé's eyes began to feel heavy. He didn't want this night to end, and he didn't want the others to think that he could not drink as much as them. The older men took turns telling their own stories, some serious, some comical, some deep with meaning. His own words fell from his lips as if he spoke through a mouthful of *maize*.

He lost track of how much *chicha* he'd drunk and couldn't remember the others leaving. He had no clear recollections of their time together, remembering only that he laughed and cried with them long into the night, feeling accepted among them not as a boy, but as a man.

SEVENTEEN

Avá-Tapé awoke to the sound of his father's voice. "Come, my son, the forest waits."

He heard the song of morning birds and opened his eyes to the first gray of day. His mouth felt dry, his head swollen. He belched and the sour taste of *chicha* filled the back of his throat. When he sat up, two fists of dull pain throbbed behind his eyes. His stomach boiled. He put his head in his hands and belched again. The acid taste of bile bit at the back of his throat and his mouth watered.

He barely made it to the door before his stomach erupted, sending last night's *chicha* shooting from his mouth and nose. He dropped to his knees as his stomach jerked again and again, until it emptied itself and jerked some more. His head pounded, but his stomach felt better. He heard his father chuckling in the *maloca* behind him.

"You have mastered the passage of *chicha* from your body."

Avá-Tapé stayed on his hands and knees until he felt sure his stomach had stopped its dance, then wiped his nose and mouth with the back of his hand and stood. His stomach had settled, but his head still pounded.

"Drink this." His father handed him a gourd. "We must go. It is time for your hunt."

Avá-Tapé took the gourd and drank a thick, sweet tasting mixture. The hot bitterness in his throat and insides gave way to cool numbness. His stomach tightened, but the drink stayed down.

His father gave him a bow, a quiver of arrows and a spear, then took him into the forest, away from the village and the mission. Avá-Tapé stumbled at first, then settled into his father's rhythm. As the day brightened, his head began to clear and his body felt stronger.

They moved swift and quiet through trees and underbrush, passing through mist-filled hollows. Avá-Nembiará remained silent, using only his hands to speak.

The cries of birds grew more insistent and the calls and rustlings of other animals filled the air, marking the forest's passage from a face of darkness to one of light. The roar of rushing water rumbled in the distance. Soon they would be at the river where the animals came to drink, the best place to hunt in the morning.

By the time they saw water, Avá-Tapé's head felt clear, his senses sharpened. His father's drink had worked its magic.

He saw the blood-red sun rimming the horizon through the trees ahead. Drawing a deep breath, he took in the sweet rotting plant smell of algae in the water and felt the cool mist from the river on his skin. The ground beneath him trembled with the thunder of the falls.

Avá-Nembiará turned upstream toward calmer waters. The plant smell grew stronger and the roar faded, leaving the gentler sound of coursing water. When they reached a quiet grove, Avá-Nembiará found a spot at the base of a tree and sat. Avá-Tapé looked to his father for guidance. Avá-Nembiará's eyes told him to go on by himself.

The sun, now a fiery orange, shone brighter as it crested the horizon. The humid air grew warmer. He followed the bank, staying close to the water's edge, his sight, smell, and hearing tuned to every nuance of his surroundings. The air hung thick and wet like the riotous growth at the water's edge. He scanned the point where the new and decaying plant life met the water, searching for subtle changes that would betray the presence of game.

The water gurgled softly, its babble lulling him like the voices of whispering spirits. He could still hear the dim roar of the falls, its powerful voice underscoring all that he knew, like the voice of Tupá.

He felt the forest watching him as much as he watched it. He had to read what it said. What mood did it have today? Would it be friendly or indifferent? He had to immerse himself in it. Whatever game it gave to him would have importance for the rest of his life.

Rounding a bend, he spotted fresh deer and boar droppings beside a wide pool where the water had slowed and swelled. A good place for game to drink.

He stopped, letting his eyes move along the water's edge. A soft grunt came from the other side of the river. He saw nothing until the tip of a reed quivered. His heart thumped.

Backing down the river, he crossed chest-deep where the sound of the water covered the noise of his passage and the danger of water snakes diminished. Invigorated by the cool water rushing around him, he crept up the bank on the other side, holding his spear in front of him with both hands.

The reeds quivered again.

He circled behind the spot and moved forward keeping low, using the tip of his spear to part the reeds. Another grunt came. Closer. Then slurping and lapping. He took slow tiny steps, straining to see any difference in coloration in the reeds ahead. A few more steps and he saw the dark, shaggy backside of a boar. Too many reeds for a bow shot.

Forcing himself to breathe slowly, he gauged how close he needed to be for a solid thrust with his spear. If he didn't make a killing strike the first time, he would be in danger of being gored. He had seen many gashes and more than one death from wounded boars. A bow shot would have been preferable.

He took another step and the boar flung its head up, sending a spray of water over the bristles of its back. The points of its tusks glistened in the early morning sun.

The boar remained immobile. Avá-Tapé held his breath and clutched his spear tighter. Still too far for a killing strike.

After an endless moment the boar lowered its head and drank again, snuffling contentedly. Avá-Tapé let himself breathe before creeping forward.

He took three more steps and the boar reared, this time grunting angrily as it whirled on Avá-Tapé. Two dark yellow, bloodshot eyes and flashing tusks charged for his legs, then darted to the side.

Avá-Tapé slipped into the flow of the moment, letting his arms and legs move in concert with the animal. A dance. Two quick steps to the right. One fluid motion. His torso weaved like a snake and his arms circled high above his head, bringing the spear down in a graceful arc that found its mark in the soft spot behind the boar's ear.

A high-pitched squeal pierced the air and the animal wrenched the spear from his hands. Blood shot from the wound, spraying Avá-Tapé with sticky heat. The boar spun, chasing its pain. Squeals of enraged fear and agony sent chills through Avá-Tapé, then the animal came straight toward him.

He sidestepped. The end of the spear nearly swept him from his feet, but he danced nimbly over it. The boar made a wider circle, stopped, and faced Avá-Tapé again. Its squeals diminished. Its breathing grew wet and ragged. Blood frothed from the beast's mouth and flowed from the wound in its side. Its tusks glistened pink. Lowering its head, it charged again.

Halfway, its legs buckled and it collapsed, twitching and kicking. Avá-Tapé stepped closer, watching the boar's bloody heaving flank. One large bloodshot eye watched him, ebbing life before widening in full awareness. Its breath rasped, weaker with each exhale, then it kicked twice and lay motionless.

The boar's eye still watched him as it shrank, life fading like a dying ember. Its lifeless, accusing glare cut through him, then the vision of Avá-Canindé's dead woman flooded his mind.

The eye of death.

The memory of her vacant gaze filled him with remorse. He stared at the boar's eye a moment longer, then went to the water and washed the blood from his legs and chest.

EIGHTEEN

"You must think about the animal you have killed," Avá-Nembiará said over the roar of the falls. The sun had risen higher and the day had grown warmer. Avá-Tapé sat with his father at the edge of the forest overlooking the falls. Flies buzzed around the boar's head. Its eye had glazed over and its tongue lolled from between yellowed teeth.

After dragging it from where he killed it, he was anxious to get it back to the village. If the jaguars smelled its death, they would come. He looked from the boar to his father. What did he mean by "think about the animal?"

"How should I think about it?"

"Think about it. That is all."

Avá-Tapé remembered the thrill of stalking the boar and how it attacked straight on before trying to escape at the last moment. It didn't want a fight. It wanted to live. And then the strange thing happened. His whole being slipped into the moment. Into the dance. By dancing, he felt as if he'd stepped outside of time. When the boar charged, Avá-Tapé danced its death dance. If he had stopped and thought about it, he would have danced his own death dance.

The gaze of the dying boar filled his mind. He looked again at its eye. A fly landed at its edge and began its own meal, living by consuming death. Avá-Tapé waved it away and studied the boar's unfocused glare. Not so different from the dead stare of Avá-Canindé's woman. The eye of death had been upon him twice. He shivered at the thought.

"The people will live from the boar's death," Avá-Nembiará

said, breaking into his thoughts, "but its flesh is heavy with *techó-achy*. Not for a *paí*. He must eat only plants so he can lighten his spirit and fly to the other worlds. To be one who eats only the sacredness of plants is a great honor."

Avá-Tapé wondered if he was strong enough to carry his responsibility. He thought of himself living like the other men and realized he would never be happy. His thoughts of his place in the world went deeper than those who lived only to keep the bellies of a mate and his children full. Like his father, Avá-Tapé felt that everything in the world held deeper meaning than what he saw on the surface. The unseen called him. He could almost feel the hand of Tupá pushing him forward into the darkness—a place he had to explore. Would Kuná-Mainó be part of this?

"A *paí* must live apart from men and travel to worlds that most never see until they die," his father said. "When he returns he will long to speak of what he has seen. No one but himself will understand."

"The same as when I killed a boar. What I learned was only for me."

His father smiled. "You must learn to control your visions and master your soul."

Avá-Tapé closed his eyes and let the thunder of the falls fill his senses. The memory of his visions flooded his thoughts. Beyond them Tupá's chant floated like the mists of the forest, almost tangible, but impossible to grasp. "I have to hear the song of Tupá first," he said. "Then I will be free to travel to the other worlds." He opened his eyes. "Tell me of your song, father."

A smile filled Avá-Nembiará's face and a faraway look came to his eyes. "I was eighteen harvests when I flew into the sky." He made a sweeping gesture. "And found myself walking to the place where the sun comes out of the earth. I saw a beautiful house like the church of the Jesuits. I knew I had come to the country of the dead, only this house held a much greater beauty. I met my grandfather and uncle there. My uncle took one arm. My grandfather took the other. Together they showed me the ladder that joins the earth and sky, then I saw people dancing in the house."

Avá-Tapé heard a tremor in his father's voice. A tear ran down the older man's cheek. Avá-Tapé's heart swelled with the knowledge that his father would share something so private.

Avá-Nembiará took a deep breath and continued. "My grandfather and uncle told me it was the place where prayers are learned. The dancers turned toward us. After I watched them dance I looked toward the rising sun to see if it was going to rain, but I knew it would not.

"They took me to a mountain to hear the chant. I saw a dead man in a pit. His body was swollen with death. Flies swarmed around his grave. My grandfather and uncle said, 'You are the one who must cure this man.' I told them I could not since I did not know how. They made me listen to their prayer."

Avá-Nembiará began to chant, then he stopped and sobbed. "As I tell you this, I live it again," he said softly.

"They made me walk three times around the body. I chanted and breathed on the dead man and he arose and spoke. Sometimes Our Father, when he hears these prayers, will restore the dead to life."

Avá-Tapé remembered the story of Jesus and Lazarus, and of how Jesus Himself rose from the dead. He had to be the great shaman of the white men. Could the son of the Jesuit God be the great shaman of the Guarani? Could Jesus and Tupá be the same, or brothers?

He wanted to ask his father, but held back. Avá-Nembiará would get angry at any mention of the Christian teachings, and Avá-Tapé knew what would happen if he tried to tell Father Antonio. The white men, who were supposed to be men of God, crucified Jesus and feared Tupá. How sad.

"The next day I chanted early in the morning as I had been taught," his father continued. "Every night my uncle and grandfather showed me the remedies to cure the sick. That is how I know the love of all things."

Avá-Tapé hoped that when he found his prayer, the vision would be as powerful as his father's. "Tupá's song lives with me," he said aloud. "I can feel it in my heart. He does not want me to know it until I am ready for its power. When that time comes he will sing and I will sing with him. Then I will remember."

"You have hunted well." Avá-Nembiará rose and held his hand over his chest. "Your words tell me that the spirit of the boar and the spirits of the forest have given you the signs. We must take the meat back to the village so all may eat."

They tied the boar's feet with vines and slid Avá-Tapé's spear between its legs and body. Avá-Nembiará led the way, carrying one end while Avá-Tapé shouldered the other. When they neared the village, Avá-Nembiará made his son take the lead.

Santo and Rico spotted them and ran ahead, announcing their arrival. People lined both sides of the path, looking at him differently than before. A little girl ran up and touched his sash, then darted back into the crowd. Though his shoulders ached from the weight of the boar, he walked straight and held his chest out. Avá-Canindé, Avá-Guiracambí, Avá-Takuá, and Avá-Karaí stood together, all smiling the same way his father had smiled when Pindé was born.

He went straight to Avá-Canindé, laid the boar at his feet, and looked up to see his mother apart from the others, holding her hands close to her bosom. Tears ran down her cheeks. His throat grew tight. He wanted to go to her. He took a deep breath and let it out slowly. His eyes burned. His own tears threatened to spill.

He saw Kuná-Mainó smiling at him. The way her eyes pulled him in made his stomach flutter. While the rest of the tribe looked at him with awe and respect, Kuná-Mainó's gaze held his heart. Like his dance with the boar, this moment felt timeless, as if no one but he and Kuná-Mainó existed. More than anything he wanted to be with her.

He looked again at Avá-Karaí and saw his friend gazing at Kuná-Mainó the same way. Didn't he see the way she looked at him? Avá-Tapé glanced back at her. Her gaze still held him. He imagined her soft warmth against him, the smell of her hair, and her eyes looking only at him…

"Make a fire." Avá-Canindé slapped Avá-Tapé on the back, breaking the magic. "Tonight we celebrate our young *paí*. We must all eat from the gift he has brought. Tomorrow, we build the dance house."

Children gathered wood, men butchered the boar, and the women roasted it on a spit. The people sang and danced. Avá-Tapé sat at the center of the festivities beside his father. His mouth watered at the smell of the roasting meat, but like his father he did not eat. The boar had been a gift from the forest. To eat what he had killed would put his spirit in danger.

He glimpsed Kuná-Mainó moving in and out of the shadows at the other side of the fire and wished she could be at his side. The war between the ways of his father and the teachings of the white men had come to an end—at least for him. Tupá. Jesus. His father. All healers. Now him.

He hoped to work out the differences between the gods, but now a new war raged. The spirits of the forest had chosen him. His heart had committed to the path of the *paí*, but his heart had also chosen Kuná-Mainó. Could he walk with his feet on both paths?

NINETEEN

When the fire burned down to embers and the last of the boar had been eaten, the celebration slowed and the people faded into the shadows, back to their *malocas*. Avá-Tapé searched the dwindling crowd until his eyes found Kuná-Mainó's. She gave him a lingering look before she too went off into the darkness. When he started after her, his father's hand stopped him.

"I have seen your eyes talk and know the hunger of your heart. This is how it was when I first saw your mother, but you cannot do this now. To join with her will put your soul in danger. You need all of your power for what is to come. After you travel in the other world and defeat the spirits of fear, you can seek her heart."

"What if she doesn't wait? What if another man comes along?"

"If she cannot wait, her heart is unsure. She is young. She might still wish to dance from flower to flower like the hummingbird before it finds the nectar it craves."

Avá-Tapé's heart beat harder at the thought of Kuná-Mainó with Avá-Karaí. He forced it from his mind. He couldn't let himself be distracted. He had to give all of himself to becoming a *paí*.

Avá-Nembiará started toward his *maloca*. Avá-Tapé followed, glancing over his shoulder one more time to where he had last seen Kuná-Mainó.

After his father had gone to sleep, Avá-Tapé closed his eyes, remembering the *chicha* he drank with the older men, his death dance with the boar, and the way Kuná-Mainó looked at him. No. He couldn't think of her. He had to think of the forest and the way it spoke to him.

He fingered the sash lying by his head. His initiation had only been a beginning. He needed to learn about the spirits of the forest from his father. He would have his true initiation when he stood at the doorway to the other world.

Father Antonio would be angry, but Avá-Tapé wasn't afraid. How could a God be angry at one who wanted to become a healer? Maybe this knowledge is what gave his father strength when he stood against the Jesuits.

He started to drift, welcoming the escape of sleep. He hoped that Tupá might come in a vision and give him his chant. With these thoughts he let the darkness take him...

The lifeless eye of the boar floated up to swallow him. He passed through it, reliving his dance and the animal's death. He felt the bloodshot yellow eye watch him as it widened in the total awareness that comes with the end, then he heard a cry.

A bird! He went toward it, sensing it the same way he had sensed the boar, immersing himself in its presence until he became one with his surroundings and the bird sang only for him. He moved steadily, guided by the song of the bird, but as he drew closer, it moved away.

Twice he glimpsed brilliant flashes of color flitting among the leaves above him.

The roar of the falls came to him and he knew that the bird wanted him there. In a blur of color and motion he stood high on a promontory overlooking the raging waters. The ground shook beneath him, and the thunder of the water filled his ears. Mists floated up, tickling his skin.

The sound of the water held him, speaking a wordless message that he understood, but couldn't articulate. His heart ached, and his feelings came forth with a rhythm that intertwined with the song of the falls.

His body moved and a song came to his lips. He danced and sang, not knowing the meaning of the words—only that they were the full expression of his yearning, then he became aware of the bird again. Its song matched his. Could this be Tupá's song? The thought startled him and his vision faded.

He opened his eyes to his father's *maloca* in the gray between the worlds. He could still hear the bird. A single cry in the darkness. Disappointment filled him. The call of a morning bird—the same cries he heard every morning.

The lone bird was answered by another, then another. A howler monkey bellowed. As light dissipated the gray of morning, the forest came alive with the cries, chitters, and screeches of animals all combining to drown out the first song of morning.

Avá-Tapé felt uneasy. Grabbing his bow and spear, he slipped past the sleeping form of his father so he could be alone in the forest. He moved in the direction of the water, letting his eyes and ears merge with the cries and colors of his surroundings, while his thoughts took their own journey.

In spite of his initiation and all the attention from his people, Avá-Tapé felt more alone than he ever had in his life, as if he'd been abandoned between worlds. No longer at home in the world of men, and foreign to the country of the dead. He didn't feel comfortable in either place, but wanted both. He'd flown past the death spirits and become one with the forest, a place he yearned for but didn't know how to find.

The buzz of insects, the cries of birds, the chatter of spider monkeys and the call of a howler all seemed to be meant for him alone. Though he couldn't hear them, the trees, vines, ferns, and flowers all spoke their own language, the way the white man talked on paper, yet different. More vivid. They spoke to more than the eyes. Each had its own scent and texture.

He strained to listen for the rumble of the falls. Even the water talked to him. If he were to hear the roar of the *añag*, they too would have something to tell him. The forest spoke to him through all of his senses, making him feel as much a part of the forest as it had become a part of him. He understood everything in a wordless way, with his feelings.

By the time he reached the falls, the sun had risen above the horizon. The combination of its warmth and the cool mist refreshed him. He climbed on top of a high rock, closed his eyes and listened to the thunder of rushing water, letting its power fill him with its wordless yearning. As with his vision of the night before, he felt the emptiness and the ache, only now it felt dull and remote. His chest tightened.

No bird sang with him.

In his mind he danced and sang with the same abandon as he had in his vision. He felt the words that were not words. Sounds that carried more meaning than those spoken by men.

Sounds of the forest...

He would give anything if only he could remember the song of Tupá.

TWENTY

The sun rose higher and grew warmer. Avá-Tapé picked up his bow and spear and followed the riverbank, moving away from the power of the falls. Upstream the roar quieted to a soothing gurgle that tickled his senses. He thought about finding a clear pool where he could cool off without danger from snakes. He knew of a spot his father had shown him. The people had begun making regular use of it.

He worked his way along the bank listening intently. Part of him stayed alert for signs of life, part focused on the sound of the water, letting the voice of the river flow through him. He had only to listen and let it speak in its own language.

He walked, paying attention to the water's message until he thought he heard voices. Moving quicker, he heard the cries and high-pitched giggles that only girls could make. Rounding a bend, he heard splashing and saw a flash of brown skin against the green backdrop. He recognized some of the older girls in a small pool. Two of them splashed each other and two swam, while the others washed their hair. None wore clothes.

He stopped, his first impulse pushing him back the way he came. He had started toward the falls when Kuná-Mainó's laughter tickled his ears and touched his heart. He caught his breath and his skin prickled. He went back to where he could see her without being seen. He saw nothing at first, then heard her laughter like the song of a bird.

Sunlight dappled the water, highlighting her brown skin and the smooth lines of her body. Her long black hair fanned out beneath her, floating in the clear water as she swam gracefully on her back. She dove under the surface and came up close to the shore.

When she rose from the water, the sights, sounds, and voices around him ceased to exist. He no longer felt the sun, saw the forest, or heard its inhabitants.

The sun glistened on her skin as her lithe body moved up the sandy shore with the grace of a deer. Slender shoulders and a smooth back arched into the delicate curve of swaying hips that tapered down to the smooth definition of her legs. He watched the taut muscles of her hips sliding beneath the sheen of her skin and felt a stirring under his loincloth.

His breath hitched when she turned toward him. Eyes closed, she dropped her head back, exposing her neck and upturned face to the sun. Her dark hair hung over one shoulder partially covering one of her breasts. The other stood out like firm fruit. Avá-Tapé drew in a long shaky breath and felt his man part growing hard.

One of the girls called out, jolting him back to the world. The clamor of birds, animals, and the song of the water rushed in as he became aware of the world around him. He saw the backsides of two of the younger girls rising up out of the water and turned away, his face flushing with shame. What if they saw him? What if someone else saw him? What was he doing? He dropped to the ground, forgetting his passion. He wanted to talk to Kuná-Mainó alone. Tell her how he felt. How could he explain the way she made him feel? Every part of him wanted her and he couldn't keep it a secret. His body betrayed the desires of his heart.

After seeing her this way he didn't know if he'd be able to look her in the eyes again, and if he did—if he were close to her… What if his body betrayed his feelings then? Is this what Avá-Karaí felt?

He heard the girls again. Closer. He peered over a fern and saw them coming. Grabbing his bow and spear, he ran along the riverbank, following the water's edge at a full trot. As the thunder of the falls grew closer, the voices of the girls faded.

When he heard nothing but the falls, he listened closely, trying to hear its voice again, then directed his attention toward the forest, trying to hear its song. They would not speak as they had before. Kuná-Mainó filled his thoughts.

Scrambling among the rocks near the top of the falls, he went toward the one he'd climbed earlier. When he drew close he saw a lone figure perched on top of it. He climbed up and sat beside his father, feeling as if they both knew they were supposed to be at that spot at that time.

"You are ready to be shown the magic of the forest," Avá-Nembiará said, looking out over the falls. "The secret lives of the plants."

Avá-Tapé pushed Kuná-Mainó from his mind.

His father looked at him with sharp eyes. "You must leave the world of men, and the yearning of your heart and body for the company of a woman."

Avá-Tapé's face felt hot.

"We must live in the forest for a time. Away from men. The plants and trees have much to teach. Much to give. They will purify us. We must live in their world and learn their language so they will know us as allies. Their spirits will help us fight the spirits of death that haunt us as men."

Avá-Tapé thought of Kuná-Mainó again. If only he could talk to her. Explain his feelings. "Will we go to the village before we leave?"

"We have everything we need…"

"All I have is my bow and spear."

Avá-Nembiará smiled. "The forest is a wise teacher and a generous host."

"How long?"

"Yacy, the moon will guide us, but we must watch him carefully. He is a trickster. He controls the bleeding times of women and takes those who have been untouched by men. When he shows himself fully, our animal sides rise up, but he is the lord of plants. He will shine with his full cold fire in the night sky more than once before we see men again." Avá-

Nembiará climbed down from the rock.

Avá-Tapé followed him to the edge of the cliff. The deafening thunder of the falls filled his ears and the ground vibrated beneath his feet. The sun hung low in the sky and a gentle breeze blew wisps of cool mist over them, soaking everything. Avá-Nembiará strode to the edge of the cliff and looked over the precipice. Avá-Tapé came up timidly behind him, keeping one hand on a boulder. Leaning out, he held tight to the rock and peered over the edge. Dizziness took him.

Sheets of water rushed over the cliffs, exploding against the rocks in sprays of white before falling farther in an endless rush of foam toward an unbroken mat of green below. Craggy outcroppings and cascading water extended as far as he could see on both sides. A lone eagle circled overhead. The power and immenseness of the whole place made him feel small and insignificant. His father stood beside him, arms crossed, his angular features firm, eyes intent like an eagle surveying his domain.

"We have reached the edge," Avá-Tapé called over the roar of the water. "Which way do we go now?"

Avá-Nembiará smiled, took the spear from his son and started climbing down.

Avá-Tapé's stomach turned as his father's head disappeared over the edge of the cliff. The sound of rushing water roared in his ears. His throat felt dry. He looked around again. Above him blue sky, below, white foam and green. His mind told him to move but his feet stayed rooted.

He took a shaky breath and forced himself to move. Bow over one shoulder, arrows over the other, he started down the face of the cliff on trembling legs. Pressing his body close to the wet rock, he worked his way down, legs stretching, toes finding footholds, hands clutching tightly to slimy stone. His knees felt as if they would give with his next move. His stomach was queasy. He forced himself to focus first on one step, then the next.

When he'd covered some distance, he looked up and saw only blue and the rock face above. Water rumbled beside him.

Anxious to make it to the bottom, he looked down and stiffened. It didn't look any closer than it had at the top. Dizziness gripped him and his stomach went cold. He closed his eyes and held tighter. A breeze gusted, blowing wet mist over him. The thought that the wind could blow him off the cliff entered his mind.

Water thundered. His eyes stayed closed and his fingers grew numb. His feet ached. Did his hands have the strength to grip again if he let go? He had to try, but fear held him. He heard another sound beneath the roar of the falls, and then his father's voice.

"Do not look up and do not look down. The secret of defeating fear lies in keeping your mind in one spot, not in what has happened and not in what could happen. Only here. Only now. Nothing else matters."

Avá-Tapé opened his eyes to Avá-Nembiará's intent scrutiny.

"Either you let the winds of fear blow your spirit like dead leaves or root yourself like a strong tree and let them rush past you like the nothingness that they are. Choose and stay rooted, or give up and abandon yourself."

Avá-Tapé let go with one hand and his fingers cramped. Clenching and unclenching his fist, he grabbed on again and did the same with the other hand, then he flexed his feet. Avá-Nembiará smiled and patted him on the back before starting his descent again.

Avá-Tapé pulled in a deep breath and took one tentative trembling step, then another, forcing everything from his mind. Soon he moved steadily down, keeping his eyes on the rock immediately surrounding him, not looking up or down.

The lower he went, the louder the falls thundered and the thicker the mists grew. The rocks beneath his hands and feet vibrated as if containing a life of their own. His arms and legs felt heavy, and his fingers and toes ached.

When the slope started to level, he turned around and sat down. The falls roared in his ears and thick mist pressed in from all sides. Whiteness and thunder—as if he lived in the sky with the gods. The rocks, his hair and skin, all felt wet and slippery. He could barely see huge boulders looming in the whiteness like guardians to another world.

Ahead the white darkened and took form as Avá-Nembiará appeared out of the mist. "My young warrior has defeated his fear," he yelled over the tumult. "And fought his way to the doorway of another world. Come." He waved Avá-Tapé forward and disappeared back into the haze.

Avá-Tapé scrambled over rocks and boulders after his father. His legs felt strong again, the trembling gone. The din of the falls and the rumbling ground faded as the swirling mists thinned to wraithlike wisps. He shuddered, thinking of the souls of the dead trying to torment him, then he remembered his father's words.

"I have seen them wandering near the burial places..."

He hurried to catch up with Avá-Nembiará.

TWENTY-ONE

A shaft of sunlight pierced the haze, reminding Avá-Tapé of the beams that shone through the stained-glass Jesus at the mission church. Ahead he saw the shadowy form of Avá-Nembiará moving through the dissipating mists.

Sunlight and patches of blue broke through the haze when he reached his father. A wall of green jungle and rolling hills loomed before them. Avá-Tapé welcomed the warmth of the sun on his back. "I feel like we've passed from one world to another."

His father smiled. "The spirits of this world carry great knowledge and power that we can bring back to the other world." He started toward the forest. "Even I have much to learn."

They followed the river along a rock-strewn path at the base of the falls into the lush green of the forest, passing from the heat and light of the sun into the humid half-light of the jungle. Avá-Tapé still smelled the green plant scent from the water, but the fragrances of the trees, ferns, and shrubs held him like an invisible hand.

"The light will be gone soon," his father said. "We are coming to the time between the worlds when the *añag* hunt. We can build a fire away from the water."

They went deeper into the forest until they came to a clearing among some rocks. Avá-Tapé built a fire while his father went off in search of food. When the shadows started to merge and the world turned gray, his father reappeared with oranges and an assortment of roots, herbs, and leafy plants. They ate beside a blazing fire that held back the darkness. By the time they finished eating, animal cries and insect sounds filled the night.

Avá-Tapé followed his father's lead, weaving fibers and vines into a hammock. "Tomorrow we learn from Kuarahy, brother of Tupá, who taught us how to speak to the plant spirits," Avá-Nembiará said. "His wisdom will show us their secret life."

Avá-Tapé looked past his father into the darkness. The screech of a monkey pierced the night, followed by the growl of a jaguar. A chill passed through him.

"We are safe from the *añag* as long as we keep our fire," Avá-Nembiara said without looking up from his work. "Without the cattle of the white man, they do not run in packs. In this part of the forest they hunt alone." His fingers manipulated vine and fiber as he wove.

Avá-Tapé moved closer to the fire. "Will we see the plant spirits?"

"We won't see their spirits, but we have seen their power. When a *paí* calls upon his allies, the plant spirits come to his aid and attack the spirits of sickness. A *paí* must know which plants to call when fighting the dark ones."

"How does he know?"

"After he sees the sickness he sleeps and learns which plants to use. Kuarahy helps him learn their meaning and power. When a healer seeks his allies, he sings to the spirit of the healing plant. The song rouses the plant's spirit to battle the spirits of sickness. When the sun comes back to the world, I will take you to where these allies live and teach you their magic."

Avá-Nembiará lapsed into silence as they worked fibers into a lattice made with the vines. They added woven fiber strips so they could hang them from trees. After stoking the fire, they stretched out in their finished hammocks to sleep.

Avá-Tapé lay awake thinking of Kuná-Mainó, Avá-Karaí, Father Antonio, and Father Lorenzo. His life rushed ahead like the rapids at the top of the falls, pulling him forward with a force that he feared would carry him over the edge. He looked at his father. Already sleeping. No fear.

Closing his eyes, he let himself drift toward sleep. A chorus of insects sang in the darkness, accented by the cries of night birds, monkeys, and nocturnal hunters. Avá-Tapé had dropped into a dreamless sleep when the song of a single bird roused him.

He'd heard morning birds as far back as he could remember, but none like this. The trill of its melody stirred a glimmer of recognition. Keeping his eyes closed, he listened, letting its lonely cries fill him with a yearning that made his throat feel tight.

He opened his eyes to the gray of morning. Mist drifted up from the jungle floor. The bird's song came from somewhere in the grayness. He sat up, saw movement in the trees and glimpsed flashes of color as a bird flitted through the mist, leading his attention to the gaze of a lone jaguar studying him from a distance.

He stiffened. His bow and quiver lay against a tree near his head. Could he raise it and aim fast enough? Smoke from the fire drifted toward him. Its flames had died to smoldering coals. How could his father let this happen?

The jaguar yawned and trotted into the haze. Avá-Tapé looked behind him and saw his father. How long had he been watching?

"He fears the smoke," Avá-Nembiará said matter-of-factly, "but his curiosity is strong. As long as there is smoke, there is no danger."

Avá-Tapé breathed deep to calm his racing heart. Except for the cries of birds, the other forest dwellers remained quiet. Avá-Tapé peered into the mist for signs of life.

Avá-Nembiará disappeared, returning a short time later with more vines and plants which he and Avá-Tapé wove into carrying baskets. When they had finished, Avá-Nembiará stretched like a cat.

"Today, we will ask the plant spirits for help and for permission to take them." He picked up the spear and a basket. Avá-Tapé slung his bow and quiver over one shoulder, his basket over the other and followed his father.

Avá-Nembiará moved with confidence through the jungle. The life of the forest grew louder as more light filtered from above. Brightly colored parrots flew from branch to branch, monkeys chattered, and lizards scampered up trees as they passed. The buzz of insects was constant. Avá-Tapé stayed close to his father, keeping his eyes and ears alert for signs of jaguars.

Avá-Nembiará stopped in front of a waist-high plant with lance-shaped leaves, square stems, and spikes of violet flowers. He picked a couple of leaves, chewed one and gave the other to his son. The bite of cool mint made Avá-Tapé's mouth water.

"It is good to taste and it is strong medicine," Avá-Nembiará said. "We must ask its spirit for help." He chanted and circled the plant three times in one direction, then three times in the other, before sitting cross-legged in front of it. His utterances shifted and their tone became conversational. The words made no sense to Avá-Tapé.

Finally, the one-sided dialogue stopped. "Forgive me for taking your life," his father said to the plant, "but I know your wisdom tells you how the fire burns in all of us. Your time has come to be consumed just as it will come for me. I hope that my end will serve a purpose as noble as yours." He made a tobacco offering, looked up and raised his arms. "I entrust myself to you as I gather this medicine so that your many messengers will bring success." He dug around the base of the plant and gently uprooted it.

"What is it that you sing?" Avá-Tapé asked. "What does it mean?"

His father cleaned the mint's root with a stick. "The sound and the words have no meaning in the world of men, but what they say and how they say it carries deeper meaning than the words of men."

Avá-Tapé remembered the way he felt when he heard the song of the morning bird. The same way he felt at the falls when he sensed the forest speaking to him. This had to be how his father felt when he sang and danced. "I know what you mean," he heard himself saying.

The sun and moon passed over many times as he and his
father made their way through the forest near the base of the
falls. Avá-Nembiará spoke and chanted to each plant before
taking it, then told his son its uses and where it liked to live.
At his father's urging, Avá-Tapé began talking to the plants and
taking some himself. He didn't chant because he didn't know
the feeling of the words.

They collected rue, mint, tobacco, sassafras leaves, sweet
citrons, and bark from different trees. Avá-Nembiará taught
Avá-Tapé how to extract resin from the roots of the jalap tree
by making it flow under the sun and how to use it to cure bile
and rheum. He made a tasteless purge from the root of another
plant with coiled flowers and the rind of the tamarind.

A remedy for sore eyes came from a healing powder
ground from thorns from the barrel-shaped trunk of the
drunken tree. A similar tree had bark that was used to treat
wounds made by jaguar teeth. The arm's length leaves of the
cupay yielded oil the color of water which stopped the flow of
blood from open wounds, healed snakebites and kept scars
from forming.

"Your heart is in another place when you sing to the plants,"
Avá-Nembiará said one day as he pounded the soft yellow skin
and seeds of an *algaroba* pod into a pulp. "Have you not heard
Tupa's chant?"

Avá-Tapé felt a flush of embarrassment. "I remember how
it felt in my dreams. But I still can't remember the words."

His father stopped working and looked straight into his
eyes. "It is not the words. It is the feeling."

Avá-Tapé stared at the ground, avoiding his father's gaze.
"How you sing to the plants," he said tentatively. "I can feel your
feeling. I cannot feel my own."

"It is time to let your spirit wander farther from your body."
Avá-Nembiará beat the pod with greater fervor. By the time he
finished, darkness had come. While crickets chirped and night
animals began their cries, Avá-Tapé gathered wood and built a
fire. Avá-Nembiará fashioned a bowl from a gourd and filled it

with the pulpy juice from the pods, then lay down in his hammock and closed his eyes.

Avá-Tapé's stomach growled, reminding him that they had not eaten since morning. "We have not eaten," he said. "I cannot sleep with a starving jaguar prowling inside of me."

"The journey of the spirit begins by lightening the body," Avá-Nembiará said without opening his eyes. "Food only ties the spirit closer to it. We must free ourselves from the hunger of our bodies so our souls can travel in the spirit world."

Avá-Tapé's stomach growled again. "I can't sleep with an angry stomach. How long do I have to let it cry out?"

"Until you hear the song of Tupá."

TWENTY-TWO

Avá-Tapé lay with his back to the fire, listening to the sounds of the night coming to him from the darkness. Emptiness hung in the pit of his stomach and his body felt worn. His mind spun. What was happening with Father Antonio and the mission? He'd seen him angry before, but now he acted like another person.

The letter to the bishop and the talk of the white settlers worried him. Would they really make his people slaves? No. The bishop was coming. A man close to the Christian God wouldn't let such a thing happen. The Jesuits wouldn't give them up that easily either, but they might try to win the people back while he and his father were away, especially if they thought the settlers wanted to make slaves. He remembered Avá-Canindé and smiled. The big man wouldn't let that happen.

He turned onto his back and envisioned Kuná-Mainó and her beauty that first night he had run from the church. Now he had glimpsed the sheen of her smooth skin, her curves, and everything else female about her. This last thought made his man part stir.

He pushed her from his mind. He had to think about Tupá and his chant. If he could find Tupá in his dreams and grasp his song, he could eat again and go back to the village.

Avá-Tapé passed more of the night awake than sleeping. When he did sleep he thought of Tupá, and while awake, all that had happened since the sickness had taken him. More often than not he saw Kuná-Mainó's smiling face, firm breasts, and smooth curves rising from the water.

When the black of night faded to gray, he felt as if he hadn't slept. The morning bird's first song came clear, crying out as if taunting. Smoke from the smoldering fire drifted toward him and a dull ache pressed down on his head. His throat felt dry, his stomach empty. Now that the day had come, he wished he could escape into sleep.

After stoking the fire he stared into the flames, wishing he could eat and wondering what he had to do to hear Tupá's song.

"Without food," his father said as if reading his thoughts, "your fire will move from your stomach to your head." He opened his eyes and sat up. "Your spirit will lighten. Your stomach will yowl like a baby but it will soon grow quiet. Put your thoughts away from your body and let them go toward the world of spirits. Tupá will hear you. You must listen closely."

A patter came from above, and warm drops hit Avá-Tapé's head as rain started to fall. His father looked up and smiled. "Maybe he is giving you a sign. Let us find more plants."

Warm rain fell most of the morning as they chanted to, talked to, and collected plants. Avá-Tapé kept his mind open for signs of Tupá, but heard only the hiss of rain and the calls and chatters of animals. He grew used to the emptiness in his stomach, but felt weak. He knew his father wouldn't eat either, until he heard Tupá's chant.

Avá-Tapé's legs felt weighted. It was all he could do to keep up with his father, and he wanted nothing more than to stop and rest, but like the warm rain falling from the sky, Avá-Nembiará kept a steady pace. When it seemed they would go on forever, he stopped, set down his basket and sat on the ground.

Avá-Tapé recognized the remains of their fire. He dropped beside his father. The rain fell heavier, running down his face, back, and shoulders. He pushed his hair out of his eyes, put his head back and let the downpour fill his senses. The noise rushed through him like the sound of the rapids. He felt as if the water spoke to him as it had that morning by the falls.

The patter of raindrops slowed to an infrequent tap, and the birds began singing again. Avá-Tapé closed his eyes and listened to their music, hoping one might sing the song of Tupá, but a dull headache hung at the back of his skull, making it hard to concentrate. He opened his eyes and saw his father holding out the gourd he had filled with the pulpy juice beaten from the *algaroba* pod.

"Drink," he said.

Avá-Tapé took the gourd. It was warm. Tiny bubbles rose in the pulpy liquid. He looked at his father, then downed the sharp tasting juice. A short while later his stomach grew quiet and warmth spread through his body. Like the diminishing rain, his headache cleared and his energy returned. His thoughts had greater clarity.

"We have more plants to gather," Avá-Nembiará said. "More spirits to speak with. This is all we can do until you hear the song of Tupá." With great care, he laid out the plants they had gathered that morning. When he finished, Avá-Tapé followed him back into the forest.

A half moon hung in the sky that second night and grew toward fullness as the days and nights passed, but no songs came. At times Avá-Tapé felt light as the mist, other times he felt weighed down with rocks. Some nights his hunger kept him awake, slipping in and out of light sleep and vivid dreams. Father Antonio came, followed by Father Lorenzo, and Father Rodrigo, all begging him to come back to their God.

Kuná-Mainó came, making him feel the warmth of her beside him. Avá-Karaí would take her away. The *añag* chased him through the streets of the mission.

Other nights he slept in deep oblivion.

He and his father drank only water. When Avá-Tapé felt he had no strength, Avá-Nembiará would pound out more *algaroba* pods. Avá-Tapé looked forward to the warm, sharp tasting, bubbly juice and the energy it would bring.

He went to sleep exhausted one night, drifting between the worlds where he slept, yet felt awake. A familiar melody came to him, speaking of feelings without words. He wanted to sing with all his heart but could only grasp it in his mind.

"You have not heard my messenger," a directionless voice said. "You struggle to hear the words of men and miss the spirit of the messenger. Stop your thoughts and listen. His voice will tell you of meanings greater than those of men."

"Is this the song of Tupá?"

The space before him shimmered like water cascading over the falls, and the form of a man appeared. Tall and majestic, he had clear eyes like those of Jesus. A glowing headdress adorned his head. He held a bow in one hand, a spear in the other. Fierce yet wise. Warrior and hunter.

"Tupá," Avá-Tapé whispered. Joy filled his heart and the image rippled as though someone had thrown a rock into a pond. The face and the feathers on the headdress shone brighter and the melody came again. Avá-Tapé yearned for it with all his being until his fervor woke him. He looked up into the bright light of the full moon. His heart felt weighted with emptiness.

The silence of the forest held him until the lone cry of a morning bird floated to him on the still air. Disappointment sank his heart deeper. The same cries he heard every morning. His father snored beside their smoldering fire.

The trees and ferns stood out in silhouettes of black and silver, highlighted by gossamer moonbeams. The lone bird sang in a melodic trill. Its sweet chirps lifted his heart as the bird broke into full-throated song. Avá-Tapé's vision blurred from tears.

He rose from his hammock and felt the bird's song carry his flourishing emotions into the surrounding trees until he sensed a presence, the same he'd felt while hunting the boar and in the dreams and visions that followed. The same that had been at the falls when the sound of the water, the sight and smell of the trees and ferns, and the cries of the animals had come to him as one.

A flash of winged silver flitted among the leaves as the rest of the forest came alive with sound. The bird's song stood out like a brilliant flower among the leaves. Every sight, sound and smell spoke in a wordless message that Avá-Tapé understood, but could not articulate. His chest expanded with emotions both full and empty. His heart ached. His tears flowed and his feelings rose, blending with the song of the bird.

Avá-Tapé's body moved and he began to sing and dance, not knowing the meaning of his words, only that they were the expression of his yearning. He became aware of the bird again, its song matching his in harmony, then the buzz of insects, the calls of other birds, and the chatter of monkeys all speaking as if to him alone.

The trees, vines, ferns, and flowers all spoke in silvery moonlight in their own language. They spoke to more than his eyes, with fragrances and textures.

His dance took on a life of its own, connecting him to everything he knew. The forest spoke through all his senses, making him feel as much a part of it as it became part of him. Everything it said he understood with his feelings; but his mind didn't know what it told him, only that it spoke to his heart.

Giving himself over, Avá-Tapé sang and danced with the same abandon of his vision. His body moved, each step, each gesture imbued with feeling and meaning that moved with his singing. Any boundaries between himself and the outer world dissolved. He saw his father sitting up, first watching, then adding logs to the smoldering fire, coaxing it to flames. As the wood began to blaze, Avá-Tapé saw tears running down his father's face and knew at last that he had heard and sung the song of Tupá.

TWENTY-THREE

Avá-Tapé sang and danced with full abandon, moving between the cold fire of the full moon and the heat from the blaze that his father built, until the silver filigree gracing the trees and ferns faded to gray and the blackened sky turned indigo. When the first rays of gold filtered through the treetops he dropped to the ground, closed his eyes, and lay on his back.

His head swam, his arms and legs trembled, and his heart thumped. His breath came sharp and rapid. Sweat poured from him. The cool ground felt good against his hot skin.

Avá-Tapé's heart slowed, his breathing grew regular and a contented feeling stole over him as though something inside had completed itself. The songs of birds and the buzz of insects spoke as if welcoming him into a new world. Never again would they be simple sounds heard with the coming of the day. Now they had special meaning.

He lay with his eyes closed, taking in the sounds, the tanginess of his own sweat, the earthy smell of the forest floor, the lush fragrances of flowered vines, sweet cedar, and the acrid hint of smoke from their fire.

Opening his eyes, he saw patches of blue filtering through a dark green canopy. The emerald green of the ferns, the pinks and violets of flowered vines and small patches of sunlight slipping through the overhead growth danced before his eyes. A flock of multi-colored parakeets flitted through the trees followed by a pair of larger scarlet macaws.

"How long have you known the chant?"

He lay still for another moment before sitting up to face his father across the smoking fire. "How did you know I knew?"

His father smiled. "How you acted in the forest. How you listened. The way you looked at the trees and plants. Tupá always sings, but his song can only be heard by those with an open heart."

"How could I know that his message was one of feeling? I only thought of it as sound."

"A chant that comes from the mouth of gods is sound with feeling. It is what gives it meaning."

"This is what I know in my heart."

Avá-Nembiará smiled. "When did you learn?"

Avá-Tapé thought of sound with feeling. This was how he sang and danced. This was how his father sang and danced. He listened to the cry of a monkey and the songs of birds, then looked around at the trees and ferns. "I first heard it when I hunted the boar."

Avá-Nembiará tilted his head back, held his palms out, and gazed skyward as if giving silent thanks.

"The forest, the animals and the water all talked to me," Avá-Tapé continued. "After I took the boar's life I heard the cry of a bird as if it sang only to me." He closed his eyes and re-lived the moment when Tupá's messenger bird had coaxed him to the falls. "The calls of birds, the speech of the water, the voices of animals, and the song of insects spoke to my ears. Trees, ferns and flowers spoke to my eyes. Smells and tastes of the plants and water spoke to my nose and mouth. Tupá spoke to every part of me, but still I did not hear his messengers."

"It was the same with me." Avá-Nembiará crossed his arms and nodded. "I became lost in my head and did not hear my feelings. I heard the song of Tupá and did not know that my heart was opened. It was only when I stopped my thoughts that I could listen with my heart."

"And now that I have heard," Avá-Tapé said, "I have opened myself to the spirits."

"In your sickness you traveled past the sleeping *añag* to the place where Urukera and Owl live. The souls of the dead wanted to keep you. I had to take you from them. Because you have not eaten, you freed your spirit from *techó-achy* and stood between the worlds, where you could open your heart to Tupá. You have only glimpsed what lies on the other side. You must still learn magical flight."

His father's words hit like a splash of cold water. "But the other world opened to me. I sang and danced…"

"But you have not flown."

Avá-Tapé's anger flashed. "What does it take to fly to the other world?"

"You will learn when the time is right. Your chant and dance and purified body will set your spirit free. This is how we will fly to the Land Without Evil and lead the people to paradise." Avá-Nembiará rose and disappeared into the foliage, leaving Avá-Tapé alone with his thoughts.

His sweat had dried and his limbs felt like wet rope, but his senses felt sharpened. His thoughts floated around the fringes of sleep. He had been at the doorway to the other world but had not passed through. His heart felt heavy like his body. He had gone without eating, had heard the chant of Tupá, and had sung and danced to the song in his heart—but he had not flown. What would it take to fly like his father? He closed his eyes and remembered the visions from his sickness. Had he flown then, or had the spirits of death carried his soul?

Death.

A sure way to pass to the other side, but you couldn't come back unless you knew how to get past the sleeping *añag*. The souls of the dead wanted you to stay. He had seen the face of death. How close to staying had he been when his father brought him back?

He had been many days without eating, and had sang and danced, wearing himself down to nothing. Was the secret of magical flight the art of dancing on the edge of death? How close could he get and still come back to the world of men? That had to be the art of the *paí*.

The fluttering of startled birds made him open his eyes. Avá-Nembiará came through tall ferns with an armload of bananas, *cassava* root, and oranges. Avá-Tapé's stomach growled and his mouth watered. How long since he'd eaten?

"You must only eat a little," Avá-Nembiará said, holding out an orange. "Too much too soon will make your insides spill like the morning after too much *chicha*. As your body remembers how to consume, you can eat more."

Avá-Tapé took the orange, held it to his nose and inhaled its sweet essence. Part of him wanted to gobble it whole. Another part didn't want to eat. He feared losing the clarity his senses brought him.

"You must eat and build yourself back to strength." Avá-Nembiará peeled an orange, pulled off a piece and popped it into his mouth. Rapture filled his face. "When you are strong we will search for power objects. The spirits of the forest have much to give you."

Avá-Tapé dug a thumb into his orange, peeled it and broke it into pieces. A painful rush of saliva filled his mouth when he bit into it, followed by cool sweetness. He forced himself to chew slowly, savoring the shadings of its flavor, then he ate the rest, followed by a banana and another orange. Though his stomach felt full he wanted more, but his father stopped him.

They spent the next few days sorting through the plants they had gathered, eating more each day until Avá-Tapé's appetite grew healthy and he could eat without getting sick. His strength returned, along with his desire to be back among the people. To see Kuná-Mainó. He was not the same person he'd been when he left. He had grown in strength and recognized the chant of Tupá, which he held in his heart and could see and hear in the trees and plants and animals. When the time was right, he would sing and dance like his father.

"When the sun comes again," Avá-Nembiará said as they lay down to sleep one night, "you will rise and begin the final part of your quest. If you please the gods, you will return to the people as a *paí*."

Avá-Tapé looked up at the patch of starlit sky above the clearing. "Will I be able to fly up into the stars?"

"When you have grown tired of your body and have danced and sung Tupá's song, your spirit will lighten and fly into the heavens, but if your soul is weighed down by *techó-achy*, it will stay close to the earth."

Avá-Tapé felt his weight sagging in his hammock, as if an invisible hand tugged him toward the ground. He remembered the lightness he'd felt when he and his father drank the sharp tasting, bubbly juice of the *algaroba*. Could he make himself light enough? Closing his eyes, he listened to the sounds of the night and let sleep creep up on him. As he drifted into grayness, he imagined himself growing lighter with each breath...

The trees above him parted, revealing a moonless sky sprayed with glimmering silver. A tiny streak of white cut the dark night like a fish darting across a sunlit pool. Avá-Tapé thought of his father's soul flashing across the heavens. His heart yearned to fly beside his father.

The feeling overwhelmed him until he felt he would burst like over-ripened fruit. He started to sing, knowing that his chant would free his spirit from the terrible longing that threatened to crush his heart.

His words came forth as pure expression, taking flight like spirit birds that carried his message of yearning to the gods. In the next moment his body flowed with his words, each gesture moving in concert with his song as he danced in front of a fire. He sensed the tribe watching. They had little importance compared to the aching that he longed to fill.

He moved to the other side of the fire and saw Kuná-Mainó looking up at him, her soft eyes taking him in as if they held the power to swallow him. Gazing into her eyes, he saw the depths of the sky graced with shimmering starlight. His voice rose and his dance quickened.

Every fiber of his being strained toward the heavens, as the unity of his song and dance became a full expression of his desire—and then his body rose, slowly at first, then faster and faster, gaining speed until he flashed across the night sky, following the path of his father and becoming one with the stars.

TWENTY-FOUR

He soared straight into the heavens while the earth below shrank to the size of a gourd. He saw Tupá standing tall and majestic, a multitude of birds flying to him, transforming his feathered headdress into a moving mass of blue, green, yellow and crimson that stood out against the twilight like a many-colored sun. Tupá stood between the worlds of darkness and light, his visage brightening the horizon the way the sun crests the edge of the world.

A tree bearing tiny fruit sprouted behind the earth-gourd and grew to full size. Fruit fell from it and flew through the air, disappearing through the skin of the gourd. Tupá nocked an arrow and let it fly. The arrow pierced the gourd and became a rattle, then a flock of birds from Tupá's head alighted on its top. Tupá shook the *mbaraká* the same way Avá-Nembiará shook his.

Avá-Tapé floated into the air while questions fluttered through his mind. Tupá gave him a knowing smile and shook the rattle more slowly. Its sound became smooth and trembling. Avá-Tapé drifted down until he felt solidness beneath his feet, then Tupá faded, and the rattling grew louder.

Avá-Tapé flashed across the sky again as the sound of the rattle transported him back to the forest. A mass of treetops rushed toward him, startling him awake in his hammock. He could still hear the rattle.

Forcing his eyes open, he thought he saw Tupá standing over him until he recognized his father shaking *his* rattle. "Where have you been, my son?"

Had the sound of Avá-Nembiará's rattle taken him to the other world? He sat up and studied his father's angular face, remembering his visions. His father and Tupá looked much alike. "I have danced in the air with Tupá."

His father's smile broadened. "It is time for you to learn of the *mbaraká*. Find the tree and seek a sacred gourd. Its voice will come from your spirit helpers."

Avá-Tapé swung his legs over the side of his hammock. "Tree?"

Avá-Nembiará pointed toward the surrounding vegetation. "You know the tree."

"How do I know which is the right one?"

Avá-Nembiará folded his arms. "The spirits will guide you."

When his father didn't move or speak, Avá-Tapé knew he would have to look, but he had no idea where. He left the clearing studying the foliage for signs that might guide him. His father followed.

One tree blended with the next. Leaves, vines, and branches all intertwined like a huge woven mat. Oneness. He remembered how it had been when the morning bird guided him. When he hunted the boar. When he had stood at the falls. The forest had spoken without words.

He walked, emptying his mind while opening his senses. Chattering birds and the drone of insects came in their own purity, without his mind imposing order.

He had no sensation of time and no sense of direction—only the flow of his existence and the immediacy of an infinite moment that held him suspended like a spider from its web. His eyes took in details without making judgments until he found himself before the tree. The same one he had seen in his dream. Small bright green leaves stood straight on full branches. Tiny dark fruit hung in clusters.

He stepped closer and saw a vine wrapped around its roots bearing a single gold-colored gourd. Never in his life had he seen a gourd growing from the roots of a tree and never had he seen one so perfect in proportion and color—except on his father's rattle. The world rushed back in all its immediacy.

Sights, sounds and smells swirled around him as if he were the center, then his father's voice.

"You know what you must do."

He began singing and dancing, giving the yearning in his heart a voice. His body moved with the rhythm of his song. When he felt he had given part of himself back to the forest, he picked a handful of fruit from the tree, plucked the gourd from its vine and followed his father back to camp.

Avá-Nembiará prepared a fire, putting in special branches and vines. A sweet fragrance filled the air as sap bubbled and dripped from the cut ends of wood. Avá-Nembiará scraped the dripping sap into a small gourd.

"You must pierce the gourd with an arrow." He took an arrow, put its sharpened tip to the end of Avá-Tapé's gourd and rotated it back and forth, then handed both to Avá-Tapé, who continued boring.

"The *mbaraká* is the symbol of our race." Avá-Nembiará scraped resin into the gourd cup. "Its holiness and magical power live in its voice. When it speaks and a *paí* listens, its voice carries his spirit to the stars."

Avá-Tapé envisioned himself streaking across the heavens. What his father said was true. The voice of the *mbaraká* had taken him to Tupá and flown him back.

"When we dance and our helper spirits join in, the voice of the *mbaraká* will take us away from this world to the Land Without Evil," his father said.

Avá-Tapé's arrow pierced the gourd. He pulled it out and looked to his father. Avá-Nembiará took the gourd and ran the arrow all the way through. After passing the shaft back and forth he blew through the opening and handed it back to Avá-Tapé.

"Hold it to the fire and dry its insides."

Avá-Tapé held it near the flames and turned it slowly.

"The sound of the sacred fruit is a call to the higher powers," his father said, holding the fruit in his palm. "The fruit are your spirit-helper family."

"They will live inside my *mbaraká* and in the spirit world?"

"From the beginning, sound and power have been part of the oneness. The *mbaraká* is the symbol of sacred sound. Kuarahy, the sun, made a rattle like this one and danced himself into ecstasy until his father, the Creator-God Nanderú Guazú, took him away. Because of Kuarahy's success, a *paí* listens for the spirit voice who calls other spirits from inside. The truest form of the fruit that live inside can be found in paradise."

While his father told him of the ancient myths, Avá-Tapé let the gourd cool and used the tip of his arrow to scrape its insides. He blew through it, repeating the process until it had been hollowed out, then put the fruit from the tree inside. His father mounted the gourd on the arrow with the tip sticking out of the top. After sealing both ends with resin, he crushed black and red berries. Avá-Tapé painted designs with the juice, following the patterns on his father's *mbaraká*.

Finishing by firelight, Avá-Tapé stood and stretched, happy to have a *mbaraká* of his own. With his plant helpers, he could battle the spirits of sickness. He had learned much from the forest spirits; he had heard their voice and understood their message. Now he could go back to the village a *paí*.

He thought of Kuná-Mainó's full-throated laughter, like the song of a bird that lifted his heart on its wings. Her brown skin and the smooth lines of her body. Long black hair. He imagined how it would feel to rest his cheek on her soft breasts and shivered at the thought of his man part sliding into the dark patch between her legs...

"Where are your thoughts?"

"I - I am ready to return to our people. We have collected plants. I have had visions and learned the chant of Tupá. My voice, my heart, and the voice of the spirits in my *mbaraká* cry to our gods."

Avá-Nembiará smiled. Firelight danced in his eyes. "Yes, my young *paí*, you are ready to return."

His heart soared...

"Once you have completed your last, most severe test."

... and then crashed.

TWENTY-FIVE

"You need to gather feathers." Their fire burned low and the night had grown deeper. Avá-Nembiará's face, illuminated by the glow of coals, hovered in the darkness like a pale flower floating on the surface of a blackened pond. "The feathers a *paí* wears and the feathers on his *mbaraká* are the souls of the birds that are his spirit helpers. They have to come from live parrots."

"Live?"

"He must also get the blood-colored feathers from the bird who drums on trees, and the blue tail feathers of another with yellow wings. Both have special power."

Avá-Tapé felt a sinking feeling in his stomach. He had heard stories of men injured and killed getting feathers. To harvest them from live birds, he had to climb to the top of the forest. He looked up at the darkened trees and felt dizzy. He had to trap the birds, pluck what he could, and let them go.

"We will find the tree together," Avá-Nembiará said.

Avá-Tapé looked into his father's shadowed face. Avá-Nembiará's darkened eyes were unreadable.

Avá-Tapé took a deep breath and hardened himself. "If this is the path, I will climb the trees to catch my spirit helpers. Tupá will guide me," he said, wishing he felt as strong as he sounded.

A smile flickered across his father's face. "When Kuarahy brings his light we will find a tree that is home to spirit helpers. Sleep now. You will need your strength."

Avá-Tapé looked up at the stars between the treetops. Tomorrow he would be among the branches, closer to the sky and the wings of the spirit messengers. Would they give him power to reach the sky, or would they send him crashing to his death like a bird with a broken wing?

He didn't remember sleeping that night; only opening his eyes to the shimmering crack between the worlds at the edge of the tree line. The first light of Kuarahy and the cold fire of Yacy shared the sky for a short time before Kuarahy would rule for the day. Avá-Tapé watched the brightening sky until the first bird began its song, then he climbed out of his hammock and gathered fruit for their morning meal. When he returned, he found his father by the fire weaving fibers into a short, thick length of rope.

After they ate, Avá-Nembiará nodded toward a pile of fiber and resumed his weaving. "Make a smaller rope that you can use for a sling."

Following his father's directions, Avá-Tapé braided the fibers into a thin length with a loop at the end. When he finished, they stacked the plants they had collected in their carrying nets and slung them high on their backs, and then set out for the falls. By late afternoon, Avá-Tapé could hear the rumbling of water. The dampness he had grown used to felt cooler. He couldn't see the falls yet, but he imagined the cool mists swallowing the forest like hungry spirits.

Avá-Nembiará stopped and looked up. "Here is the tree," he said, pointing to the thick trunk of a palm. "Here you will find the wings of your spirit messengers."

Avá-Tapé followed the tree's smooth trunk with his eyes until it disappeared into the lush foliage above. His father set down his load, pulled out a short rope, and wrapped it around the tree trunk. Sliding it up, he used his feet, then the rope, alternating the two until he almost disappeared into the leaves. He clambered down as quickly as he had gone up. His breathing came heavy, and a sheen of sweat covered his body.

Avá-Tapé's throat went dry when his father handed him the rope. He hung the sling over his neck and wrapped the rope around the base of the tree. It bit into his hands as he worked his way toward the top of the forest. Near the top, the trunk thinned and shook with his movements. He looked down when he reached the base of the foliage. The height made him nauseous.

He climbed again until his hands and feet found palm fronds. A screech startled him. A monkey skittered up the trunk and leaped to another tree. Avá-Tapé hung the thicker rope around his neck and scaled to the top of the tree through the fronds. He knew his father had chosen a good tree when he couldn't avoid putting his hands and feet in the greenish-white droppings that splattered the upper branches.

He heard the cooing and cries of parrots. Rustling feathers and squawks greeted him when he popped his head through the top layer of leaves. The birds took flight, leaving behind a sunset that shaded the horizon in a pink glow. A cool wind gusted. He held on as his vantage point swayed in the breeze.

In spite of his dizzying height, Avá-Tapé still felt small when he gazed up at the falls. As the day faded, he watched the billowing mists rise toward the heavens before disappearing. When the earth swallowed the last spark of the sun, Avá-Tapé readied himself for the night.

He made a blind by bending over fronds while the crown of the tree swayed in the dusk. Holding on with one hand, he laid his sling around the palm fruits and waited for the parrots to come and roost for the night. Several had to be trapped, plucked, and let go without robbing them of their ability to take wing. He would have to stay at the top of the tree for a long time.

His first chance came when the light of the sun had gone and the dark of night had not yet come. A large red and yellow parrot landed near his sling and started eating fruit. Avá-Tapé pulled on the sling when the bird stepped close. The parrot flapped frantically and rose into the air. He felt a tug before the bird broke free, flying toward the place where the sun had fallen from the sky. Avá-Tapé cursed himself. To gain a spirit messenger at the time between the worlds could bring powerful magic, but to lose one—not a good omen.

He laid out the sling again and waited until stars began dotting the sky. His arms and legs began to ache, but he didn't move. He wasn't leaving the tree until he had his feathers. He couldn't go down without messengers. He would have no power.

Fluttering in the darkness. Another parrot landed. This one in the middle of the sling. He waited until it dropped its head to eat, then jerked hard on the rope. The parrot squawked and flapped. Avá-Tapé lunged forward, fingers grabbing at its tail. The sling loosened, but not before his fingers grasped feather. He felt a pull as the bird thrashed and broke free, leaving him clutching two large tail feathers.

His confidence grew.

He set them aside, laid out his sling again and waited. More stars speckled the horizon as Yacy appeared above the treetops. Avá-Tapé hoped that the light of Yacy's fire would smile down on him.

He quickly trapped two more parrots, harvesting more tail feathers before the night grew quiet. As more time passed, his arms and legs burned. He fought the urge to stretch, almost giving in, when he heard more flapping. Twin shadows floated into the treetop close to his sling. Silver moonlight glinted off feathered wingtips as two of the largest macaws he'd ever seen stretched their wings skyward. Avá-Tapé tightened his sweaty grip on the sling as their heads bobbed in the moonlight, picking at fruit. One stepped close and moved away again, still pecking.

Avá-Tapé's legs trembled. The macaw's head popped up and the bird looked straight at him. He held his breath. Legs, arms, and lungs ached as the moment stretched into a bubble of stillness outside of time.

The bird stepped into the middle of the snare and Avá-Tapé yanked. Startled squawks and rustling feathers filled the night as the two birds took wing. One flapped into the darkness. The second one rose in a flurry, then came down hard as Avá-Tapé pulled again and lunged for its tail. The macaw's wings beat against his face. He felt sharp pain as a claw raked him below the eye. He swayed and fell on his side, clutching the rope. The macaw squawked and flapped. Avá-Tapé grabbed with his other hand, no longer caring about holding on.

Only the feathers mattered.

Another claw cut into his hand before he grasped the bird's tail. Claws slashed again as the macaw scrabbled to free itself. Hot pain lanced through his arm when the bird bit the back of his hand. He let go of the rope but held fast to the tail.

The macaw took to the sky, flying unsteadily toward the moon, silhouetted by the cold fire of Yacy, leaving Avá-Tapé shaking. His hands and face ran with blood. He clutched three huge tail feathers.

TWENTY-SIX

The climb up through the mists at the base of the falls took much longer than the climb down. Avá-Nembiará bundled their plants into nets and he and Avá-Tapé worked their way up the falls, pulling their load behind them.

Avá-Tapé's arms and legs shook near the top of the ascent, but terror no longer controlled him. He carried his fear, studying it as if from a distance. His body felt brittle from lack of sleep, and dried blood had crusted on his face and hands, but the wetness from the mists washed them clean by the time he crested the top.

Scratches criss-crossed his body where palm fronds had cut him, and his hands had been pierced. The bite on the back of one hand bled the most. Avá-Nembiará had wrapped the gash with herbs and strips of fiber, but a thin stream of blood still flowed from the cut. The wounds on his hands and the one below his eye throbbed with the pulse pounding in his ears, but he felt strong and proud.

He had his spirit messengers.

Avá-Tapé envisioned Kuná-Mainó's beautiful face in the glow of a fire, the brightness of its flames dancing in her eyes. He wanted to go to her now. Share his heart.

Avá-Nembiará led them to his *maloca*, where they sorted the plants until darkness approached. "We must make the new *paí* ready for his people," he said, smiling.

He cleaned Avá-Tapé's cuts with a solution of herbs and water. Using red and black paints from crushed berries and ash, Avá-Nembiará painted his son's face, arms, and legs with warrior stripes and patterns. Avá-Tapé wove his new feathers into the soft cotton of his headdress and donned his sash, while his father dressed in his own ceremonial feathers.

"A fiercer warrior I have not seen," Avá-Nembiará said when they finished. "The spirits of death will fly from your power. We must bring you to the people."

His father's words made his heart beat faster. Kuná-Mainó. The full cold fire of Yacy had gone and come again to the night sky since they had gone over the falls. He followed his father to the village, clutching his rattle. Darkened forms moved in the twilight, silhouetted by flames. Behind the fire, a huge *maloca,* the House of Dances, stood at the village center. Avá-Nembiará stopped and held up his hand.

Murmurs filled the air when Avá-Nembiará strode into the village and talked to some of the men. Three small boys darted into the surrounding *malocas.* A short time later the people straggled into the clearing amidst hushed conversation and whispers. When most of them had gathered, Avá-Nembiará led his son out before the fire.

Silence swept through the gathering like a ripple on a pond. Avá-Tapé felt their eyes on him. The village had grown since they'd gone. Where was Kuná-Mainó? Not with Avá-Karaí, he hoped with a sinking feeling.

Women and men watched him walk toward the fire. Little boys and girls looked up at him wide-eyed. He held his head high, for the first time noticing the other men and their feathers. None had as many as him except for his father, who had more.

At first he didn't recognize anyone, then he spotted Avá-Canindé's wide grin, like a proud father. Beside him, Avá-Guiracambí and Avá-Karaí stood like brothers. Santo and Rico jumped up and down. His mother's eyes shone like the dew. Even Pindé said nothing. She only stared open-mouthed.

Avá-Canindé regarded him with the same expression he reserved for Avá-Nembiará. Others had expectant gazes. With the attention, he felt the added weight of responsibility. Where was Kuná-Mainó? What message would her eyes have?

They stopped in front of the new dance house. Avá-Nembiará closed his eyes, held his arms high, and chanted softly. Avá-Tapé wondered if he should chant, but something told him no. He looked into the crowd, searching each face, each set of eyes.

"The healing spirits have spoken." His father lowered his arms. "The messenger birds have come. The voice of the spirit lives in the *mbaraká*." He took his son's wrist, raised his arm and the *mbaraká*, and shook it. The sound of the rattle stirred something in Avá-Tapé.

"The *paí* is the meeting place of the worlds. When he dances the spirits dance with him." Avá-Nembiará held his arm out toward the new dance house. "Here we will dance as one. Here our new *paí's* spirit will fly into the sky and pass through the door, past the sleeping *añag*, to the country of the dead."

While his father spoke, Avá-Tapé kept his vigil, his mind partially on what his father said, his heart yearning for a glimpse of Kuná-Mainó. He saw her at the edge of the crowd and sought out her eyes, but couldn't make contact in the darkness.

His father's hand came down on his shoulder and the people came forward, touching his hands and arms, their eyes searching his. Avá-Canindé and Avá-Guiracambí gave him powerful hugs. His mother gave him a tender embrace. He gave each his attention, longing to feel the touch of Kuná-Mainó, but when the last of the people greeted him, she faded into the shadows, never coming forth. His heart sank. Didn't she care? He thought back to when he had gone away. They had been close. Had he only imagined it?

His insides felt cold and empty. Avá-Karaí must have talked to her. Avá-Tapé's emptiness turned to anger. He would have to find her and know her heart.

His father, Avá-Canindé, and Avá-Guiracambí huddled in hushed conversation. Beside them, he glimpsed fear in Avá-Takuá's eyes. Avá-Nembiará nodded and seemed to be giving reassurances. The last thing he heard before the group separated was a whispered word that sounded like, "Cristobal," but he couldn't be sure.

"What is it?" he asked when he and Avá-Nembiará moved through the darkness back to his father's *maloca*.

Avá-Nembiará seemed distracted. "There is new sickness at the mission," he said. "Tomorrow we must see if your healing spirits are strong enough to battle the spirits of death."

Avá-Tapé had looked into the face of death many times and had seen different faces, but the eye of death always had the same look. One that stared past the here and now into the world beyond. He would have to look upon it again, but knew he couldn't choose the time and place. It chose for you. Without warning. He didn't want to face it this time. Not because of his fear, but because of his longing.

He wanted to find Kuná-Mainó and know her heart. What had changed since their last time together? The first chance he got he would seek her out, but for now the small sickness in his heart would have to wait. The greater sickness of his people came first.

TWENTY-SEVEN

Avá-Tapé opened his eyes to grayness and the call of the morning bird. Its song sounded different, like a warning. Then it stopped. He sat up in his hammock and looked out at the lines and shadows of early morning. The silence continued. Too long.

A flash lit the *maloca*, followed by a deafening boom and the crackle of thunder. Avá-Tapé's heart slammed in his chest. He looked over at his father whose eyes were open and alert.

"The gods are angry," Avá-Nembiará said, climbing out of his hammock. "The spirits of darkness have grown strong at the mission. There is much death."

Avá-Tapé remembered the look of fear in Avá-Takuá's eyes from the night before.

Thunder clapped again, and the patter of rain came hard like countless monkeys scampering across the roof. Avá-Nembiará stoked the fire and heated *maize* mash and *cassava* bread. While Avá-Tapé ate, his father gathered herbs and bundled them into nets. "There is much healing to do," he said as he worked. "Many have gone to the country of the dead and will not return, but many stand at the doorway, pulled by both worlds."

Avá-Tapé felt cold in the pit of his stomach. "I have not passed through the door by my own power. I am not ready. You said it yourself. Not until I have danced at the dance house…"

"You have strong allies. Do not weaken them with fear. Fear gives darkness its power. You cannot yet travel between the worlds, but your spirit helpers can join with mine and bring more magic to the battle."

152

"My spirit cannot fly through the door. What can I do as a man?"

"You may not have the freedom of a warrior's spirit, but you have his heart. Soon it will be free." Avá-Nembiará gathered up the nets and handed one to his son. Avá-Tapé grabbed his spear. His father took the bow and quiver, and the two walked out into the gray morning.

The forest came alive with the patter of rain. Big warm drops soaked them, falling faster each moment. Avá-Tapé thought of the time he had gone to the mission and faced the jaguars. A shudder passed through him. It had rained then, too.

When they came to the path from the village to the mission he kept closer to his father, peering through the hazy shadows and gray sheets of water in search of movement.

They passed through the forest without seeing other signs of life, only the din of the rain blurring sight and sound. It fell harder when they stepped into the clearing near the hulking buildings of the mission.

Avá-Tapé slogged through ankle-deep mud behind his father, wondering how much sickness lay in wait for them. Would they see Father Antonio or the other priests? If so, how would the Jesuits act when they saw him as a healer, a *paí* like his father? He remembered the night they chased him from the House of their God because they feared his father.

Now he was a *paí*. They would fear him, too. He couldn't understand how a man of God could fear a man who healed, but the whites had killed the son of their own God who had been a healer. Avá-Tapé shook his head. He would never understand.

The mission streets ran swift with muddy water. Most of the houses looked dark and abandoned. Because of the rain, he couldn't tell if any fires burned. He and his father moved from door to door, peering into blackness. How many had stayed in fear of the Jesuit God? From what he had seen the night before, most had moved to the new village. He secretly hoped they would find no one, but knew that would not be so.

Avá-Nembiará stopped, held his hand out and stayed rock still, staring straight ahead. Avá-Tapé clutched his spear tighter and strained to see what held his father's attention. At first he saw nothing, then a dark shapeless mass emerged from the shadows of a doorway, moving low to the ground. His first thought was of the *añag*, but this looked too long.

It moved into the street and started toward them. Avá-Tapé wanted to run, but his father remained immobile. Did he ever show fear? Avá-Tapé raised his spear. Avá-Nembiará removed the bow, nocked an arrow, and trained it on the form.

The mass kept coming.

The moment Avá-Tapé saw the jaguar dragging a man, an arrow left his father's bow with a twang. All four paws left the ground as the man-sized cat flew into the air with a short, high-pitched mewl. It spun, hissing and biting at the arrow in its neck. Avá-Nembiará nocked a second, took aim, and loosed it. The cat jerked and stopped its spin. The second arrow jutted from its shoulder. The jaguar came at them, rapidly cutting the distance in a lopsided scramble. His father nocked a third arrow. Avá-Tapé ran up the side of the street, spear forward. The jaguar went straight for his father.

Avá-Tapé lunged, making the cat turn on him, and the third arrow passed through its flank, poking out the other side. It spun back toward his father and Avá-Tapé moved in, putting all his weight behind the thrust of his spear.

It caught the jaguar behind its foreleg and broke, wrenching Avá-Tapé's wrist. The cat toppled into the mud, clawing and hissing at the air. Avá-Tapé backed away, wrist stinging. His father readied a fourth arrow, drew back and waited. The cat's hisses weakened, until they were swallowed by the softer hiss of the rain. Its head rolled and its tail twitched.

Avá-Tapé drew closer. The jaguar's flank heaved with slow, labored breaths. Blood trickled from its maw and ran in streams from its muddied wounds. Avá-Tapé looked into one of its huge yellow eyes, feeling it on him, knowing that it spoke of death. It blinked and watched him as if all the cat's life were contained in it, then its fire faded and went still. His father lowered the bow.

Avá-Tapé shuddered. His breath came hard. His wrist ached. His heart thumped in his ears. The rain danced steadily, causing streams of blood and mud to run in the black and yellow of the jaguar's fur. The hiss of the rain filled his senses.

Avá-Nembiará looked up the street and gestured with his head toward the motionless form the jaguar had abandoned. Avá-Tapé moved slowly, knowing what he would find. His father walked beside him, keeping the bow out and an arrow nocked. No fear.

They found a man face up in the mud, mouth open, his head cocked at an obscene angle. His lips looked blue, his mud-streaked body, fish-belly white and emaciated. His torso had been clawed and slashed, one arm gnawed off at the elbow. His eyes stared off in two directions, destroying any semblance of intelligence that may have remained at his moment of death. Rain streamed from the dead man's eyes as if he were crying.

Avá-Nembiará pulled what looked like a small strip of skin from the man's stomach and held it close. Avá-Tapé leaned forward and watched it writhe between his father's fingers. Avá-Nembiará squeezed it between his thumb and forefinger and flicked it away. "Worms killed him before the *añag* did."

"Worms?"

"From the white man's meat. *Techó-achy.* Fat and easy prey for worms and the *añag.* It draws darkness to itself and to men. Not like game from the forest."

Avá-Tapé looked at the body, now washed clean from the rain. He wanted to move it but couldn't bring himself to touch it. The man would have to be buried when the rain stopped. Holding his breath, he grabbed the corpse by the feet to drag it under the veranda. Its skin slipped off and hung loose in his hands. He shook the sloughing skin off and felt his stomach turn.

Dropping to his knees, he washed his hands in the mud. His father went into the doorway and emerged a moment later with an ox skin. He rolled the body in it, bound it with fiber, and dragged it under the veranda.

"We will come for the *añag* later," Avá-Nembiará said, pointing toward the jaguar. "The dead will stay in the country of the dead. We must find those who still wander there and guide them back to the world of men."

Though he had washed the man's skin from his hands, Avá-Tapé wanted to wash again. He looked up at the sky. Since leaving the *maloca* it had brightened, but the rain continued hard and steady. His father started down the street, checking doorways. Avá-Tapé followed, his senses alert for danger. Most of the houses on the outer streets had been abandoned. The people who remained at the mission clustered toward its center, close to the church.

They passed many doorways before they found signs of life. The first family were all healthy, but they spoke of the sickness, pointing out which houses held the stricken. Avá-Tapé had just begun to dry by the fire when they had to go back out in search of those needing healing.

He followed his father to the next house, stopping at the door. His stomach jerked as if he'd been punched. He had been here before. A woman in the corner in shadow, two children thin as *maize* stalks, and a big man lying before a cold hearth. His father went in without hesitation.

Avá-Tapé stood inside the door, unable to take his eyes from the still form of the woman. Remembering the way he had found Avá-Canindé's woman, he went to the body, anxious to wrap her in a skin so he wouldn't have to see her tortured features. Her eyes were open and unmoving as if studying him. He knelt beside her, grabbed the edge of the skin that she lay on, and started to roll.

Her eyes widened.

He cried out and fell backward, his heart jumping as though a jaguar claw had ripped it. Avá-Nembiará leaned toward the wide-eyed woman, put a hand to her head, smiled and stroked her cheek. The fear in her eyes receded. "Forgive my son," he said. "He has walked among dark spirits and looked on those that have come to your door. He thought you had passed on to the country of the dead." Avá-Nembiará dropped his net and unwrapped it. "Do not fear. Our magic is strong. The spirit of the plants will battle your sickness."

Avá-Tapé wanted to speak but could find no words. He had let fear strike his heart but he wouldn't let the darkness steal his soul again. He would help his father drive it from this house and these people.

"It is the white man's cattle that has brought the sickness," Avá-Nembiará said. "It is full of *techó-achy*. Only more time in the fire can kill the sickness that lives in it, but still it is heavy for the spirit—and still it brings the añag in hunting packs."

The woman watched in silence while Avá-Nembiará chanted and shredded tobacco leaves into a gourd. Avá-Tapé went back out into the rain, collected wood, and started a fire in the hearth. After adding small portions of other herbs and water, his father stirred the mixture over the fire, producing a strong, bitter-smelling liquid. When it grew sticky, he propped the woman up in the crook of his arm and held a cup to her lips.

"Drink fast," he said. "Do not think of the taste."

The woman looked up at him, put thin trembling fingers over his, and tipped the cup up. After two swallows, her hands dropped, but Avá-Nembiará kept the cup to her lips, forcing her to drink the rest. She grimaced and a gamut of agonies passed over her drawn face before she grabbed her stomach and tilted to the side. Avá-Nembiará put a gourd bowl beside her.

She jerked twice and vomited a thick stream of brownish-white fluid into the gourd. She retched, heaved, gave two more spurts, and heaved again, this time producing nothing but an agonized moan.

A gooey, brown-white mass of worms writhed in the bowl. Avá-Tapé's stomach spasmed and he tasted his own bile. The woman rolled onto her back, her face blanched like ash. Her body shook and tears streamed from her eyes. Avá-Nembiará mixed a second drink of juice from lemon, rue, and mint, which he strained. The woman sipped tentatively, finishing it all.

She grabbed at her stomach again and twitched, but didn't vomit. Avá-Nembiará made her lie back and close her eyes while he blew tobacco smoke over the length of her body, shook his rattle, and chanted.

He then treated the rest of the family the same way, each time getting similar results. By the time they left, Avá-Tapé had grown used to the sight of worm-thickened vomit.

He followed his father through the rain and mud to the next house, determined not to show weakness. When they reached the third house, Avá-Tapé made his own mixture and treated half the people, while his father worked on the others. Twice, the smell of death greeted them. Without hesitation, Avá-Tapé rolled the bodies into their skins and dragged them from the house, keeping alert for jaguars.

The third time, the sickly-sweet odor hit as though someone had thrown it in his face. From the doorway he saw a number of silent forms, stretched out on the floor like so many pieces of wood. The whole family had passed on. Only the husks of their bodies remained. He remembered the way the skin had come off the first man and shuddered at the prospect of touching these. The stench invaded his nose and mouth. His stomach boiled, and for the third time that day he tasted bile.

He rushed outside, turned his face to the sky, and let the rain fall upon his eyes, into his mouth, down his cheeks, and through his hair, as if cleansing him of the smell and taste of death. Part of him grew stronger with every confrontation, part of him weakened as if each healing took something from him. Death seemed to be seeping into him a little at a time, robbing him of life.

He closed his eyes and let the hiss of the rain wash over him. The unbroken sound lulled him until he felt as if something watched him. His skin prickled. His spear had been broken killing the jaguar. His father had the bow. He opened his eyes and peered down the street through a curtain of rain. A dark form huddled over one of the skin-wrapped bodies he and his father had dragged into the street.

TWENTY-EIGHT

His heart raced. What if it attacked? Could he get to the bow in time?

It moved.

It would take more than one arrow.

And rose.

A spectral smudge of black against a haze of gray moved toward him as if floating. A dark-hooded figure. A Jesuit. Avá-Tapé's legs started to shake.

The priest peered out from the folds of his hood before pushing it back, revealing the balding head of Father Lorenzo, who clutched his rosary. Water ran down his face and fingers. Gaunt and ashen, his once bright blue eyes looked hollow and empty. Desperate. Muddied robes hung from his thin frame like rags on a tree. "So much death," he said softly.

The sound of the rain hissed between them. Avá-Tapé could find no words. He thought only of the sickness. Why hadn't the Jesuits done anything? How could they let things go so far? "Where are Father Antonio and the others?"

"Gone."

Gone? They had chased him from the church. Had the gods...

"For three weeks now. To Asunción. The sickness came days after they left. I've tried everything I know, but I am no healer. Your father..."

"Why did they go?"

The priest's eyes flashed fear, then faded back to sorrow. "Bishop Cristobal." His voice came louder, as though praising

God's name. His eyes said something different. Avá-Tapé remembered the fear in Avá-Takuá's eyes. Father Lorenzo's eyes
grew wider. He stepped back.

"Many have died from eating the meat of the white man's
cattle."

Avá-Tapé flinched at the sound of his father's voice.

"I don't understand," Father Lorenzo said softly.

"Worms."

Father Lorenzo's mouth hung open. His eyes took on a faraway look. "What can I do?"

"Bury those who have gone to the country of the dead. The
añag are hungry as it is. We will try to save the living who have
not gone too far from the door between the worlds. Our magic
is strong. We can save many, but not all."

Father Lorenzo blessed himself and kissed his rosary. "I will
say a novena and pray for their souls."

Avá-Nembiará grunted. "Pray to your God for their lost
souls. I will fly to the country of the dead and bring them
back." He turned and started up the street.

Avá-Tapé watched Father Lorenzo a moment longer, trying
to read past the fear in the older man's eyes. The priest stared
at the ground the way Pindé did after her mother had scolded
her. Avá-Tapé hurried to catch his father, looking over his
shoulder one more time to see Father Lorenzo standing alone
in the rain, head bowed as if in prayer.

When they finished the last of the treatments, the gray sky
had begun fading to darkness. Using two poles, they bound the
dead jaguar and carried it back through the rain and shadows
to Avá-Nembiará's *maloca*, reaching it in darkness.

Avá-Tapé coaxed flames from smoking tinder and added
wood until a small fire burned. He felt himself start to dry,
thankful that he wouldn't have to go back out into the rain.
They had been wet all day.

Avá-Canindé and Avá-Guiracambí brought them fish, *cassava* bread, and *maize*, which they cooked. Avá-Nembiará sent
them back to the village with the jaguar. After they had gone,

father and son sat near the fire, each silent in his own thoughts. Exhausted and drained from the long day, Avá-Tapé felt himself drifting toward sleep when his father's voice brought him awake.

"You don't have the strength to pass through the door, but your soul has grown lighter with your knowledge of the other world. On this night, while you travel in your visions, watch for the souls of those who have tasted our magic. If you see them wandering, try to guide them back to the world of men."

"And if I see the *añag?*"

A slow smile came to his father's face. "Today my heart soared at your bravery. You have grown as a warrior..."

"But fear held my heart."

"And still you acted. You chose the moment, and thought not of death or fear. Only acting."

All Avá-Tapé could remember was his revulsion at the sight of the worms and the way he had run from the house of death. He couldn't meet his father's eyes. He felt unworthy. Avá-Nembiará had shown no fear.

"A true warrior would not feel fear," Avá-Tapé said. "I couldn't stay in the house of death. You did not run. You did not feel fear."

"Because I didn't show fear doesn't mean I did not feel it." Avá-Nembiará's face remained impassive, as it had most of the day. He showed little but had much knowledge.

Avá-Tapé wondered if his father felt as much as he did. How else could he sense the presence of spirits, plants, and people? Avá-Nembiará's gaze met his. His face didn't change but his eyes said much. Father and son studied each other for a long moment until Avá-Tapé could no longer bear the weight of his father's stare.

Avá-Nembiará went to his hammock. "I have many souls to seek this night," he called from the darkness. "When the light comes to the world again, we will go back to the mission. Sleep now. Seek out lost souls in your visions."

Avá-Tapé went to his hammock and fell into a deep sleep.

He saw no wandering souls and no jaguars. He dreamed of
Kuná-Mainó, her mouth parting in anticipation. He went to
her, anxious to touch his lips to hers.

When he drew close a worm wriggled from between her
teeth. He blinked and stared into the drawn and laughing face
of Avá-Canindé's woman, her gaping mouth full of writhing
worms. The sound of her voice invaded his body, shaking him
until he awoke, still hearing her laughter.

He sat up in semi-darkness, listening before realizing that
her laughter was the shriek of a spider monkey. A light patter
of rain fell on the roof. He saw the silhouette of his father
crouched before the fire, preparing plants for the day's healing.

After a meal of fruit and *maize* mash, they started toward the
mission, visiting the houses they had been to the day before. At
each one, Avá-Nembiará leaned over and made sucking sounds
near the sick person's stomach before repeating the tobacco
juice and herb drink.

On the way to the third house, Avá-Nembiará's manner had
lightened. "A *paí* can cure by sucking out the sickness because
Kuarahy once brought dead birds to life in the same way," he
said. "Kuarahy and Yacy had great sadness after killing many
birds. Kuarahy wanted to bring them back to life, so he made
a basket of vine. With Yacy's help he put the dead birds in it.
He took them out one by one, sucked their throats, and the
birds lived again. The first bird he brought back was the pheasant. That is why it has a bare neck where no feathers grow."

"Why do you sing and blow smoke?" Avá-Tapé wondered
aloud.

"Chanting is the way Kuarahy raised his dead mother,
Nandé Cy. The chant calls down the power of the *paí's* helper
spirit. A *paí* blows smoke because this is the way Kuarahy revived
his brother. Yacy had been eaten by the *añag*. Kuarahy talked
them into leaving the bones whole. He took his dead brother's
bones into the forest and breathed on them until flesh returned. When a *paí* breathes on the spot on the head where the
soul enters, power leaves the *paí* and enters the sick person.

This magic wrestles with the dark spirit and forces it to leave the sick person's body."

In each house they visited, Avá-Tapé saw and felt the change in its occupants. A flicker of life had come back into the eyes of most, as if his father had indeed traveled to the country of the dead and brought their souls back.

The sky remained slate gray and the rain fell steadily. The only sense of passing time came from the growing weariness that crept over Avá-Tapé with each healing.

A small but growing group of mission Indians followed them from house to house, gasping when they saw the worms expelled from the sick, becoming silent when his father chanted and shook his rattle. True to his word, Father Lorenzo had taken the bodies of the dead from the streets.

They saw no jaguars.

TWENTY-NINE

The rain stopped on the third day. Since Avá-Tapé and his father had begun their healing, no more of the tribe had passed over to the country of the dead. They saw little of Father Lorenzo, and when they did, he remained in the shadows, disappearing if they went in his direction. They saw no sign of Father Antonio or Father Rodrigo.

The crowd that followed them around the mission grew with each passing day. More than once, Avá-Tapé heard the name of Cristobal whispered, but when he asked, those he spoke to shook their heads and turned away.

On the fourth day, most of the sick had recovered. The group that had followed them around the mission went back to the village with them, leaving only a handful of families behind.

When they reached the village, Avá-Tapé searched the waiting faces, longing for a glimpse of Kuná-Mainó. His heart rose when he saw Avá-Guiracambí, but Kuná-Mainó didn't follow, only Avá-Canindé and Avá-Takuá. Avá-Canindé's eyes showed concern. Avá-Guiracambí's, worry. Avá-Takuá's held fear.

Avá-Canindé looked around before leaning close to Avá-Nembiará. "We must speak where none can hear," he said in a hushed voice. "Many things have happened since you went below the falls, but we could not speak of them until you battled the sickness at the mission."

"I felt this," Avá-Nembiará said, nodding. "Come to my *maloca* when the insects begin their night song." He walked out of the village, leaving its new members in the care of the older ones. Avá-Tapé glanced back at Avá-Takuá. The look in Monkey Face's eyes made him uneasy.

That night, as crickets chirped and monkeys chattered, the three men entered the *maloca* in silence, seating themselves around the hearth. The firelight made Avá-Canindé's nose look even bigger on his broad face, but his sleepy expression showed nothing. Avá-Guiracambí's big ears and pug nose looked smaller in the midst of his round worried face. Avá-Takuá's wiry frame looked fragile between the two bigger men. His too-close eyes darted like moths diving into a fire.

Avá-Nembiará stared into the flames. The others looked everywhere but at him. Avá-Tapé decided to study the fire like his father. He knew they would speak when they were ready.

Avá-Canindé cleared his throat and glanced from Avá-Takuá to Avá-Guiracambí, then back to Avá-Nembiará. "Most of the people have come from the mission to live with us," he said. "Father Antonio, Father Lorenzo, and the other priests came many times to the village, and then Father Antonio came alone. He put the fear of his Christian God into our hearts with his words. Some went back to him, but most did not. He became angry, then sad. He cried like a child."

Avá-Canindé looked at his companions, who nodded but said nothing. "One day he came no more. The hearts of the people grew lighter. My heart felt like it would slip over the edge of the falls. After many days I went to the mission to talk to those who still lived in fear of the Jesuit God. They told me that Father Lorenzo still said the Mass, but Father Antonio had gone in much sadness."

"Where?" Avá-Nembiará cut in, speaking for the first time.

"Bishop Cristobal called for him."

The name struck Avá-Tapé's heart like an arrow. He had heard it many times from Father Antonio and Father Lorenzo, always spoken with reverence, sometimes with fear. Bishop Cristobal. Father Antonio had written to the Bishop asking him to come, and now he had gone to him.

In the divine order of the church the Bishop was closer to

the Christian God than most men. Father Antonio said that the
mission existed because of the Bishop's grace. Cristobal spoke
not only for the leaders of the church, but for the white settlers.
The Bishop was powerful in the world of men and in the world
of their spirits.

"Do you fear this holy man of the Christian God?" Avá-
Nembiará said, his voice even.

"Only the power he has over the white men," Avá-Canindé
said.

"Your heart does not lie. They are many. We are shrinking. The word of Tupá is true. The time of destruction has
returned. The Earth is old. Our tribe is no longer growing.
The world is bloated with death. *Techó-achy* has made our
souls heavy. We have eaten the food of the whites. Now the
growing weight of our faults has brought us to the end. The
sun will disappear and there will be nothing for us to do on
this Earth."

"He comes," Avá-Takuá blurted. "Some of our men were
gone many days in the forest. Hunting and fishing. They saw
canoes on the river. Father Antonio was with them. Other white
men, too—and people of the forest like us, but not Guarani."
He stopped as quickly as he had started, his eyes wide.

All faces turned to Avá-Nembiará. The fire crackled and a
howler monkey cried out. This new knowledge changed things.
How many whites came in canoes? Were they settlers? Did
Bishop Cristobal come with them? What of these other people?
Would they take over the mission?

"We do not have to fall under the weight of *techó-achy*," Avá-
Nembiará said. "We must lighten our spirits and reach perfection. If we stay, the white men will destroy us. Those not destroyed will become slaves."

The tightness in Avá-Tapé's stomach grew hot with anger.
"We can fight!" The words flew from his mouth before he could
catch them. "We are warriors."

"We can fight and die quickly at the hands of the white men
or we can die a slow death as their slaves," Avá-Nembiará said. "It

doesn't matter how the end comes. To die fighting is noble, but is foolish when it is a battle we cannot win. They are many, but our numbers lessen with each passing moon. Why fight and die in a time and place chosen by the white men when we can dance in our own time? Sing to our own gods? We must dance until our bodies rise above the earth and fly to the Land Without Evil."

"How can we know that the white men will make slaves of us?" Avá-Tapé couldn't believe that Father Antonio and Father Lorenzo would let such a thing happen.

"We should move back to the mission where we are safe," Avá-Takuá said, his eyes blinking like a monkey's. "The Bishop will protect us..."

"Men who put the son of their God to death are men who will not stop feeding their lower natures," Avá-Nembiará said. "I have heard from other Guarani who have traded with us. The whites have made slaves of many. They say that as long as the Guarani sing praise to the white God in the white man's church, the Jesuits have the power to keep the settlers from making slaves of us. Now that the Jesuits do not have us in their church, other whites come."

"We will go to their church," Avá-Takuá said. "Pray to their God. Show them..."

"We must flee," Avá-Guiracambí said, speaking for the first time.

"We will not run from the whites," Avá-Nembiará said. "We will journey to the Land Without Evil. To the house of our gods. My visions show that the end of the world is coming. We must travel across the land to the great sea, build a dance house, lighten our bodies, and purify our spirits. We must dance with pure hearts until we rise into the sky and enter the door of heaven."

Avá-Tapé looked at the faces of the men and saw their acceptance of his father's word, except for Avá-Takuá, who stared at the ground.

"Go to the people," Avá-Nembiará said. "Tell them we will make a long journey. Gather food. Make the hunters ready. Fish must be caught and dried. Any who don't want to come can stay, but if they stay, they will live back at the mission."

"When will this journey begin?" Avá-Canindé asked.

"When Yacy shines full in the night sky," Avá-Nembiará said. "Go now. You know what to do."

Avá-Canindé, Avá-Guiracambí, and Avá-Takuá stood in unison. Each man nodded to Avá-Nembiará and each met Avá-Tapé's eyes, giving silent commitment with their expressions.

After they left, Avá-Tapé stared into the coals and remembered his visions, wondering what his part would be in all that would happen. The crickets and animals went quiet as if a dark wind had passed through the forest, leaving a silence that settled over the gathering like the morning mist. The moment hung indeterminably, outside of time until the night insects and his father's voice came together as though they had agreed to speak as one.

"We must prepare our hearts, thoughts, bodies, and spirits," Avá-Nembiará said. "Do not eat. Drink only water. You must lighten your spirit for the dance. My wish for you was to have more time to learn the knowledge of the *paí*, but the world is moving faster now that the end is coming. We must trust the spirits of the forest to show us the way to the Land Without Evil." He fell silent. The night song of the insects continued.

Avá-Tapé's eyes grew heavy. The weight of all that happened felt as if it pushed him into the earth. Still, he had not seen Kuná-Mainó. He had to talk to her.

"There is much to do," his father said, breaking in on his thoughts. "When the sun comes back to the world, you must go to the mission and look upon those who have been sick. The healing has been done. Only their spirits need to be comforted. Go quietly and tell them of the journey. Do not force your words on their ears. Speak and let them decide with their own hearts."

THIRTY

Avá-Tapé lay awake in the darkness listening to the rhythm of his father's breathing. The chirp of crickets floated to him on the cool damp air. The change in sounds since he'd first gone to his hammock told him he'd been sleeping, but he felt as if he hadn't. His father's words floated through his mind.

"Go and tell them of the journey. Do not force your words on their ears. Let them decide with their hearts." How much had he, Avá-Tapé, decided with his heart? His first impulse said yes, he had chosen his path, but he couldn't help feeling that more powerful forces pushed him along it. Had he really had a choice?

His father said Tupá chose him. If Tupá had chosen *him*, then he had no choice. If that were so, did Jesus choose the Jesuits? Did the God of the white men choose the Jesuits as warriors against the gods of his grandfathers or did the white man make his God out of his own mind? Could the Christian God be false?

Avá-Tapé searched his memories for signs from the white man's God but found none—only stories, symbols, books, and buildings. Tupá spoke through his father, and the Jesuits broke the magic with their own fear the same way their grandfathers had crucified the son of their God. Maybe the Christian God was not false, but simply refused to speak to those who killed his son.

Could it be that gods would not speak to men who lived in fear? Avá-Tapé remembered his pleas to the Christian God his last night in the church. He had held no fear, only yearning. The

Jesuits drove him from the church with *their* fear. What choice had they given him but to run? Now he would go back to the mission without his father to give those who stayed a choice. One that would not be thrust on them in fear and anger.

He closed his eyes and let his thoughts drift. What would he want if he could choose? A vision of Kuná-Mainó rising up out of the water filled his mind. The curves of her body. Her eyes and the way they spoke more than what she said with words. He felt a stirring in his groin. His body remembered her as well as his mind did. He thought of the little time spent with her. The first time he'd seen her. And Avá-Karaí. Two moons had passed since he had gone below the falls with his father. What had passed between Kuná-Mainó and Avá-Karaí while he was gone?

The crickets stopped and silence filled the forest before the cry of the morning bird floated to him across the quiet like the voice of Tupá, urging him toward those who needed healing. He climbed out of his hammock. He would go to the mission alone, his first time by himself in a long time. When he saw that the spirits of the sick were no longer in danger of getting lost in the country of the dead, he would come back to the village, find Kuná-Mainó, and ask her why she had hidden herself when he returned from below the falls.

He moved about the *maloca* in darkness, collecting the plants he needed for the day's healings. The worms had been purged. He had only to nurse those who had been sick so their spirits wouldn't stray from their bodies.

By the time he had the essential plants, darkness had turned to gray. He looked back to see Avá-Nembiará squatting beside the fire. Avá-Tapé had been so busy, he hadn't heard his father rise, but he knew that if all the forest had been without sound, he still would not have heard his father.

"Your knowledge of the plants and the strength of your allies will help you today," Avá-Nembiará said without looking up. "I would go, but there is much to be done at the village."

"I have my allies and the strength of your spirit."

"You are your own man now."

"We are part of the same healing power. We have the same allies." Though he couldn't see his father's face, he sensed Avá-Nembiará smiling in the darkness.

"Go now. Hold back the darkness with the light of your wisdom. Show the people that you are a healer."

Avá-Tapé gathered the plants, grabbed his spear and bow, and stepped out into a warm, mist-filled morning. Monkeys chattered, insects buzzed, and the cries of birds filled the air. The sounds told him no jaguars were near, but that could change with one leap from a tree, or one soul-piercing screech.

He looked up at the tops of the trees lost in thick fog and started toward the mission, keeping his senses alert for signs of danger. Huge wisps of mist floated up from the ground like slithering snakes, joining the mass that hung in the treetops. He moved quickly, anxious to get his work done at the mission so he could get back to the village and find Kuná-Mainó. He had to know her heart.

When he reached the edge of the forest, the sky had brightened and the air had cleared. Fog still clung to the ground in cottony swirls. Feeling vulnerable, he scanned the clearing once for jaguars, and then hurried across the open space.

The outer streets of the mission showed no signs of life. As he neared the center, he heard a familiar chorus. Rounding a corner, he stood at the edge of the main square and heard voices raised up in song.

Ave Maria.

The skin on his arms and the back of his neck prickled. His throat tightened as sadness and longing filled him. He remembered being at the front of the church with Father Antonio and Father Lorenzo, dressed in the sacred robes of the whites, the voices of the people raised up in song. If only there had been some way to live in both worlds.

He listened, forgetting all differences, letting the words carry his heart like wings on a breeze. When the song finished, he crept up the steps to the church, cracked the door and peered inside. Father Lorenzo stood at the altar in his gold and purple robes holding a chalice above his head, speaking in Latin before lowering the cup and drinking the blood of Christ. Warrior tribes drank the blood of their enemies to take on their spirit. The Jesuits drank the blood of Christ to take on His spirit, but Jesus was not their enemy. He was the son of their God.

He looked up at the crucifix behind the altar. The holes in the hands and feet of Jesus. Their words spoke of love for Him, but they had treated Him as an enemy. Avá-Tapé remembered the last night he had been here. Like they had done to Jesus, the Jesuits had treated him as an enemy.

Easing the door shut, he leaned against it, listening to Father Lorenzo's words echoing through the hollowness inside. Words that pleaded and questioned, but never got answers.

Day after day, the same pleas, prayers, and songs, only to be answered by the silence of stone and wood. Avá-Tapé shook his head and went down the steps. Enough of the Jesuits and their God. He had the spirits of the plants as his allies. Together they would defeat the sickness.

He found an empty house where he could sit and watch the church without being seen. After more songs and chants, the doors opened and a small group of people came down the steps and made their way back to their homes. Father Lorenzo stood in the doorway, head bowed as he watched them move down the street.

When they disappeared into their houses and the doors of the church closed again, Avá-Tapé stepped into the quiet street and made his way to those who had been sick. At the first house, he found a man and woman sitting beside their hearth. The man wove a reed basket while the woman ground *maize* into flour. Avá-Tapé recognized them as two who had come out of the church.

"Your soul has stayed with your body," he said. "That is good."

Two sets of eyes looked up with worried frowns before looking down again. Avá-Tapé recognized the fear he had seen in Avá-Takuá's eyes. It made his stomach queasy. "No more healing is needed," he said, as he prepared a mixture of herbs. "Drink this to be sure that the worms do not have a place to live."

"Your magic is strong," the man said without looking up. "We will drink but we will also pray to Jesus."

Avá-Tapé could think of nothing to say. Their words neither hurt nor angered him. He ground his herbs, added them to water, and put the mixture over their fire. "Do what is right in your hearts," he said. "You have stayed at the mission to live as whites. I have also done this. But I can only ask. Who has healed you, the spirits of the forest or the God of the white man?"

"We must pray to Jesus," the man said again.

Avá-Tapé heard a tremor in the man's voice and felt his fear. He fought back anger. "Then I know where your heart lies," he said, "but I tell you this so you can choose."

"We have chosen," the woman said.

Avá-Tapé continued as if she hadn't spoken. "We will soon be taking a long journey to the Land Without Evil. To the house of our gods. We will travel to the great sea. There we plan to build a dance house, lighten our bodies and purify our spirits. We will dance with pure hearts until we rise into the sky and enter paradise."

The man looked up again, his eyes pleading. "Father Antonio comes with one who is closer to Jesus. A Bishop." He looked to his wife.

"Cristobal," she whispered.

"A man of great power," the man said. "A man close to God…"

"Men who put the son of their God to death are men who cannot stop feeding their animal natures," Avá-Tapé said, feeling his anger rise again. "It is because of their *techó-achy* that you have had this sickness."

"Father Antonio and the Bishop will protect us."

"Other Guarani say that the white men have made slaves of many and that as long as the Guarani sing praise to the white God in the white man's church, the Jesuits can keep the settlers from making slaves. Now that the Jesuits do not have all of the people in their church, other whites come."

Avá-Tapé heard a hiss and saw that his mixture had boiled over. He removed it from the fire, strained it, and made two drinks. The actions helped him regain his composure.

"Forgive me," he said. "I didn't mean to speak in anger of men and gods. I have come as a healer. I only want you to know what your people have chosen so you can join them if you want. Pray to Jesus if it brings comfort to your heart, and drink the magic of the forest so you can heal your body." He gathered his things.

"When does this journey begin?" the man asked when Avá-Tapé was halfway out the door.

"When Yacy shines full in the night sky."

"And how will you know which way to go?"

"The spirits will guide us."

Avá-Tapé went to the other families still at the mission, made the herb drink for those who had been sick, and told of the journey. All of them accepted his healing, but insisted on staying at the mission and praying to Jesus. He didn't let his anger come forth as it had with the first man. He simply told them of the plans and left them to their own thoughts. By late afternoon he had visited all who had stayed at the mission.

The setting sun flared on the red-rimmed horizon like an angry eye. If he hurried he could make it to the village and find Kuná-Mainó before dark. Starting down the street, he headed toward the outskirts of the mission. He passed his old house, shivering at the memory of the night the jaguars had been at the door.

Toward the end of the street he saw two big men appear from a darkened doorway, carrying short sticks. The falling sun made it hard to see, but he could tell by their movements that they were not white men. He squinted, trying to recognize them, but the angle of the sun made it impossible. Avá-Canindé and Avá-Guiracambí? What would they be doing at the mission? One of the sticks glinted in the late afternoon sun. Strange.

Both men moved toward him, one staggering, the other moving in an unsteady gait, as if sick or injured. Avá-Tapé's heart beat faster. He had never healed anyone by himself. Was his magic strong enough to help them?

Up close he saw narrow faces, flat noses, and long black stringy hair. Not Guarani. Their skin looked darker and their dress strange, half that of forest people, half of white men. One had a red cloth on his head. Their sticks shone smooth and shiny like the candle holders in the church, only these had a piece of wood growing out of the end. The men stopped in front of Avá-Tapé, no longer moving, but still swaying. The man with the cloth on his head clutched another shiny object Avá-Tapé recognized as a bottle. He had seen Father Antonio drink from one.

The man without the cloth on his head smiled through rotted teeth and spoke in a strange tongue. His breath hit Avá-Tapé like a slap of pungent, sour-smelling effluvium that reminded him of his father's breath after a long night of drinking *chicha*, only stronger.

"I am Avá-Tapé, son of Avá-Nembiará, *paí* of the Guarani," he said, holding himself up straight.

The man with the cloth on his head frowned and handed the bottle to the one with rotted teeth, who took it and drank. Some of its contents ran down his chin. He wiped it away with his forearm, belched, and squinted at Avá-Tapé. "*Ay Tay say o Aba Naria,*" he said in a mincing voice.

The words were unintelligible, but Avá-Tapé got their meaning. His hand tightened on his spear as his anger surged. These men had no sickness other than *techó-achy* from the white man's drink. He didn't need to talk to them. He adjusted the net of plants on his back and started past them. The one with the red cloth on his head pressed the hollow end of his stick into Avá-Tapé and pushed him backward, leaving a red circle on his chest.

Avá-Tapé held his spear in front of him. The cloth-headed man looked at his rotten-toothed companion, lowered his stick and laughed. Did they mean him harm or were they playing?

He rubbed the red ring on his chest. If they were playing, the drink made their play rough.

He glanced up at the sky. The sun had settled lower. Darkness would come soon. He had no time to get caught in a game. He started past them again and they moved in front of him. He tried to go around the other side and they blocked again. Both erupted in a burst of angry, guttural sounds, that seemed more animal than human.

Avá-Tapé looked into glazed red eyes, saw dullness and a look he could only think of as animal. His father's words filled his mind. "As men, another soul is added to the vital word. This second soul develops as a man grows. *Techó achy kué*, the animal soul responsible for the lowest passions and evil appetites." He tried one more time to dart to the side, but they blocked, so he bolted between them.

The man with the red cloth on his head caught Avá-Tapé across the chest with the smooth metal of the stick. Avá-Tapé pushed harder and both men drove him backward, sending him sprawling to the ground. His spear slipped from his hand and plants spilled from his net. Arrows scattered from his quiver. He grabbed for his spear and felt the smooth tip of a stick against his throat. Looking up, he saw rotted teeth twisted into a hideous snarl and bloodshot eyes glaring through a dark frown. More guttural sounds. He opened his mouth to speak and the man pressed the stick harder, choking off his words.

A burst of pain shot through his ribs, followed by a flash of light. Breath rushed from him. He glimpsed a red blur from the corner of his vision before another jolt stabbed through him. Still no breath. He rolled onto his side, feeling metal bite into his throat and saw the foot come again. Agony exploded in his midsection. He closed his eyes and trapped the foot, curling his body around it. The man pulled and staggered. Avá-Tapé held on, aware of the other man moving behind him. The foot slipped. Avá-Tapé opened his eyes to a muscled calf inches from his nose. The man pulled again and Avá-Tapé sank his teeth into the hard meat of the man's leg. An animal howl filled his ears and his tormentor tumbled to the ground. Avá-Tapé clenched his jaws tighter, tasting blood. The man wailed.

More pain lanced through Avá-Tapé's shoulder. He spit flesh and rolled to the side. A stick whistled by his ear, slamming the ground. Broken Tooth straddled him and raised it again. Avá-Tapé brought his foot up hard into the man's groin, doubling him over. The cloth-headed man yanked him by the hair. Avá-Tapé grabbed a handful of dirt and flung it into his enemy's eyes, causing the man to howl and let go.

Avá-Tapé staggered to his feet and saw the rotten-toothed one curled on the ground, clutching his groin. Flinging another handful of dirt in the man's eyes, Avá-Tapé grabbed his spear and ran for the forest, leaving plants and arrows scattered in the street.

THIRTY-ONE

Avá-Tapé ran straight for the path, then darted sideways away from it. Glancing back, he saw a violet-hued sky; ahead, darkening shadows. He ducked under a vine-laden tree, tripped and fell into some brush, scratching his face on prickly branches. Startled parrots flew in a flurry of squawks and color. He lay still, heart pounding in his ears. Sweat flowed from his face, stinging the scrape on his throat. His side throbbed where he had been kicked. He worked a stringy clot of skin from between his teeth and spit it out, still tasting blood.

He forced himself to breathe deeper, feeling his chest shaking with each breath. He had to get to the village. Warn his father. These men who spoke and acted like animals had to be the ones seen on the river with Father Antonio and Bishop Cristobal. The bottle had been a sure sign of the white man's *techó-achy*.

What did this mean? Father Antonio chased him from the house of the Jesuit God after Avá-Tapé had learned his ways. He knew Father Antonio had angry moments, but he would never allow anyone to hit another.

He heard guttural noises, peered up into the fading light, and saw the shadows of night creeping in. He had to move. He crawled through the undergrowth to the base of a tree, propped himself behind it, and scanned the clearing. The two men came around the corner of a building, holding their sticks out in front of them.

Avá-Tapé's breathing had slowed, but his heart quickened. He worked his way to the clearing and grabbed a handful of rocks before fading back into the jungle, angling toward the path.

A flurry of broken branches and angry voices crashed into the forest. Avá-Tapé listened to them come noisily toward him, snuffling and grunting like angry boars. He didn't want them to find the path to the village or his father's *maloca*.

Keeping their sounds in front of him, he moved further from the path. After putting some distance between them, he snapped a branch over his knee and cried out. Two angry voices bellowed and crashed through the jungle toward him. He trotted beneath trees and vines, stumbling in the shadows until the men sounded far away. He threw a rock and evoked more rustling branches and angry sounds.

He did it twice more, leading them farther into the forest each time. Away from the path and the village.

The fourth time he threw a rock they fell into silence. Avá-Tapé strained to hear sounds other than the chirp of crickets and the buzz of insects. A lone macaw cried out. He crouched low and listened. Time passed. The night sounds grew louder. No sound from his tormentors. He waited.

A twig broke. Too close for him to run. He hid his spear beneath a bush and crawled until he found a tree, which he climbed slowly, hoping to hide and get a glimpse of his pursuers. A short way up he came eye-to-eye with an anaconda hanging from a branch. Its head floated toward him in the darkness, tongue darting in his face. Avá-Tapé blew at it and it reared back. Careful not to disturb its perch, he moved past it.

A few more steps and he heard rustling and a grunt below. Looking down, he saw a red cloth hovering in the darkness. An arm's length away he could barely make out the shaggy head of the one with rotted teeth.

He held his breath as they paused beneath him, sticks held straight in front like spears, moving from side to side. Avá-Tapé's chest felt as if it would burst. The moment they moved, he let his breath out slowly through his nose.

When he could see them no more, he hurled a rock into the trees. A moment of silence followed, then a crash of branches, a deafening boom, and a blinding flash close to the ground that jerked his heart into his throat. Thunder echoed, a monkey screamed, and parrots screeched. Wings fluttered in the dark.

He heard shouts and the men rushing toward where he had thrown the rock. His whole body shook. An acrid smell drifted up to him. His skin felt clammy. What magic did these men have that brought thunder to the forest? Did the *techó-achy* of the white man's drink give them this power? Had the God of the whites finally spoken? His own heart thundered as if touched by the power of this bitter smelling magic. White thunder.

Avá-Tapé listened as the thrashing and breaking of branches moved away. His arms, legs, and chest all trembled. Such power in the hands of men. Their noises faded and the forest grew quiet for a long time. No insects sang. No animals cried.

A single cricket began its song like a scout checking for danger. Another answered, then the rest joined. A spider monkey chittered from somewhere, a parrot squawked, and the sounds of the night resumed.

Avá-Tapé clung to the tree, breathing slowly, calming himself, feeling the sweat dry on his body. His ears rang. Were his enemies quiet because they stalked him, or had they moved in another direction? He remembered hunting the boar and how he had immersed himself in the forest.

Closing his eyes, he opened his senses, listening for changes in the songs and cries of the night that warned of danger. When the rhythm felt right, he inched his way down the tree, once more sidestepping the anaconda. Crouching at the bottom, he checked again for any changes in the sounds before retrieving his spear.

His flight from the men and the onset of darkness had caused him to lose his direction. The only thing he felt sure of was that he had moved away from the mission and the village. Looking up at where he had hidden, he knew the way the men had gone. He crept off in the opposite direction, moving through the dark more in fear of the men than of jaguars. He moved slowly. No moon. No light. Only the thick canopy above.

He walked a long time, eyes open, ears poised, nose taking in the scents, his mind searching for signs of the mission or the village, until his eyes and limbs grew heavy. He should have come to a familiar place, but hadn't. He needed rest, but had to watch for danger. A fire would keep the jaguars at bay, but it would attract the men.

He propped himself up at the base of a tree. The raw spot on his neck where the stick had scraped it burned from his sweat, and his ribs throbbed, but exhaustion ruled his body. He laid his spear across his legs and fell into a restless sleep. His last thought was of the two men moving through the forest with the white man's thunder. Would they find the village?

THIRTY-TWO

Avá-Tapé awoke to the hum of insects and the song of birds. Thick fog enveloped him like the hand of a giant ghost. Every part of him ached, and his limbs were stiff. He moved and felt sharp pain in his side. Groaning, he pushed himself up, gingerly touching the scab on his neck where the stick had scraped him.

His stomach growled, reminding him that he hadn't eaten. He had no idea where he was or what direction to take. He listened, hearing nothing out of the ordinary, wondering about the two who had chased him. Were they still in the forest? Had they found their way back to the mission? He didn't think so. He didn't think they had found the village, either. Most likely they were lost, too.

Using his spear as a support, he pulled himself to his feet, wincing from the pain in his side. Turning in a slow circle, he scanned his surroundings, seeing nothing but white and the blurred outlines of trees, vines, and ferns etched into the haze.

He couldn't see more than a short distance in any direction. Only his senses of smell and hearing could guide him, but these would be no help unless he were close to people, the river, or some other strong presence. Without landmarks or paths, the forest had a sameness that could go for days in any direction. To go blindly could lead him farther from the village. He had to stay here until the mist cleared.

He thought of his father and mother. His sister. Avá-Karaí. Kuná-Mainó. Would he ever get to see her alone? Would these strange and angry forest people bring as much death as the whites? More? Could the Jesuit God be showing his anger now that the Bishop had come to this part of the world? His legs shook at the memory of the crack and flash of their thunder, its bitter odor, and the overpowering smell of the white man's drink.

He had to get to the village to warn his father and Avá-Canindé of their dark magic. He studied the outlines of trees swathed in fog, which had thinned in the upper branches. As time passed he could see farther. Closing his eyes, he relived the night before, retracing the way he had come, then he walked in the opposite direction. Pain shot through his side with each step.

Visibility grew until the mist cleared, but Avá-Tapé still had no sense of where the village or the mission might be.

He made a paste from the leaves of a plant his father had shown him, and put it on his neck. Its cool wetness soothed the itch. He found oranges. Remembering his father's admonition to purify himself, he drank their juice, but didn't eat. He kept moving, stopping only to listen and smell for familiar sounds and scents. In spite of being lost and hurt, he smiled, thinking of the men who had chased him. If he couldn't find his way in a forest he had grown up in, surely they were lost too.

The day remained overcast. He glimpsed patches of light through the leaves, but couldn't see the sun. After walking for a long time, he noticed the light fading and knew the day was coming to an end. He found a high spot with a good vantage point among some boulders. The pain in his side had dwindled to a dull ache that made it hard to get comfortable, but his weariness from walking and not eating brought sleep quickly.

Something startled him awake. He opened his eyes to blackness and lay still. A noise came from the darkness near his feet.

"Umppf...umppf."

Only one animal made a noise like that. The back of his neck felt like hundreds of tiny spiders ran across it. He clutched his spear, held his breath and heard the snuffling grunt again. Closer. Something warm and wet touched his foot. He swung his spear, yelling when it thumped something. A startled grunt and the rustle of leaves followed, then quiet. His heart thumped in his ears, echoed by the ache in his side. The sounds of the night drifted back to him on the still air.

He lay awake a long time, holding his spear until he felt comfortable, gradually falling back into an uneasy sleep, awakening to gray morning and wispy tendrils of mist. Maybe today he could glimpse the sun.

He stood on stiff legs, studying the place near his feet where his "visitor" had been. A short distance from where he had slept, he saw a break in the leaves. He brushed them away and saw an impression in the dirt from a jaguar paw.

He went in the same direction as the previous day, until he saw a glint of sunlight. Finding a tall tree, he climbed past squawking macaws and chattering monkeys until he could poke his head through the growth at the top. To his right he saw the sun climbing into the sky. Looking down, he saw where he had been standing. He closed his eyes and pictured where the sun came and went from the village, then he climbed down and headed in a new direction.

As he walked, the cries and songs of the animals grew more boisterous. Late in the afternoon, he stopped to rest and drink more juice from oranges.

For three days he had been gone from his father's house. Would they make the journey without him? Where were the strange men now? Had Father Antonio and Bishop Cristobal been to the village? Had men like the ones who chased him gone to the village? Had the thunder gone with them?

It had been so long since he had talked to Kuná-Mainó. Since before he had gone with his father. Three moons? He thought of how her soft skin would feel under his hands. Touching his lips to hers. Then he thought of her in Avá-Karaí's arms and his heart ached.

He closed his eyes and listened for the place in his mind

where the forest talked to him, yearning for a sign that would guide him back to his people. He thought he heard the wind rustling through the trees, then realized it wasn't the wind, but the river. Water! He stood, slowly turning his head until he sensed the direction of the sound, then ran, dodging vines, bushes, and branches in the fading light.

He stopped once to listen again before breaking through the trees in time to see the last of the sun sinking in a fiery ball that dappled the water's surface in red, orange and gold. He didn't recognize anything along the banks, but knew he was above the falls. The village had to be downstream.

He moved along the bank, watching for jaguars that might come to drink at the time between the worlds. He had trouble keeping his footing among the roots when darkness fell, finally stopping when it became too difficult to see. He found a spot among some fallen trees to rest for the night. At first light he would head down river and find the village.

Lying on his back, he breathed in the green algae smell of the water and gazed up at the spray of stars in the night sky, trying to read meaning into their patterns and wondering how many were homes of gods, and which ones shone on the Land Without Evil. Sleep stole upon him, and in his slumber he floated toward the stars, as if lifted by giant hands that pulled him faster and faster, until the tiny points of the stars blurred into a rush of silver that flowed and bubbled like the river.

He saw the people gathered as he had in his first visions. Women carried small children in slings. Men carried bows, spears, and blowguns. Pottery, tools, food and other implements were piled high on branches lashed with netting. Excitement filled the air. He saw his father standing before them.

"*Paí guazú*," someone whispered. "The great shaman."

Behind Avá-Nembiará, a mist swirled and took the ethereal form of a giant wearing colorful feathered bands on his head and arms. Tupá.

"Abandon this darkened land so you can live in happiness instead of slow death at the hands of the white man." Tupa's voice floated on the air, strong and powerful, yet soothing like the cool mist from the falls. Eddies swirled at Tupa's feet until a huge eye formed out of the vortex, sending a stab of cold into Avá-Tapé.

The eye hung in the air a moment, then rushed toward him in a boom of thunder like the one he'd heard from the men who chased him.

More booms, and he saw a jaguar dragging a corpse in the muddy street.

Boom.

Flesh coming off in his hands when he tried to drag the body.

Boom.

The jaguar's eye upon him when he drove the spear home.

Boom.

Children vomiting worms.

Boom.

A pair of glowing amber orbs blinked back from a blackened doorway. A low growl, and the man with the red cloth and the one with bad teeth emerged from the darkness carrying their strange sticks.

Boom.

Father Antonio huddled in the street, face twisted in anguish, his mud-spattered robes torn and bloody...

The image faded with the sound of Tupá's voice. "The old ways tremble at their beginnings and balance on the edge of destruction. The world must change. You must change worlds. Leave the imperfect world of men for that of the gods. The spirit of the people lives in you."

Avá-Tapé saw the muddy streets of the mission, darkened houses, and the church with its leaning walls. No sign of people. The sky brightened and rain fell. He looked into the brightness until it formed into a feathered cross, the meeting of time and space.

"To live in the old world is to live as a slave to *techó-achy*. It brings death to the old ways and to the people. The time has come to leave that which brings death, so you may embrace life.

You are the one to carry the knowledge of your people. Their survival lives in you."

Healthy children played in fields of *maize* and *manioc*. Brightly feathered men sang and danced amidst a feast of beans, sweet potatoes, peppers, pineapples, meat and fish. Avá-Tapé's heart swelled with equal parts of yearning and hope. A sob shook him and his eyes filled with tears.

Tupá stood at the head of a table holding a feathered cross. He made an expansive gesture, turned and started to walk. The cross shimmered gold light. An excited murmur passed among the people, who then followed him into the forest.

Avá-Tapé gazed at the golden glow, blinked and opened his eyes. Through his tears he saw the jagged blur of the full moon. The smell of water filled him. The soft gurgle of the river caressed his ears. He sat up. Holding on to the bitter-sweet feeling in his heart, he wiped away his tears and peered at the lines of silver that stretched across the forest and glistened on the water.

THIRTY-THREE

Avá-Tapé moved through the moonlight, following the gurgle of the water, driven by the urgency stabbing at his heart. He had to get to the village.

The light of Yacy, the moon, faded and the first sign of Kuarahy, the sun, glimmered on the horizon with the first blush of dawn. Avá-Tapé paused, listening and watching the banks for signs of animals coming to drink by first light. A huge white egret fluttered from the reeds and sailed slowly to a perch in a high tree. A tapir poked its head through some bushes on the far bank, and a group of monkeys jabbered from a low hanging branch.

The moon had dropped low in the sky when the first beams of sunlight struck the river in reds and golds. Avá-Tapé stepped up his pace. The early morning coolness turned to warmth as the sun rose higher. He studied the river banks for familiar signs while straining for sounds that spoke of people—or jaguars.

When the sun had risen high, he stopped for a drink of water and found a shady spot beneath a cypress. Stretching out, he closed his eyes and let the gurgles of the water bubble through his mind until he dozed. Soon another sound came to him beneath the rush of the water. Voices! Young women and little girls. Grabbing his spear, he hurried downstream, heart racing, his excitement rising as the voices came closer with each bend in the bank.

He recognized the terrain before he spotted brown bodies bobbing in the water and moving on the shore. His eyes scanned each of them until he saw her sitting apart from the rest with her knees drawn up into her chest. Joy filled him. "Kuná-Mainó!" he cried out, forgetting his former embarrassment.

Her head popped up and one of the little girls screamed. The rest scrambled from the water, huddling like frightened monkeys.

"Avá-Tapé?" she said incredulously. "Avá-Tapé?" She rose, forgetting her nakedness, her beautiful mouth open in surprise, then she grabbed her shawl, slipped it over her head, and sent the rest of the girls running back to the village.

"Avá-Tapé!" She said, running toward him. He met her by the edge of the pool and held her close, savoring the tenderness of her touch, the feel of her against him and the smell of her hair. He tried to speak but words wouldn't come. Only the happiness of holding and being held.

"They said you had gone to the country of the dead," she whispered. "We heard the thunder in the forest. They said the thunder spirits took you. When you didn't come back, your father went to the mission and couldn't find you."

He held her by the arms and looked into her eyes. "You have been in my thoughts every day and every night for three moons."

"And you have lived in mine."

"What of Avá-Karaí? Why did you hide when I came back from below the falls with my father?"

She looked away. "I wanted to be with you and talk to you of the plant spirits, but my father told me not to get in the way of your thoughts. He said that if I let my feelings touch yours, you would be in danger."

He pulled her closer. "You have not given yourself to Avá-Karaí?"

She pulled back, frowned, and shook her head. "He came to me and told me his feelings, but my heart has been with you."

"You have lived in my thoughts since I first saw you by your father's fire. My visions of you were the last I saw before flying into the world of spirits. You were the first I saw when I returned."

She laid her head on his shoulder. His heart felt as if it would explode. All this time she had had the same feelings.

"We have to get to the village," she said, letting him go. "Your father searches the forest by day and the land of the spirits at night. He says he cannot find your soul. Your mother is in mourning. The people are getting ready for the journey. We are to leave when two suns have passed."

Avá-Tapé remembered the two men he had lost in the forest, and felt a rush of fear. His father would be in danger. He looked into Kuná-Mainó's eyes once again and felt a flush of warmth. He wouldn't tell her what happened. He didn't want her to live with the fear that he carried.

He followed her to the village, wishing he could stay with her by the river. Any time alone with her was precious, but the safety of the people came first. He had to warn his father and Avá-Canindé of the strange men and their powerful magic.

Halfway to the village he saw his mother hurrying up the path followed by a group of women and children. The men followed. "Avá-Tapé," she cried. "My son!" She embraced him, then held his face in her hands as her eyes searched his. Tears streamed down her cheeks.

"We heard thunder from the forest and saw a clear sky. They said that thunder demons took you to the country of the dead. I didn't want to believe it, but you didn't come back." She hugged him again.

He looked past her to his father, Avá-Canindé, and Avá-Guiracambí. Their faces brightened when they saw him, but he sensed their apprehension. He hugged his mother once more, pulled Kuná-Mainó closer, and walked back to the village in silence, his mother on one side, Kuná-Mainó on the other.

When they reached the village, he saw the House of Dances filling the spot that had been empty. Bigger than the other houses, it had one side opened to where the sun rose. In front of the open wall sat a large cedar trough in the shape of a canoe. In front of it, three cedar posts. The two outer ones were topped with feathered sticks that held candles. The center post had a cross. A taller, thinner branch and a small arrow stood beside it. Everything had been decorated with feathered bands.

Alongside the dance house he saw piles of farming implements, tools, spears, bows, pottery, nets, and gourds. His vision of the journey flashed in his mind. When his gaze met his father's, he nodded once, gave his mother and Kuná-Mainó one more hug, and then followed the men to his father's house.

Daylight had faded to long shadows when he entered the *maloca*. Avá-Nembiará, Avá-Guiracambí, Avá-Canindé, Avá-Takuá, Avá-Karaí and the other men sat around the fireplace, leaving a spot for Avá-Tapé beside his father. He took his place and studied each man, meeting each set of eyes, holding them the way he had seen his father do so many times before. When Avá-Tapé had made eye contact with them all, Avá-Nembiará broke the silence.

"I knew your spirit had not gone to the country of the dead, but I feared that you had been taken by whites."

His father's comment startled him. How much did he know? Were the stories of the white settlers and slavery true?

"We heard the thunder from the forest," he continued. "The people believe that you have battled with thunder demons that stole your soul. Now that you have returned they will say that your magic is powerful."

Avá-Tapé nodded. "They were demons. Man-demons full of *techó-achy*, but not white men. Their skin had our color, but they spoke in an animal tongue I have never heard."

"The men who came in the canoes with Bishop Cristobal and Father Antonio," Avá-Takuá said.

"Two men carrying shiny sticks attacked me at the time when the sun falls to the earth. They pointed their sticks at me, knocked me to the ground, and kicked me. I fought and escaped." Everyone's eyes widened when he said this.

"I ran into the forest and hid. When darkness came they hunted me. I hid in a tree and played a trick. It must have angered them because that was when the thunder struck."

"*Guns!*" Avá-Canindé said. "Their shiny sticks carry death."

Guns? Avá-Tapé had never heard this word before. "I had great fear."

"You acted wisely," Avá-Nembiará said. "There has been talk of these men from those who trade with us. They come with the white settlers from another part of the forest. They kill and take others as slaves for the plantations."

A chill crept up Avá-Tapé's spine and his scalp tingled. "After the thunder I stayed quiet until they had gone. By leading them away from the path, I became lost myself and wandered for two nights."

"Many canoes came down the river with Father Antonio and Bishop Cristobal," Avá Guiracambí said, speaking slowly. "Many men. White men, not priests. Forest people, not Guarani. The first to see a healer of our people—a *paí*—and they hunt him like an animal."

Avá-Tapé couldn't believe that the men hadn't come to the village. The realization that they would come filled him with dread. They would come sooner or later.

"It is the beginning of the end," his father said, as if reflecting his thoughts. "We must have our last dance in this part of the world before we take our journey, or we will be crushed under the white man's *techó-achy*. Those who have come with the priests have been unloading their canoes and moving into the houses at the mission. When the fires burn in their hearths they will come for us."

THIRTY-FOUR

Avá-Tapé walked among the people, watching women weave nets which men stretched between branches. Others stacked dried fish, smoked meat, *maize, manioc,* pumpkins, potatoes, sugar cane, gourds, clay pots, and digging sticks in nets. Hunters made reed arrows with wood points, while those who fished gathered the vines that made fish float on the water when thrown in. Younger boys gathered saplings for spears, while girls ground *maize* into flour. Kuná-Mainó and the other young women kept charge of the children too small to be of any help.

People smiled and laughed, oblivious to the danger from the white men. Avá-Canindé, Avá-Nembiará and the few who knew the real danger, moved in silence, their stoic expressions not betraying their knowledge. Only Avá-Takuá showed fear. Avá-Tapé met his gaze and tried to convey calm, but Avá-Takuá's pained expression intensified. His eyes darted like frightened monkeys. Avá-Tapé looked away, feeling his own fear fluttering in his heart, but he didn't let it show.

His vision had become real. He and his people would follow his father, guided by the spirit of the great shaman who would take them on a journey to the edge of the world. There they would purify their bodies, lighten their souls, and dance until the gods came down out of the sky and lifted them to the Land Without Evil.

What part would he, Avá-Tapé, have in all that would happen? In his visions he had flown into the sky. In his sickness he had passed through the door to the country of the dead, but his father had brought him back. He hadn't passed through the door alone. His magic wasn't strong enough. He remembered Tupá's words. "You are the one to carry the knowledge. The survival of your people lives with you."

Avá-Tapé looked to Avá-Takuá again and saw him back away, eyes widening. Avá-Tapé looked behind him, heart pounding, his first thought, the men who had chased him from the mission. He caught his breath when Father Antonio emerged from the edge of the clearing dressed in gold and purple robes, carrying a crucifix as if he were leading a Mass. Had Avá-Takuá known he was coming?

Father Lorenzo and Father Rodrigo stood behind Father Antonio, heads bowed as if in prayer. For a moment, Avá-Tapé had a wild thought that Father Antonio was the great shaman come to lead them to the Land Without Evil.

All activity stopped and the people fell into silence, their eyes on the priest. Father Antonio held the cross out. Dark rings looked like smudges beneath his once fiery eyes. His shoulders slumped as if he'd been beaten. His face looked like he had aged many harvests instead of a few moons. When his eyes met Avá-Tapé's, their sadness touched his heart.

"My children," Father Antonio said in a quavering voice. "Blessed is he who comes in the name of the Lord." His eyes stayed on Avá-Tapé as if speaking to him alone, but his words were for all. "Come unto me and be blessed. I offer forgiveness and beg my stray lambs to come back into the safety of the fold before the lion rises up…"

"The lion has already risen," Avá-Tapé said, feeling his anger burst at the memory of the two who had attacked him. "He prowls at the mission, hunting like a jaguar. You brought him and his brothers in your canoes."

Bewilderment flashed across Father Antonio's face. His reaction surprised Avá-Tapé. Didn't he know of the man with the red cloth, and his brother with rotten teeth? His reaction said no. Father Antonio could be angry, but he wouldn't allow beatings and he wasn't a man of lies. He didn't know what these men had done.

"Yes, it is true that others have come down the river with us. We make this no secret, but they are only to protect us. Bishop Cristobal has willed it."

"What do they protect you from?"

"Jaguars. Hostile tribes. Dangers in the jungle."

"Why do you need protection now? You didn't need it before."

"You lived with us before. You were part of the mission. You protected us."

"Now that we do not live in your mission, you need to be kept safe from us? It is we who need to be kept safe from your protectors." Avá-Tapé watched Father Antonio to see if his words carried any power.

The priest stared at the ground, then looked up, eyes pleading. "They told me no harm would come to you. They gave me their word. I had no reason to disbelieve. I came of my own free will, without their knowledge, to bring you back to the church in peace. Come with me. I will guide you. The blessing of our Lord Jesus will protect you."

"If the Lord Jesus will protect us, then He must watch over you, also."

"He watches over all his children."

"Then why do you need the protection of strange men who speak and act as animals and drink the white man's *techó-achy*?"

Father Antonio frowned, obviously unaware of his fight with Red Cloth and Rotten Tooth. "What are you saying?"

A low murmur came from the crowd. Avá-Tapé heard movement behind him and thought of his father. Two moons ago, he had trembled in fear of Father Antonio and would have needed his father. Now his knowledge and anger gave him strength. He didn't need his father to stand up for what he knew to be right.

"These men who you say are protectors have brought more death," Avá-Canindé said. "They have brought the white man's thunder demons to the forest."

"Thunder demons?"

"Guns."

Father Antonio's mouth formed a small "O". His face went white. "They told me they were hunting game," he said, almost in a whisper. "They didn't—they couldn't... Has anyone been hurt?"

"We want only to live in peace in the ways of our ancestors," Avá-Tapé said. "We have no need of your food or your sickness. Leave us to live as we choose."

Father Antonio stood silent, his imploring eyes gazing at Avá-Tapé, steadily at first, then wavering before looking down. Avá-Tapé thought the priest was about to leave until Father Antonio dropped to his knees and clasped his hands tightly in front of him.

"I beg you. I implore you. I cannot stress how important it is for your welfare. Come back to your rightful place at the mission." His urgency alarmed Avá-Tapé.

He stared at the priest, puzzling over what had brought him here in such panic. His father's words came to him. "Those who have come down the river with the priests have been unloading their canoes and moving into the houses at the mission. When the fires burn in their hearths, they will come for us."

"They are coming for us," Avá-Tapé said simply.

Father Antonio nodded quickly.

"They don't know that you're here?"

He shook his head.

Avá-Tapé turned away, his last image of Father Antonio burned in his mind: kneeling in the dirt in his sacred robes. "We have much work to do," he said, feeling tired. "Much preparation."

When he looked back, Father Antonio had gone.

"We must dance tonight," Avá-Canindé said.

"And begin our journey tomorrow," Avá-Tapé answered, thinking of the two who had attacked him. "They will come bringing guns, thunder, and death."

THIRTY-FIVE

The sky darkened as the sun sank, streaking high wispy clouds in bold strokes of red and purple. Stars winked on the horizon where the sun would return, and the first of the crickets began their song. Avá-Tapé hadn't eaten for days and felt lightheaded, surely a sign that his spirit would float easily from his body. Tonight he would dance with his father and pass through the door to the other world.

People moved around him, finishing the last of the preparations for the night. He felt their excitement and heard it in their voices, which made his own heartbeat quicken. His father would be expecting him soon so they could speak of the flight of their souls. Together they would prepare for the dance.

He scanned the faces around him. He had to speak to Kuná-Mainó before nightfall, to let her know that she lived in his heart and would be with him when he flew to the stars. Looking up at the sky, he saw the light fading quickly, and knew he had little time.

He found her with his mother and Pindé, stacking cloth and pottery on a net. He spoke to his mother and sister first, embracing them both, then took Kuná-Mainó by the hand and led her to the edge of the clearing.

"Much has happened that has made it hard to have time to myself," he said softly. "In those small times when I am alone, I have visions of you dancing in my thoughts."

Her eyes stayed on his, her rapt expression taking in his words.

"My life hasn't been like that of others," he said. "The people and the powers that move it have pushed me onto a path that I have to follow. I cannot turn away from the needs of the people, but in my times of aloneness my greatest wish is to be with you. It is as if my life belongs to everyone but my- self. I don't know if it will ever belong to me again. My spirit yearns for the wisdom that will come when I soar to the Land Without Evil, but my heart and body cry for you."

She blushed and turned away, then to his surprise, she embraced him. His body responded, taking in her curves, soft- ness, and the smell of her hair. Every place he touched her he tingled, followed by a stirring under his loincloth.

"You also live in my thoughts," she whispered, her moist breath tickling his ear.

He held her tight, savoring the moment, knowing it would end, wishing it wouldn't. "Tonight I will dance for the people, but I will also dance for you. When my soul rises into the sky I will carry you with me in my heart."

She looked up at him, her big brown eyes once more swal- lowing him. He put this vision of her in his mind to savor at a later time. She opened her mouth and stopped.

Footsteps. Avá-Tapé and Kuná-Mainó remained quiet, eyes speaking more than words. The steps came closer. Men. He held her close until he saw the outlines of two people coming toward them, then took her hands in his and brushed her cheek with his lips.

"Your father waits," Avá-Canindé said, lumbering into view followed by Avá-Takuá. Avá-Canindé looked past Avá-Tapé to Kuná-Mainó and smiled sheepishly. "I am sorry to have come now, but the time is near."

"I know." Avá-Tapé gave one last look at Kuná-Mainó and then followed Avá-Canindé and Avá-Takuá.

The first fires of the night burned in the clearing. The smell of roast tapir, beans, and potatoes drifted to him, making his mouth water. It had been days since eating. He hurried, trot- ting down the path to his father's *maloca*, reaching it by the final light of day.

A small blaze burned in the fireplace, but no food cooked

on its coals. Avá-Nembiará sat gazing into the flames.

"The others make ready the House of Dances while we prepare our spirits for the dance," he said when Avá-Tapé sat down beside him. "Tonight you will dance among the men and sing your song before the people. If you sing with a pure spirit, Tupá will take you into the sky and carry you to the other world."

Avá-Tapé's heart beat harder at his memory of the vision that sent him shooting into the sky toward the stars. "I hope my song is powerful enough for him to take me."

"A *paí* becomes a healer because of the power of his dreams and the strength of his songs. If he is strong, his songs will bring back the spirits he meets in his dreams. Avá-Canindé and Avá-Guiracambí both have their own songs, but yours has more power. It can bring back the spirits from the place where you found your chant. Your song is a bridge which lets you move between the world above and the world below. Every man sings his song to the god that reveals himself in that man's dreams."

"Tonight I will sing to Tupá."

"When you sing the chant given to you in your dreams, you must bring its magic to the world by singing your song before the people. The song you heard in your dream is what tells the world that you are a *paí*. It comes from the Creator, Nanderú Guazú."

"How did your song come to you?"

His father stood, donning his sash and headdress. "Nanderú Guazú told me I must not eat meat or fat. I was to follow his orders so I could care for the people. He made me listen to his prayer so I could chant it."

Avá-Nembiará dipped his fingers in two small gourds and painted his face with black and red lines and circles. When he finished, he helped his son put on his headdress and sash. In Avá-Tapé's mind, the weight of the headdress equaled the weight of his responsibility to his people.

"After I awoke from my dream," his father said, while painting Avá-Tapé's face, "my father prepared a space for me to perform the song that I heard. Through my dream-song, Tupá gave me a way to free myself from the world of dreams. To sing the dream-song brings back your meeting with Tupá and makes it real. The spirit world comes to life in the presence of the people."

Avá-Nembiará stepped back and appraised Avá-Tapé from head to foot, nodding slowly before handing him his rattle. "My son is a man now," he said quietly. "One who dances and speaks with gods. Tonight, if it is their will, he will sing the song they have given him, and he will fly through the door to the other world."

Avá-Nembiará picked up his feathered cross and rattle. The combination of black and red face paint, and scarlet, green, and blue parrot feathers, made him imposing. Avá-Tapé wondered if he looked half as fierce as his father. Would Kuná-Mainó see him the same as his father?

Avá-Nembiará led the way down the path. Halfway, Avá-Tapé heard the voices of the people. When father and son drew near to the village, his father made him go first.

Avá-Tapé moved to the edge of the clearing, stopping when he saw the House of Dances looming before him. Fires dotted the open space, painting the dance house in swirls and flickers of yellow and orange that brought it to life.

A knot of people gathered in front of the open wall. The painted faces of Avá-Canindé and Avá-Guiracambí towered above the others, their headdresses standing out like huge birds, but neither had as many feathers as Avá-Tapé or his father.

He took a deep breath and started across the clearing. The people parted before him as though giant hands pushed them aside. The canoe-shaped trough was filled with *chicha*, and many of the women had painted their faces red. A hush fell over everyone when Avá-Tapé moved to the center of the dance house. He looked back and saw his father walking proudly.

The men formed a line across the dance house, facing the trough and posts. Avá-Tapé and his father stood at the center, flanked by Avá-Canindé and Avá-Guiracambí. Behind them the women with painted faces spread out in a line. His mother and Kuná-Mainó stood toward the far end. The rest of the people sat in front, behind the drink trough and cedar posts.

A cross stood high on the central post, symbolizing the structure where the Creator placed the world. Beside it stood a taller, thinner branch with a small arrow to show the adventures of Kuarahy and Yacy, sun and moon, the twins who ascended to heaven along a chain of arrows. The two outer posts had feathered sticks with candles burning on top.

The women beat their *takuapú* sticks, keeping rhythm while the men began to chant and dance. His father shook his rattle and moved in time with the women, singing his song in a low voice. The others sang their songs, each unique and personal, each projecting their own yearning. None sounded as powerful as Avá-Nembiará's.

Avá-Tapé shook his rattle and danced. His movements felt stiff and awkward, and his song didn't feel right, here in this place with the others. It had been his gift from the forest, but he didn't know if he could share it. He listened to the others. Each sang as if no one else was there. His father's song rose above the rest, its power clear and uninhibited.

Avá-Tapé remembered the feeling his own song gave him and the words came to his lips, no more than a whisper at first, then gathering power with each utterance. His heart swelled and his song flowed through him as though he were alone in the forest. His body fell into its own rhythm, dancing with the spirit that moved through him. His voice and movements became one. All he had seen, all he had done, all he had experienced, erupted inside of him. A yearning flowed out, taking form in sound and motion.

He danced with all of his being until his muscles burned and his breath came hard and sharp. Sweat filmed his body and dripped in his eyes. He felt as if nothing else existed, save him, his song, and his dance; then he became aware of the other dancers.

Their songs danced in his mind, the beat of the *takuapú* moved through his body, and the sound of his and his father's rattles flowed into oneness. At times the rattles sounded strong and wild, transporting him higher into his spirit, then they came smooth and trembling, as if the desire of his people for the Land Without Evil cried inside of them.

The sounds he heard and those he sang were not words, but expressions of feeling that held more meaning than words. He let go, losing himself, flowing with the sounds that pulled him into the currents like a twig rushing toward the falls. Through the din, he recognized his father's voice, but it was also the voice of Tupá. He felt light, as if floating outside himself, at the same time becoming part of all he saw.

His father danced beside him in time with the rhythm, until his movements became shorter and jerkier. It looked like the feathers on his headdress glowed and a thick plume of smoke floated from the top of his head, taking the form of his body. The smoke form of Avá-Nembiará smiled beatifically and hung in the air, watching the dancers from above. Below, Avá-Tapé saw his own body moving with the others, the fluidity of their combined movements swaying the line of dancers in one motion like a long undulating snake.

At the center of all, Avá-Nembiará's steps grew fitful. His eyes rolled back and his mouth moved. The form above him smiled and swayed gracefully while his body lurched and spasmed, still in time with the others. His face contorted, taking on the features of another and his head glowed with a soft orange ball of fire that swirled, flickered, and flared. The face of Tupá took shape.

"The sun will disappear and there will be nothing to do in this world," Tupá's voice said. "This will be the moment of *arákañí*, the last day you will see the Earth. The white man's *techóachy* is full upon you, bringing death and darkness. Your ancestors departed in life without dying, and left no trail for you to follow. It is they who thunder from where the sun rises, they who left with their human bodies. While your ancestors dance, you too will dance as a chief danced long ago when his feet did not touch the earth. This is why you must eat only those things Nanderú has commanded."

Avá-Tapé felt lighter with each word. He thought of his time below the falls, how he had purified his diet and how even now, for this dance, he had gone without food. Part of him knew he still danced with the others.

He floated farther from his body.

"Only those who have purified their spirits can hear the message." The glowing face of Tupá flowed into the face of his father, so that man and god became one. Avá-Nembiará's body glowed with the same radiance. He smiled and looked into Avá-Tapé's eyes.

When Avá-Nembiará spoke again, his voice sounded as much his own as Tupá's. "Your heart is pure, but your spirit is heavy. *Techó-achy* does not weigh on your body, but the darkness of others lays heavy on your heart. Your travels in the world of men carry much pain and sadness, but your flights into the world of spirits bring joy to your heart."

Avá-Tapé felt something pull him higher above the dancers, then up through the roof. He felt himself dancing with the others, at the same time floating over the dance house until a shimmering rectangle of gold opened up in the sky. He felt and saw a presence streak past him, disappearing through the opening. An instant later he too shot upward, following through the doorway to the other world.

THIRTY-SIX

He flew past the sleeping *añag*, flashing toward the edge of the world where the sun climbed into the sky, landing in a field of golden *maize* where children played and adults ate from a table piled high with food. Beautiful women sang with sweet voices, and men danced.

A man who could have been his father's brother came toward him. When he came close, Avá-Tapé saw that it was Tupá. His muscular body had perfect proportions and his skin had a gentle glow that brightened around his eyes. Avá-Tapé looked into them, hoping to find answers to what troubled his heart. The power of their compassion and his own flush of emotion made him feel exposed and vulnerable.

"The end of the world is coming," Tupá said, speaking quietly. His voice carried great power. "It is also a beginning. You are the seed of your people."

How can something that ends be a beginning? Avá-Tapé thought.

"It is all one," Tupá answered.

What magic is this? You can hear my...

"Your questions are known to me."

Tell me of the beginning and the end. How are they one?

Tupá smiled. "As a man moves through the world, he watches the sun and moon rise and fall. He sees new growth, flowering, and fruit, followed by death and rotting. From death comes new life, which grows again. You are this new life.

"When a man is awake and thinking and moving, his mind is in flower. All that is around him has order. Each beat of his heart is a step in his dance of life. Each beat is order, as is each time of waking. Between the beats he dreams and sleeps. He tastes death. Between the beats is chaos. Fire. The essence of all. Within the fire there is no passing of seasons. No order. No darkness. No light. Only being. Only fire."

The *maize* field turned orange and began to undulate in blurry tendrils of fire. Tupá continued speaking while the flames danced.

"The order of a man's life is what keeps the fire of chaos from burning out of control. His passing life is a line that gives order to all he sees, does, and thinks."

Do we become one with the fire when we die? Do we lose ourselves in it when we sleep?

"The art of the *paí* is to become one with fire without losing himself. He must give himself completely and allow it to consume him so he can learn its secrets."

Must he give himself to death?

"He has to sacrifice himself to the fire to become its master."

Avá-Tapé looked at the burning field and felt fear as he had never felt it before. An imminent sense of finality filled his heart like an ember threatening to burst into flame. He looked to Tupá, wishing for comfort. Tupá gazed back impassively.

His panic quickened.

"It is your choice," Tupá said, sounding far away. "Give yourself to the fire or go back to the world of men. You must act now. Once you give yourself there is no return."

Images raged across the fiery field, each coming faster than the last.

The mission.

Father Antonio.

His father.

Mother.

Kuná-Mainó.

More thoughts. Faster still.

Ants.

The crumbling altar.

Writhing worms.

Burning, rotting corpses.

Red Cloth and Broken Tooth.

His thoughts fragmented until he saw only fire. He couldn't go back. He had to find its secret. Tupá gazed at the burning field, the roiling flames reflecting in his eyes. Avá-Tapé felt the heat on his face. Behind him only blackness, as if the earth did not exist. In front of him, raging fire.

Tupá walked into the flames, leaving Avá-Tapé caught between the darkness and the light. A jaguar roared, shaking the ground. Its power pierced his heart like countless fangs. His legs felt liquid. His body trembled. His mind felt devoid of energy as if the fire had stolen his will. He walked straight into the flames.

Pain singed his hand, driving panic deeper into his heart. When he tried to move back, the fangs of a jaguar closed on his wrist. Its twin eyes of death flared up into the form of Avá-Canindé's woman. She wrapped her arms and legs around him, pressing her withered body firmly to his, grinding her hips into his groin. He felt arousal and opened his mouth to cry out. She pressed her lips to his, her tongue thrusting into his mouth like a sensuous snake until he gagged.

Pain shot through his other hand as a second jaguar closed its mouth on his wrist. Avá-Canindé's woman pushed against him, causing him to tumble onto his back. Her weight increased until she became a black jaguar. Her huge mouth hovered above his head, teeth glistening in the blackness. More pain flared and burned his feet. Tugging. His arms and legs strained. Agony.

He felt his arm pull loose. Spreading warmth. Fuzziness. His other arm popped, then his legs. Teeth ripped into his torso. Brightness flashed through him, turning his being into light and flame until he felt himself one, dissolving into a liquid fire that blossomed and scattered into the heavens like ashes in the wind.

He embraced chaos.

THIRTY-SEVEN

He had no sense of himself. No sight, sound, or feeling; as if he were everywhere at once, at the same time at the center of everything. Pure awareness.

He understood the meaning of the cross. Where time and space came together. Where he danced. Here the two worlds became one. Being and not being. Order and chaos. Man and spirit. One. Where spirits could speak through man the way Tupá spoke through his father.

Tupá. His father.

He remembered dancing with the other men, women beating time on their *takuapú*. He and his father shaking their rattles. Now that he had come here, where were they?

The thought sent him spinning, bringing weight to his being. The world rushed back. The mission. The priests. His mother. Kuná-Mainó. The sick. The dead. All that had happened crashed through his head like startled parakeets. He became aware of himself spiraling through time and space, gathering substance the way moisture collected on a leaf until it ran down in a single stream of water.

Falling.

Plummeting through the darkness, gaining speed until he stopped. His stomach lurched. His throat felt dry as bark and his breaths came shallow and rapid. He smelled the earth, and felt it sticking to his sweaty skin. Orange danced behind his eyelids. Where were the dancers? The songs? The rattles?

He opened his eyes to flickering candles, fire, and the people standing around him, strangely mute. His father writhed

on the ground beside him, breathing short and fast, eyes rolled
up into his head, showing only white. His mouth moved without speaking. Avá-Nembiará blinked twice, his eyes came back
to normal, and confusion etched itself across his features, resolv-
ing in the hard lines of anger.

Avá-Tapé rubbed his eyes and scanned the crowd. Behind
him stood the people. In front, at the edge of darkness, he saw
black robes topped by white faces illuminated in the fire's glow.
The Jesuits moved aside in silence, creating an opening in the
wall of black.

A short, bulky red figure emerged from the darkness like
a worm crawling from a blackened bud, stepping into the full
light of the fire. Pallid and soft, his pulpy face seemed the essence of *techó-achy*. His eyes shone milky blue-white from deep
sockets, the opposite of the clear, sharp gaze of Avá-Nembiará.
He wore a red pointed hat with peaks in front and back. Beneath it, his hairless head caught the firelight with a muted
glow that reminded Avá-Tapé of a pale harvest moon. Avá-
Tapé knew it was Bishop Cristobal, a man closer than most to
the Christian God. One who had great power in the world of
white men.

The eyes of the people widened when his father rose to face
Cristobal. Avá-Takuá's wild-eyed expression showed fear greater
than any. Avá-Nembiará showed none. Avá-Tapé stood on trembling legs beside his father, hoping his eyes looked as clear and
strong as his father's.

Father Lorenzo stood timidly behind the others, as if not
wanting to be seen. Where was Father Antonio? Did he hide in
shame? Avá-Tapé's stomach went cold when he glimpsed Red
Cloth and Broken Tooth at the edge of the crowd, holding the
thunder sticks that Avá-Canindé called guns. More white men
with hair on their faces stood with them. His heart beat like fists
and his knees felt like water. Could his father's magic stand up
to power such as this?

"We cannot tolerate pagan acts in the kingdom of the Lord,"
the bishop said in a sing-song falsetto. "We will forgive your

transgression this once. In the future, any man caught in these satanic acts will be whipped until the demon flees from him."

Avá-Nembiará showed no reaction. Could he still be feeling the power of Tupá?

"We are benevolent men of God," Bishop Cristobal continued, "and do not believe in the wanton use of force unless the power of Satan and his minions makes it necessary. The church of God and His only begotten son, Jesus, is a kingdom of peace and love where men may worship freely. It is for your own protection that we ask you to come back to the mission as children of God. To show you our good grace, we will leave you so you can come of your own free will. Never let it be said that any man under the kingdom of God did not come unto the love and protection of the church without acting of his own free will." He turned to leave.

"And if we choose to live in the forest in the ways of our grandfathers?" Avá-Nembiara asked evenly.

Bishop Cristobal turned back. "Surely, that is your choice, one that we dare not stand in the way of. It is our wish that you come back into the fold of your own will. To live like animals only puts you at risk." He nodded toward Red Cloth and Broken Tooth. "There are hostile Indians that have come to this area. The plantations to the north use them to hunt runaway slaves. Down here we can't control everything they do and we can't take responsibility for their actions if they get out of control." He turned to leave and stopped once more. "We can only guarantee protection if you are with us inside the safety of the mission."

He walked off into the darkness, the black robes filling in the space behind him. Avá-Tapé followed them to the edge of the clearing, where Bishop Cristobal went into a tiny house on poles. The man hunters raised the bishop's house onto their shoulders and carried him down the path to the mission, followed by a swarm of white men. Red Cloth and Broken Tooth took up the rear along with the other gun carriers. Red Cloth hobbled, favoring the leg that Avá-Tapé had bitten.

Avá-Tapé realized he was shaking. He would never be safe at the mission as long as animals like these roamed its streets. Red Cloth and Broken Tooth must have seen him, but showed no sign in front of the Bishop. Regardless of what happened, they would be coming for him. They would catch him alone and try to finish what they started at the mission.

He thought of Bishop Cristobal's words about hostile Indians. Their meeting at the mission had been no accident. They had attacked on purpose. Had this been the wish of Father Antonio? It didn't seem like his nature, but then again the man who chased Avá-Tapé from the church had not been the Father Antonio he once knew. Avá-Tapé's heart felt weighted. He didn't know what to think. His magic was not strong enough to stand against their power.

Regardless of who wanted him gone from the world of the living, these two had come as messengers. They would not stop once they killed him. They would come for his father as well.

THIRTY-EIGHT

Avá-Tapé turned back to the dance house to see Avá-Nembiará immobile, his face expressionless, as if he had neither seen nor heard the Bishop. The people stood around in silence, expectant looks on their faces. Avá-Tapé thought his father had gone back into his trance, until he spoke.

"We leave now!" he said.

Avá-Takuá's face showed dismay. "In darkness?"

"Any who live in fear of the whites or the *techó-achy* that comes with their guns and thunder can live at the mission. Those who believe in the gods of our grandfathers and the spirits of the forest can journey to the Land Without Evil. Gather what you need. We go before the sun comes back to the world."

Avá-Takuá stared wide-eyed at Avá-Nembiará while the others scattered.

"Is it a choice to be whipped for reaching out to the gods of our grandfathers?" Avá-Nembiará said. "Or does greater freedom lie in the forest where we choose our own ways and live among the spirits who cure the sickness of the white man's *techó-achy?*" He put his hand on Avá-Tapé's shoulder. "Stay, my son. Be the point where the people gather. I will go to the *maloca* for what we need. The forest will provide the rest." Avá-Nembiará disappeared into the darkness, leaving Avá-Tapé and Avá-Takuá alone in the dance house.

Avá-Takuá turned his frightened gaze on Avá-Tapé. "In darkness," he whispered, before fading into the shadows.

People moved in and out of the firelight while Avá-Tapé remembered his visions of the great journey. In them the people had come together happily in the sunlight, children running everywhere, women smiling and men working beside each other. Now, all moved in darkness. Unsmiling women clutched little ones, bleary-eyed from being wakened. Grim-faced men carried heavy loads. Some, like Avá-Takuá, openly showed fear; other faces revealed confusion.

Avá-Tapé thought about his vision of this night. He had gone through the door to the other world and returned safely, only to find the dangers here as terrifying as any encountered in his visions, but he would not give life to his fear. He would stand tall beside his father.

Avá-Canindé returned first, his face a study of resolution. Beside him, Santo and Rico, their expressions mirroring their father's. Avá-Guiracambí came next, solid and unshakable. Having brothers such as these made Avá-Tapé feel stronger. Together they would face whatever dangers came their way.

Kuná-Mainó followed her father. Her eyes found Avá-Tapé's, looking to him with concern and hope. If he had any power they would go to the Land Without Evil as one.

In spite of the fear he saw, Avá-Tapé expected Avá-Takuá to appear next, but he didn't. Others came, adding to the knot of people, all speaking in hushed tones. He spotted Avá-Karaí. Avá-Tapé felt shame, wishing he could talk to his friend alone so they could come to an understanding about Kuná-Mainó, but then Avá-Nembiará appeared, solidifying the strength Avá-Tapé felt from the others. Soon all of the tribe stood in front of the dance house, ready for the journey.

"Go quickly," Avá-Nembiará said. "Build your fires high and hang a gourd of tapir fat over them so they think we are cooking. We will move into the forest in quiet before light comes back to the world."

The people followed Avá-Nembiará's instructions, coming back a short time later amidst giggles and whispers. Avá-Nembiará held his cross high and shook his rattle. The crowd fell silent. "The world we have known has come to an end. *Techó-achy* has brought sickness and death. It has become an evil land, heavy with sadness and the weight of our faults. The time has come to make a sacred journey to the end of the world where the great water awaits us."

He held his hands wide, cross in one, *mbaraká* in the other. "There we will lighten our spirits until the gods come down from the heavens and raise us into the sky so we can dance among the stars."

He hoisted a net bag to his shoulders, retrieved his bow, and walked through the crowd toward the river where the sun rose from the earth. Avá-Tapé picked up the other net his father had brought, grabbed his spear, and fell in step behind Avá-Nembiará. The rest followed, moving through the darkness in single file.

Avá-Nembiará sent hunters ahead in search of game. He left two to the rear to cover their tracks, and a small group to make a false trail from the village to the edge of the falls. The biggest men dragged poles with nets full of food, cooking utensils, and tools. Older children carried smaller nets, and mothers carried infants in slings, while the others dragged and carried what they needed.

Avá-Tapé moved back and forth along the path, sometimes taking the lead with his father, sometimes walking with Kuná-Mainó, his mother and Pindé, or Avá-Canindé and Avá-Guiracambí. He glimpsed Avá-Takuá once at the rear of the line walking head down with a sullen expression.

They reached the riverbank and followed it toward the place where Avá-Tapé had killed the boar. Silver moonlight rippled on the water as they waded to the other side. "Now that we have crossed the river," his father said in a low voice, "the trail will not be found. We have to keep moving through the night so we will be too far for them to find us." He started off again, moving at a steady pace.

A long time after passing the river, the stark black and silver of night faded to gray. Avá-Tapé felt lightheaded with the coming of the new day. His arms and legs hung heavy, his eyes burned and his back ached, but he said nothing.

He wanted to stop and rest, but dared not speak of his discomfort. He had to be strong. He pushed himself, feeling his legs shaking beneath him, then he stumbled, putting every effort of his will into remaining upright and moving forward. The voices around him faded in and out until the first call of the morning bird came to his ears, giving him strength.

He put his mind on the bird's singing and pushed the protests of his body behind, letting the sweet melody carry him along the path until he lost awareness of his feet and felt as if he floated on the wings of its song. Fuzziness swarmed over him and he lost sensation in his legs. One moment he moved at ease with no protest from his body; the next, he pitched forward, stumbling headfirst into darkness.

THIRTY-NINE

Avá-Tapé felt soft hands on his face and dreamed of Kuná-Mainó. Her smell filled his senses. He imagined himself with his head in her lap, dimly aware of throbbing pain in his temples. The sounds of the morning drifted to him, increasing in volume alongside the ache that hit harder with each beat, driving him toward full consciousness. He felt another caress, opened his eyes, and looked up into the concerned face of Kuná-Mainó.

The pain in his head blossomed and his stomach turned. His arms and legs felt useless. "Where are we? What happened?" His voice made the pounding worse.

"No fires," he heard his father say. "No cooking. The smell of smoke and food will bring them like hungry jaguars. We are not far enough away to be safe."

Avá-Tapé turned his head and saw people hanging hammocks and hoisting full nets into the trees to keep the food safe from animals. His father stood nearby.

"You fell as if your spirit left your body," Kuná-Mainó said, stroking his hair.

"It is a long time since you've eaten," Avá-Nembiará said. "And then you danced and freed your spirit." He handed Kuná-Mainó a gourd cup and asked Avá-Tapé, "Did you pass through the door?"

In spite of the pounding in his head, Avá-Tapé couldn't help smiling.

His father beamed back. "After dancing, you moved through the forest carrying a load. Your spirit had not come all the way back. When your body could carry the weight no more, your spirit fled."

"I had no visions. Only darkness."

Avá-Nembiará gestured with his head. "Drink. Eat and bring strength to your body. We need you strong for the journey."

Kuná-Mainó propped Avá-Tapé's head up, and held the gourd to his lips. He enjoyed being in her arms, but hated for her to see him weak. He sipped, wincing at a tingle at the back of his mouth, then the cool drink of orange, mint, and herbs ran down his throat. His stomach churned and bubbled until coolness spread through his insides.

"Eat slowly as we did in the forest," Avá-Nembiará said. "Bring your spirit and body together again. Our people need strong leaders." He moved off toward the others.

Avá-Tapé's head cleared, but his body still felt weak. Kuná-Mainó smiled down on him and gave him another sip. He drank more the second time until she pulled the cup away.

"Slowly," she whispered, stroking his head.

The day came on full. The air was warm and damp. He heard people talking around him, but couldn't make out their words. He looked up at Kuná-Mainó. "What do they speak of?"

"They say things will never be the same," she said wistfully. "They are scared, excited, happy, sad, confused, and full of hope. They look to you and your father for strength."

Avá-Tapé felt his face flush. How could he lie weak and helpless when they needed him? He tried to sit up, but she pushed him back.

"Rest and let your strength return. You are tired from traveling in two worlds."

"You will stay with me?" he asked, resting his hand on her arm.

She took his hand and squeezed. "As long as you want me, I am here."

He knew she meant she would be here in his moment of weakness, but he also felt that if he stayed in this place for the rest of his life, she would stay with him.

He watched a mother put two small children to sleep in a hammock. Another man hoisted a net full of food into a tree while his young son tied it off. Little ones chased each other around a tall cedar. "It's been so long since I stayed with them," he said. "I don't know their thoughts anymore."

"There is fear of journeying to where they have never been. Each day brings a world that is strange and different."

"The world that we knew is dead," Avá-Tapé said. "All that we knew has been killed by *techó-achy*. If we had stayed at the mission there would have been nothing but death and slavery. The white man, his guns, his dark magic, and his sickness have ended the world that we knew. Nothing is ours but our dance and our dreams. They have even tried to take those."

His chest tightened in anger. "A man should be free to choose his path. He can bow to the God of the white man or he can dance in the forest with Tupá. The Bishop told us we have a choice, and gave us none. As free men we will seek the one place to live in happiness."

"The hope of the people is in the dream that they share," she said. "They have nothing else."

"Those who journey to the Land Without Evil are led by hope. Those who stay at the mission are led by fear." Avá-Tapé's eyes grew heavy as if the weight of his talking pressed down on them. He saw the weariness in Kuná-Mainó's eyes. Sleep would come soon. Most of the people were already dozing. "I have hope *and* fear," he said, fighting sleep. "Fear does not control me. I live in hope that I will find happiness, but it won't be full unless I share it with you."

Kuná-Mainó said nothing, but he saw the answer he wished for in her eyes. She fed him an orange piece by piece, then a small scrap of *cassava* bread before his father came and helped him to his hammock. He fell into it, wishing he could stay in Kuná-Mainó's lap, but he had no will to argue. Deep, dreamless sleep came swiftly.

The feeling of being watched pulled him from his sleep in a panic. He opened his eyes and looked up to see Avá-Karaí standing over him. He wanted to say something, but words wouldn't come.

Finally, Avá-Karaí broke the silence. "I have seen the way she looks at you," he said quietly. "I went to her while you were gone and I shared my heart, but her words were only of you." He hung his head.

"It's my fault," Avá-Tapé said weakly. "I should have said something sooner. I had the same feelings for her as you. When you told me how you felt I should have spoken, but I couldn't bring myself to hurt you."

Avá-Karaí looked up, sadness in his eyes. "She has chosen. Nothing you or I can do will change it." He smiled. "You have always been a brother to me." He put his hand on Avá-Tapé's shoulder. "If you are happy and she is happy, then I too can be happy. I will watch out for you both."

Avá-Karaí walked away before Avá-Tapé could answer. He felt his friend's pain, wishing things could be different. Feeling melancholy, he closed his eyes again.

He didn't remember falling asleep, but he awoke to hunger and the fading light of day. The people moved about, lowering food from trees and repacking their nets and carriers.

"We move again through the night," his father said in a low voice. "When the sun comes again we rest in quiet until it reaches its highest point, then we move again until it falls. We sleep that night and journey by light the next day."

"When will we build fires?" Avá-Guiracambí said.

"If our hunters see no signs of danger, we will build small fires on the third night."

Avá-Tapé's stomach felt empty and his throat had gone dry. Dizziness washed over him as he sat up, and a dull ache throbbed at the back of his head. He stood on wobbly legs and went to look for something to eat. Kuná-Mainó came to him with oranges and cold *maize* mash. He wanted to eat more, but stopped himself. He would eat through the night, a little at a time. "Have you seen our fathers?" he asked her.

"They are searching for Avá-Takuá."

"Avá-Takuá?" Avá-Tapé recalled the fear he'd seen in Monkey Face's eyes, and Avá-Takuá's sullen look when he walked at the end of the line.

"No one has seen him since the dance."

"I have to find my father." He stood quickly. His head went fuzzy, then cleared.

"Go and find him," Kuná-Mainó said. "But go slowly until you are strong again. I don't want to see you hurt."

In spite of his urgency, Avá-Tapé couldn't help smiling. Kuná-Mainó spoke as if she were his mother.

He held himself straight as he walked among the people, who he sensed were looking to him for strength. He wouldn't allow himself to show weakness. He circled the camp until he saw Avá-Guiracambí, Avá-Canindé, and his father gathered in hushed conversation in the shadow of a large cedar.

"Avá-Takuá is lost in the forest," Avá-Canindé said as Avá-Tapé joined them. "We have been searching since the sun fell low in the sky."

"I saw him at the end of the line when we left the village," Avá-Tapé said, "but that is the last time." He lowered his voice. "I saw much fear in his eyes."

"I've seen it, too," Avá-Guiracambí said. "It has been growing. I asked, but he hasn't spoken of it."

"He isn't lost," Avá-Nembiará said.

"Maybe he's gone in search of game," Avá-Canindé said.

Avá-Guiracambí shook his head. "Avá-Takuá was not a hunter and he fished little. He liked to work in the fields with the women and children..."

"At the mission," Avá-Nembiará said. The others looked to him. "That is where he has gone."

FORTY

The people gathered for the second night as darkness approached. Their mood felt lighter. Avá-Tapé overheard mothers telling their little ones of the Land Without Evil. Avá-Canindé's sons, Santo and Rico, boasted to the younger girls of how they would fly past the stars. Men reassured their women of the happiness that awaited them.

Avá-Tapé ate steadily, a little at a time, feeling his strength and appetite grow. His body felt close to weightless, his spirit strong. He could easily walk all night. The game trails they followed from the riverbank had thinned to nothing. On this second night, their only guide to the promised land would be the moon.

At his father's urging, Rico climbed to the top of a tree to catch a glimpse of the setting sun before they all started off in the direction of the night.

"When Yacy follows Kuarahy once more across the sky we will come to a place near the river where we can build fires," Avá-Nembiará said when they set out. "But we must be sure that the whites and their man-hunters are far enough away so they won't find us. If it's safe, we will make canoes and let the running river carry us toward the great waters."

Avá-Tapé led the way, hoping they had escaped Bishop Cristobal and the man-hunters, putting distance between himself and the others so he could be alone to think. When he no longer heard them, he walked in the fading light with his head down, trying to understand all that had happened.

Avá-Takuá had gone. What did that mean? He remembered

the look on his face when they'd left the village. By going back he had given up his freedom. What would Father Antonio do? Avá-Tapé remembered the last time he had seen the priest dressed in his finest robes, kneeling in the mud, begging them to come back.

How different from Bishop Cristobal, with his perfect red robes and herd of white men, man-hunters, and his house on poles that other men carried. Bishop Cristobal had spoken of choices that weren't choices, promising whippings if they danced in the ways of their grandfathers. Father Antonio could be an angry man, but he would never allow such a thing. Where was he when the Bishop came?

Avá-Tapé looked up to see the last shafts of fading crimson sunlight piercing the shadows and highlighting a nearby hilltop in a blaze of red. He saw movement around what appeared to be a man-sized black bird with outspread wings atop the hill. He hurried toward it, thinking that *Paí-guazú* had come in the form of a giant bird. Halfway up the hill he recognized the movement as birds. Spirit messengers! They fluttered away as he neared the top.

He stopped, feeling as though a fist had slammed into his midsection. Confusion engulfed him as an image burned itself into his mind, each detail adding another layer of horror. Not a giant bird—a man! Wearing the robes of a priest, the man hung like Jesus on a crudely built cross.

Gold and purple robes looked brown and red in the last rays of blood-colored light, except for the man's blackened midsection. Glistening entrails dangled raw and pink, poking through shredded cloth.

Bile rose in Avá-Tapé's throat. Twin trickles of red ran down the grimacing man's cheeks like tears of blood. The eyeless face of Father Antonio glared down from the cross, as if accusing him. Avá-Tapé stared, unable to bear the sight, unable to turn away. His stomach churned and his heart rose in his throat. His skin went hot and prickly.

He understood everything.

With his understanding came an impulse that made him turn and run down the hill. Thunder burst around him.

Ripping sounds tore through the leaves above and behind like the patter of angry rain. Panic made his legs buckle, and he stumbled, falling face-first into a tangle of ferns. He scrambled to his feet and continued to run. More thunder erupted. More ripping around him.

"Get down!" he yelled, running toward the stunned crowd. "On the ground!"

As a woman stood screaming, thunder burst and her face erupted in a shower of crimson. She dropped to the ground like a sack of *maize*. Avá-Tapé dove into the leaves beside her and rolled her over. Her eyes told him death had taken her.

Thunder exploded on all sides. Children screamed. Flashes lit the darkening forest. A man he'd healed only days before ran past. Thunder roared and the man's stomach exploded in a blur of ragged flesh. He continued running until his legs collapsed, propelling him face-first to the ground.

The acrid smell of death drifted to him, reminding him of the night Red Cloth and Broken Tooth had chased him through the forest. He crawled on his stomach looking for Kuná-Mainó and his father, and found another man face-down in a pool of blood, clutching his bow. Avá-Tapé pulled the bow from the man's fingers, slipped the quiver from his still body, and crawled behind a tree. A line of flashes and thunder came from the hill. Nocking an arrow, he took aim and tracked the advancing flashes. At the next boom, he let an arrow fly. A scream of pain followed.

"Aim for the fire!" he yelled, pulling another arrow from the quiver. "Spears and arrows! Aim for the fire!" He shot at another flash and heard nothing. The twang of another arrow followed his, and a second voice cried out, changing to an anguished moan.

The sound of bowstrings filled the night, nearly silent compared with the boom of guns. More screams pierced the darkness and the thunder stopped. The sound of running feet and breaking branches followed, until nothing remained but the cries and sobs of his people.

Avá-Tapé's heart beat in his ears. His hands shook. Another anguished moan came from the hill, and then silence fell once more. How many had been taken by the white man's death? How many lived? The healing powers of his magic couldn't stand against power such as this. His father! Mother…

A hand grasped his shoulder. He jumped as if fire had singed his heart. A yelp flew from his lips. He rolled to one side and saw Avá-Nembiará crawling toward him out of the gray.

"We go now," Avá-Nembiará said in a sharp whisper. "Gather the people. Take them toward Yacy before he rises in the night. I will send our warriors to watch for white men and man-hunters."

The force of his father's words chased the fear from Avá-Tapé's limbs. He moved quickly, finding people in hiding, sending them to find others, gathering the living toward the far end of the clearing, leaving the dead where they lay. Others crept out of the forest, bleeding and wounded.

He found Avá-Canindé and Avá-Guiracambí, and directed them to lead the people toward the rising moon. Kuná-Maínó moved by him, her face shining with tears. He wanted to go with her, but knew he had to stay behind and be sure the rest had been found. He touched her cheek and grasped her fingers, then sent her after her father.

More people rushed past, with terror, shock, and pain etched in their faces. As their numbers dwindled, a sense of dread grew in Avá-Tapé.

Moving back in the direction of the cross, his bow drawn and an arrow nocked, he scanned the ground and surrounding trees in search of his mother and sister. His heart jumped when he saw shadowy forms of rocks and undergrowth, reminding him of the man-hunters, but he remained intent on finding his family.

He found more people hiding in the shadows and sent them toward the others. His dread grew with each passing moment, as did the inevitability of checking the dead.

He stopped and breathed deeply, trying to regain control of his rampaging heart. How could he find his family? He breathed in again, trying to still his terror and focus on the world around him. No birds cried. No animals stirred. Only the crickets dared sing.

He moved in a crouch, recalling where he'd seen the dead fall, remembering Avá-Canindé's woman and the eye of death which now beckoned him. A strange calm came over him, as if he watched himself from a distance. Another sound. Breathing. No, the silent cry of a stuttering heart. Even in her wordless grief, he knew the sound of his mother's anguish. His heart fell.

He found Kuñá-Ywy Verá behind a tree, the limp form of Pindé dangling in her arms like a broken sapling. Dark blood covered her arms and torso. His mother looked straight ahead, eyes wide and unseeing, as if her soul had been sucked down into blackness with her sorrow.

Avá-Tapé trembled as his own sobs threatened to steal his heart. He pried Pindé from his mother's grasp, remembering her as a little girl three harvests old, smiling when she brought him food his mother had cooked. He recalled the way she had tucked her hand in his, making him feel as tall as a tree in the forest, and how she had imitated his mother...

He forced the images from his mind.

Kuñá-Ywy Verá held tight until Avá-Tapé whispered to her. Her eyes came into focus and met his. She gave one last sob and let Avá-Tapé take his sister's bloody corpse. Hot tears burned his eyes. Sobs wracked him, but he forced them back and gently laid Pindé's limp form beside a tree.

He went to his mother, pulling her to her feet to guide her away from the clearing. Away from the evil of the white man's magic. Away from the lifeless body of her little girl.

FORTY-ONE

Avá-Tapé moved through the darkness, alert for danger. Still no sound but the crickets. His mother clutched his arm, moving beside him in silence. Images of his sister's frail body lying beside the tree and Father Antonio hung from a cross burned in his mind. If the *añag* smelled blood they would come hunting. He wouldn't allow himself to dwell on what they would do when they found Pindé.

He remembered Father Lorenzo and his "proper Christian burial." There was nothing "proper" about the white man's thunder. Only death. With Father Antonio gone, no one would protect them from the whites. Now he understood the urgency of Father Antonio's pleas the last time he'd come to the village.

Avá-Tapé saw the first shimmer of Yacy rising in the night sky and gave one last look back, then he moved into the forest, heading toward the cold fire of the night.

Moonbeams shone through the trees casting long shadows. His mother's eyes glistened silver in the cold light, staring straight ahead, seeing but not seeing. He put an arm around her and felt her trembling. He wanted to give her comforting words, but found only loss and emptiness when he looked within. Just as well; maybe silence was better.

They walked steadily, passing through the trees from scattered light to darkness where the overhead growth shut out the sky. When blackness enveloped them and they could no longer see, Avá-Tapé found a spot beneath a tall cedar. His mother curled into a ball and rested her head in Avá-Tapé's lap, while he sat against the tree trunk, keeping his senses alert. He felt wetness from her tears on his leg as her body shook with sobs. His own eyes burned and his heart hung like a cold stone, but he wouldn't allow himself to cry. He had to be strong.

Darkness gradually passed, and the first gray of the new day filtered from above. The song of the morning bird conveyed the grief that he could not. Avá-Tapé hadn't slept and he was sure his mother hadn't, either. Neither had spoken since leaving the clearing. Now that he could see again, so could the others, both friends and enemies. Avá-Tapé and his mother had to keep moving.

He rose on cramped legs and helped Kuñá-Ywy Verá up. She looked at him as though not looking. He couldn't bear seeing her pain. Holding one of her arms, he guided her through the gray morning, farther from the mission and the death that followed, into the unknown forest which loomed before them. He moved as fast as he could, aware of birds calling, the growing buzz of insects, and the jabber of monkeys, listening for changes that warned of danger.

The day brightened and grew warmer. He found wild oranges and berries, which he tried to persuade his mother to eat; but she would not. He needed strength, so he ate what he'd collected, hoping Kuñá-Ywy Verá would eat later.

Fear pinched his heart, fueling a growing dread that he'd lost track of the people. He breathed deeply to still his thoughts, and sensed a difference in his surroundings. His heart quickened. He glanced at his mother, who showed no sign that she'd heard or seen anything. He pulled her closer and continued walking, glancing behind and ahead.

After cresting a small hill, he saw Avá-Guiracambí and a group of hunters crouched behind trees with bows and spears at the ready. When he waved, they came and led him to a hollow where the rest of the tribe waited.

Kuná-Mainó ran to him and threw herself into his arms, hugging him fiercely. Her eyes said everything. Fear. Loss. Her worry for him. Avá-Tapé held her and his mother until Avá-Nembiará appeared. Kuñá-Ywy Verá began sobbing when she saw her husband, who gently led her away, holding her close. Avá-Tapé felt Kuná-Mainó trembling in his arms, then her tears on his shoulder.

He looked past her and saw the people huddled in small groups, stony looks in the eyes of the men, anguish on the faces of the women. Some had crusted blood from wounds on their sides, arms, and legs; others were motionless on the ground. He didn't know if they slept or had passed on.

Much healing was needed quickly. They couldn't stay here long.

Their questioning stares pressed on him, seeking guidance. Kuná-Mainó clung to him. He felt them all drawing on him for strength he couldn't find, so he withdrew and searched, yearning for a spark of wisdom, finding nothing. His eyes felt heavy, his limbs cumbersome. His whole body sagged, craving the escape of sleep.

His father and his mother reappeared. "Kuná-Mainó," Avá-Nembiará said softly. "Stay with her. There is much healing to do. We have to gather the people and keep them moving. The fear of the white man took Avá-Takuá. He has given us away and brought us death. We cannot stay here."

Avá-Tapé looked at Kuñá-Ywy Verá, who still stared ahead as if looking at nothing. Kuná-Mainó put an arm over his mother's shoulder and led her away.

"Those who have come this far can make it the rest of the way," his father said solemnly, "but they need healing. We must dress their wounds and continue our journey."

Avá-Tapé marveled at his father's resolve, a quality he couldn't seem to find in himself. He started to speak, but the limp form of his sister appeared in his mind. An unexpected sob wracked him.

"What is it, my son?"

"Pindé," he whispered.

Avá-Nembiará took him by the shoulder and held him with a steady gaze. "Your sister has gone to the country of the dead. We can travel there. If we can lead the people to the great waters and teach them to dance and purify themselves, we can all rise to the Land Without Evil. If our hearts are pure, our brothers and sisters who have been taken by the white man's evil can join us there. We can all be together again, living and dancing in peace and happiness. You and I must lead."

My father gives me strength, Avá-Tapé thought. I have to be strong to give the people strength. He and I will bring the living and the dead together.

Something inside him shifted from hopelessness to anger. The struggle had meaning again. He was a *paí*. A healer. One who had faced his fear and walked into the fires of chaos.

"Let Tupá and the spirits of the forest help us heal," Avá-Tapé said, feeling the tremor in his voice. "We will heal those who have been hurt and move swiftly like the *añag*. The forest will protect us from the white man's thunder."

Avá-Nembiará squeezed his shoulder, then father and son moved among the people, first dressing a young boy's eye with a poultice made from herbs, then wrapping an old woman's bleeding leg before chanting softly over a hunter's bloody arm.

They circled outward, giving attention to all who had been hurt, whispering words of encouragement and hope. By the time they had tended the last of the injured, Avá-Tapé's eyes began closing by themselves. His father led him to a hammock.

Death ravaged his dreams. Thunder burst around him and the acrid smoke of death filled the air. Over and over, he saw the woman's face erupting in a shower of crimson, the man's stomach exploding in a blur of entrails, and Red Cloth and Broken Tooth, whose twisted grins lit up in the flash of gunfire. Smoke pressed in, thick and suffocating, burning his nose and throat. The cocoon of white threatening to swallow him swirled and floated outward, revealing two shadowy forms. He recognized the spindly frame of Avá-Canindé's woman. His heart caught when he saw Pindé holding her hand.

They both smiled and held out their arms. He tried to back away but his legs wouldn't move. Avá-Canindé's woman took one hand, Pindé took the other, and they pulled him toward them. He cried and thrashed against them until something shook him. When his eyes opened, he looked up into the grave eyes of his father.

"Our warriors have found the whites and their man-hunters," Avá-Nembiará said. "Our best spear and bow men have hidden themselves. The evil ones can come no closer, but they will not go back. They want to talk."

Avá-Tapé breathed deeply, trying to slow his pounding heart. The moist heat of late day hung in the air. Sweat soaked him. He climbed out of the hammock and followed his father back the way they had come, feeling the eyes of the people on them as they went to face the men who hunted them.

They came to a large tree a short distance away. One of their hunters stood behind it, an arrow nocked and aimed, but not drawn. Avá-Nembiará pointed to a number of places high and low that surrounded a small clearing. Avá-Tapé saw the points of spears and arrows. He smelled smoke. Following the arrow tip of the hunter with his eyes, he saw a fire, then the red cloth he had come to recognize as evil.

A group of white men with hairy faces and Red Cloth's people sat around the fire cradling their guns. Avá-Tapé's stomach tightened in anger. He wanted to send an arrow straight through Red Cloth's heart, but they would answer with thunder. More would die.

His father waved to a man in a tree who waved to another, passing the signal along until all had been alerted, then he motioned for Avá-Tapé to hide himself.

"Let us go in peace," Avá-Nembiará called out. "We only want to live in the ways of our ancestors."

The men around the fire stood, guns ready.

"I'm sorry, but that's not possible," a man said in an accent which Avá-Tapé had never heard. The group around the fire parted, revealing a heavyset man with shaggy hair that covered his face and head like a strange animal. He wore dark clothes and black boots. A long knife hung from his waist. "In the best interests of the church," he continued, "you are needed at the mission to work in the fields and supply the good people of Spain with food."

"Can't they feed themselves?" his father asked.

"They have more important matters to tend to."

"And we do not?"

The big man grunted. "We gave you a chance to come back of your own free will, and you ran into the jungle like thieves. Bishop Cristobal was hurt by your actions. He only wants you to live in safety back at the mission. No harm will come to you."

"Just as no harm came to Father Antonio," Avá-Tapé blurted.

The hairy one looked at the ground and shook his head. "An unfortunate accident. The Jesuit tried to stop us from coming after you. One of my men mistook him for an animal. I'm sorry he had to come to such an end. I am told he was a good man."

"Your words say one thing. What you do tells another," Avá-Nembiará said. "To go back to the mission would be to walk into the arms of death. Your true wish is to see me and my son dead so you can hold the hearts of our people in your hand of fear."

The hairy one continued looking at the ground and shaking his head. "They said you were stubborn. It's obvious you won't listen to reason, but I had to try. Aeore," he said in a harder voice, "bring him!"

The men stepped aside and Red Cloth came forth dragging Avá-Takuá by the hair, pressing the end of a gun under his chin. Red Cloth's lips twisted into a cruel smile. The man beside Avá-Tapé drew back his bow and aimed at Red Cloth.

"You leave us no choice," the hairy one said. "We can kill you all. Bows and spears are no match for our firepower. It would be much better if you came without resistance."

Avá-Takuá stood motionless, head cocked to one side, his eyes wide with the fear that ruled his heart. The anguish radiating from his eyes made Avá-Tapé's stomach turn. Avá-Takuá's fear had caused many deaths, including Pindé's. Avá-Tapé looked to his father. Avá-Nembiará had not moved.

"You would take the life of one who came to you of his own will?" his father asked evenly.

"I grow tired of this game." The man jerked his thumb over his shoulder. "I lost three of my best men back there. I don't want any more problems. Give yourselves up."

"If I do I will be like the priest. What you have called an 'unfortunate accident'."

"If you don't, the death of this man will be on your hands."

"Another unfortunate accident. It is you who brings death."

"I'm afraid so." He nodded toward Red Cloth.

Avá-Takuá's face exploded in a muffled thunderclap that sprayed red mist into the air and rained flesh and bone into the foliage. An arrow twanged, piercing Red Cloth's neck. He grabbed at it, making a wet gurgling sound. His gun slipped from his hand, and Avá-Takuá dropped to the ground in silence, blood spewing from the pulpy mass that had been his head. Men scattered as Red Cloth clutched at his throat. Blood spurted through his fingers. He stumbled over Avá-Takuá and crumpled to the ground on top of the man he had killed.

A long moment of quiet followed before thunder and arrows filled the forest. Avá-Tapé, his father, and the others dropped to the ground while their archers rained arrows and spears into the clearing, sending the men who had hunted them scattering into the forest beyond.

"After them!" Avá-Nembiará shouted, then lowering his voice, he added. "Keep them running so we can lead our people away. Work your way back to us when they are scattered. The river is close to a day's journey. If we can reach it and build our canoes fast enough, we can escape down the river."

While the Guarani hunters followed their enemies, Avá-Tapé and Avá-Nembiará went back to gather the people and get them moving toward the river.

FORTY-TWO

They ran to where they had camped, finding no one until Avá-Tapé spotted Santo and Rico hiding in a tree. "Come down," he said. "Hurry! Help find the others. We have to get to the river. Our warriors are keeping the man-hunters from finding us, but they can't keep them away for long."

The brothers clambered down and disappeared into some bushes. Moments later, timid faces poked out. "Come," Avá-Nembiará said. "We will lead you to the river before the evil thunder comes again. Find your families. Bring them here. We leave now."

Gunfire thundered in the distance as families and belongings emerged from behind trees and bushes. Avá-Nembiará made a quick search of the area, calling softly to those who were in hiding. Avá-Tapé saw Kuná-Mainó come from behind a tree with her arm around his mother's waist. Kuñá-Ywy Verá's eyes still had a faraway look. She didn't respond when he spoke to her, but she flinched at each gunshot.

Avá-Tapé kept waiting for more people until it struck him that there would be no more. Seeing how quickly their numbers had diminished made his heart heavy. Close to half had been killed. Avá-Nembiará sent Avá-Canindé and his sons to lead the quickest and strongest men and boys to the river ahead to start building canoes. He and Avá-Tapé stayed with the others to guide them, while their warriors kept the white men and their man-hunters busy.

They left behind most of their belongings so they could move faster. Avá-Tapé still heard gunfire, but it wasn't as frequent or as loud. His fear lessened with each step. The image of Avá-Takuá's exploding face kept intruding on his thoughts. He had seen more death in the past few days than in his whole life.

He kept pushing thoughts of the dead from his mind, but knew he couldn't escape. When it came time to sleep and his spirit wandered from his body, he feared that the dead would come and try to make him stay with them. It would take all of his magic to move among them without getting caught. He had to be strong to lead the living to the Land Without Evil.

He heard the calls of birds and animals and realized that the gunfire had ceased. He hoped their warriors had been successful. Looking up, he saw that the gray light of the forest had dimmed. Another day would soon pass. They had to travel in darkness until the thickness of the forest robbed them of light, then they would stop. Their enemies had to stop, too.

He moved up the line of people until he found Kuná-Mainó and his mother. Kuñá-Ywy Verá's face looked drawn in the fading light. She stared ahead as if seeing something no one else could. The blankness of her gaze reminded him of the eye of death. He couldn't look at her for long.

"How is she?" he asked.

"She doesn't eat or speak," Kuná-Mainó said quietly. "I talk to her, but I don't know if she hears." Her voice trembled. "I think her soul is with your sister. If she doesn't eat she will stay there."

Avá-Tapé felt torn between staying with his mother and leading the people. Everyone needed him. The three of them walked together in silence for some time until darkness came.

"Thank you for watching over her," he whispered to Kuná-Mainó. He kissed her on the cheek. "I have to watch out for all of us. I will come find you later." He dropped back and let the others pass until he walked alone, watching and listening for signs of enemies.

They moved long into the night, until the darkness became so complete they could barely see. Avá-Tapé and Avá-Nembiará helped the others hang their hammocks, urging them to get what sleep they could. As soon as light came they would move again. Before his father could ask, Avá-Tapé told him to sleep while he kept vigil. Avá-Nembiará hadn't slept for a long time.

"I'll wake you when the light returns," Avá-Tapé said.

Avá-Nembiará slipped into the darkness without a word, leaving Avá-Tapé alone with his thoughts. Avá-Tapé propped himself against a boulder and listened to the night. His eyes burned and his limbs ached, but he had no desire for sleep. He feared the souls of the dead clamoring for him in the other world.

Other than the songs of insects and the calls of night birds, the only sounds came from frightened cries and whimpers, and whispered reassurances. When the song of the morning bird came and the black of night lifted, Avá-Tapé went to wake his father. He found Avá-Nembiará already awake.

"Have our warriors returned?" Avá-Nembiará asked.

"No one has come. I hope they are safe."

"I don't know. They may have stayed to watch for our enemies. Wake the people so we can start our journey again. We should reach the river before the sun is at its highest point."

They had the tribe moving again in a short time. Early in the afternoon, when the full heat of the day beat down on him, Avá-Tapé heard increasing animal activity, which told him water was near. He walked faster until the familiar rush and burble called to him like an old friend. He kept moving until he heard something in the bushes. His skin prickled. He jerked his head to one side and saw Rico running toward him.

"We're down river," he said, pointing. "We worked through the night. Two canoes are built. My father sent me to watch for you."

Avá-Tapé took a long breath. His heart pounded. "You have done well, little brother. You have a warrior's heart. We need to find the others and tell them the river is near." With Rico at his side, they went back and met the people coming through the forest.

Tired, troubled faces met them. Avá-Tapé looked to each, trying to impart strength. His heart sank when he saw his mother. Though his eyes found hers, she didn't see him.

Rico led them to the river's bank, and then downstream, until they heard the familiar clumping sound of tree trunks being hollowed by axes. They rounded a bend and saw Avá-Canindé, Avá-Guiracambí, and the others hard at work, finishing a third canoe. Wood chips were scattered everywhere, and the smell of cedar filled the air. Avá-Tapé, his father, and the few men who had come with them took over the work and gave Avá-Canindé and his men a rest.

"We will take turns," his father said, "and build as quickly as we can. When our warriors return, they can help. We cannot stay long."

By late afternoon two more canoes were built, but still their warriors hadn't come. Avá-Tapé had a cold feeling in the pit of his stomach, but he didn't let his fear show. Although he pushed it from his mind, the faces of death rushed in, taking its place. He couldn't control his thinking and had to concede that as much as he feared it, he needed sleep.

He found himself staring at the ax in his hand, trying to make sense of all that had happened. His throat grew tight. His heart felt as if it would burst. It took all his strength to hold in his emotion, but his body began to betray him and his eyes grew bleary. He dropped the ax and walked up the riverbank to cry alone, so no one would see his weakness.

FORTY-THREE

Night fell and Avá-Tapé tumbled into his hammock without eating. He dreaded the souls of the dead who waited on the other side of sleep, but he couldn't keep his eyes open any longer. To his amazement, no visions, nightmares, gods, or dead came to him.

He awoke to the fresh smell of cedar. The warmth of the sun told him he'd slept past the morning bird's song. He sat up, and the events of the past few days filled his mind like water crashing over the falls. Father Antonio, Pindé, Avá-Takuá, the others—gone. Death and thunder had ravaged the forest.

He listened to the rush of the river, letting its voice calm him. The sound of someone chopping wood and the hushed voices of people brought him out of his hammock, anxious to see if their warriors had returned and whether his mother had grown stronger.

Two more canoes had been built. Men, women, and children worked on three more. He spotted Kuná-Mainó scraping the inside of one canoe with a rock. Kuñá-Ywy Verá sat off to one side, her face expressionless, her posture stiff. Avá-Canindé and Avá-Guiracambí dragged another felled tree into the clearing. A smaller circle of women made paddles out of branches.

He waited until they had dropped the tree before approaching Avá-Canindé. "Where is my father?"

"Gone to look for our warriors."

Avá-Tapé's heart lurched. "They haven't come back?"

Avá-Canindé shook his head. "If they don't, no more canoes need to be built. If that is so, we are still in danger from the

man-hunters. We have to go down river before the sun leaves
the sky."

Avá-Tapé grabbed an ax and began chopping branches off
the log which had just been dragged in. Avá-Guiracambí joined
him, while Avá-Canindé went to check on the work of the others. Avá-Tapé put all his energy into hollowing out the log.

By the time the sun had risen to its highest point, his father
still hadn't returned. Avá-Tapé's trepidation grew. If Avá-
Nembiará didn't come back he would have to lead, and he
didn't have the strength. Where were the gods? Where had
Tupá gone? Was the God of the white man angry because the
people had listened to Tupá?

He closed his eyes and saw the eyeless face of Father Antonio glaring down from the cross. How could a God let such a
thing happen to one of his servants? Was it the same as allowing his only son to be killed?

Tupá wouldn't let his people do such things, but he didn't
have the power to stop others. Did his power only come from
the spirit world? Could the people only be led to the Land
Without Evil through death?

The day grew warmer. He stopped chopping and went to
the river to wash off the sweat. When he came out of the water, Kuná-Mainó waited with a gourd of water. He drank and
touched her cheek, whispering thanks. She smiled and brought
water to Kuñá-Ywy Verá, but she didn't drink. Avá-Tapé knelt in
front of his mother. Her face looked haggard, her eyes empty,
as if she no longer lived in her body.

"You cannot go on like this." He took the gourd from Kuná-
Mainó and held it to his mother's lips. "If you don't eat and
drink, you will die!" he said, louder. "Do you hear me?" Water
ran from her mouth and dribbled down the front of her shawl.
Her eyes didn't move.

He shook his head and handed the gourd to Kuná-Mainó,
who took his hand and pressed it to her face. "Your mother's
body is with us, but her spirit is gone."

Avá-Tapé heard something coming through the trees. Watching for movement, he spotted his father running toward him.

"Our warriors are gone," Avá-Nembiará said breathlessly. "They fought and killed many of the man-hunters, but they could not stop the thunder. We have to go in the canoes now. Avá-Canindé, take one canoe of men to lead, then the women, children, and ancient ones. Go now. Fast!"

His words ignited a flurry of activity. Men dragged canoes to the water. Women and children tossed belongings into them. Men grabbed paddles and pushed off. The first of the canoes drifted into the water and disappeared around the bend. Two more were dragged to the shore, loaded and shoved off. Avá-Tapé hustled his mother and Kuná-Mainó into the next canoe, while Avá-Guiracambí grabbed bows and spears and started toward the path Avá-Nembiará had taken to find them.

"How close?" Avá-Tapé said.

"They are coming down the riverbank by now," his father said.

Most of the canoes had made it into the water. The one with Kuná-Mainó and his mother drifted toward the bend. One canoe remained.

"Go," Avá-Guiracambí said to Avá-Tapé. "The people need leaders. I will stay until you are in the water. We cannot let the enemy get a canoe."

Avá-Tapé, his father, and the remaining men pushed off in the last canoe. As it slid off the bank, Avá-Guiracambí ran down after it.

Thunder burst from the trees and Avá-Guiracambí stumbled face-first into the water. Avá-Tapé ducked. Kuná-Mainó's scream sang out over the water. He thought she'd been hit, but then a long, anguished cry pierced his heart and he knew that she cried for her father.

More thunder boomed. Water splashed and bullets thwacked the side of the canoe, but the currents pulled them along. After more shots, the thunder stopped. Avá-Tapé ventured a peek over the side of the canoe and saw one of the man-hunters pull Avá-Guiracambí from the river by the hair and fire a muffled shot that sent parts of his head scattering over the waters.

The river carried him around the bend until he heard nothing but the ripple of water and the heart-wrenching cries of Kuná-Mainó. Her grief tore his heart more painfully than any weapon he could imagine.

Once out of range of the guns, they sat up and paddled furiously. By the time the whites and their man-hunters built canoes and got them into the water, the people would be too far ahead to catch, but their freedom had been costly.

Kuná-Mainó's cries quieted, but for Avá-Tapé, their pain continued to haunt him. When he pushed her sorrow from his mind, other thoughts flooded in.

The eyeless glare of Father Antonio.

The limp body of Pindé.

The bloody death of Avá-Takuá and the cruel attack on Avá-Guiracambí.

He tried to free himself by calling forth good memories: playing with his sister when they were smaller; Father Antonio's happiness when Avá-Tapé learned to talk on paper; and Avá-Tapé's initiation, when he drank *chicha* with the men. These scenes he clung to, but they slipped away, leaving him with an emptiness he couldn't fill.

Tupá's prophecy had come true. The world he knew had come to an end.

They paddled throughout the next day and night without touching land, each man alternating between sleeping and paddling. At the end of the third day, they pulled to the shore and made camp. Warm food and fires helped revive their sagging spirits, but sorrow still hung over them like a darkened cloud.

Avá-Tapé brought food to Kuñá-Ywy Verá and Kuná-Mainó. Kuná-Mainó ate little and said less. He wanted to give her words to soothe her grief, but could find none. He could only see to her needs and hold her close.

His mother wouldn't eat, drink, or speak. Her once smooth skin had tightened over her face, giving her a skeletal look. Her eyes still stared, their attention fixed on something distant. Avá-Tapé feared that she saw only the other world.

When he'd done all he could to make them comfortable, Avá-Tapé walked among the people, offering encouragement, then he went looking for his father. He found Avá-Nembiará sitting alone in the shadows by a smaller fire.

"Kuná-Mainó eats little," Avá-Tapé said. "Mother doesn't eat at all. I'm afraid she has gone and will not come back."

Avá-Nembiará sighed. His face stayed hidden in shadow. His voice sounded far away. "Her eyes do not see and her ears do not hear. Much darkness has come. My little girl is gone from this world. I can only visit her in the other. Two more of my brothers have been taken by the white man's evil."

When Avá-Nembiará turned his head, Avá-Tapé thought he saw tears glisten in the firelight, but his father's voice remained even.

"Mother's eyes," Avá-Tapé heard himself saying. "They have the look of death."

"Her body is here, but her spirit has gone to look for your sister. When I sleep, I visit my brothers and my little one. Your mother is always there. I have tried to bring her back many times. She won't leave her little one. My heart tells me she won't return, but still I must try."

"I haven't been able to free my spirit," Avá-Tapé said. "I haven't been able to fly past the stars. Sadness has held me to the Earth. I don't know if my magic is strong enough to look upon the faces of those who live in the country of the dead. I am afraid that if I go there, I will be like my mother, who won't return to the world of the living."

"It is wise not to go there in this time of sadness," his father said. "You have to stay strong for the living. When our sorrow has had more time to pass, you and I will raise the spirits of the people and lead them in dance. When your spirit doesn't carry so much weight you will be able to fly again."

Avá-Nembiará fell into silence. Avá-Tapé wanted to say more, but couldn't think of words that carried the strength of his father's. It was better to remain quiet. They sat together a long time. When the fire had burned down to embers, Avá-Nembiará spoke again.

"The people are lost in sadness. We have to lead them out of it so we can bring them to the Land Without Evil." His voice grew stronger. "There we will all live in happiness."

FORTY-FOUR

Though they felt confident that danger had passed, the men took turns keeping watch throughout the night. Avá-Tapé slept soundly, and for a second night had no dreams. He awoke to the smell of cooking fires and the voices of the people talking quietly among themselves. The events of the past few days still shrouded his thoughts, but his father's talk had given him hope and a new determination.

He wanted to pass this feeling on to the others, especially Kuná-Mainó and his mother—if she'd listen. He splashed water over himself and went into the forest to gather fruit. He took what he picked, along with two bowls of warm *maize* mash, to Kuná-Mainó and Kuñá-Ywy Verá.

He found Kuná-Mainó rocking back and forth, her hands clutching her knees as she wept silently. Kuñá-Ywy Verá remained in her hammock.

"What is it?" Avá-Tapé asked, sitting beside her and pulling her close.

She didn't answer, but he understood her silence. He went to Kuñá-Ywy Verá's hammock and saw that his mother's eyes were empty. No breath moved in her chest.

Her spirit had gone.

Avá-Tapé's eyes filled with hot tears. He didn't care if anyone saw. Didn't care if they thought him weak. He shuddered, his body expressing what his mouth could not. Emotion flooded through him in a release that both relieved and angered him. The white men and their man-hunters had destroyed his world.

Somewhere in his emptiness, Kuná-Mainó came to him and the two leaned into one other, weeping together, life clinging to life. The loss of those they loved gave them a new bond that made them one as they shared their sorrow.

They stayed together a long time, not speaking, only holding. Avá-Tapé held her to his heart, gently stroking her back. She felt fragile in his arms. Her vulnerability brought out a fierce protectiveness in Avá-Tapé.

"My mother has gone to the country of the dead to stay with your father and my sister," he said softly. "I am here to see that you're not alone with the living."

She pulled away and gave him a tremulous smile, then her tears flowed again. Avá-Tapé took her hands and kissed her on the forehead the way his mother used to, then led her away from Kuñá-Ywy Verá's lifeless body. With each step, he felt a deepening numbness that he thought of as a protective shell.

They buried his mother in an unmarked grave, the first of their dead they had been able to return to the earth. Avá-Tapé gained some comfort knowing that predators and scavengers wouldn't make a meal of his mother's body. Father Antonio and Pindé had not been so lucky.

When they pushed their canoes back into the river, Avá-Tapé made sure that Kuná-Mainó came in his. From this time on he wouldn't let her go far from him.

After Kuñá-Ywy Verá's death, his father grew distant, but his strength and resolve remained. Avá-Tapé's own feeling of separation made this distance feel greater, but he understood. His father needed to be alone. He would speak of the deaths when the time was right. Avá-Tapé kept his own shell hard and hid his sadness, sharing it only with Kuná-Mainó. To all who approached him, he maintained the same appearance of strength and dignity as that of his father.

Days on the water passed uneventfully. The sun, the moon, the flow of the water, and rainstorms which ended as quickly as they started, were constant companions. Men fished and hunted along the riverbanks while closely guarded women and children gathered fruits, berries, and roots.

Every couple of days, the people beached their canoes and slept overnight on the shore, the men taking turns keeping watch through the night. Avá-Tapé always slept within arm's reach of Kuná-Mainó.

After weeks of little communication, their mood lightened. All had lost loved ones. Now they looked to each other for comfort and companionship. When Avá-Tapé wasn't seeing to the needs of the people, he spent every moment with Kuná-Mainó. Sometimes they talked long into the night, sharing memories and hopes for the future; other times they stayed in each other's arms, neither one feeling the need to speak.

As more time passed, sleeping and waking blurred. Avá-Tapé slept deeply, either not dreaming or not remembering. He didn't try to travel to the country of the dead, and the souls of the dead didn't come for him. He felt thankful and protected. He didn't think he had the strength to travel to the country of the dead without being trapped there with his mother and sister.

Avá-Tapé sat in the stern of his canoe one morning, guiding it on the lazy currents. Kuná-Mainó dozed in front of him. He spotted a row of turtles sunning themselves on a log, lined up from smallest to largest. He tapped Kuná-Mainó on the shoulder and pointed. The biggest turtle plopped into the river, and the others followed in order, as though they were all tied together. A tiny smile came to Kuná-Mainó's face, but it didn't last. Still, it warmed Avá-Tapé's heart.

He couldn't remember the last time he'd seen her smile.

Two days later, she brightened when they rounded a bend, pointing to a cove full of bushes with huge blooms, and shrubs with shiny red flowers. Some trees looked hazy with pink, white, and yellow blossoms. Others hung enmeshed in nets of pale pink morning glories.

Macaws swooped low over the water, streaking the air with color. Smaller birds darted, yellow and brown, black and scarlet. Others flashed iridescent wings, breasts, and backs. A pure white egret sailed overhead and perched in a tree to observe their passage. Kuná-Mainó watched simple things with growing interest, as if she'd been wandering in the country of the dead and had rediscovered life among the living.

One day the high-pitched screeches of monkeys startled them. Two monkeys on a low branch squabbled over a piece of fruit. One slipped and tumbled into the water. Kuná-Mainó burst into giggles watching it scrabble frantically toward shore. After so much solemnity, her laughter sounded foreign and beautiful. Avá-Tapé's giggles followed hers, setting off a new round. Their laughter fed off one another until Avá-Tapé laughed so hard, he nearly dropped his paddle while grabbing at his stomach.

When their mirth subsided, tears streaked their faces. Avá-Tapé leaned forward, dropped his arms over Kuñá-Mainó's shoulders, and pulled her close. She grabbed his hands, stroked his arm with her cheek, and kissed it.

Late one afternoon, his father pulled astern and pointed toward the shore with his paddle. "Watch for a place to stay," he said. "The danger has grown weak. Only passing days can heal us. It's time for the people to chant and dance. We have to make ourselves ready for the great waters. Keep your eyes open for a spot. I'll tell the others our plan."

It wasn't until the sky shone red with the falling sun that Avá-Tapé saw a suitable place. He waved to the other canoes and angled in toward a clearing.

"Tonight we eat and rest." His father pulled his canoe onto the bank alongside his son's. "Tomorrow we build a bigger fire and dance."

As people built fires and prepared the night's meal, Avá-Tapé and Avá-Nembiará went from fire to fire, giving words of strength. Avá-Nembiará's already strong resolve had grown. The lines in his face had deepened, reflecting the intensity of his quest. He seldom smiled now, and spoke less. When he did speak, each word seemed to carry more weight. His whole being focused on reaching the great water.

That night, Avá-Tapé and Kuná-Mainó slept in each other's arms. While his father had withdrawn and developed a harder shell, Avá-Tapé felt something open inside him, as if his own shell had dissolved and allowed Kuná-Mainó to fill his emptiness. He had lost his mother and sister, and his father seemed to be slipping further with each passing day. The more distance he felt between himself and his father, the closer he grew to Kuná-Mainó.

The next morning, he awoke to find her gone. He lay listening to the excitement in everyone's voice. The words sounded louder than they had in days and a few laughed, a welcome sound. Kuná-Mainó brought him hot *cassava* bread and a huge leaf filled with fruit. The warm bread felt good in his stomach. He ate, then took her arm and walked among the people, anxious to share in the excitement.

He found Avá-Canindé and Rico smoothing and reattaching new feathers to the older man's headdress. The smaller boys collected firewood under the supervision of Santo. Avá-Karaí had taken a hunting party out. Women mixed face paint, while men fussed over their headdresses.

Avá-Nembiará had gone into the forest. His absence filled Avá-Tapé with longing and the knowledge that he, too, would have to go off alone to listen for the voices of the forest spirits.

"I have to be alone like my father," he whispered to Kuná-Mainó. "I have to go into the forest and open my heart, so the spirits will know that they can come to me. If they know my heart, they will hear my chant and come to my dance."

"Go." She squeezed his hand. "You are a *paí* like your father. With all the evil that has come, we need the healing that the forest can bring." She nodded toward some women working by the riverbank. "The dance takes our minds and hearts away from the pain. It brings us together and gives us purpose."

Avá-Tapé took her hands in his, looked into her eyes, and held her gaze a moment before letting go. "It is all we have," he said.

FORTY-FIVE

A vá-Tapé moved up the riverbank carrying his bow and spear, hoping the forest spirits would guide him. He had no answers for all that had happened. He knew only yearning.

Moving quietly, he listened with his whole being, remembering how he'd followed the song of the morning bird and hunted the boar. The ripple and bubbling of the water filled his mind. Birds sang, insects hummed, and animals chattered. The fragrance of blossoms floated to him on the moist air, and beneath it, the algae smell of the water.

Each detail spoke its own language, combining with the others to carry him away from his sadness. Part of him felt calm among the plants and animals; another part felt a growing urgency to reach the Land Without Evil. So much death had come so swiftly. It could come for him at any time. He felt it hovering close, giving each moment more depth and his yearning greater poignancy.

Leaves rustled, followed by a small splash. On the water, he saw what appeared to be a drifting piece of wood until he noticed it cutting across the current toward the far shore. A moment later, a sleek jaguar burst from the water onto the muddy bank, its black rosettes contrasting with the wet yellow of its coat.

The cat shook itself before vanishing into the jungle. Its nearness reminded Avá-Tapé of the closeness of his own death. He had to understand death and help his people overcome it before it took him from the world.

Farther upriver, he spotted the tail feathers of a strange bird sticking out from a bush. He approached quietly, expecting the bird to take flight, but when he drew close, it didn't move. The feathers were tied to the end of a stick. He pulled the stick free, discovering an arrow made by hands other than those of his people. It had a stone tip and tiny red and blue feathers. The shaft looked straight and smooth. He sniffed it, trying to determine what kind of wood it was made of, then put the arrow in his quiver and made his way back down river, reaching camp as the sun sank to the earth.

A huge bonfire had been built, but not yet lit. Women cooked over smaller fires, while men painted their faces and donned headdresses. Kuná-Mainó came to Avá-Tapé, her face painted bright red. He wanted to tell her about the arrow he'd found, but decided not to. He didn't want the specter of fear overshadowing their dance. The people needed to be strong so they could dance as one and join their hearts with the forest spirits. Fear had no place here.

With Kuná-Mainó's help, he painted his own face, put on his headdress, and took his rattle. When darkness came, someone lit the fire. As it roared, Avá-Nembiará appeared, his face painted as a warrior. The feathers on his head, rattle, and cross shone bright in the firelight. Avá-Tapé walked to meet him, hearing the whispers of the people as he passed.

"Will the voice of Tupá speak through our *paí*?"

"Will Tupá lead us away from the white death, or will he be angry and not speak?"

"The spirit is strong in our *paí*. You can see it in their faces. Tonight the spirits will dance with us."

Avá-Tapé met his father by the fire. Avá-Canindé, Avá-Karaí and the other men flanked them, and the women lined up behind.

"We must all dance." Avá-Nembiará held his arms wide. "And sing. Everyone should have a song. If your heart is pure, a song will come to you. Only by singing together will the spirits hear our voices and come to us."

Those who had never danced looked at each other, then at the dancers. One of the men started to rise, but his woman pulled him back.

"Let him dance," Avá-Nembiará said. "His heart will tell him what to do. You, too, will dance when you are ready."

The man looked nervously back at his woman and then rose again. Kuná-Mainó painted the man's face. Others came and helped one another paint their faces until most of them had come to the fire. Avá-Tapé, Avá-Canindé, Avá-Karaí, Avá-Nembiará, and the original dancers made an inner circle, while the newer dancers made a larger circle around them.

Avá-Tapé's heart pumped harder when the first beat of the *takuapú* came to his ears. He shook his rattle in time and moved slowly and uncertainly at first, then faster. The outer circle moved awkwardly, trying to follow the grace of the inner. Seeing the others looking to him, Avá-Tapé gained more confidence. He didn't notice when his father began his song and didn't know when his own song came, but his body moved without thought, and his song flowed from his lips as if spoken by another.

Hoping to open himself to helper spirits, Avá-Tapé tried not to think while he sang and danced, but his thoughts came anyway. His dance didn't feel the same without Avá-Guiracambí. He felt the loss of his friend as well as his little sister, his mother, and Father Antonio. Thoughts of them made his throat tighten and his eyes blur. He felt their loss as a hollowness, while his yearning increased, until the ache of his emotion flowed from his emptiness, expressing itself in his song. He listened to and looked at the others. They, too, sang with great pain.

Avá-Tapé moved with abandon, remembering the words of Tupá, hoping to be taken away from the anguish of living by escaping into the joy that a vision could bring. His muscles burned and sweat stung his eyes. His breath came hard. Something shifted in his father's step, and Avá-Nembiará broke rhythm, his dance becoming a disjointed stagger-step. Tupá would speak soon.

The songs of the others grew softer as the dance continued. Avá-Nembiará slumped to the ground, body jerking to the music. Avá-Tapé closed his eyes, ready to be transported by the voice of Tupá, but when the voice came, nothing happened.

"Your brothers and sisters have been forced into the spirit world by the dark magic of the white men," Avá-Nembiará said in a voice not his own.

The other dancers stopped, but Avá-Tapé continued, still hoping for a vision. His father rose from the ground, his features twisting into the familiar contortions of Tupá's face transposed on his.

"The world that you knew has died, never to return. Your numbers are fewer. You are a new family. The last of your people. Purify yourselves of *techó-achy* and find your way to the great waters. Build a dance house there. If your hearts are full and your desire is pure, your songs and dances will reach up to the Land Without Evil. We will hear your cry, and you will be lifted up to the place where you will live in peace."

Avá-Nembiará's head slumped forward and his body sagged. Avá-Tapé knew a vision wouldn't come to him this night, so he stopped his dance. The people stayed silent, all eyes on Avá-Nembiará. No more words came. Avá-Tapé's heart told him that Tupá had gone.

Why had no vision come? Why had nothing come to him in the forest? Why had so many died? Why did Tupá seem so far away? He looked around and saw disappointment in the eyes of the others. Their hopes had been high. They, too, had expected more. He looked at his father, who still hadn't moved.

"We have lost many of our people," Avá-Tapé said. "Our hearts are heavy. We need to take our pain and put it into our songs. Then the gods will come."

Avá-Nembiará's head bobbed, and his eyelids flickered. His features looked blank, then his normal expression returned. "My son speaks the truth," he said. "Put your pain into your songs, and the gods will come."

FORTY-SIX

Avá-Tapé lay awake that night, holding Kuná-Mainó close, her head resting on his chest. He couldn't understand why Tupá had spoken so briefly through his father.

Most of the people had danced, but their songs and dances didn't have the strength and purpose of the old days when Avá-Takuá and Avá-Guiracambí had danced. Most had never danced before. Their magic wasn't strong enough. That had to be the answer. It would take time for them to learn their songs, but they had a long journey ahead, and not enough time. When they danced again, their magic would be stronger.

He closed his eyes, aware of Kuná-Mainó beside him. Her warmth made his man part hard, something with which he had been struggling. Since the deaths of his mother and Avá-Guiracambí, Avá-Tapé and Kuná-Mainó had slept in each other's arms every night. This was taboo in the eyes of the church *and* in the eyes of the ancient ones, but in the aftermath of the slaughter, huddling together in sorrow was natural. Avá-Tapé's desire stayed in the background, overshadowed by grief. He did nothing more than hold her close, but as the days passed, his desire grew and his body betrayed him more often.

He wanted to take her as his woman and felt sure she wanted him, but with the old order destroyed, the old ways had become uncertain. Most of the elders who carried the traditions had been killed.

Tupa's words came back to him. "The world that you knew has died, never to be the same. Your numbers are fewer, but you are a new family. The last of your people."

A new family.

How could he join with her? Kuná-Mainó had no family, and he had only his father, whose thoughts were with the people. Avá-Tapé's body and his heart knew, but he remained unsure. Kuná-Mainó still cried in her sleep, waking with her father's name on her lips. The time wasn't right, but that time was coming. With these thoughts, he quieted his passion and drifted into troubled sleep.

In his dreams he hunted game, gathered fruit and *maize*, and went to the house of Avá-Guiracambí, dragging a net full of food to ask for permission to take his daughter. Avá-Guiracambí smiled and nodded. A happy Kuná-Mainó waited with outstretched arms, wearing a white shawl hung with shells and feathers. Her hair was braided with flowers, and a delicate pink shell necklace graced her throat. Avá-Tapé took her in his arms and closed his eyes.

When he opened them, he saw his mother and sister wearing white shawls decorated with feathers and flowers. Avá-Canindé, Avá-Guiracambí, and Avá-Karaí all stood nearby, dressed in their finest loincloths and feathers. Avá-Nembiará stood at the front, his headdress, *mbaraká*, and feathered cross all bursting with color.

Avá-Tapé looked from his father to his mother and his sister. His heart soared, knowing they were close. He tried to hold on, but their images slipped from his mind, replaced by the feeling of being watched.

His heart jumped and his eyes flew open. The sky looked gray with the first light of coming day. Kuná-Mainó slept beside him. He grabbed his spear and waited, scanning the surrounding foliage. He saw nothing, but the uneasy feeling stayed with him. As the sky brightened, he kept his spear ready, eyes and ears open for danger. The sounds and smells of his people starting the morning meal came to him, and his uneasiness passed, but he didn't think the danger had.

Kuná-Mainó stirred and opened her eyes. Avá-Tapé kissed her on the head, climbed out of their hammock, and made a slow circle of their camp, looking for signs of man or animal. When he found none, he went in search of his father.

He found Avá-Nembiará beside a fire eating fruit and hot *cassava* bread. He handed Avá-Tapé a leaf full of food and gestured for him to sit.

"No visions came to me when we danced," Avá-Tapé said. He laid down his bow and spear and took the food.

"And Tupá did not stay long with me," Avá-Nembiará answered between mouthfuls. "Our numbers are small, and two of our best dancers were killed. It weakened our magic. We have to dance more. The others will learn from us and our power will grow strong again."

"Next time, I will go without eating and prepare myself better."

"If I thought our magic could be stronger, I would have prepared you myself, but losing your mother and sister..." His eyes took on a faraway look. "And Avá-Guiracambí and Avá-Takuá..." His voice sounded closer to a growl when he said Monkey Face's name.

"This morning, when I opened my eyes," Avá-Tapé said. "I felt..."

"Hunters!" Rico ran toward them, eyes wide.

Avá-Tapé grabbed his bow and spear.

"The edge of camp," Rico said breathlessly. "People of the forest."

Avá-Tapé and Avá-Nembiará followed him back, meeting Avá-Canindé and the others on the way. "Did you see any thunder sticks?" Avá-Tapé asked, dreading the answer.

"Only bows and spears," Rico said.

They stopped when they saw a man as big as Avá-Canindé standing alone at the forest's edge. He had a headdress of huge white egret plumes, a long spear with scarlet, green, and yellow feathers hanging near its tip, and blue and white feathered armbands. His red, yellow, and black face paint looked fierce. He held a bow, and a quiver hung from his shoulder. Avá-Tapé recognized the red and blue tail feathers on his arrows.

No one spoke or moved. The man stared straight at them, eyes unblinking. Avá-Tapé wished he could see his father's expression, but he didn't want to take his eyes from the man. His action might be seen as a sign of weakness.

"We have come in peace," his father said. "We are on a great journey to the Land Without Evil."

The man gave no indication that he'd heard.

"What does he want?" Avá-Tapé asked, not letting his gaze waver.

"He wants to know our intent," his father said. "He might be angry because we are in his hunting grounds." Avá-Nembiará started toward the strange warrior. The man didn't move, but the bushes and trees around him sprang to life as warriors appeared, bows drawn and spears at the ready. Avá-Nembiará halted.

Avá-Tapé stepped around his father with his arms held wide. Slowly, he withdrew the blue and red feathered arrow from his quiver, holding it in front of him with both hands. Still no one moved.

Feeling all eyes on him, he approached the warrior holding the arrow out, never letting his eyes stray from the other man's. The man remained still as a tree, his eyes boring into Avá-Tapé until the two men were within touching distance, then a huge grin broke on the older man's face.

He took the arrow and turned it slowly in his hands, studying the tail feathers, then he put his hand on Avá-Tapé's shoulder. His eyes softened. Avá-Tapé heard more rustling from the bushes and trees. Spears were lowered and bow strings relaxed.

Kuná-Mainó came to his side with a net full of *cassava* bread, which she held out to the warrior. He bowed, took a piece and chewed thoughtfully, then spoke for the first time in accented Guarani. His men faded back into the forest.

His father said a few words similar to the man's, and the grin returned.

"He speaks our tongue?" Avá-Tapé asked.

"He is Guarani," Avá-Nembiará replied. "There are many different Guarani scattered all over this part of the world."

A small group of men appeared behind the warrior. Avá-Tapé and his father led them into the camp and had the women bring more food. Avá-Nembiará and the man spoke haltingly, both straining to understand the other. Because of the man's accent, Avá-Tapé didn't understand most of what he said.

Avá-Nembiará showed the warrior their canoes and spoke using expansive gestures, telling of the people's journey to the Land Without Evil.

Some of the chief's men returned with fish, berries, and smoked meat. Avá-Nembiará, the chief, Avá-Canindé, Avá-Karaí, and Avá-Tapé sat around the remains of the previous night's bonfire. The others spread out around them. The two older men obviously enjoyed each other's company, laughing together and trading stories, the same way he had shared his with Avá-Canindé, Avá-Guiracambí, and Avá-Takuá the night they'd drunk *chicha* so long ago.

They spent the whole day around the fire, until the sun settled into the earth. Their voices lowered, but their conversation continued in spurts, each man looking to Avá-Tapé between pauses.

"He admires your bravery," Avá-Nembiará said. "He didn't know our intent but saw in your eyes that you had heart. He wishes he had a son like you, but his wife has only given him daughters."

Avá-Tapé felt his face flush.

"His warriors heard our singing and thought we might be a war party," Avá-Nembiará continued. "I told him of the man-hunters and how they took our best warriors with their thunder sticks, and of our wish to go in peace to the Land Without Evil. He hopes that we find our way, and has given us gifts to help us." Avá-Nembiará smiled. "He asks us to say good words to our gods for him and his people. Someday, they will travel to the Land Without Evil, but their spirits are not ready."

"Tell him I will ask the gods to bring him a son who will grow to be a great warrior like he is," Avá-Tapé said.

After Avá-Nembiará spoke, the man broke into a belly laugh and rose. His warriors followed suit. Avá-Tapé and his father stood. The old chief came around the fire, put a hand on Avá-Tapé's shoulder, and squeezed, then he and his warriors turned to leave.

Avá-Tapé took an arrow from his quiver and handed it to the chief, who smiled and took it, then he and his warriors disappeared into the forest.

FORTY-SEVEN

Feeling safe with the knowledge that friendly Guarani lived nearby, Avá-Tapé walked with Kuná-Mainó beneath the bright moonlit sky near the edge of the clearing. The smells of roasting meat and cooking fires drifted to them on the night air, adding to their comfort. His heart had blossomed this day when she had shown her bravery by bringing food to the visiting chief. Now, being close to her like this in the darkness, his heart opened again.

He took her hand and felt a gentle squeeze from her in answer to his grasp. Together, they looked up at the spray of stars shimmering in the sky, then looked down, his gaze meeting hers. Her big brown eyes looked soft and inviting beneath the questions he saw in them.

He pulled her to him. His lips brushed hers and their tongues met, thrusting toward each other in mutual hunger. Avá-Tapé pressed against her, touching as much of himself to her as he could. She pressed back and his man part came to life. His hips moved into hers and she answered with her body. He slid his hands beneath her shawl and ran them along her smooth curves until she sank to the ground, pulling him down on top of her. Her hands caressed his back, while his lips moved from hers, trailing down her neck and across her throat.

"I want you," she whispered. "Inside me." Her breath came hot and moist in his ear, sending an exquisite tingle down his spine that peaked in his man part. "I want to be one with you." Her hands slid down his sides and tugged his loincloth down. He pulled her shawl over her head and climbed on top of her, every part of him seeking every part of her. She let out a tiny squeal when his man part slipped inside, then she arched her back, taking more of him inside of her as they moved together, expressing with their bodies what words could not.

They joined twice more during the night, each time lasting longer than the one before, until the light of the moon passed overhead and began to fall from the sky. Avá-Tapé and Kuná-Mainó went back to their hammock hand in hand, falling asleep in each other's arms.

They awoke soon after the first light of the sun hit the waters. A short time later, nine long canoes with ten people in each moved languidly down river. Avá-Tapé paddled steadily, his thoughts lost on the pleasures of the previous night.

The day grew hot and humid long before the sun reached its highest point, so they paddled little, letting the currents do most of the work. Avá-Tapé splashed water on himself from time to time to keep cool, but even the river water felt warm. Kuná-Mainó sat in front of him, dozing in the heat.

Days passed with little change. When they found a suitable clearing, they stopped for the night, built a bonfire, sang and danced. At every opportunity, Avá-Tapé and Kuná-Mainó slipped away to a private place to share their love.

Tupá didn't speak through his father, and Avá-Tapé had no visions. Their dances didn't have the power of their first ones. He and Avá-Nembiará didn't prepare the way they had in the past, and those who danced with them hadn't been dancing for long. Their movements were clumsy and awkward. Avá-Tapé thought of their river dances as practice, just like Father Antonio had made them practice singing in the church. While the others had made their first faltering steps, he had become an example, perfecting his own movements and feeling his song.

Some nights the forest pressed in so close, they couldn't beach their canoes. Trees and undergrowth came right to the water's edge. Only the sound of the flowing river and the hum of insects floated to them over the water, punctuated by the cries of birds.

Each day blurred into the next. They ate fish, fruit, heart of palm, *cassava* bread, nuts, and roots. On nights when they stopped, someone always hunted, bringing back deer, boars, armadillos, partridges, tapir, and beehives full of honey.

When they pushed off from camp one morning, Avá-Tapé thought the water was moving faster. As the day wore on, he watched the shore. The current had picked up. Faster water meant falls ahead. What would they do when they reached them? He paddled harder and caught up with his father.

"The water's moving faster," he said.

"I felt it when we came back on the river," Avá-Nembiará said. "Many rivers branch from one. If we don't watch each other, we'll drift apart. Tell the others to stay close."

Avá-Tapé dropped back, and warned everyone; then took his place at the rear. The currents gained speed. Avá-Nembiará led the canoes closer to shore, keeping within arm's length of the riverbank. Avá-Tapé fought to keep his canoe straight while rocks close to the surface battered his paddle. One moment they followed close to the bank, and in the next they shot out into the middle of a wider, faster flowing river.

"Paddle!" His father yelled, pointing to a hazy mass of brown on the horizon. "We have to reach the shore before the big water carries us too far down."

Avá-Tapé and the man in the front of his canoe dug in with their paddles, moving across the river while being pulled downstream. The people with them grabbed paddles and helped. Whitecaps splashed over the front, showering them with cool spray. Kuná-Mainó hung on to the sides as the canoe rocked in the fast moving waters. The others paddled hard, but the distance between the canoes widened as currents pulled the slower ones faster downriver. Somewhere past the middle of the river, they saw a break in the tree line farther down the shore. Avá-Nembiará pointed to a rock upstream from the break.

"Paddle toward that," he said. "If we head straight for it, we'll end up at that break in the trees. That's where our journey continues."

Avá-Tapé's hand blistered from sliding on the wet paddle, and his arms and shoulders ached, but he didn't lessen his stride. Avá-Karaí's canoe and a second one drifted farther down river. "Paddle upstream!" he yelled to his friend. "Toward us." He couldn't tell whether they heard over the noise of the rushing water, so he yelled again, getting no response.

Because he was in the last canoe, it was all he could do to keep up with the others. His muscles burned and his breath came hard and fast. The shore looked closer, as did the break in the tree line, but the current remained strong. He looked back and saw that the two downstream canoes had drifted almost even with the break in the trees. Did they know to head for it?

"Push!" he yelled when he paddled. "Push!" he yelled with the next stroke.

"Push!" his bow man yelled with the following stroke.

"Push!" the others cried, keeping time. Their paddling made the canoe surge forward with each stroke. Avá-Tapé saw the two slower canoes drifting past the opening. Paddles flashed in the sunlight, slower than in his canoe. They didn't paddle together.

He angled his canoe upstream as the tree line opened before them. His canoe closed on the opening and started to slide past. With a strong forward momentum, the canoes ahead kept the same course. He watched them make the opening one by one as the two slower canoes drifted farther downriver. His canoe landed close to the downstream side of the opening, passing the peninsula that separated the two tributaries.

Avá-Tapé's muscles quivered and his hands ached. He rested his paddle across his knees, letting the current of the new stream pull him along. Falling in behind the other canoes, he looked back, hoping to see the two lost ones round the bend, but they didn't appear.

At the first opening on the peninsula, they pulled their canoes onto a sandy beach and collapsed on the shore to rest and wait. When the other canoes didn't show, he and his father set off across the span of woods between the two rivers to search for them. If they could find the two canoes, they hoped to carry them across the peninsula to the new stream.

The sun blazed high in the sky when they disappeared into the swampy undergrowth between their group and the big river. The rush of the water faded to a muffled roar behind them, eclipsed by the roar of the bigger river ahead.

After pushing through vines and chest-deep stagnant pools, the darkness ahead grew brighter. Scrambling over a small leaf-covered hill, they came to the water's edge. Avá-Tapé and Avá-Nembiará searched up and down the riverbank for signs of the other canoes. They heard only the rush of the river and saw nothing but a vast expanse of flowing water and the hazy blur of the far shore.

"Maybe they've gone past and are waiting with the others," Avá-Nembiará said in a low voice.

Avá-Tapé followed his father up river with a sinking feeling in his stomach as the sun fell toward the far shore. They reached the tip of the peninsula and stopped to watch the fiery red ball hang at the edge of the blurred horizon, before starting back along the river's bank, scrambling over, under, and around low-hanging branches. Night came quickly, swallowing their surroundings in blackness like that which hovered over Avá-Tapé's heart.

They reached camp, guided by the glow from cooking fires. Avá-Tapé's hopes rose when he saw the first canoe, and sank when he saw only seven lining the shore.

"They still might come," his father said, as if reading his son's thoughts. "This night we build a great fire and sing and dance. If they seek us, our fire and the cry of our songs will bring them."

After a quick meal, they assembled the others, built up the fire, and danced. Avá-Tapé had little energy, but he sang as loud as he could. Tired after the hard paddle, the men danced for a short time. Avá-Tapé's whole body shook with each step. He wanted to stop with the others, but his father continued dancing, so he pushed himself, not allowing his mind to give in to his fatigue.

His head felt lighter, then he drifted up from the agony of his burning muscles and his body seemed to drop. He had the sensation of floating, but didn't streak toward the stars. As before, he saw himself and his father from above, dancing around the bonfire, surrounded by smaller cooking fires. He rose further and saw a huge white bird gliding beside him.

The fires below receded until Avá-Tapé saw a crescent moon above, and below, two silver spangled rivers that came together in one point. His camp and its tiny constellation of fires surrounded the bigger bonfire like the stars and moon.

Farther down the big river, another glow caught his attention, drawing him and the white bird toward it. He floated on the breeze, thinking himself like the egret he'd seen a few days before. He and the other bird swooped down toward the second glow, and saw two canoes and a group of people circling the fire. He opened his mouth to cry out and the fire blurred.

He felt the ground hard beneath him, as if he'd flown into it. Sweat ran down his face and chest. His eyes clouded and dirt stuck to his arms, legs, and back where sweaty skin had touched ground. His head ached.

Kuná-Mainó knelt beside him, holding his head up. She wiped his face with a wet cloth and gave him a sip of water from a gourd. He looked around and saw the others staring, with expectant faces. Had a vision come? Had he seen the lost canoes? He didn't know what to say, so he remained silent, looking across the fire to his father, hoping for an answer.

Avá-Nembiará sat cross-legged, his gaze fixed on his son, as if he, too, possessed the same knowledge. His silence gave power to his gaze. Avá-Tapé wanted to speak, but something held him back, as though his words would break the magic. Instead, he thought of his flight into the night and the bird that had flown beside him.

FORTY-EIGHT

With Kuná-Mainó's help, Avá-Tapé made his way to their hammock on rubbery legs. Sleep took him without dreams. He awoke alone, to full daylight and the sound of running water. The smell of cooking food made his stomach gurgle.

He stood on stiff legs and looked around. His hands stung from broken blisters on his palms and fingers. The sun shone clear and bright on the water. Women cooked and children played. He walked to the big fire and found his father and Kuná-Mainó. Avá-Nembiará sat in silence, a distant look in his eyes. Avá-Tapé wondered if they had shared the vision, but he couldn't bring himself to ask.

"A *pai* must always follow his visions," his father said. "We will search for the lost canoes."

Was he speaking of a shared vision? Avá-Tapé thought he knew, but didn't voice his thoughts. If his father didn't confirm what he thought, he feared the magic would be lost. Since the whites and their man-hunters had brought so much death, the magic of his people had been weakened. He didn't want to risk weakening it any more with his doubt.

They followed the shoreline back to the big waters so they wouldn't miss the canoes if they came back up stream. By the time they reached the place where the rivers separated, the morning sun blazed off the big waters, burning his eyes. He looked down stream, scanning the river's middle and the two shores, but he saw nothing.

He and his father worked their way down river, following the tangled growth along the bank, alternating between wading

and walking. When the sun reached its highest point they
stopped to rest at a small sandbar. Avá-Tapé splashed water on
his face and looked for life down stream.

"If we don't see them soon we'll have to go back," his father said.

"They should have heard our songs."

"The voice of the water is strong. Its song travels farther."
Avá-Nembiará squinted, then stood and shaded his eyes.

Avá-Tapé followed his father's line of sight, seeing nothing,
then a glint down stream on their side. They stared a long time
before it flashed again. His heart thumped as he followed Avá-
Nembiará into the currents. They saw another flash, then a
dark mass close to the shore. Avá-Tapé recognized the two canoes first, then the men and women, waist deep in the water,
pushing the canoes up river.

"Here!" he yelled, waving his arms. "Here!"

Excited voices answered and arms waved back.

"We waited, and you didn't come," Avá-Karaí said when
they got close. His eagle eyes looked amused. "We followed
the big waters until you disappeared into the forest. By that
time we couldn't get back and the other canoe had gone farther. We caught it after darkness, and found a place to sleep
for the night."

"You did the wise thing." Avá-Nembiará smiled for the first
time in days. "There is still a long way to travel to reach the
others. We can push the canoes up river until the sun falls, then
drag them onto shore and go to the camp. When the sun
comes again, we will come back with more men."

That night, they led the lost people back to the camp in
darkness. Excited cries greeted them, and everyone ate, sang,
and danced long into the night. The next day, half their number went back and took turns pushing the two lost canoes up
river. By late afternoon, they beached the lost ones next to the
seven others.

On the second night, they sang and danced with greater
energy than any time since the attacks by the man-hunters. Avá-

Tapé had no visions, and Tupá didn't speak through his father, but Avá-Tapé was undaunted. He had believed in his vision, and the people were back together. Their magic had grown stronger.

Later that night, he lay in his hammock with Kuná-Mainó. The warmth and softness of her skin against his and the silkiness of her hair filled him with pleasure.

"It feels right that we are with each other," he said softly. "Together our bodies sing like the song of the morning bird."

"Your arms protect me in the night," Kuná-Mainó said dreamily. "Your strength keeps the dark spirits from my heart." She kissed him on the chest, sending a delicious tingle through him.

"We are made to be together," he said.

She snuggled closer. If they went no farther on their journey, he could stay in this place with her for the rest of time.

They had almost lost two canoes crossing the big river. What if she'd been in one, lost to him forever? He didn't want to think about it. The lives of their families had passed from the Earth too quickly. How many more peaceful moments would he have alone with her? How much time did they have left together?

He remembered his dream of taking gifts to Avá-Guira-cambí. His mother, sister, and all of the dead whom he had known and loved were there. With so many gone, how could he follow the traditions of his people?

Kuná-Mainó's soft kiss awakened the ache of the release he enjoyed so much. She had no family. Only him. Their people had no ceremonies. Only the dance. Their hearts were one. So it was with their bodies.

His man part grew hard at the thought. His heart beat higher in his chest and his breath grew shallow, as if holding back his passion. He turned toward her and pressed his hardness against the warm curve of her thigh, and saw by the slow rise and fall of her breath that she had fallen asleep.

FORTY-NINE

A warm drop of water hit Avá-Tapé on the forehead. He opened his eyes to an overcast sky. Kuná-Mainó stirred beside him. She opened her eyes and smiled until more drops fell and the rain began. They ate a cold meal, packed the canoes, and started down river on the smaller branch they had fought so hard to reach. With the big waters behind them, the terrain returned to the way it had been before the rivers met, but the current still moved swiftly.

"Falls ahead," Avá-Nembiará said through the hiss of rain, which had come steadily since morning. "If the waters rise, there is greater danger."

They guided their canoes side by side, letting the faster currents carry them. Avá-Tapé savored the break from paddling. His blisters still stung. "What will we do at the falls?"

"Beach the canoes and make ropes to lower them to the bottom," his father said.

Avá-Tapé remembered his last experience climbing down falls. His heart thumped at the memory of his fear. Now his father wanted to lower the canoes by rope. How would the others overcome their fear? None had ever been over falls. "That won't be easy," he continued. "It will take time…"

"Two days," his father said. "No more."

Avá-Tapé looked down at Kuná-Mainó, who rested her back against his legs. He couldn't imagine her climbing down the falls.

"Watch how high and fast the water climbs," Avá-Nembiará said. "Keep your eyes open for rocks and branches. If the water rises too fast, and the rain keeps coming, it will be harder to know when we come to the falls." He pushed away, paddling his canoe up to the front of the line.

The rain continued. As the afternoon light faded, muddy streams of water ran from the shore into the river, clouding it in swirling pools of brown. By the time darkness fell, the waters had risen two hands up the bank. Avá-Nembiará found a small lagoon, where they tied the canoes to large tree trunks. He and Avá-Tapé took turns keeping watch on the rising waters, while the others slept through the night under skins tied over the tops of the canoes.

Avá-Tapé slept restlessly as rain roared down, sometimes building to a deafening crescendo, then fading before starting the cycle again. Kuná-Mainó hugged him close, an ever present distraction. Beneath it all came the steady roar of rushing water.

The new day came with a gray that never brightened. When Avá-Tapé came up from under his jaguar skin, he saw that the waters had risen well over the roots of the tree they had tied their canoe to. They ate cold food and moved forth cautiously from the lagoon into a mass of rushing dark brown that swelled high up over the river's banks.

"Try to find an opening on the shore where we can beach the canoes," his father called back as the river drew him toward the middle. "We can drag them far from the water and wait for the rains to pass."

Avá-Tapé watched the shore and the swirling waters. Branches and tree limbs floated past, sticking out from the water like claws. Everywhere he looked, the forest crowded the river's edge. Water rose against trees and plants, swallowing them with its own hunger. They saw no breaks in the tree line.

His canoe surged forward as though pulled by an unseen rope. Rocks and branches scraped its bottom as Avá-Tapé fought foamy eddies and whirlpools. The other canoes hurtled ahead, spinning in the torrent. Two drifted sideways, banging rocks and branches, sloshing water over their sides. Another spun backward and a third crashed against a boulder with a loud crack and stopped. Rushing water foamed over its side.

"To the shore!" Avá-Nembiara yelled. "Paddle fast. The falls are near."

Avá-Tapé's paddle glanced off a rock and broke. His canoe moved sideways. He threw the broken paddle away and another appeared in Kuná-Mainó's hand. He dug in again, fighting the water as his bow man and the others paddled frantically. "Push!" he yelled. "Like the big river. Push together. Push! Push!"

Their paddles moved in unison as he angled the canoe toward a rocky shore. They moved swiftly down river and sideways at the same time. He felt and heard the roar of the falls beneath the hissing rain.

A wall of mist rushed toward them. The canoes disappeared into fog ahead, still heading for the rocky shore, leaving behind the one trapped by the boulder and the two that drifted sideways. The mists swirled and cleared, giving Avá-Tapé a shadowy glimpse of the foundering canoes. One moment he saw them clearly against a wall of haze, in the next he saw an open space where canoes and Earth disappeared, swallowed by the roar.

His heart dropped as if it, too, had gone over the edge. Panic drove his paddle with greater urgency. The fog swallowed him again, and the roar filled his ears. He paddled with all his strength, expecting the earth to drop out at any moment. Two more strokes, and his canoe smashed into something hard, throwing him forward onto Kuná-Mainó. Water washed over the edge and the canoe slammed sideways. Avá-Tapé pulled himself up, seeing that they had crashed into a rocky shore. He saw other canoes up river with men and women struggling to drag them out of the torrent.

"Out of the canoe!" he shouted. "Grab the rocks and hold tight. Don't let the water pull you down. We have to get to the shore." He steadied the canoe with his paddle while everyone scrambled out. It bobbed up and down, rising higher in the water as each person stepped out, leaving Avá-Tapé alone to fight the rushing waters.

Avá-Karaí and two others came and dragged his canoe out of the water. Once they had it high up on the rocks, he joined the others. Wide eyes, sobs, and soft crying met him along with stony-faced silence and faraway stares.

Only six canoes had made it to the rocks. Two had fallen off the edge of the Earth, and one had broken against a boulder. Water poured steadily from above, and the ground shook from the thundering falls. White mist and gray haze hung everywhere.

The men dragged two canoes apart and stacked the other four across the top. Stretching skins over the canoes, they made a shelter where they huddled to wait out the rain. The day grew darker and slipped into night. Avá-Tapé wished for a fire to dry by, but the rain wouldn't let up.

By morning, the waters had risen more than five hands and the rain showed no sign of stopping. Few words were spoken and little sleep was possible. Most of the people hunched miserably beneath their shelter, wrapped in the silence of their own thoughts. They got what little comfort they could from each other, and from cold food.

On the morning of the second day, the rain ended, leaving the roar of the falls below and the silence of the mist above. Avá-Tapé climbed from beneath the shelter and looked around. He couldn't see far. He walked among the shadowy forms of mist shrouded rocks, trying to get a sense of himself and his surroundings. A washed out sun tried to reach the land beneath. Avá-Tapé's heart lightened. If the rains stayed away, the sun would break through and the fog would pass. They could continue their journey.

The clouds thinned and patches of blue appeared, then the warmth of the sun broke through. Avá-Tapé ran back to the shelter and pulled Kuná-Mainó out into the light. The mists faded, the ground began to dry, and their visibility increased. Below the falls, a thick mat of green stretched as far as he could see. Dark water cascaded over the top, splashing to the rocks below in a frenzy of foam and mist. They had pulled out only a short distance from the precipice, in the last circle of boulders before the drop.

They opened the shelter and laid out the canoes and skins to dry in the sun, then a group of hunters climbed the rocks up toward the forest in search of game, while Santo, Rico, and the other boys followed in search of wood and a place to build a fire. It could be days before the waters would lower enough to continue their journey.

While the others searched for food and shelter, Avá-Tapé and his father walked the shore, and scanned the area below the falls for the lost canoes. The broken one by the boulder had washed away. Avá-Tapé couldn't forget seeing the other two, in his sight one moment, gone from the face of the Earth the next. Three canoes full of people. Gone.

He noticed that the lines on Avá-Nembiará's face had deepened, and his eyes looked unfocused, as though something else had his attention. When Avá-Tapé spoke, the intensity of his father's gaze frightened him.

They walked back to the others in silence, each in his own way bearing the weight of the three lost canoes. Avá-Tapé didn't want to tell anyone that the canoes were gone, but he sensed that they knew. He walked behind his father studying the water level, when he smelled the smoke of new fires. Kuná-Mainó would be waiting with hot food. Tonight they would lie in each other's arms, sharing their grief and the comfort each gave the other.

FIFTY

Avá-Tapé trailed his father up over the rocks, following the smell of smoke until they came to a tangle of trees and vines. Fires burned among the uneven rocks. Children ran back and forth into the dense growth, returning with small pieces of firewood. The men and women crouched beside smoky fires, building them slowly with wet wood. Others brought out what food they had to cook. No hunters had returned.

When Avá-Tapé and his father drew close, the others stood, expectation on their faces. Avá-Nembiará walked straight into their midst, saying nothing. His silence and the expectation of the people urged Avá-Tapé to speak for him.

"The waters have taken them," he said simply.

All eyes went back to the ground, everyone continuing their work in silence. His words had come as no surprise, but there had been hope.

He found Kuná-Mainó and sat with her. Avá-Nembiará sat apart, his eyes looking far away, the lines of his face creased with thought. Kuná-Mainó looked from Avá-Tapé to his father and back again, but said nothing.

The smell of hot *cassava* bread and *maize* mash filled the air. Few words were spoken until the hunters returned with a huge tapir. Cooking the butchered animal brought mouth-watering smells of roasting meat, the first they'd eaten in days. A dark mood still hung over everyone, but the fresh meat loosened tongues and stirred conversation.

Avá-Tapé ate ravenously, summoning all his willpower to avoid the sweet-smelling meat of the tapir. What he did eat filled him with warmth, a pleasant change after days and nights of continual dampness. Avá-Nembiará kept his distance from the others, shrouded in silence. He didn't eat.

Wispy pink and red clouds streaked the sky when the sun dipped below the tree line. They built their fires higher and drew together. Avá-Tapé sat, his back to a rock, with Kuná-Mainó snuggled beside him. When the last light of day faded, Avá-Canindé appeared out of the shadows and squatted beside Avá-Tapé. "The spirit of the people is weak. They had been growing strong after losing their families to the man-hunters, but losing more to the falls—they don't feel purpose burning in their hearts, and have little hope for the new day."

The truth of Avá-Canindé's words gripped Avá-Tapé's chest. He, too, felt like a canoe with a broken paddle, spinning in the currents. Where had their guidance gone?

"It is as if your father isn't with us," Avá-Canindé said. "With all of the people who have passed to the country of the dead, his spirit is spending all of its time trying to guide their souls. The dead don't want him to come back to the living."

Like my mother, Avá-Tapé thought. She couldn't leave Pindé and the others. They took her soul. She couldn't find her way back.

"Your father's magic is strong," Avá-Canindé said. "He has the power to fly between the worlds, but there are too many crying out for him."

"I can travel between the worlds," Avá-Tapé said, "but my magic is not as strong as my father's. I don't know if I could find my way back from the country of the dead. I have waited for them to come to me in my sleep, but they haven't." He felt Kuná-Mainó's eyes on him and wondered how much she knew of these things.

"It is Tupá's wish," Avá-Canindé said softly. "Your father's soul is heavy with the weight of the dead. They seek him and he goes to them with an open heart. The living don't see this. They, too, are troubled by the souls of the dead. Avá-Nembiará cannot be in both places at the same time. I am sure this is why

Tupá has kept the dead from coming to you. What your father does when he is guiding souls in the country of the dead, you must do in the land of the living. Only a *paí* has the power to do this."

Avá-Tapé looked to Kuná-Mainó, who nodded slowly. His father had grown distant and spoken less. Avá-Canindé had been pushing them, making decisions and being strong for them all, but Avá-Nembiará had been their leader. Tupá had spoken through him. While the souls of the dead took the power of his father's spirit, it fell to Avá-Tapé to bring strength to the souls of the living. Besides his father, only Avá-Tapé had heard the chant of Tupá.

"Your words bring strength," he said to Avá-Canindé. "Like you, I have to be strong for the people, and bring the power of Tupá's magic to them. I will speak the words my father cannot. Go now. Build one fire for all. I will speak."

Avá-Canindé broke into a wide grin. He patted Avá-Tapé on the back, turned his smile on Kuná-Mainó, and slipped into the darkness.

"I will be strong for them," Avá-Tapé said, pulling her close.

She pressed her face to his neck. "And I will be strong for you."

He wrapped his arms around her and they held each other, watching shadowy forms move from fire to fire. Soon the flames of one grew higher, while the others diminished. Avá-Tapé saw the dark mass of people gathering around it and heard their hushed voices.

He led Kuná-Mainó through the rocks toward them. When they drew close to the circle, he squeezed her hand and let go, walking toward the fire. Silence greeted him when he reached the middle. Walking around the fire, he searched for the eyes of each person, meeting each gaze the way his father had done so many times before.

"Much death has come to us," he said slowly. "Our brothers and sisters have fallen to the hunger of the white man and the hunger of the waters. Our hearts have gone with them, leaving an emptiness that cries to be filled. Their souls long for us to journey to the other world, but the danger is great. Our magic is not strong enough to go there and find our way back. My mother's heart went to the other world when my sister passed over. Her spirit didn't come back, and it too passed from the Earth." He stopped and circled the fire again, letting the weight of his words carry their message.

"We are living in the world of men!" he said, banging his chest with his fist. "This is where our hearts live. This is where our souls must live. Here is where we have the greatest power. Not in the country of the dead. Only a *paí* can travel between the worlds, but his magic can be weaker than the will of the dead. My father has powerful magic, but even he must struggle with the dead."

He stopped and saw that he had their rapt attention. "Do not let your hearts wander too much with the thoughts of our dead. Their souls cry out, but if your heart cries back they will linger in your thoughts and dreams. Let go of them so they can find their place in the country of the dead with those who have gone before them. Give them their freedom, so you can have yours.

"To reach the Land Without Evil, you cannot wait for the magic of others. The power of your own spirit must be rooted in this world, not the world of those who have passed on. It has to be strong so its magic can join with the power of your brothers and sisters here in the world of men. It should add to the power of your *paí* in the same way that his will is with the will of the gods. One people. One will—following the path of our ancestors."

"How can we do this?" Avá-Canindé asked, rising from the back of the crowd. "How can we know each other's hearts? How can we know they are one?"

"I have a song given to me by Tupá. If we seek with all our desire, each one of us can find his or her own song. Some of you already have. We all must find our songs. When our intent is pure, we will sing with all of our yearning. When the time is right, the power of our songs will rise to the heavens and be heard by the gods. They will come down from the sky and raise us up." He felt his voice growing higher and louder. "There we will live together in peace and happiness. This is our purpose."

The others rose with his last words, and he knew to stop. Without another word, he strode through the crowd and went into the darkness to be alone. He felt as though, when his words had gone out from his body, they had taken his life's energy with them, and the people had taken all he had given.

FIFTY-ONE

Avá-Tapé sensed a change in the people the next morning. Their mood had shifted from quiet listlessness to boisterous purpose. Had his words carried that much power? Had his father heard his speech? He wanted the hope to stay alive. Without it, they'd lose the will to go on, and without that, they could lose the will to live.

He walked among the people greeted by smiles, offers of food, and a place by their fires. He stopped at each fire before moving on in search of his father. Eventually, he found Avá-Canindé, Santo, and Rico with Avá-Karaí, making arrows and sharpening spears.

"Avá-Karaí is taking us on a hunt," Rico said, running toward Avá-Tapé waving a spear.

Avá-Karaí looked up and smiled. "He has the eye of a hunter."

"I see we have a gathering of wise men." Avá-Tapé nodded toward Santo and Rico, winking when he gave the same nod to Avá-Karaí. "We don't have much food, and we'll be in this place for some time. It is a wise man who hunts."

Santo and Rico smiled at each other, and Avá-Karaí nodded sagely. Avá-Canindé's pleasure showed in his eyes. "Go now," he said. "Avá-Tapé and I must talk."

Avá-Karaí led the boys into the forest, looking back once to wink at Avá-Tapé and Avá-Canindé.

"You spoke like a true *pai* before the people," Avá-Canindé said. "Your words and your power brought joy to my heart and made me feel like a proud father."

"It was because of your words spoken to me like a father," Avá-Tapé replied. "I wouldn't have said anything if you had not pushed. I spoke strong words, but I am not sure what to do. My father has grown quiet the way my mother did. I'm afraid he will lose his soul."

"I haven't seen Avá-Nembiará since the rains stopped, but I do not fear for him," Avá-Canindé said, folding his arms. "He is a powerful man. The souls of the dead are taking his thoughts, but they will not take his spirit."

Avá-Tapé gestured toward the other fires. "They won't wait. They will grow restless…"

"We know what has to be done," Avá-Canindé said, gesturing toward Avá-Tapé and himself. "You will be the voice and the heart. I will be the legs and the hands. We have to weave ropes and nets to lower the canoes over the falls. The river will bring us toward the great waters. It is the only way. We must all gather and weave while our hunters bring back game. Below the falls, the earth will change. There may not be as much to eat. We don't know. We have to smoke as much meat as we can for harder times."

"We'll spread the word and start making ropes," Avá-Tapé said.

"The time it takes to braid them will give the waters time to lower. It will keep the people busy. There will be less danger when the water has gone down."

Avá-Tapé stood and rested his hand on Avá-Canindé's shoulder. "I am lucky to have two fathers."

"We are all brothers," Avá-Canindé said with a dismissive gesture. "The same family."

"I'll look for my father, then we'll begin the work."

He searched up and down the river and in the forest, but Avá-Tapé couldn't find Avá-Nembiará, leaving him with the realization that his father wouldn't be back until his magic was complete. Putting anxiety aside, Avá-Tapé joined Avá-Canindé, and they started the people on the huge task of gathering fiber and weaving it into ropes and nets.

That night they danced for the first time without Avá-Nembiará. Everyone danced, including the women and children. Though eloquence and the usual purposeful steps didn't come, each dancer moved in his or her own way, struggling for words. What they lacked in performance, they made up for with conviction. Avá-Tapé listened to the halting cadence of their chants, feeling every dancer searching for a song. Avá-Tapé didn't think the gods could ignore the feelings which the people poured into their songs.

He awoke the following morning to find his father sitting beside his fire sipping from a gourd. When Kuná-Mainó saw them together she went to another fire. Avá-Tapé had taken things into his own hands, and now he wondered if his father approved.

"Everyone danced and tried to sing their own songs," he said, sitting across from his father.

Avá-Nembiará leveled his gaze at his son. Avá-Tapé forced himself to meet his father's eyes.

"They sounded like dying monkeys and danced like birds with broken wings," Avá-Nembiará said without expression.

Avá-Tapé's anger flared until his father spoke again.

"But the pureness of their intent came to me in the forest and touched my heart," he said in a low voice. "In time, their steps will be true and their songs will be right." A smile flickered across his lips. "I heard you speaking to them the night of the big fire. Your words could have been mine. You have done a good thing. It brings me much happiness."

Avá-Tapé's pride bloomed in his chest and throat. When he spoke, he heard a tremor in his voice. "We are weaving rope to lower the canoes over the falls. Our hunters are hunting game for the journey ahead."

Avá-Nembiará nodded. "Below the falls there will be big places with no forest. Game will be scarce. We need all we can bring."

"Then I have done the right thing."

"I knew you would."

"And you have spent much time in the country of the dead."

"There is more work to be done there," Avá-Nembiará said. "I am sorry my spirit has been far from you. I hold you close in my heart. Never forget that. As I have been the voice of Tupá, you will be my voice. You have acted wisely..."

"I was nothing without Avá-Canindé's words and wisdom."

A tiny smile returned. "It is the same with me. He is a true brother."

The people danced that night with Avá-Nembiará, but things had changed. When he walked among them, all showed him great respect, but he never spoke and always stayed near the edge of all that happened. Avá-Tapé found himself at the center. The voice. The people feared Avá-Nembiará's solemn mood, but respected his silence. He still led them, but his wishes came through Avá-Tapé, the only one who dared speak to him besides Avá-Canindé.

Days passed, and the pain from the loss of families and friends lessened as the ropes grew in length. They worked every day from first light to the coming of darkness. By the time they had stretched the first length of rope from one end of camp to the other, the waters had receded, letting them walk to the edge of the cliff and dangle ropes over the side to check their length. One length of the camp went just a short distance down the face of the falls. More work and longer ropes were needed.

One day, Avá-Tapé heard soft humming from many of the people while they worked. He realized he'd heard it for a few days, but had only now noticed it. Acting as though his attention was on something else, he listened to one of the men.

He didn't recognize the tune until it struck him that the man hummed a personal song. When they danced that night, Avá-Tapé listened closely. The man sang the same tune he had been humming. The others who hummed while working also sang their own songs when they danced.

Every few days they threw their ropes over the cliff. Each time they fell farther and farther. Groups of weavers gathered, each making their own rope and all going to the top of the falls at the end of the day, betting feathers, skins, and arrowheads to see whose rope would reach the bottom first. The farther their ropes fell, the greater the excitement, until the day Avá-Karaí stood at the top of the falls with one end of a rope tied to his waist, a huge coil beside him, and a rock tied to the end. He hurled the rock and stepped back, watching it arc over the face of the cliff, the rope playing out at his feet.

A cheer went up when the rock hit the ground below and a few loops of rope remained beside Avá-Karaí. That night they ate a small feast with plenty of fresh game. When darkness came, they built a huge bonfire and danced long into the night with great fervor. As the dancers tired, they stopped one by one until none danced but Avá-Tapé, his father, and Avá-Canindé. When they stopped, Avá-Canindé stood alone in front of the fire, arms upraised.

"Soon we will lower the canoes over the falls with our ropes and continue our journey," he said breathlessly. "Our hunters have brought game, and we have gathered plants. Our spirit is strong. Our canoes are full. Let us move on to the great waters and dance our way to the Land Without Evil." He raised his fist and everyone cheered, then they all straggled back to their hammocks.

After most had fallen asleep, Avá-Tapé lay awake with Kuná-Mainó, her head resting in the crook of his arm. Above, he saw the stars scattered across the sky. A crescent moon hung on the horizon. Leaning over, he buried his face in her hair and kissed her head. She gently kissed his chest. Her soft lips brushing his skin shot through him like lightning, making his man part jump.

He pulled her closer, threw his leg over her hip and pressed his groin to hers. She kissed his nose and pressed her forehead to his.

"I know that your body cries out for mine. I have felt you pressing against me in the darkness of these long nights. Sometimes I have pretended to be asleep, feeling you next to me tighter than a stretched rope." She drew her head back and looked him in the eye. "You cannot bring my father game and gifts to ask for my hand in the old ways. I have no father, but my love for you is stronger than the power of the water at the falls."

"I will protect you and hold you close," Avá-Tapé promised.

She nodded. "My father was so proud of you. Like his own son. He would want us to be one."

She kissed him on the nape of his neck, sending a chill down his spine. He put his lips to hers and they came together, moving with slow intimacy, sharing each other's pleasures.

FIFTY-TWO

Using the longest line as a guide, they finished cords and fashioned nets. With ropes tied around their waists, Avá-Tapé and Avá-Karaí went over the edge of the falls, lowered by the others. Avá-Tapé felt his old fear rushing back as he took the first steps, but he didn't look down. His legs trembled when he neared the bottom and thought about the souls of the people who had died going over the falls. The mists rising up to swallow him did nothing to calm him. What would he see? Would their spirits come to him? Did anything remain of their bodies or had they been washed away?

He looked at the falls when his feet touched wet rock, seeing only plumes of mist and the shadowy forms of boulders.

After untying the rope from his waist, he let it go and watched it bounce back up the rocky face of the cliff. He and Avá-Karaí moved back as the first canoe full of food and necessities came slowly down the face of the cliff, hung by lines and nets. Not quite halfway, its stern caught on the edge of a jutting rock. The men at the top raised and lowered the canoe three times, but each time it caught. Remembering how fear had frozen him last time, Avá-Tapé scrambled up the rocks toward the canoe.

He looked nowhere but up, grabbing slippery handholds and footholds, angling toward the snagged canoe. When he drew close, he studied it, wondering how one man could get it loose. The outcropping that held it jutted from the cliff, making a V that fit the bottom of the canoe.

Yelling for those above to raise the canoe again, Avá-Tapé propped himself against the cliff and pushed against the side of the canoe with his feet. When it swayed outward he yelled "Lower!"

It moved down in two jerky movements, and its side scraped the rock, tilting the canoe up. Avá-Tapé crawled toward it and looked down. His head spun and his stomach churned. Closing his eyes, he waited for the spell to pass, then pushed the canoe out again when the men lowered it more. The canoe leveled and continued its descent until it reached the bottom.

After untying it, Avá-Karaí dragged the canoe aside while the second one came down. Avá-Tapé pressed himself against the cliff face, breathing deeply to calm his thundering heart. When the second canoe came within reach, he pushed out until it cleared the outcropping and made its way down, too.

By late afternoon all the canoes had been lowered. While men below carried them farther down river to find a camp, Avá-Tapé climbed back to the top and helped lower people to the base of the falls, sympathizing with their fear. Kuná-Mainó stayed with him until the last person went over. When her turn came, he looked into her eyes, seeing her terror.

"There is nothing to be afraid of," he said, pulling her close. "Don't look down and your heart will grow still. I once went up and down with no rope. It can be done."

He held her tight until her trembling stopped, then he gently lowered her from the top, threw the rope over, and took one last look at the river, the forest, and the sun falling in a blaze of orange behind him, then he started down the face of the falls, moving with confidence, never once looking down.

He reached the mists in gray shadow, thinking once more of those who had met their end there. His thoughts, the cool mists and the fading light caused him to shiver. He hurried through the cool whiteness, anxious to reach the warmth of fires and the comfort of the living. He found them a short time later, in a small clearing at a bend farther down river.

Exhausted after a long day of lowering and carrying canoes,

they didn't dance that night. The roar of the water sounded different from below, and for the first night in many, the ground didn't shake. Avá-Tapé had grown used to the constant rumble and found it hard to sleep without it.

The next morning, they pushed off into smooth, fast-moving currents. It felt good to be back on the journey. Men laughed and joked, children splashed each other, and women giggled. Avá-Tapé still thought about those who had gone over the falls. They had seen no signs of them or their canoes. Had they been smashed to nothing? It seemed so, but the river had swelled from the heavy rains. Avá-Tapé watched the branch and tree-strewn banks for signs of the dead.

The waters slowed as the river narrowed and the day grew warmer. The cool dampness felt near the falls turned hot and wet. Trees overhead crowded in, cutting off most of the sunlight. Stringy weeds and algae hung limp from low-hanging branches like soggy hair, evidence of high water from the recent flood.

They paddled when they could, sometimes snagging on branches below the surface or tangling their paddles in weeds. The plant scent of the water grew stronger until a sickly-sweet, rotting odor overpowered everything else.

Ahead, Avá-Tapé saw the trunk of a huge tree blocking their way down river. On the bank, the massive ball of its roots stuck out of the mud like a broken fist. Its branches jutted haphazardly from the water. The river had backed up in front of it, catching branches of rotted wood, leaves, and weeds.

Avá-Tapé held his hand up for the others to stop while he guided his canoe along the log, prodding it with his paddle. "It will take many hands to move this," he said, pushing against the waterlogged wood. He paddled to the bank and tied his canoe. The others followed, tying up behind him. Wading into the warm water, he went to the far end of the tree to see where they could cut it to let the canoes through.

Branches and green leaves still grew from its top. Avá-Tapé pushed into the bushy mass, holding his arm in front of his face to keep from getting poked in the eye. A shadowy form huddled among the leaves. He moved closer, pushing aside a leafy branch.

A putrid smell and a horrible visage invaded his senses. Bony white ribs stuck out from beneath its chest. Above it, a waxy, brownish-white, grease-like substance covered what remained of once human flesh. He gagged and stumbled backward, breaking off the branch and falling into the water. He vomited through his fingers, unable to take his eyes from the silent horror.

The drawn skin of the face had the same waxy coating, and its hair stood out in tufts. Its lips and eyeballs had been eaten away leaving gaping holes, and the face was split in a wide, sardonic grin. A ragged mix of skin and tendon hung from a bony arm which splayed out as if pointing.

He heard water splashing behind him and turned to face the others. "Don't look," he said, waving both hands. "It is the face of death. We have to cut the tree in the middle and let the water carry the branches away."

Avá-Canindé and Avá-Karaí splashed back to their canoes, returning with machetes.

"Here," Avá-Tapé said, moving to the middle of the river. He scrambled to his canoe, avoiding another look at the corrupted, grinning rictus among the leaves. Grabbing his machete, he hurried to join the others, hacking through the trunk in a frenzy.

"What is this face of death that makes you swing your machete so hard?" Avá-Karaí asked, starting past him.

Avá-Tapé blocked his friend and looked over his shoulder at the darkened mass. He didn't have to go nearer to see the face again. The grinning skull would stay with him for the rest of his life. "Don't look," he said. "The smile of death will steal whatever is in your stomach."

"I have to see."

Avá-Tapé dropped his arm. A moment later he heard Avá-Karaí retching and gagging. Avá-Karaí came back tight-lipped and white faced. When he attacked the tree with his machete this time, he chopped with more abandon than Avá-Tapé had ever seen.

FIFTY-THREE

After chopping through the middle of the tree, it took six men to push the trunk far enough for the canoes to pass. No one else dared to look at the death's head. Avá-Tapé took the lead, flinching each time his paddle snagged a branch or rock, thinking that the hand of one of the dead might pull him into the water.

The current slowed as the day wore on. The river widened and the waters became shallow. The wider river opened the leaf cover above, letting more sun through. Gradually, the tree line thinned and the tangled vines and undergrowth diminished, leaving grassy patches and wide clearings.

When the sun sank behind them, they camped in one of the clearings. The grass was soft and mushy beneath their feet when they dragged their canoes out of the water. Avá-Tapé and Avá-Canindé walked a short way into the swamp to look for drier ground, but found none.

With darkness came swarms of biting insects. Everyone slapped and scratched until Avá-Nembiará brewed a sweet smelling mixture of tapir fat and ferns, which they rubbed on themselves from head to foot. The annoying, high-pitched insect buzz remained, but the biting stopped. The people couldn't find a good spot for a bonfire, so they didn't dance. They went to their hammocks, anxious to sleep through the night, eager for an early start.

At first light they moved back onto the water. Once in the middle of the river, the insects finally left them alone. Kuná-

Mainó dozed, her head resting on Avá-Tapé's knees while he paddled steadily down river.

The following day, some of the elders and the youngest children grew feverish. Avá-Tapé and Avá-Nembiará tended to them with herb drinks, chants, and rattles, but the pattern persisted: high fever, night sweats, and loss of appetite. They kept the sick in one canoe and took turns ministering to them, but the pace of the fever quickened. The old ones passed on within a few days of each other. The children hung on longer before succumbing. Avá-Tapé spent many days trying to revive the youngest, but his efforts failed.

They found no good place in the marshes to bury their dead, and the humid weather brought insects swarming to the bodies soon after life passed. They kept the canoe with the sick at the end of the line. Each time the fever took a life, they waited until dark to drop the body over the side.

All but two children died. The survivors went back to the other canoes when they recovered, leaving the one canoe empty. With heavy hearts, Avá-Tapé and Avá-Karaí emptied it and dragged it into the marshes, while those who lost loved ones wept. The others looked on stone faced. Avá-Tapé grew firmer in his resolve.

Five canoes remained.

The terrain shifted, bringing the river through a wide, grassy plain that stretched as far as they could see. When the sun didn't beat down, the rains came swift and sudden, swelling the river. They took what skins they had and made covers to block the rain and sun. At night, after the rain passed, the moon and stars sparkled against the dark sky as if washed by the storm, covering the heavens in countless points of silver.

Each part of the shore they touched had the same mushy grass and swarming insects that had brought the fever-death. They continued day and night, taking turns paddling without touching shore, eating smoked meat, what fish they could catch, and the remainder of their fruit and vegetables.

"We have to eat less," Avá-Nembiará said one day. "We have

seen no game since leaving the forest. Our food is going fast. All we can harvest are fish. Soon there will be no plants left to eat."

One day blended into the next with no change. The water, wide open fields, and the vast sky all had a maddening sameness. No sounds could be heard except the splash of their paddles, the quiet ripple of the water, the cries of far off birds, and the sound of the wind whispering through the grasses.

Avá-Tapé and Avá-Nembiará had to forgo their vegetable diet and eat fish and small pieces of smoked meat as the others did. More days passed and their food supply dwindled. Their hunters went on long treks across the marshy plains in search of game, coming back with nothing more than a few small birds. Those and the fish they caught sustained them. While two men paddled each canoe, the others fished.

Hunger made the fish palatable, but the smell and sight of it began to turn Avá-Tapé's stomach. He didn't know how much longer he could go on eating it. Each day, when faced with the raw offering, he forced himself to eat.

How long since they had left the falls? How long since they danced? How long since the deaths of the others? His life with Father Antonio felt as if it had been a dream.

One day as Avá-Tapé paddled, Kuná-Mainó turned on her knees to face him. He saw the bones standing out under the skin on her face. Looking down, he realized with equal shock that his own arms and legs had withered.

When they stopped to stretch, he leaned over the side of his canoe to study his reflection in the waters and saw the face of an ancient one. He looked to the other canoes and saw the same gaunt faces and hollow cheeks. Even Santo and Rico looked like old men.

Each stroke of the paddle took all his effort. He could tell by the expressions of the others that they too had little energy, but the water still flowed, carrying them forward when their arms could not.

More days passed until the river grew wider still and a huge body of water opened up before them.

"The great waters," Avá-Karaí said breathlessly. "We are at the end of our journey."

Avá-Tapé looked out and saw nothing but blue as far as he could see. Had they come to the end of their journey? He dared not think it. He couldn't bear to be disappointed.

A cool breeze blew across the waters making small white-caps. Avá-Tapé pulled his paddle across his knees and let the wind ruffle his hair.

No one paddled. No one spoke. The canoes drifted out onto the open waters in silence as the people all stared, eyes and mouths wide open.

Avá-Nembiará dipped his hand into the water and touched it to his lips. "Not the great waters," he said in a hoarse voice.

Avá-Tapé's hope spilled from his heart like water from a cracked gourd. The pain he saw in the faces of the others exceeded his own.

"How much further?" Avá-Tapé asked.

His father didn't answer. He only pointed, first toward the sun falling in the sky behind them, then forward to the place where the moon would rise, and then began paddling.

FIFTY-FOUR

"D o you think it's wise to keep heading for the place of the rising sun?" Avá-Tapé asked. "Maybe we should turn to the side, find land, and follow it."

"We could go for as many days to the side as ahead," Avá-Nembiará said. "Maybe more. There is no way to know."

"Some think we have taken our canoes into the great waters and paddled off the edge of the Earth." Each word came to Avá-Tapé with great effort, as if his body didn't want to give what little energy he had to speaking.

They floated side by side in front of the three other canoes, nothing but azure sky above and dark blue water below. No land in sight. They had been days on the water with less to eat than in the marshes, and they hadn't been able to stop and stretch. Avá-Tapé longed for the feel of earth beneath his feet, soft or not, and his stomach ached for food. Deeper water made it impossible to spear for fish, forcing them to depend on what little they could net.

As before, Avá-Nembiará put his hand to the water and touched it to his lips. "These are not the great waters," he would say, resuming his paddling. "The river still carries us. We will see land again before we reach the end of our journey."

More days passed. Avá-Tapé imagined seeing the shore in the dark of night, twice calling out to Kuná-Mainó and pointing, both times regretting it when he saw her excitement and the disappointment that followed.

He imagined land more frequently after the sun had fallen behind them, or when the new day glimmered on the horizon, but he had learned his lesson and refused to believe what his mind told him. When the thought of land seized him, his mouth watered and his mind filled with memories of succulent roast tapir, juicy oranges, and the soothing minty taste of one of his father's herb drinks.

Thick strands of mist drifted along the surface of the water one gray dawn, reminding Avá-Tapé of the way it covered the ground in the forest. He paddled steadily, fighting the urge to step out of his canoe and test the ground. The sun would come soon, showing only—he hit something and his canoe slid to the side and stopped. His father's canoe hit the back of Avá-Tapé's and scraped its length. Before they could voice their shock, the other canoes ran into them, jamming one against another.

Dismay engulfed Avá-Tapé for a long moment before he realized what had happened. How could the canoes hit something in the middle of the waters? He pushed with his paddle and met resistance, but he saw nothing until the fog parted, revealing the trunk of a submerged tree. Behind it, reeds and bushes. Land!

His howl echoed off the waters, startling Kuná-Mainó and those around him. She looked up, wide-eyed and open-mouthed. "Land!" he cried, emotion cracking in his voice. "We've found land!"

"Land?" Avá-Canindé's incredulous voice came out of the haze behind him. "We have come to land?"

"Not only land," Avá-Tapé said, his eyes filling with tears. "We are near the forest. My canoe hit a fallen tree!"

"We have to wait until the sun burns away the mists so we can see where we are," his father said.

The words made sense, but Avá-Tapé couldn't bear the thought of waiting another moment. To walk on land. Food. Game. "I'm stuck on a log," Avá-Tapé said, barely able to contain himself. "We have to back our canoes away so I can free mine."

Paddles splashed, followed by the scrape of wood as the canoes backed off, giving Avá-Tapé room. Two hard strokes and his canoe slid free. He looked up and saw the first shimmer of daylight blooming through the mist.

"Land," Kuná-Mainó whispered. Her eyes shone in the feeble light, looking too big inside the thin mask of skin that covered the bones of her face. Avá-Tapé vowed that he would be the first to gather food and the first to hunt. She would be the first to eat.

The haze burned off as the sky brightened. They followed the shoreline until they found a break in the reeds where the river passed into the forest. They paddled hard toward the first solid land that jutted into the water.

Avá-Tapé's heart rose when the bottom of his canoe scraped against rock. Those in front clambered out and fell repeatedly as they tried to walk. After watching them struggle to beach their canoes, Avá-Tapé tried to stand.

Holding tightly to the side of his canoe, he lowered himself into the water and stood on quivering legs. The water felt good, but nowhere near as good as the feel of solid ground beneath his feet, or the stretching of his muscles when he stumbled toward shore.

While the others beached their canoes, Avá-Tapé took Santo, Rico, and Avá-Karaí into the forest in search of food. A short way in, they found roots and berries which they gathered, gobbling as they went. The taste of the first berries made Avá-Tapé's mouth water to the point of pain. They brought roots and berries back to the others and showed them where to gather more, then the men left with bows and spears in search of game.

They followed the riverbank until they came to a trail on which they found fresh deer spoor. Avá-Tapé nocked an arrow and Santo and Rico readied their spears. Avá-Karaí took up the rear with an arrow nocked.

Avá-Tapé pulled back on his bow when he spotted a deer grazing on bushes. He needed all his strength to let the arrow fly. It sailed high over the deer's back.

The animal's head popped up, its ears cocked, and then it bolted. Santo and Rico heaved their spears. Rico's caught it in the hind quarter, causing the deer to falter, but it bounded away, taking the spear with it. Avá-Karaí couldn't get a shot off.

They found a trail of blood, which they followed for a long time before finding the deer again, still standing but swaying. Avá-Tapé nocked another shaking arrow, but Santo's spear flew before he could shoot, catching the deer in its midsection. The deer took three leaps before collapsing in a tangle of legs.

The four of them ran to find it thrashing on the ground. Avá-Tapé held the tip of his arrow close to the shoulder where the heart would be and released an arrow, stilling the deer. Making a small slice at the base of its throat, he cupped his hands, filling them with warm blood, which he held out to Rico.

"Drink first," he said. "The heart of the deer is yours."

Rico looked wide-eyed, first at Santo, then at the others, as if silently asking permission. Santo and Avá-Karaí nodded and Rico drank from Avá-Tapé's hands. Blood ran down his chin onto his bony chest.

"A warrior and a hunter," Avá-Tapé said, smearing the blood across the boy's ribs with his fingertips. He went back to the deer, drew more blood, and repeated the gesture with Santo, who drank without hesitation. Next Avá-Karaí drank, and then Avá-Tapé allowed himself to swallow the coppery richness.

The warm blood filled him with strength, as if the life of the deer had passed from its blood to his. His insides kicked into motion, and the dullness of his senses slipped away like a snake shedding its skin, giving the world a new vibrancy. He looked at his companions and smiled when he saw a new fire burning in their eyes.

They tied their spears together, reinforcing them with a sapling, bound the deer's feet, and slipped the pole through them. Avá-Tapé and Avá-Karaí shouldered the carcass and began the long journey back.

By the time they reached camp, darkness had fallen and fires had been lit in anticipation of fresh meat. Outside the range of firelight, Avá-Tapé shifted the carcass to Santo and Rico, who carried the deer, with Rico taking the lead.

A cheer went up as they struggled into the firelight with the deer. Avá-Tapé and Avá-Karaí waited until the butchering began before quietly stealing into camp. The sweet smell of roasting venison filled the air. Avá-Tapé watched the hungry eyes of the people widen in anticipation of the feast. They reminded him of the hungry eyes of jaguars.

He took the deer heart and roasted it on a separate spit. As the first strips of meat were cut, Avá-Nembiará stood by the main fire and called the people together in a rare moment of speaking. "We must thank the gods for giving us such great hunters," he said, gesturing toward Santo and Rico.

The two boys looked at the ground and shuffled uneasily.

"Eat wisely of this gift from the forest," Avá-Nembiará continued. "It has been many days since you tasted fresh game. Your mouths will cry for more, but your stomachs won't be ready. Do not eat too much too soon. Your stomachs will throw this good meat back to the earth."

As the long awaited feast began, Avá-Tapé split the heart down the middle, giving half to Santo and the other to Rico. After eating a small portion of venison himself, Avá-Tapé took his turn before the main fire. "The heart and the spirit of the deer have gone to the hunters whose spirits are as swift as the deer."

Santo and Rico looked up, eyes shining. Avá-Tapé glanced over at Avá-Canindé and saw that his eyes shone, too.

"I knew the people had great need of meat, so I took the best hunters I could find," Avá-Tapé continued, speaking dramatically. He looked and saw that all eyes held him. "We found a game trail near the waters and followed it, but my legs could barely carry me. My strength came from the cries of my stomach and the knowledge that my brothers were as weak as I was. We found the deer grazing alone. I drew back on my bow, but my arms were not strong. The arrow flew past the deer. I feared my weakness had lost the hope of the people until a spear flew from the hand of a strong hunter.

"A second spear flew before I could raise my bow, bringing the deer down." Avá-Tapé made a fist and raised it. "You eat now because of the strength and bravery of the sons of Avá-Canindé!"

His old friend's face shone with pride. Avá-Tapé remembered how it had felt such a short time ago when the same look had been given to him by the same man.

FIFTY-FIVE

They ate the entire deer that first night, except for its hoofs and horns, even baking its bones in the coals to break open and suck out the marrow. Everyone went to sleep satisfied, except for those few who'd eaten too much. As Avá-Nembiará had warned, they spilled the contents of their stomachs.

Avá-Tapé awoke before the first gray of day. His heart warmed when he heard the notes of the morning bird's song, which he had missed after so much time on the waters. Kuná-Mainó stirred beside him. The frailness of her body troubled him, and hunger gnawed at his gut. He'd tasted something other than fish and wanted more.

"I will hunt when the game come to drink at first light," he whispered. "When the sun comes, take the others to gather food, but stay close to the canoes. Most of the men will come with me. Tonight we will have a true feast."

"We will eat every kind of food on the earth," Kuná-Mainó said.

"Except fish."

She shook with laughter, which Avá-Tapé hadn't heard in a long time. He kissed her on the shoulder and climbed from the hammock. After gathering his bow and spear, he roused Avá-Karaí, Santo, Rico, Avá-Canindé, and the other men. They separated into six hunting parties.

Avá-Tapé, Avá-Karaí, Santo, and Rico went to the place where they had found the deer, concealing themselves upwind in bushes to wait. Not long after they settled in, Avá-Tapé spotted movement. His heart jumped when a huge jaguar came slinking down the game trail toward the water. When it dropped its head to drink, Santo and Rico started to rise with their spears. Avá-Tapé motioned for them to stop and waved for Avá-Karaí to come closer with the other bow.

"Two arrow shots together," he whispered. "Then you must be fast with the spears." He looked hard at Santo and Rico. "*Añag* die harder than deer. If he sees us, he will come for us."

Standing side by side, Avá-Tapé and Avá-Karaí drew back on their bows and aimed as one. To his relief, Avá-Tapé felt strength in his arms. When the two men both had a steady bead, Avá-Tapé whispered, "Now," and released his bowstring. The twang of Avá-Karaí's bow followed.

All four of the jaguar's feet left the ground when the first arrow caught it behind its foreleg. The jaguar hissed, spun, and the second arrow buried itself in its side, near the first. The cat scrambled for the water.

"Spears!" Avá-Tapé yelled. Rico's fell short, but the tip of Santo's caught the jaguar in the flank.. The cat turned and nipped at it while thrashing in the water. Avá-Tapé charged with his spear and ran knee deep into the water, driving the spear's tip into the jaguar's back. Avá-Karaí came in close behind, piercing the animal's midsection.

The jaguar's movements slowed and the currents pulled it toward the middle of the river. Avá-Tapé waded after the cat, keeping his distance as it splashed in its death throes. When the cat's head sank under water and its body went limp, Avá-Tapé and Avá-Karaí dragged the animal to shore.

"It will take all of us to carry this one back," Avá-Tapé said, gulping for breath. "He is bigger than all of us. To catch a jaguar on the first hunt of the morning is a strong sign. Santo and Rico, your hunting magic is powerful. I am honored to have you in my hunting party. And you, my friend," he patted Avá-Karaí on the shoulder. "You are a skilled hunter." Avá-Tapé turned to Santo and Rico. "Did you see how he came in close and fast behind me? That is the sign of a great hunter. If he'd been slow, this monster might have gotten away or turned on us."

Before the sun fell, they killed a wild pig and a handful of birds. The rest of the parties had been lucky, too, but none had killed a jaguar. The people marveled at its size. Avá-Tapé took its teeth and claws and put them on small cords. He tied one cord each around the necks of Santo, Rico, and Avá-Karaí, keeping one for himself.

They feasted that night, reminding Avá-Tapé of the feasts he'd seen in his visions. While they ate, members of each hunting party stood in front of the fire and told the stories of their hunt. They left the story of the jaguar for last. When it came time, Avá-Tapé nudged Avá-Karaí and let him have the attention he deserved.

It rained steadily for the next few days. They stayed in the same camp, moving into the forest each day, men building their meat supply while women gathered roots, berries, nuts, and heart of palm. No one fished.

Avá-Nembiará went into the forest alone every day. He didn't hunt, and he spoke to no one.

Three times a day they ate. As their appetites increased, taut faces and withered limbs began to fill out again, and vigor returned. Avá-Tapé tanned the deer and jaguar hides, splitting the deer skin, giving half each to Santo and Rico. He gave the whole jaguar skin to Avá-Karaí, who proudly showed it off.

When the rains stopped, they danced again for the first time in a long while. Avá-Tapé was thrilled to feel the movements of his body flowing with his chant, and the sound of his song brought him joy. His father, who had become the quietest of them all, abandoned his silence when they danced. His song flew from his lips with power and authority. Only Avá-Tapé's came close, and his song sounded little more than a whisper beside the power of Avá-Nembiará's.

Kuná-Mainó's face grew full again, like the moon. The curves of her body softened from a sharp, bony outline back to the graceful contours that stirred Avá-Tapé's passions. His own body and those of the others filled out as well.

After stacking their canoes to overflowing with smoked meat, nuts, berries, and fruit, the people started off again. They followed the river away from the big waters, deeper into a new part of the jungle. As the days passed, they settled into a steady downstream paddle. They stopped each night to eat, dance, and sleep, hunting when they saw the first signs that their food supply was diminishing.

FIFTY-SIX

The forest became lush, as it had been near the mission. Food and game were plentiful, making Avá-Tapé wonder how long it would be before they met other people. He hoped the contact would be peaceful. If they encountered Guarani, it would be even better.

Each night they danced and each night their movements gained unity and fluidity. The days were still warm, but less humid, and the nights had cooled.

Avá-Tapé began covering himself and Kuná-Mainó with skins before going to sleep, knowing that the time just before the sun would be coolest. He enjoyed waking to find her pressing her body close for warmth, her arms over his shoulders and her knees behind his.

They beached their canoes when the rains came, built fires, and made shelters from canoes and skins, staying off the water until the weather cleared. The loss of the canoes over the falls had made a deep impression. The warm rains they'd always known posed no problem since the people could stay wet for days with no harm, but the cooler rains chilled them, especially when darkness came.

After three days of rain, they hunted to keep their food supply stocked, and then set out again on the swollen river.

The dancers had grown sure-footed and the group's movements flowed as one. More and more dancers sang their own songs as confidently as they danced. Avá-Tapé couldn't help smiling when he thought about how close his people had become, and how much their power had grown. The oneness of their songs and dance made their magic the strongest it had been since they left their village—maybe stronger.

The time had come for Avá-Tapé to change the way he ate. No meat. He expected to hear the voice of Tupá any day. They had a good food supply and his body had regained its weight and strength. The people had grown stronger too. He could go back to eating plants and purifying his body, so his spirit would lighten. Soon, he would fly toward the stars again.

The river widened and the trees parted overhead, letting the sun shine on the waters for the first time in days. The warmth felt good after so many cool, rainy days and cold nights. The songs of birds and the sound of flowing waters lulled Avá-Tapé into contentment. Kuná-Mainó stretched out in front of him and rested her head against his knees. Holding his paddle beside the canoe as a rudder, he put his head back, closed his eyes and enjoyed the moment's peace.

A small splash jolted him, followed by a startled cry and a staccato patter. He opened his eyes and saw arrows and spears arcing in the sunlight. Screams pierced the air. An arrow stuck out of the back of one man in his canoe. A spear had struck another man's shoulder

"Pull skins over your heads! Lie down in the canoes!" Avá-Tapé yelled, pushing Kuná-Mainó down in front of him. The rain of spears slowed, but arrows continued splashing around him. Kuná-Mainó pushed a skin at him. He ducked and spread it over his back and the sides of the canoe. Two arrows thumped against the skin in quick succession.

Keeping low, he peered out and saw the other canoes being covered too. A moan came from his bow paddler and Kuná-Mainó sobbed. Sticking an arm and paddle from beneath the skin, Avá-Tapé risked two paddle strokes and straightened his course. More arrows splashed around him, thumped against the skin, and thwacked the side of his canoe, reminding him of the man-hunters and their guns. His anger surged. He wanted to shoot back, but couldn't see the attackers.

Though the assault continued, he heard no more cries from his people. One arrow pierced the skin close to his head and another came through, grazing his arm. The splashes, thumps, and thwacks diminished until he heard only soft cries, gurgling water, and the song of birds. Peering from beneath his skin, Avá-Tapé saw the canoes still moving down stream. Arrows stuck out from the sides and poked from the tops of the skins, like reeds at the water's edge. More arrows floated in the water. One of the men slumped over the side of his canoe, a spear sticking out of his back like a sapling.

The spears and arrows told him that forest people had attacked from hiding spots on the riverbank. Avá-Tapé's people had been exposed in the middle of the river, unable to fight back.

His arm stung where it had been grazed, and a thin stream of sticky blood ran down into his hand. He wanted to raise his head to look around, but decided against it. The enemy could still be hiding. Best to wait. He peered out again and saw that his canoe was drifting toward shore. He thrust out his arm and paddle once more, half expecting another rain of arrows, but none came.

"Paddle!" he yelled. "Stay low and keep the skins up. Paddle hard!"

He steered the canoe toward mid-stream, where the currents flowed stronger, and then slowly raised himself, letting the skin slide from his back. The sun shone, the birds sang, and the soft rush of the water filled his ears. The other canoes looked like big animals brought down in a hunt by many arrows.

One more slow scan told him they were safe. "Come up from your skins!" he called. "The danger has gone. Paddle swiftly down river and find a safe place to land."

Skins moved aside and heads popped up, revealing wide eyes and a few sprawled bodies with arrows sticking from them. Two had been impaled with spears.

"Two men in each canoe," Avá-Canindé ordered. "Take your bows and make your arrows ready. Watch for the enemy."

They continued paddling until the sun began to fall, beaching their canoes on the opposite shore from where the attack had come. Avá-Canindé sent out two parties to scout for the enemy, while Avá-Nembiará dressed Avá-Tapé's wound, then father and son tended the others.

Four men and three women had been killed, and a dozen others wounded—four of them seriously. They dragged the dead away from camp amidst anguished cries and shouts of anger. Others buried the dead while Avá-Nembiará and Avá-Tapé gave their attention to the wounded, wrapping wounds with bandages of herbs and leaves. They built no fires and had no dance. The men took turns keeping watch through the night, spears at the ready and arrows nocked.

Avá-Tapé spent the night holding a trembling Kuná-Mainó close with one arm, the other throbbing dully, his spear and bow within easy reach. When daylight came, four more had gone to the country of the dead. After re-dressing the wounds of the survivors, they ate a hasty meal, pulled arrows from the canoes and skins, and set out again.

Four canoes remained.

Avá-Canindé took the stern of one, Avá-Nembiará another, Avá-Karaí the third, and Avá-Tapé, the fourth, which took up the rear. In each canoe, one man watched the shoreline, bow ready.

Avá-Tapé's heart hung heavy. The day before their magic had been strong. Now they had been weakened again. Fear and anger showed in everyone's eyes and to make matters worse, Kuná-Mainó hadn't spoken or eaten since the attack. Avá-Tapé's stomach knotted at the thought of her soul wandering back toward her father and the country of the dead. He paddled steadily, watching the forest, at the same time studying the arrow he had put in front of himself.

Black and dark blue tail feathers. Shorter than most arrows, it had a pointed tip cut at the end of its wooden shaft. Not a stone, claw, or fang arrowhead, like he was used to. If he ever saw a hunter with arrows like this, he would not offer one as he had to the other chief. He would offer the pointed end of his spear.

FIFTY-SEVEN

"Canoes!" Rico shouted pointing behind them.

The men holding bows turned back and trained their arrows behind Avá-Tapé. A handful of smaller canoes paddled after them. "My bow," he said to Kuná-Maino.

She didn't move.

"Bow and arrows!" he said louder. "Now!"

She jumped, grabbed his bow, passed it to him, and fished out his quiver. Arrows flew toward them, making his anger flare. "Under the skins!" he said loud enough for all to hear. Arrows splashed into the water around them. He snatched one from the water.

Black and dark blue feathers.

His anger burst into fire. He stood and braced his feet against both sides of the canoe for balance. A line of smaller canoes closed in behind them, spanning the river from one side to the other. Each canoe carried three men, two paddlers and an archer in the middle who fired arrows in quick succession. The canoes in the center surged forward.

While arrows fell around him, Avá-Tapé took the blue and black feathered arrow, fitted it to his bowstring and drew back, taking aim at the archer in the center canoe. Closing one eye, he saw the man draw down on him. Avá-Tapé took a deep breath and released the arrow.

His enemy flew backward, capsizing the canoe. The attack faltered. Avá-Tapé drew one of his longer arrows and let it fly, catching a second archer high in the shoulder. He heard the twang of bowstrings behind him and saw arrows flying toward the enemy, hitting more of them. The smaller canoes crashed into each other and tipped. Men cried out and fell into the river.

"Paddle!" he heard Avá-Nembiará order. Avá-Tapé almost lost his balance when the canoe lurched forward. He looked behind him and saw Kuná-Mainó paddling. Kneeling, he pulled out another arrow and let it fly toward the canoes, which had bunched in the middle. The others kept shooting toward the same spot. The distance between their long canoes and the smaller ones grew.

Avá-Tapé shot one more arrow, saw it fall short, then grabbed his paddle and stroked with the others. The four canoes lunged through the water with each stroke, leaving the enemy far behind. Avá-Tapé felt a "Whoop! Whoop! Whoop!" rise in his throat and sing out over the waters. His pent-up emotion flew from him like the release he felt when he sang and danced, only more savage. The other archers cried out as he did, matching his shout in force and intensity.

None of their people had been hit.

At least four of their attackers had fallen.

The cries of the enemy and the sight of their canoes faded. Four archers remained vigilant; everyone else paddled. When the sun reached its highest point, the paddlers rested, watching the waters behind them. No canoes came.

They moved through the afternoon and into darkness as they had when the whites chased them. Taking turns sleeping, they paddled straight through the night, watching moonlight pass into the next day. They didn't stop until sunset the following day. They built no fires. Half of the men kept watch while the others slept. They pushed off again at first light.

The new day wore on, and the river grew narrower and deeper. The banks and forest sloped upward from the water. Clouds hugged the tall peaks of tree covered mountains in the distance. As they moved toward the mountains, the banks grew higher and the peaks loomed closer until they towered on both sides of the river which snaked along a canyon bottom. In spite of the high banks, they still found places to camp near where game came down to the water to drink.

With the mountains came longer, colder nights. Avá-Tapé huddled close to Kuná-Mainó in his hammock, wrapped from top to bottom in skins. He watched the sky, hoping no rain would come. Cold nights were hard enough, but he dreaded what might happen if the people turned cold and wet.

They skinned the large game animals their hunters had brought down, and tanned hides to ensure that no one would be cold at night. The height of the mountains blocked out much of the morning and afternoon sun. The warmth that did come later in the day didn't stay long.

The sun disappeared behind the mountains long before darkness came, bringing cooling winds to the forest. They made camp and gathered wood well before the first star appeared. Twice, in the middle of the day, Avá-Tapé spotted people watching them from far up on the banks, but the watchers took no action.

Gradually the mountains turned into rolling hills and forest. They found a big clearing where the land became flat again. After a successful hunt, they feasted, sang, and danced for the first time in days. Though awkward at the start, they soon fell into step, singing softly, with much feeling. Since the attack by the black feathers, they had recovered quickly from their grief, dancing sooner than they had in the past, venting their fear and anger through their songs. The loss of families had weakened their magic, but it had brought them closer. Their magic still had power.

When the women and children went to sleep, the men stayed awake long into the night, speaking of their bravery in the canoe battle. Avá-Tapé could think only of those killed in the first attack, and the anger that sent his arrows into the hearts of the enemy. The magic had been strong, but he didn't like the feel of its power. It wasn't right for a healer to take the lives of others. He didn't speak of his bravery, but he did listen to the stories of others.

Their days settled into an endless rhythm, the way it had when their journey began. They saw no signs of other people, so the archers relaxed and the dancing continued. When the forest started to thin, Avá-Tapé sensed marshlands ahead.

After Avá-Tapé shared his thoughts with Avá-Canindé and his father, they stopped to hunt and fill their canoes with as much meat as they could. They didn't want to risk losing any more to starvation.

"We will be walking soon," Avá-Nembiará said in one of his now rare pronouncements. "The river will end before we reach the great waters."

"How do you know?" Avá-Tapé asked, trying to fathom his father's logic. His instincts told him the river would continue, but he couldn't ignore the conviction in his father's voice.

"That is how my grandfather spoke of the great journey," he said. "Our search will end with a journey through the forest, after crossing the mountains. We will reach the great waters on foot."

Two days later, they came to marshes where the river grew shallow and the banks closed in. Thick reeds impeded the river's flow, leaving them bogged down and unable to paddle any farther in the grasses of a muddy swamp.

FIFTY-EIGHT

"Our numbers are small," Avá-Nembiará said. "We can leave our canoes and scout on foot. If we find more water, we'll come back for them. If not, we will continue our journey on land."

Standing ankle-deep in mud beside his canoe, Avá-Tapé looked through reeds and swamp grass, seeing forest on both sides, and swampland in front of him.

"It is the wise thing to do." Avá-Canindé pulled his skins and spears from his canoe. "We will carry what we have the way we did when we left the mission. Our legs can carry us now instead of our arms."

"I will send out two men to hunt and look for danger," Avá-Tapé said. He lifted Kuná-Mainó from the canoe, and set her feet first in the mud. The sun had begun its fall, reflecting gold and yellow on the surface of the shallow water, which once had been a flowing river.

They stretched skins and nets between their spears and filled them with food and other necessities. Avá-Tapé ran his fingers over the holes where his canoe had been struck by the white man's thunder, and fingered the gashes where the black and blue feathered arrows had stuck. This canoe had been home for many days and nights. He was reluctant to leave it, but if the land stretched out the way his father had predicted, the canoe would no longer be needed.

After packing smaller nets and loading them on their backs, they set off through the marshes, away from the setting sun, slipping and stumbling between tall grass and pockets of mud.

Avá-Canindé took the lead, and Avá-Nembiará followed. Avá-Tapé stayed close to Kuná-Mainó, happy that she had begun talking again.

They stepped onto the first solid island of dry land among a grove of palms as the red sun dipped into the horizon. Not long after darkness fell, their scouts returned with a huge length of anaconda and a pheasant.

As the aroma of roasting snake lingered in the air, insect songs and bird calls pierced the darkness. After their meal, Avá-Tapé sat with an arm around Kuná-Mainó in front of a fire. His father sat beside them, along with Avá-Canindé, Santo, Rico, and Avá-Karaí.

"We will come to the great waters soon," Avá-Nembiará said.

Avá-Tapé looked up, somewhat surprised that his father had spoken. Orange fire danced across the older man's shadowed features, darkening his eyes.

"Then it will be time to build a *maloca* and a House of Dances," Avá-Canindé said. "There we will hunt and dance and sing until the gods come down from the sky and carry us over the great waters."

"Our magic grows strong again," Avá-Tapé said. "All who are left dance with us now. Their steps get stronger with each dance. Much darkness has taken our brothers and sisters to the country of the dead, but those who still live dance with pure hearts and sure steps."

Avá-Karaí tossed wood onto the fire, sending a shower of sparks into the air. He gestured toward the dying embers. "So many have passed so quickly. Their souls have scattered swifter than the embers. Their power is not with us in this world."

"So many voices," Avá-Nembiará said. "I hoped to lead them to the Land Without Evil, but too many have gone too quickly. I cannot save them all. Now that we are close to the great waters, we have to free ourselves from the weight of their spirits. They weaken our magic."

"We can dance together," Avá-Tapé said. "The living and the dead…"

Avá-Nembiará stepped closer to the fire, waving his hand over the flames. "Avá-Karaí's word is true when he speaks of souls scattering like embers from the fire. The souls of the dead fly apart when they die. Their breath is the lighter spirit that goes from them at death. Their scattered parts cannot reach paradise, but still they try.

"Their spirit has to tiptoe past the sleeping jaguar who stretches his hammock across the path to the other world. If the *añag* awakens, he devours the soul. If the spirit gets past him, it lives a life of happiness drinking *maize* beer and honey. These spirits will dance with us — if they can be found, and if they have not been devoured."

"What of the heavier spirits?" Avá-Tapé asked. He shuddered, knowing what his father would say.

"As adults, these soul parts have touched animal souls by eating game. They cannot enter the Land Without Evil. Urukera, the second *añag*, calls to the souls of the dead if any of their heavier soul parts try to cross into the Land Without Evil. Any spirit who crosses becomes a wandering soul who can be dangerous, especially if death was sudden."

Kuná-Mainó huddled closer to Avá-Tapé, burying her head in his shoulder. He felt her shaking. When he thought of all the death he had seen, sickness tickled the pit of his stomach. Did his father battle these heavy souls? "The lower souls are still with us," Avá-Tapé heard himself saying.

"We have a growing tribe of dead who follow us." Avá-Nembiará looked directly at Avá-Tapé. "It is they who roam the Earth. They who weaken our magic. The time has come for us to see that they go to their right place. We have to do this before we reach the great waters, so when we dance our spirits will be free. The weight of these heavier spirits make it difficult to fly out of our bodies. They wait in the darkness for us."

Avá-Tapé closed his eyes and saw Avá-Canindé's woman, arms outstretched, worms writhing between her lips. He looked over and saw Santo and Rico staring at his father, eyes wide and mouths open. "This is why we have no visions," Avá-Tapé said.

"This is what weakens our magic."

Avá-Nembiará nodded.

"How can we stop them?" Avá-Karaí asked.

Avá-Canindé looked to Avá-Nembiará, who nodded. "A special dance," Avá-Canindé said. "The *yoasá*. A dance that crosses one thing with another. It is difficult and dangerous to the spirit. The *yoasá* catches the wandering souls in a magic place and gives them to Tupá, who brings them to the place of lost souls. If the wandering soul part is heavy with *techó-achy*, it carries even more danger. It will make your spirit angry, and hungry for the flesh of animals."

"So we who live must dance and trap the spirits of the dead by dancing a special dance," Avá-Tapé said.

"A dance that is a hunt." Avá-Nembiará raised himself up on his haunches. Firelight flickered in his eyes, giving him a haunted, wild look, as if the lost and angry spirits raged inside him. Avá-Tapé couldn't remember the last time his father had spoken with such power. "The *yoasá* is the final ordeal for the lower soul. The spirit meets its end by becoming the prey of the living. A brave warrior is joined by two men and a woman, who are his hunting companions. He has to kill the spirit with sacred weapons."

The sputtering of their fire and the hushed voices from the other fires filled the night. Even the insects had grown quiet. Avá-Tapé looked up at the orange firelight dancing on the trees and wondered about the hunt, dreading the thought of facing the dark spirits on the other side. He didn't know if he was strong enough.

A warrior had to be the hunter if their tribe were to break free from the darkness hanging over them. He knew without looking that all eyes were on him. Closing his eyes, he took a deep breath and summoned the will to speak.

"I will be the hunter," Avá-Karaí said.

Avá-Tapé opened his eyes and saw his friend standing before the fire, a glint of determination in his eye. "Show me what I have to do and I will hunt the heavy spirits of the dead. We cannot have this shadow of dark souls hanging over us when we dance before the great waters. We need our magic to be its strongest for the gods to raise us to the Land Without Evil."

FIFTY-NINE

They started out the next morning, moving between groves of solid land and mist covered swamps. While Avá-Tapé and Avá-Canindé led, Avá-Nembiará and Avá-Karaí lingered behind, engrossed in discussion about Avá-Karaí's part in the upcoming hunt for wandering souls. Avá-Tape hadn't seen his father speak this much since leaving the mission.

He felt a twinge of jealousy in spite of the fact that Avá-Karaí was the best man to be the hunter. Avá-Tapé and his father had discussed the hunt long into the night. Avá-Tapé, Avá-Canindé, and Kuná-Mainó would be his hunting companions, and Avá-Nembiará would direct the hunt and dance. Avá-Tapé hoped that the spirit of Avá-Canindé's woman would be trapped and sent to the place of lost souls.

The stretches of solid ground lengthened as the day wore on, but they still walked long distances in water, which was sometimes waist deep. They moved slowly, avoiding ropy vines, fallen trees, hollows, and holes that couldn't be seen beneath the brown water. They camped that night in the middle of a dry stretch of land. While the people gathered around small fires, Avá-Nembiará and Avá-Karaí disappeared into the darkness. No one saw them until the next morning.

The watery places became less frequent, and the forest grew dim from the leafy canopy which blocked the sun. Tall palms and clumps of smaller ones dotted the landscape with hairy trunks and tops like tail feathers. Huge ferns hung like dying trees. Mats of pink, lavender, and scarlet petals covered the ground, but the flowers they fell from were too high in the trees to be seen. Every time they came to a clearing they checked the position of the sun, moving steadily toward it in the morning and keeping it to their backs after it had passed over them.

That evening they came across a huge fallen tree. Again they camped and ate with no sign of Avá-Nembiará and Avá-Karaí until full darkness had come and the night insects sang. The two men emerged from the darkness and sat across from Avá-Tapé, Avá-Canindé, and Kuná-Mainó.

"If the spirits of the forest are strong again tomorrow," Avá-Nembiará said solemnly, "and we are close to a place of power, we will dance the *yoasá* and hunt the wandering souls of our people under the full light of Yacy."

The hairs bristled on the back of Avá-Tapé's neck. He looked around at the others, seeing only solemn expressions, except for Kuná-Mainó's, whose widened eyes gazed up at him from the darkness.

"I will be happy to see their souls put to rest," he said, breaking the silence. "I am tired of carrying them."

His father's eyes met his, and a silent understanding passed between them, then Avá-Nembiará and Avá-Karaí slipped back into the darkness. Kuná-Mainó clung to Avá-Tapé as they went back to their hammock to sleep. All night he could feel the tension in her body. Neither slept much.

The next day passed in a blur of fear and anticipation. Toward evening, Avá-Tapé felt his heart cold and hard in his chest. They built fires in a small clearing and ate little as they waited for his father. The night sky shone clear through the break in the trees. A handful of stars scattered across the sky. Yacy rose slowly, large and orange like a dying fire.

A light breeze blew, bringing with it cool, damp air. Mists drifted in feeling cold on Avá-Tapé's skin, their wet chill touching his insides when he breathed the cool dampness. He'd never seen mists in the night. They had always appeared in the morning. Now the world seemed turned around, as if the worlds of the living and the dead had crossed. His father's words filled his mind. "A dance that crosses one thing with another."

Avá-Canindé, Santo, Rico, and Kuná-Mainó all sat close to the fire, faces expectant. No one spoke. The breeze gusted, bringing a wall of fog that vanished as quickly as it appeared. Leaves whispered on darkened trees, flashing gossamer and silver, while moonbeams danced in the blackness amidst a thinner haze. Avá-Tapé moved closer to the fire. The chill touched his bones. No matter what he did, he couldn't warm his hands and feet.

Beyond the fire the mists swirled and two shadows appeared. Avá-Tapé's heart jerked before he recognized the faces of his father and Avá-Karaí floating toward him. Both men stepped into the circle of firelight wearing full headdresses and feathered armbands.

Their faces and bodies were painted with strange colors and patterns. Both wore jaguar skins over their shoulders. Their faces had been painted white and their eyes black, making them look like skulls. Avá-Nembiará held his feathered cross and rattle. Avá-Karaí held a bow with dark red and black feathers dangling from it, and a necklace of jaguar teeth, claws, and arrowheads.

"We have found a place where the power is strong," Avá-Nembiará said, gesturing behind him and looking to Avá-Karaí, who nodded, then the two started back into the fog. Reluctant to leave the warmth of the fire, Avá-Tapé took Kuná-Mainó's hand and led her after them. Avá-Canindé followed. Santo and Rico stayed behind.

Avá-Nembiará led, followed by Avá-Karaí, Avá-Tapé, Kuná-Mainó, and Avá-Canindé. They stayed close, passing between trees and low hanging vines and branches. Fog and moonlight alternated around them like a dance of two worlds. Soon they came to a small, low lying clearing.

Avá-Nembiará held up a hand and put it to his lips to silence them. His head looked like a floating skull bobbing above his body in the hazy moonlight as he disappeared into the hollow.

A moment later the sound of his rattle floated up from the darkness, followed by a low, pleading chant. When the sounds faded, Avá-Karaí went down into the hollow and Avá-Nembiará reappeared. He took Avá-Canindé first, then Kuná-Mainó. Avá-Tapé gave her shoulder a squeeze to quell the terror he saw in her eyes, then she went down into the mist.

His father led him to a tree and gave him a *takuapú*. "When you hear the voice of the rattle," he said, "hit the tree with the *takuapú* to call the spirits."

Avá-Tapé imagined Avá-Canindé's woman floating through the haze toward him with outstretched arms. He shuddered. Avá-Nembiará disappeared again.

The sound of his father's rattle followed, joined soon after by Avá-Nembiará's chant. Avá-Tapé rapped the side of the tree with the *takuapú*. Two other beats rang out from each side of him. As the rattle and his father's voice grew in volume, he and the others beat louder. The haze thinned and lifted, revealing a silvery shadow near the base of a tree on one side of Avá-Tapé, and two more on the other, all pounding their own beats. Avá-Tapé stood at the place where Yacy had risen while whomever was across from him matched the place Yacy would fall. A third person stood to one side below the bright star of the night, the last across from the third. His father stood in the middle, dancing a strange backward dance in the full moonlight.

Avá-Nembiará's rattle moved, first above his head, then toward the middle of the clearing. Avá-Tapé felt a cold wind pass through him. A small patch of fog swirled in the hollow where his father's rattle pointed. Avá-Tapé beat the tree harder, finding comfort in the force of his sound. The rattle shook faster and lower, and the mist appeared to spin into a silver cocoon. Avá-Nembiará's rattle pointed straight at the mist while his chant became soft, fast, and continuous, before falling quiet. Everyone stopped beating the trees. A hush covered everything. No birds, no insects, no wind.

Avá-Tapé looked around, not daring to breathe, then a bone-jarring cry pierced his ears, melting his insides. Kuná-Mainó shrieked, followed by the twang of a bow and the thump of an arrow.

Silence followed.

Avá-Tapé didn't know whether to run to Kuná-Mainó or stay in his place. He looked again at the bottom of the hollow. The misty cocoon had vanished. A low cry came from his father, who knelt on the ground close to where the cocoon had been. Avá-Tapé's insides chilled, picturing an arrow piercing his father's stomach. He ran down the hill, dreading what he would find.

Avá-Nembiará rocked back and forth clutching his stomach and weeping. Avá-Tapé knelt beside him and saw the arrow stuck in the ground where the cocoon had been. He helped his father to his feet and saw tears streaming down his face. Great sobs wracked his body as Avá-Nembiará whispered:

"I have sent them to Tupá. He has taken them to the place of lost souls."

SIXTY

After another sleepless night, they started off toward the rising sun. The day felt warm, but a cool, steady breeze kept it comfortable. No underbrush blocked their way, allowing them to move freely over a mat of dead leaves. Small trees mingled with the trunks of giants whose upper branches merged into a leafy roof. Vines hung from above. No one spoke of the previous night, but Avá-Nembiará moved with a new purpose, bouncing as though he'd dropped a load that had been too heavy to bear.

The forest sloped upward, then down again in gently rolling hills. Late in the day, they topped one of the hills and saw marshes spreading out before them. The breeze blew steadily with a strong, clean scent which was unlike anything Avá-Tapé had ever smelled.

"We will sleep here tonight," Avá-Nembiará said, "and go into the tall grasses tomorrow. There is no way to know how long we will travel there."

That night they all sat by the fire, telling stories of the old days and the old dances. Avá-Tapé smiled, seeing the delight on Kuná-Mainó's face when his father spun tales of hunts, gods, and magical flights. Avá-Nembiará hadn't spoken like this since leaving the mission.

"Like you I was once a hunter of spirits," Avá-Nembiará said, turning to Avá-Karaí. Everyone exchanged nervous glances. None of them had spoken of the eerie experience.

"Many of the old ones passed on from our people in the same season," his father said. "We lived in fear. My grandfather, our *paí*, walked in the darkness talking to spirits of the dead. The people feared him and went away when he came near until he talked to no one but the dead. I had spent many days in the forest learning from him. I feared the dead with all my being, but I loved my grandfather more. I went to him and asked what I could do to bring him back to the living. Two moons later, we hunted the dead."

"What did you see when your grandfather danced the *yoasá?*" Avá-Tapé asked.

"Two hungry eyes of fire," Avá-Nembiará said in a lower voice.

"What did you do when you saw the *añag?*" Avá-Karaí asked.

"What any warrior would do. I fired my arrow and ran screaming into the night."

"What of your grandfather and his magic?" Avá-Tapé asked.

"He said I had chased the dead into Tupá's hands. He stopped talking to them and came back to the living."

The same as you, Avá-Tapé nearly said aloud. He wished he could have danced the *yoasá* when his sister and the others had been killed by the man-hunters. It might have kept his mother with the living.

His father and Avá-Canindé talked by the fire long after Avá-Tapé went to his hammock with Kuná-Mainó. He fell asleep to the sound of their voices, waking to other voices as if he'd only closed his eyes a moment. The morning air felt cool and he didn't want to leave Kuná-Mainó's warmth. At times like these, he wished they slept in a warm *maloca*.

He could tell by the smells of food and the voices that the people were preparing to resume their journey. He smiled, realizing that the change that had come over Avá-Nembiará had brought new excitement to the others. Maybe they, too, had been freed from the encumbering spirits of the dead.

Leaning over, he kissed Kuná-Mainó on the back of the neck and climbed out of the hammock. "We go into the marshes today," he said. "We should eat before we go. We don't know how long we will be in there."

She smiled. Her soft eyes and ruffled hair made him want to climb back under the skins with her.

A short time later, they stood at the top of the hill, their belongings packed on their backs or in spear and skin carriers. Below them, reeds and high swamp grass spread as far as they could see. The breeze blew steadily from the direction of the marshes bringing the strong, clean scent that Avá-Tapé had first smelled the day before.

His father led them into the marsh. Thick reeds and cattails grew high, blocking the view in front of them. They saw the sun above, clearly showing them the direction to follow. For most of the day, they heard nothing but the steady wind whispering through the reeds and grasses.

Some time after the sun passed over, Avá-Nembiará held up his hand, stopping them. He put his finger to his lips and cupped his hand to his ear. Avá-Tapé heard what sounded like birds, but they didn't sing like birds of the forest. Their calls came as high-pitched cries. For a long time everyone stood motionless, listening in awe to the new sounds, before Avá-Nembiará waved them forward, moving faster.

The sun fell behind them, bathing the undulating tops of the marsh grasses in waves of orange fire. Soon the forest appeared. Avá-Nembiará hurried out of the marshes toward the trees, once more holding up his hand. The strange cries grew louder, then another sound came, this one low and steady like the roar of the rapids, but this rumble peaked and faded to a hiss before starting again. The strange scent smelled stronger than ever.

Avá-Nembiará's eyes widened. He set his load down and trotted away into the trees. Avá-Tapé dropped his things and followed the sunbeams that streaked through the branches. The clean smell filled his chest with moist coolness, and the rising and falling roar became louder, like far off thunder. Avá-Tapé leaped over roots and dodged fallen limbs and trunks, keeping his eye on his father, who ran ahead.

The trees thinned and opened wide to nothing but blue. Avá-Tapé broke into a sprint, nearly catching his father before the trees ended and the ground dropped out from under them. Avá-Nembiará shouted at the top of his lungs as he leaped a short distance onto a sandy beach. Avá-Tapé jumped down beside his father, who stood motionless, chest heaving, tears running down his cheeks.

Water spread out before them as far as they could see. Man-sized waves thundered onto the shore, leaving a white foam that disappeared as new waves washed over. Huge white birds floated and circled on the breeze above, making the high-pitched cries they had been hearing. Avá-Nembiará ran for the water, splashing into a wave. Avá-Tapé followed, reaching the shore in time to see his father put his hand in the water and touch it to his lips. He grimaced, spit it from his mouth, knelt in the roiling water, and smiled beatifically.

"We have come to the great waters," he whispered.

SIXTY-ONE

"We will build our dance house in the sand near the waters," Avá-Canindé said. Wrapped in skins, they all huddled around a bonfire among the trees a short distance from the beach. Darkness had fallen not long after everyone had seen, touched, and tasted the saltiness of the great waters. A light fog hung in the air, giving the fire a hazy glow. The roar of the surf pounded in the background.

"We should build a *maloca* first," Avá-Tapé said, pulling his jaguar skin tighter around his shoulders. "It is colder here and the air is wet. We need a warm place to sleep while we work on the dance house."

Avá-Canindé nodded. "When the light comes again, we'll send out hunters while the others build a *maloca* here." He pointed to the ground.

"We have to be strong and pure in our hearts and diets before we dance," Avá-Nembiará said. "Our spirits need to be light enough to rise over the great waters. The gods will not take us if we are heavy with *techó-achy.*"

"How soon can we dance?" Avá-Karaí asked.

"We need to gather food and build a *maloca* first," Avá-Nembiará said. "The days and nights grow cold. It is past the time of harvest. We have to hunt and gather enough food to take us to the time of sprouting. When the days grow longer and new seeds break through the ground, we will lighten our diets so our spirits can break free and rise toward the sun like the young plants."

At Avá-Nembiará's urging, everyone gathered on the beach the next morning in darkness to watch the sun rise from the waters, a new experience. Once it shone bright, Avá-Karaí led a hunting party, while Avá-Canindé put the others to work building a *maloca* big enough for all.

Santo and Rico led the children, collecting palm fronds and reeds for the *maloca's* walls and roof, while their father took the men to chop down bigger trees for the frame and roof beams. While the hunters butchered and smoked fresh game, builders worked steadily from first light to darkness.

By the time the sun came and went four times, all slept indoors, out of the cold winds. Two days later they had the inside walled off for privacy. They built a fireplace at one end of the *maloca* in an open space where the women shared the cooking.

No sooner had they thatched the roof when rain and cold winds came, showering them for days before stopping, and then starting again. They spent much of their time around the fire, listening to Avá-Canindé share his plans for the dance house, or to Avá-Nembiará speaking of preparing for the dance.

As the days grew colder, sniffling, wheezing, and coughs filled the nights. Days were spent before the fire drinking Avá-Nembiará's warm preparations. He and Avá-Tapé spent much of their time chanting and healing the sick. Most of the people recovered, but some coughs and runny noses led to fever, and some fevers to death. By the time the rains ended and the first of the warm breezes came again, three of their number had passed on.

When the ground began to dry, Avá-Nembiará sent everyone away from the *maloca* and went through it, blowing smoke and shaking his rattle in its corners to chase away the spirits of sickness. When the people returned, he had them sit around the fire.

"We have lost more of our family," he said. "I have chased the spirits of sickness from our house. The time of death has passed. The season of new growth comes swiftly. Now is the time for building." He looked to Avá-Canindé. "Our brother the builder will show us."

"We start the new dance house when the sun comes again," Avá-Canindé said. "We who have lived through so much death are strong in our hearts. The gods have chosen us because they want the strongest dancers." He shook his fist. "We will build the dance house and dance until the gods raise us up."

That night, Avá-Tapé lay with his eyes open, unable to sleep as he wondered whether the dance house and the power of his yearning, his father's yearning, and the desire of the people would be strong enough to bring the gods down from the heavens. Their numbers were nothing compared with what they had been, but Avá-Canindé's words rang true. Those who survived came through with stronger hearts. They *were* the strongest dancers. Every one of them had a personal song. How could the gods ignore the oneness of their dance?

Avá-Tapé hoped the magic of his own song would be a bridge to carry him between the worlds. He hoped his song and dance had the power to bring back the spirit of Tupá that had come to him in his dream.

Kuná-Mainó stirred beside him. He slipped out of their hammock without waking her and made his way toward the beach. Looking up, he saw countless stars. No moon.

He closed his eyes and sat near the waterline, listening to the waves, hoping they would speak to him like the water near the falls. A warm breeze whispered past him, as if teasing with half-remembered promises. He remained still for a long time, closing his eyes to the night while opening his ears and heart to the voice of the wind and the sighs of the water.

When he opened his eyes, a line of indigo rimmed the horizon, gradually brightening to violet and blue. The new day lit the sky like the hope in his heart, blossoming in red and orange, finally sparking to white fire that streaked the high, wispy clouds of the morning sky with bold strokes of red.

Today they would start work on the House of Dances.

He rose when full sunlight hit the beach, coloring the sand like fire, and walked back to the smell of cooking and the sound of excited talk. The food reminded him of the emptiness in his stomach, but he wouldn't eat. On this morning he would start purifying himself.

Inside, Avá-Canindé sat by the fire surrounded by people, drawing his plans for the dance house in the dirt with a stick. He sent groups of men in search of cedar for the roof and frame, and the little ones in search of palm fronds for thatching. Avá-Tapé didn't offer to help, knowing Avá-Canindé wouldn't allow it. It was understood that the others would build a strong frame and solid walls while he and his father built strong spirits.

Avá-Nembiará disappeared as soon as the building began. When Avá-Tapé wasn't off trying to hear the voices of the spirits, he spent his time away from the others, watching them build the frame first, and then the walls and roof. Their songs drifted to him on the breeze as they worked, sometimes coming as a lone voice, other times as many singing as one.

In the first days, he ate only vegetables. As the building continued, he stopped eating and drank only juices, longing for the warm, sharp-tasting *algaroba* that had energized him in the past.

From behind, the new dance house looked like their *maloca*, but was bigger. The side facing the water had no wall. In front of this open side, they put a cedar trough in the shape of a canoe. In front of that, they planted three cedar posts, decorating the outer two with feathered sticks. The middle post represented the cross. Beside it a taller, thinner stick with a little arrow showed Kuarahy's and Yacy's climb to heaven. Bands of feathered ornaments covered the walls, doorway, and posts.

The day they finished, Avá-Nembiará reappeared late in the afternoon as the sun faded behind the forest. A full, blood-orange moon loomed on the horizon above the great waters. Avá-Tapé wondered if the timing of the completion of the dance house, his father's appearance, and the full moon were coincidental or intentional. Afraid of jeopardizing the magic, he didn't question it.

Having eaten nothing for days, Avá-Tapé felt lightheaded and giddy, a strong sign that his spirit would float easily from his body. Tonight he would dance with his whole being and try to bring the gods down from the sky.

People rushed around preparing for the dance, their excitement growing with the rising moon. Avá-Nembiará put his hand on Avá-Tapé's shoulder and led him to a small hut hidden near the reeds in the forest beyond the edge of the trees.

"The others make ready the House of Dances while we prepare our spirits," Avá-Nembiará said, kindling a small fire. "Tonight, we dance and sing with pure hearts. If our magic is strong, Tupá will take us into the sky." He brought out two small gourds and painted his face in black and red lines and circles. When he finished, Avá-Tapé did the same. Both put on their headdresses and sashes.

The eyes of father and son met in silent affirmation before Avá-Nembiará picked up his feathered cross and rattle. The fire in his eyes, his face paint, and the bright colors of his headdress, cross, and rattle combined, giving him a fearsome look.

They walked to the House of Dances together, finding a bonfire in front of the open space facing the water. Flames reflected against the dance house and off the water, dappling the walls in orange flickers that looked like dancing birds and insects. Everyone gathered in front. In the middle stood Avá-Canindé, Avá-Karaí, Santo, and Rico, all wearing smaller headdresses and feathers. A hush settled over the gathering as Avá-Tapé and his father moved to the center of the dance house and faced the great waters.

From where they stood, all they could see were the trough, posts, and a strip of moonlight wavering over the dark waters. The dance house seemed to hold them between the worlds, with the trees and plants beneath them, and a bridge of moonlight leading them toward the silvery doorway to the other world.

The rest of the men, including Santo and Rico, formed a line facing the water. Avá-Tapé and Avá-Nembiará stood at the center, flanked by Avá-Canindé and Avá-Karaí. Behind them, women and children with their cheeks painted red fanned out in a line with Kuná-Mainó in the middle.

She looked to Avá-Tapé, then to Avá-Nembiará, before starting the first beat of her *takuapú*. The others joined in and the men began to chant and dance. Avá-Nembiará shook his rattle and moved with the women's beat, beginning his song with a low voice. The others followed, all projecting their own yearning.

Their heartfelt cries brought an unexpected flurry of faces to Avá-Tapé's mind. Those of Pindé, his mother, Avá-Guiracambí, Avá-Takuá, Father Antonio, and others. His throat tightened and his eyes filled with tears. He shook his rattle as if to chase them away, and he began to dance.

Avá-Tapé closed his eyes and cried out, putting his anguish into his chant, drowning out the others. His heart pumped and his song flowed through him as if he were alone. His body fell into step, dancing with the spirit that rose from inside him as a longing that poured from his mouth and limbs in a unity of sound and motion. He let himself go, flowing with the sounds that pulled him headlong like water rushing toward falls.

Avá-Tapé danced with all his being until his arms and legs burned and his breath came hard. Sweat dripped into his eyes. He heard the songs of the others, the beat of the *takuapú*, and his father's rattle, first strong and wild, then smooth and trembling, as if the desire of his people for the Land Without Evil cried inside them all. His head buzzed and he felt lighter with each word. Part of him knew that he danced with the others, but he could feel himself drifting farther from his body.

The face of the moon blurred and the glowing face of Tupá filled his vision. "Tupá!" he cried out.

"Only those who have purified their spirits can hear," Tupá said. "You are the future of the people. You are the seed. Prepare yourself. Your heart is pure, but your spirit is heavy. *Techóachy* does not weigh on your body, but the darkness of those who dance with you holds them to the Earth."

Something pulled him higher until a shimmering rectangle of silver opened in the sky. He rushed toward it. For an instant he had no sense of himself as if he were everywhere, at the same time at the center of everything.

The weight of Avá-Tapé's body plunged through the darkness, gaining speed until his stomach lurched to a stop. He felt sand sticking to his sweaty skin and his heart fluttering. His breathing came shallow and rapid. At first he saw nothing, then the faces of his father and the other dancers swam into view above him.

SIXTY-TWO

Frowns and puzzled stares greeted Avá-Tapé while Tupa's voice still rang in his ears. "You are the future of the people. You are the seed. Prepare yourself. Your heart is pure but your spirit is heavy. *Techó-achy* does not weigh on your body, but the darkness of those who dance with you holds them to the earth."

"You cried out to Tupá and fell to the ground," Avá-Nembiará said. "I had no vision. Has Tupá touched your heart? What is his message?"

Avá-Tapé sat up and a wave of blackness swept over him. You are the future of the people, Tupá had said. What did it mean? His stomach heaved, but nothing came. Kuná-Mainó stood close, worry creasing her brow.

"We are too heavy with *techó-achy*," he said, feeling his heart tighten at the words. "The spirit of the white man and his unnatural foods have made us cling to the Earth with much weight. To reach the Land Without Evil, we all have to stop eating animals as my father and I have done." He looked around and saw slumped shoulders and saddened eyes.

"The gods do not want us," someone said miserably.

"We have become too much like the whites," another said. "Their soft ways have weakened us."

"We must follow the voice of Tupá as our young *pai* has told us," Avá-Canindé said, helping Avá-Tapé to his feet.

Avá-Tapé felt another wave of queasiness as he rose on trembling legs. Kuná-Mainó took his arm over her shoulder and helped him back to the *maloca*. She tried to make him eat, but he took only water and juice from oranges. His heart hung heavy and his disappointment grew. What did Tupá mean? He breathed in slowly and deeply, knowing one wrong word would bring tears.

"We have to try again while Yacy shows his full face," he said when his father came to his hammock with an herb drink. A tremor shook his voice. He spoke deeper to drive it out. "While his light is full, the power is strong and the door is open the widest. If we dance with all our hearts, we can still rise above the weight of our *techó-achy.*"

Avá-Nembiará smiled. "I knew we wouldn't rise with our first dance. It will take many dances before our spirits are right. Our magic is strong and the powers of both worlds have crossed in our hearts, songs, and dance. When all of these become one, we will rise."

Avá-Tapé's heart lightened at his father's words, but doubt wormed its way into his thoughts. For the first time, he pondered the possibility of not reaching the Land Without Evil. He knew he and his father could rise. They had done so in the past, but he couldn't speak for the hearts and intent of the others.

That night, chaotic dreams filled his sleep. He danced endlessly, singing in a hoarse voice, his arms and legs screaming for release from the agony of his relentless dance. The ache of his body paled alongside the pain of his yearning. His surroundings shifted back and forth between the living and the dead. More often than not he danced among the dead. When he awoke, he was relieved to see that the light of day had returned.

He felt weak and his head throbbed all day, but that night they assembled again under the full moon. As before, he danced with all his heart, but what little energy he had left him sooner than the previous night. At the point where their chants and dance steps came together, he collapsed without hearing the voice of Tupá. Kuná-Mainó tried harder to get him to eat, but he only drank water and juice.

He tried again on the third night and fell even sooner, as he did the next night, and the next. As the moon waned, he lost strength sooner each night, his fading energies paralleling the diminishing light of the moon, until his father put a stop to the dances.

"It is time to eat and build back your strength," Avá-Nembiará said. "When you have grown strong, you and I will return to the forest to be alone with the spirits. When the light of the moon is full, we will dance again."

Avá-Tapé ate slowly, gathering strength and weight the way he had so many times before. He spent his days alone looking out over the great waters, struggling against the doubt that haunted him whenever his mind grew still.

He walked for long stretches on the beach, looking at the ground. Small pink shells stood out in the sun against the white sand, reminding him of Kuná-Mainó's delicate beauty. He started collecting them, wondering if he and Kuná-Mainó would ever reach the Land Without Evil together. He had been pushing himself so hard, his desire for her had nearly vanished. Now that he grew strong again, his passion reawakened.

When he had more shells than he could carry, inspiration struck him. Working many days from first light to darkness, he made holes in the shells using the tip of an arrow. He did the same with two of his prized jaguar claws and a fang.

Weaving a small string from palm fiber, he strung the fang first, with a claw to each side and shells on both sides of the claws, making a striking pink necklace that he hid in his quiver.

His father built a bonfire and called the people before the dance house one night as the last of the sun flared red on the horizon behind the forest. A warm, steady breeze blew in from the ocean, and the first of the bright stars dotted the sky.

"We have all made many sacrifices to come to the great waters," Avá-Nembiará said to the gathered tribe. "Our spirits are strong, our songs are full of hope, and our dance is one with our bodies, but some of our hearts are not true."

Avá-Tapé thought of his doubt and felt a pang of guilt. Had his weakness betrayed them?

"When the sun comes back to the Earth, my son and I will go into the forest to purify our bodies and ask our helper spirits to strengthen our magic. We will return when the face of Yacy is full. Our power will be greater than the last time we danced, but we cannot do this magic alone. Each of you must look into your hearts and strengthen your spirits by purifying your bodies. No animals can be eaten. Only plants. We have to free ourselves from *techó-achy*." He looked out over the waters and held out both hands. "We have traveled on a dangerous journey to reach the end of the world. Only the great waters block us from reaching the Land Without Evil."

"How do we journey past them?" Avá-Karaí asked. "Will we truly float over them?"

"Will our magic dry up the waters so we can pass?" someone else asked.

"It doesn't matter if we fly over, or dry them up." Avá-Canindé stepped out beside Avá-Nembiará. "What matters is that we dance with true hearts and light spirits."

Another asked, "If our magic is strong, why hasn't this happened?"

"Because men like you with doubt in their hearts have killed Tupá's messenger birds," Avá-Canindé said in a rare flash of anger.

The crowd fell silent.

"Our spirits grew heavy from too much of the white man's food," Avá-Nembiará said, breaking the silence. "Now we stand at the end of the world." He pointed to the water again. "The time of chaos and destruction has returned. The Earth is old. Our numbers grow smaller. There is no place left for us on the Earth. This is why we dance. Either the lower spirit of the Earth will draw us down into death, or our pure spirits will rise and dance with the gods. The choice lies in your hearts."

He turned and walked into the last fading light of day.

Avá-Canindé followed, and the crowd drifted apart, heading to the *maloca*. Avá-Tapé stayed behind, sitting alone in front of the fire. Tomorrow, his father would lead him into the forest and for the first time since Kuná-Mainó's father died, she would be alone. He had to find her, to give her the necklace. While he stayed in the forest with his father, she could look at it, think of him, and know that when she held it, she held his heart.

He found her in the *maloca* by the fire with the other women. Hiding the necklace behind him, he took her hand. She looked up, smiled and let him pull her to her feet. He heard giggles from the other women as he led her into the night, walking hand in hand down to the fire, away from the others.

Alone beside the dance house, Avá-Tapé pulled her to him, kissed her gently on the forehead and stepped back, letting go of her hand. He paused, savoring the puzzlement on her face, before pulling forth the necklace with a flourish.

Her eyes widened and her mouth formed a small "O". Avá-Tapé felt great happiness when he pulled her close and draped the necklace over her head. She touched the fang and claws and examined them by the light of the fire before turning her back to him. Her shoulders shook.

His heart rose in his throat. "What is it?" he asked. "Don't you like it?"

She faced him again, and he saw tears streaming down her face. "It's beautiful," she whispered, pressing it to her cheek. "No one has ever given me a gift as beautiful as this."

He sighed, and words came forth like rushing water before he could stop himself. "Tomorrow I will go into the forest with my father. When I come back, I will dance with the people. My time alone with you is precious, but you live in my thoughts. Each time you look at this, think of me and know that you live in my heart. Wear it always and know that I am with you. My fang and claws lie over the center of your being to protect your heart with the fierceness of my love."

The crackling of the fire and the mild roar of the surf filled the space between them. A breeze gusted, gently lifting her hair from her face. Bathed in soft firelight, her eyes sparkled and her skin held a warm glow. Every fiber of Avá-Tapé's being ached for her. Shaking back her hair, she took his hand and led him up the beach to a clearing deeper in the forest, far from the *maloca*. Ferns bordered its edge and a cluster of slender trees stood in the middle.

Kuná-Mainó sank to the ground and pulled him down beside her. Avá-Tapé stretched out next to her, cradling her head in the crook of his arm and the two lay on their backs, looking up, neither speaking. A breeze rattled in the palms, and leafy branches stretched black against a sky that darkened to thin transparent blue, still luminous with the day's afterglow. They watched the first stars pierce the darkness with faint spots of light which grew in number until they crowded the sky with brilliance. In the shadows by the trees, other points of light darted, hovered, and disappeared as fireflies danced in the bushes.

Her eyes sparkled like star fire. She kissed him on the cheek and his lips moved to hers. Their tongues danced, parted, and danced again. She pulled her shawl up over her head, revealing breasts, curves, soft skin, and the dark patch between her legs. Avá-Tapé slipped from his loincloth and took her in his arms, pressing his flesh to hers, reveling in the contact. Every part of him felt alive at her touch.

His mouth found hers and their tongues danced again before his lips trailed down her neck. She shivered under his touch and a low, breathy moan rose from deep inside her. His mouth went to hers again and he climbed on top of her. She opened herself to him and let out a throaty moan of pleasure when he slid inside her and the two became one.

SIXTY-THREE

Avá-Tapé stood with his father at the edge of the forest near the beach. The sun shimmered on the horizon, lighting the cresting waves in gold and silver. Each man carried a bow, and arrows, a spear, and a hammock. All the people had come out from the *maloca* to see them off. Avá-Canindé, Avá-Karaí, Santo, Rico, and Kuná-Mainó stood in the morning sunlight, each vowing to eat only plants and purify their spirits so that when the two *país* returned with stronger magic, all would rise easily.

Avá-Tapé's eyes burned from lack of sleep. His body was worn and his limbs heavy. His mind raced as the events of the previous days filled him with images and sensations, each as poignant as when he experienced it, at the same time strangely distant, as if the events hadn't really happened. He couldn't keep his gaze from Kuná-Mainó, whose dreamy eyes stayed on him without wavering. He wished he could stay by her side and never leave.

Avá-Nembiará turned to go and Avá-Tapé followed, stopping to look back at her one more time. She ran to him with open arms. He caught her and pulled her tight.

"Come back safe, my love," she whispered. "My heart is empty without you."

He looked into her eyes and took in her essence, burning her face, scent, and feel into his mind to carry with him on his journey, then he kissed her and trotted up the beach to catch up with his father.

They walked along the shore, away from the place where the bright star of the night shone. Avá-Tapé stayed a few steps behind, his head down and his thoughts on Kuná-Mainó. The two men followed the shoreline until it curved inward before Avá-Nembiará spoke.

"You have taken Kuná-Mainó as your woman," Avá-Nembiará said. "My heart soars for you. She is a good woman. Your mother loved her as her own and hoped for this day. My only sadness comes in knowing she is not here to share your happiness."

Avá-Tapé found no words, and his father said nothing more, so they continued in silence. When the sun had passed above them, Avá-Nembiará turned from the beach and walked into the forest in the direction in which the sun would fall, passing from the wide spaces of the trees near the shore to the denser jungle farther inland. The silence between them felt comfortable. Avá-Tapé needed to free his thoughts from Kuná-Mainó and concentrate on making his spirit lighter. The sooner he and his father made stronger magic, the sooner he could be back by her side.

Shadows lengthened and the overhead growth closed in, bringing the day to an end. Avá-Nembiará chose an open space where they built a small fire and strung their hammocks. After a silent meal of roots and berries, they climbed into their hammocks. Exhausted from the day's walk, Avá-Tapé fell asleep instantly.

The song of the morning bird woke him as it had in the forest near the mission so long ago. Its melody touched his heart. He missed the warmth and company of Kuná-Mainó. Lying with his hands behind his head, he listened to the bird's song floating above the silence. He had grown used to the steady wash of the surf and the cry of the gulls, and until this moment, he hadn't realized how much he missed the morning peace of the forest.

The rest of the birds and animals came to life as the sky brightened. Avá-Tapé sat up, not surprised to see his father's hammock empty. After gathering wood, he sat in front of the fire wondering what Kuná-Mainó would be doing. Avá-Nembiará appeared a short time later with heart of palm and an armload of plants, which he ground into a thick paste that he wrapped inside broad leaves. After splitting the leaf wraps into two piles, he pushed one toward Avá-Tapé and ate the other.

After eating, they went deeper into the forest. Avá-Tapé felt strong, particularly when he thought of how he had felt the day before. It wasn't until they came to the end of the second day that he realized he had no hunger. They made their fire that night without seeking food. As the flames leaped up and the insects sang, Avá-Nembiará broke the silence.

"Tupá has not taken us to the Land Without Evil because our people stand at the end of the world, each having to make his own choice. They need to be apart from us as much as we need to be away from them so they can know the way of their own hearts without our urging."

"What do you mean when you say each has to make his own choice? I thought our people did that when they took the journey."

"The time of destruction has returned. Our people stand at the end of time, at the end of the world before the great waters. They have to choose which path their souls will take."

"Don't they do this when they dance?"

"If they had made the choice, we would be eating at the table of the gods. Deep in their hearts, they haven't chosen…"

"I don't understand. Two paths? Two ends of the world?"

"The bad end comes from the gathering weight of *techó-achy*. Our faults make our souls heavy and powerless to rise to the place that can bring new life. All the time spent at the mission eating food not made by gods, and not living the customs they gave us has made our souls weak. The gathering weight has brought the end of the world by the fleeing of the light. The sun will disappear, and there will be nothing for us to do on this earth. This will be the moment of *ará-kaní*, the last time we see the Earth."

Avá-Tapé's stomach felt queasy. "This is why our people haven't risen with our dance?"

Avá-Nembiará stared into the fire, only half aware that his son had spoken. "It is the only reason I can think of," he said softly.

Avá-Tapé's heart pumped faster. "We have come back to the forest to lighten our spirits..."

"And to give our people the chance to lighten theirs and to let them carry their destinies in their own hands. I do not know Tupá's mind in this. It is a long time since I have had visions. Our people can only make the choice for themselves. We cannot do this for them."

They both fell silent. Since the white men had come, Avá-Tapé had seen more and more death with each passing season. Had their unnatural ways doomed his people? He couldn't accept that. There had to be another way. "Tell me again about the other end of the world."

Avá-Nembiará smiled. "A paradise where great *país* master special arts that lighten their bodies and bring wisdom. Spiritual perfection so great that flames spring from their chests." He threw both arms out in a dramatic gesture and his voice rose. "They defy the pull of the Earth. Their lean bodies rise to fly across the great waters to the Land Without Evil. They lead other dancers on the same magical flight and escape death. It is a real world that lies toward the place where the sun rises. Only dancing believers live there."

"Do their spirits leave their bodies back on the Earth?"

"Going to this new world changes their bodies."

"How do the gods know they are ready? How do they choose?"

"The people show their faith when they change their diet," Avá-Nembiará said. "Their yearning shows in the intensity of their dance and the sincerity of their chant. Their belief changes their bodies into spirit forms."

"The success of our dance is in our people's hands," Avá-Tapé said. "Not ours."

Avá-Nembiará smiled. "Many, many harvests ago, our people migrated to this land in sacred canoes. Our ancestors departed life without dying and left no trail for us to follow. It is they who thunder in the place where the sun comes to the world. They who departed with their bodies of flesh. While those who went away dance, we too dance. In those times, the chief danced and his feet did not touch the Earth. This is why, in order to dance, we eat only what Nanderú has commanded us."

Avá-Tapé and Avá-Nembiará spent days traveling deeper into the forest, while the moon diminished to a sliver. When it began growing fat again, they traveled back toward the place of the rising sun. Each night, Avá-Tapé dreamed wildly, sometimes of dancing with the gods, sometimes of joining with Kuná-Mainó, sometimes of a huge darkness swallowing the sun.

As the moon waxed, his resolve grew with it. The people would dance again on the beach, between the worlds. This time, all their spirits would be strong and light. This time, they would rise easily. He saw a change in his father that tracked the growing light of Yacy. Avá-Nembiará spoke more and more of flying over the great waters, the power growing inside him, and his conviction that their magic had the strength to carry them.

As the moon neared fullness, they ate nothing but the leaf-wrapped herbs, which killed their appetites. They only drank juices and water. The growing sense of his father's power made Avá-Tapé feel stronger than he'd ever felt before.

One evening, they reached the forest near the beach as the last red of the sun rippled over the waters. Anxious to see Kuná-Mainó, Avá-Tapé wanted to travel by the light of the moon, but his father insisted that they spend this last night alone in final preparation for the dance.

They camped near the beach as the moon rose on the horizon and shone full on the waters. Avá-Tapé's heart rose with it. With the new day, he would be back with the one he loved. Hand in hand, they would rise over the waters and live in paradise.

SIXTY-FOUR

Anticipation rushed through Avá-Tapé, keeping him awake long into the night. He imagined over and over how it would be to return to the arms and warmth of Kuná-Mainó. He thought of the look on her face when she saw him returning with powerful magic to lead the people. They would dance and he would take her hand and bring her to the place of the gods where they would be together forever.

He looked up at the pale light of the moon, then down at the shining sand on the beach. Silver-capped waves crashed endlessly on the shore, contrasting with the quiet of the forest and the soft cries of birds and animals. A big sound of power, yet gentle. Moonlight pierced the treetops, striping the trees and spotting the ground with silver. Tomorrow he would dance beneath the moon and rise with Kuná-Mainó to the shimmering doorway to the other world.

He didn't remember falling asleep, but when he opened his eyes, a red-rimmed sky greeted him. He watched it brighten, then joined his father by the fire. Avá-Nembiará handed him a gourd of strong-smelling drink that reminded him of the leaf-wrapped herbs they'd been eating. He drank it in silence, feeling its energy.

When full sunlight came, they followed the shoreline toward the place where the bright star of the night appeared. Avá-Tapé kept getting ahead of his father, then slowing down to wait. He suspected that Avá-Nembiará timed his walk so they would reach the people as the moon rose, when the power of their dance would be the greatest.

When daylight faded, Avá-Tapé kept his eyes trained for signs of the dance house. Soon they would be lighting the fire. His heartbeat quickened when he saw a dark shape. His legs moved faster until he trotted and then broke into a run, reaching the dance house as the last beams of red sunlight flushed the sky.

The structure loomed before him dark and empty. Where were the dancers? The fire? He slowed his breathing, then stilled it, straining to detect signs of the people. The lonely cries of the gulls and the roar of the waves came to him. He looked back to see his father staring at the dance house, his face expressionless.

Kuná-Mainó!

Avá-Tapé's breath stabbed in his chest like lightning. He ran for the forest, scrambling over roots and past trees toward the *maloca*. The acrid smell of old fire bit into his nostrils, shooting an icy pang into his core. His stomach dropped.

A few steps more and he broke into the clearing, seeing the charred and broken frame that had once been the *maloca*. His breath came harder, as if some other force pulled it out of him. Dropping to the ground, his body twitched with his jagged breathing until an anguished cry ripped through him.

No answer came except the endless susurration of the surf and the cry of a lone gull.

SIXTY-FIVE

Time and awareness blurred as cold emptiness engulfed Avá-Tapé. A hand on his shoulder snatched him back. He turned and saw his father staring vacantly at the broken remains of the *maloca*. The dark wings of grief swooped down and stole Avá-Tapé's soul a second time.

When he came back to himself, he sprawled in the dirt, sobbing. He summoned the strength to stand and saw that his father hadn't moved, and that his odd blank expression hadn't changed.

Moonlight highlighted the twisted frame of the *maloca*, making it look like the broken carcass of some great animal. Tears filled Avá-Tapé's eyes, starring his vision with shards of cold silver. He stumbled through the moonlight, trying to make sense of his horror. He could hardly bear it—hardly breathe past it.

A white blur caught his eye from the darkest corner of the *maloca* where part of the wall and a section of roof still hung. He staggered forward, seeing more white, coming to a halt when he recognized skeletons of all sizes huddled in the darkness.

"No. Kuná-Mainó. No," he whispered.

He stared uncomprehending, then his mind began to work slowly, as if in a cocoon, far from his present agony. He saw arms wrapped around smaller skeletons, recognizing the protective postures of mothers. Some clung to each other, the largest those of men. Not all of the people had been burned. What had happened to the others? Had Kuná-Mainó escaped? Had the others been shot by man-hunters? He felt a fleeting hope that they might have been taken to the Land Without Evil, but the reality of the empty dance house crushed it.

"We have to dance," his father said, touching him again on the shoulder.

"Dance?" Avá-Tapé whispered, speaking for the first time. "What kind of dance? Do we dance the *yoasá* to hunt the souls of the dead? Who will be the hunter?" He picked up a charred piece of timber and smashed it against the blackened door frame, causing a section of the roof to collapse. "Who will hit the trees to bring the spirits out?"

"We dance because that is all we have left," his father said.

Avá-Nembiará faded into the moonlight, leaving Avá-Tapé to face the skeletons alone. A short time later, the lone utterances of his father's song floated to him on the night air. Its plaintive cry pulled at his heart, drawing him away from the charred death. As if disconnected from his mind, his feet carried him to the beach, leaving behind the acrid smells of fire and death, for the fresh scent of ocean breezes.

Orange flickered over the sand behind the House of Dances, and embers drifted on the breeze. Avá-Nembiará's voice rose into the night with the flames. Avá-Tapé moved to the front of the dance house and stood before its open side, watching his father shake his rattle and dance.

Tears glistened on Avá-Nembiará's cheeks as emotions flew from him. In the profound sadness of his father's cry, Avá-Tapé heard the anguish of all his people. Avá-Tapé's throat tightened, his vision blurred, and his head began to bob in time with his father's steps. As Avá-Tapé's feet began to move, his own grief bubbled forth in an outpouring of impassioned song and tears.

They danced before the dwindling firelight, seeing no visions and experiencing no magical flight, only release, complete and exhausting, until they collapsed on the sand, spent and drained. Avá-Tapé welcomed the escape that came with sleep, but soon drifted back to consciousness, cringing from the pain that came with the knowledge of his loss. Kuná-Mainó. Gone. The thought possessed him as the brunt of his grief descended, its talons piercing his heart at its core. His stomach knotted, his head throbbed, and his throat grew tight. Sobs wracked him.

When his emotion had spent itself, he became aware of the warm sun on his back, the roar of the surf, and the cry of gulls. Sunlight reflecting off the waves hurt his eyes.

His father had gone. What could he do now? What reason did he have to live? He thought of the burned *maloca*, shuddering at the thought of the huddled skeletons. He couldn't bring himself to look there again, but he had to know if Kuná-Mainó might have escaped.

Feeling oddly detached from all that he did, Avá-Tapé walked the beach and circled the clearing, searching for signs. He found spears and arrows. Moving outward, he caught the sickly sweet odor of death.

Soon he found the remains of a handful of warriors, three of them his own people, one with a spear through his middle. The two others had been shot full of arrows. A number of the enemy lay sprawled, spears and arrows jutting from their bloated corpses.

Too much time had passed. He couldn't recognize any of the dead. He could only tell that they'd been attacked by forest people, not the man-hunters. He examined the tail feathers on the arrows. Red and green. He'd never seen such arrows.

In the days that followed, he wandered in a stupor, searching for Kuná-Mainó, sometimes alone, sometimes following his father. They found only death. Each night, they went back to the dance house and slept on the sand. Neither spoke of the *maloca*, and neither had gone near it since the first night.

The moon faded and then waxed strong again. Avá-Tapé's trepidation grew with the coming of the full moon. His father would want to dance. Avá-Tapé didn't think he had the strength.

"Come," Avá-Nembiará said when the moon shone full on the waters. "We have only the dance, nothing more. We are the last of our people. We must sing to the gods so they will come."

"Our people have been taken by the spirit of *techó-achy*," Avá-

Tapé muttered bitterly. "They have gone the way of the lower souls."

"The ways of the white men weakened their hearts," Avá-Nembiará said. "We live to dance because we are *paí*."

Avá-Tapé saw the resolution in his father's face; he knew it would be useless to argue. Although the fire in his heart had all but gone out, he danced to please his father.

Nothing happened. No miracles, no visions, no signs from Tupá. They waited for another moon, and then another. With each cycle, his father grew more distant.

They spent their days gathering food and sitting in the shade of the dance house gazing over the great waters. Avá-Tapé dreaded the nights and the dreams of Kuná-Mainó that brought him awake to tears and emptiness. When he didn't dream of her, he dreamed of his mother, Pindé, Father Antonio, or one of the others.

Days and nights blurred, and Avá-Nembiará spoke less and less. When he did talk, his words became increasingly incoherent. Avá-Tapé suspected that his spirit wandered in the country of the dead, trying to guide the souls of the lost.

The warm season passed, bringing cooler weather and the first of the rains. Avá-Tapé didn't think he and his father would last long, sleeping in the open-walled dance house on the beach. He pondered what he should do as he and his father sat together one night, watching the rain fall.

"I have seen her," Avá-Nembiará said, as if they had been in the middle of a conversation. "Walking in the darkness of the burned *maloca*."

Avá-Tapé thought he spoke of Kuná-Mainó, until his father continued.

"Kuñá-Ywy Verá comes to me in the night and cries for me to stay with her and our little one. Sometimes when the sun has gone and the night has not yet come, she walks in the shadows. Each time I see her, I find it harder not to follow."

"What of Kuñá-Mainó?" Avá-Tapé blurted. "Have you seen her in the country of the dead? Has she come to you?"

Avá-Nembiará shook his head slowly. "So many come…"

"Have you looked for her?"

His father's eyes locked on his with a hopeless, penetrating stare that Avá-Tapé couldn't bear to hold. He shuddered as cold fingers tickled his spine. They had stayed here at the end of the world long enough. When the new day came they would go back to the forest, away from this place of death to find safety where the magic of the plant spirits grew stronger. To stay would mean that slow death would draw them into the world of lost souls.

If Kuná-Mainó walked among them he would go happily, but he hadn't visited there, and his father didn't say she walked there. Puzzling over his loss, he fell asleep listening to the patter of rain, dreading what might come to him in dreams.

A loud crash jolted him awake. His heart fluttered in confusion. Lightning flashed, illuminating the beach in whiteness. In the flash, he saw Avá-Nembiará dancing and singing in a downpour, his words and movements different from any Avá-Tapé had ever seen. His father's steps quickened and grew jerkier until Avá-Nembiará fell to the ground. He tried to get up, but his legs wouldn't hold.

Avá-Tapé dragged his father back through the wet sand to the shelter of the dance house. Avá-Nembiará's eyes looked wild and far away, as if seeing another world. His skin felt hot. He babbled names and snatches of songs, none of which made sense.

SIXTY-SIX

The rain stopped when daylight returned. Avá-Tapé went into the forest and found a clearing away from the *maloca* where he built a small lean-to and a fire. When it grew warm and comfortable, he went back to the beach and helped his father away from the windy exposure of the open-sided dance house.

Avá-Nembiará coughed and shivered, speaking in a steady stream of disconnected phrases about reaching the center of the universe. Avá-Tapé prepared a hot drink and persuaded his father to drink it.

Avá-Nembiará's fever raged for three days while the rain started and stopped. Their shelter and the growth around them kept them dry.

Avá-Nembiará's fever broke on the fourth day. He sat up and stared into the fire for a long time. "We haven't gone the way of *techó-achy*," he said wearily. "Our magic was strong but our people were weak. The Guarani live in many different places. Some of them live in the forest toward the bright star of the night. We can teach them to dance and still find our way to the Land Without Evil."

"As soon as your strength returns, we are going farther into the forest," Avá-Tapé said. "Away from the end of the world. Away from the great waters. Only death lives here."

"That is what I'm telling you," his father said. "We have to go back to the forest. Back to the center of the world. There our people wait and dream of finding the Land Without Evil. We can lead them."

The thought of leading other people to this place of death wasn't something Avá-Tapé wanted to consider; nor did he want to talk of it. Nothing had meaning anymore, not even the dance. He had lost everything he loved. He had danced with all his strength and had found only emptiness. He had no heart for anything more, but he needed a reason to take his father back into the forest. "When you are strong again, we will journey back to the center of the world and search for the Guarani."

Two days later, they began their journey, moving slowly through the forest toward the place between the setting sun and the bright star of the night.

Full moons came and went, but they didn't dance. Avá-Nembiará's health wouldn't allow it. They saw signs of other people, but had no contact until Avá-Tapé awoke one morning to see a lone hunter standing beside the fire. Avá-Tapé eyed his own spear, then looked back at the man, recognizing his armbands and headdress. He stood tall with big hands, broad shoulders, and a flat nose that reminded Avá-Tapé of Avá-Guiracambí.

"How do you come to be here?" the man asked in accented Guarani.

Avá-Tapé could find no words.

"We are *paí* of the Guarani," his father said, appearing from the trees behind him.

"I am Guarani." The man pointed to himself. "I have never seen you or your people in this part of the forest."

"We have been in search of the Land Without Evil," Avá-Nembiará said. "We have danced at the end of the earth, but the spirits of our people have been taken by the darkness of *techó-achy*. We are the only ones left whose magic is strong enough to live, but we have lost all. We have only our dance."

The man's face brightened. "Our men dance tonight," he said. "The face of Yacy is full. We hope to hear the voice of Tupá or Kuarahy."

Avá-Nembiará beamed. "My son and I have heard the voice of Tupá."

The man's eyes widened. "You have heard Tupá?"

"He has given me a song," Avá-Tapé said.

When the man spoke again, he lowered his voice and looked at the ground. "It would be a great honor if you would dance with us."

"The honor is ours," Avá-Nembiará said.

They spent the better part of the day following the man through the forest, reaching a village as the sun fell. A warm feeling came over Avá-Tapé when they smelled cooking and heard voices. Seeing *malocas* and hearing the children's noisy play made his heart shrink. How long had it been since he and his father had danced? He wondered if his father's health would allow it.

"Our people are strong," the warrior said, interrupting his thoughts. "Many of them have come from around us, chased from their villages by white men. Our numbers are shrinking, and the Earth is growing old, but we stay together and keep each other safe."

Avá-Tapé smiled. "You are a wise man."

"I only wish to see our people strong again. Come, the fire is built. We will dance and then talk of other things."

Avá-Tapé's excitement rose when he saw the other men wearing headdresses and face paint. The sound of their rattles brought out long dormant feelings. He looked up and saw the full moon shining low and orange on the horizon. The sky held no clouds.

"Their magic is strong," Avá-Nembiará said quietly. "They will see the power of our dance. Together our magic can take us to the Land Without Evil."

The men stood around the bonfire arrayed in feathers and paint. Avá-Tapé felt attention centered on him and his father, the way it had been in the old days.

"We would be honored if you would lead us," the warrior said, to Avá-Tapé's surprise.

Avá-Nembiará nodded and looked to his son. Avá-Tapé felt queasy, but tried not to show his discomfort. His father rose and the other dancers stepped back, making room.

Avá-Nembiará began the same way he had so many times before, his steps coming sure and strong, as if he'd never been weakened. Avá-Tapé looked at the other dancers and saw awe in their faces at the power of his father's song and dance. He felt his own body move with that of his father.

The intensity of his own song frightened Avá-Tapé as passion and emotions he had not felt for so long flew from him like birds, taking away all the pain and loss he had experienced. The ring of dancers stepped back wide-eyed and open mouthed when he cried out. Stunned gasps and whispers came from them, but Avá-Tapé barely heard.

Tears filled his eyes as his song joined with his father's. Their movements fell into rhythm, father and son dancing as one. The other dancers did not join. They only watched.

The old familiar burning came to Avá-Tapé's chest and sweat came to his eyes, mixing with his tears. As in the old days, his thoughts lightened as though they would float from his body. His father moved fluidly, then began jerking the way he did before Tupá would speak.

Avá-Nembiará twitched and spasmed, then dropped to the ground. His eyes widened, his face contorted and his mouth twisted. Avá-Tapé expected to see the face of Tupá looming over his father's at any moment, but Tupá did not appear. Instead, Avá-Nembiará reared back, spreading his arms wide as if embracing the cosmos, and pushed his chest out. Avá-Tapé saw flames spring from him, erupting in sparks of silver that coalesced into the shimmering form of a gossamer bird, which took wing. Its sparkling form merged with the rising sparks of the fire, spiraling up into the starlit sky, its essence becoming one with the stars.

"*Kandire*," Avá-Tape whispered as his father's body jerked twice and went slack. Avá-Nembiará's eyes widened the same way the eye of the boar had when Avá-Tapé took its life. The same way the jaguar's had in the muddy streets of the mission.

The eye of death.

Silence fell over the gathering. Avá-Tapé looked up and saw a cloud pass before the moon. Avá-Nembiará stared into nothingness, his body motionless as a rock. Avá-Tapé went to his father's side and closed Avá-Nembiará's eyes. The others stayed back, hushed whispers expressing their confusion.

Avá-Tapé understood, even as emptiness engulfed him. He was alone in the world. The only one left of his people. His father's prophecy and visions had come true. The end of the world had come, and Avá-Tapé had seen it. He had danced with his people. His father. His brothers. Now he had only the dance. The knowledge. The history. No one else had lived to see it. None of his family lived so he might pass his knowledge on the way his father had passed it to him.

He danced alone.

He felt vaguely aware of people gathering around him and then heard a woman's cry. He looked up through tears and saw a necklace of pink shells, with a jaguar fang and two claws hung from its middle, then he saw a face that touched his heart. Her eyes spoke to him saying more than words could ever say.

SIXTY-SEVEN

Avá-Tapé stared up at the blurred visage of Kuná-Mainó, thinking that a cruel vision had come to him, until she wrapped her arms around his neck and he held her close. He tried to speak but his words caught in his throat.

"How?" he whispered between sobs. "How did you escape?"

They clung together, her cheek pressed to his, their tears mixing. "I was out gathering roots near the marshes when I heard screams and smelled smoke," she said in a trembling voice. "I ran to the *maloca* and saw the evil ones destroying everything. I saw none of our people, so I ran back into the marshes to hide and lost my way in the darkness. I wandered for days toward the bright star of the night until a hunting party from this village found me."

The crowd parted, making room for a fierce warrior. The man, wearing a full headdress, armbands, and face paint, knelt in front of Avá-Tapé. The set of his jaw reminded Avá-Tapé of Avá-Karaí, though in the man's face he saw his father, then Avá-Canindé and Avá-Guiracambí—as if all of those he had loved and lost now lived in this man. The warrior's stare penetrated Avá-Tapé, softening, when he asked:

"*Paí*, will you lead us in dance?"

AFTERWORD

As we enter the 21st century, the Guarani Indians of South America are still facing the struggle for survival that has plagued them since the European conquest of the Americas 500 years ago. Prior to that invasion, the Guarani were driven to search for the paradise promised by their myths: the Land Without Evil.

During the 18th and 19th centuries, the threat of extinction brought on by disease, slavery, and massacre lent urgency to their quest. Fear of world destruction shook their society and world order, and the shaman rose to the highest level of importance as the route to salvation.

Impelled by hope and anxiety, masses of Guarani, inspired by their shaman-prophets, abandoned their homes and set out for the promised land. Against devastating odds, one group, led by the shaman-prophet Nimbiarapony, arrived at the sea via the route that follows the Rio Tieté. Nimbiarapony soon realized the impossibility of crossing over to the Land Without Evil from the eastern seaboard and decided to follow an alternate tradition, which located the promised land not on the world's eastern periphery but at its center.

All but two people died during the trek.

Undaunted, Nimbiarapony returned to Mato Grosso, gathered a new following, and set out across Ivinhema and the state of Paraná in search of the center of the universe. After 35 years of mystical wanderings across rugged and treacherous terrain, Nimbiarapony died, still on the march, in 1905.

Today, the struggle for survival is more intense than ever. In Brazil alone, the Guarani commit suicide at a rate that's 50 times greater than that of the general poplutaion—the highest suicide rate among all native peoples in the Americas. The Guarani attribute this to the weakening of their traditions.

To this day, the quest for spiritual transcendence retains its poignancy for the Guarani, who continue to sct out on messianic wanderings in search of the Land Without Evil.

Acknowledgments

First and foremost, I want to thank Dr. Lawrence Sullivan, Director of Harvard University Center for the Study of World Religions, for his support, encouragement, and for *Icanchu's Drum*, which inspired me, along with Professor Chuck Wallace and his Forest of Symbols course at San Diego Mesa College. I also owe thanks to the work of Miguel Alberto Bartolomé, and to Dr. Stanley Krippner for his enthusiasm and encouragement.

I'd like to thank my mother, Colleen Kennedy, for her support and selflessness, and Joan Oppenheimer, my literary mother, for teaching me so much. From the heart, thanks to Lynn Ford, Ashley Butler Geist, Rick Geist, John H. Ritter, Ken Reeth, Eric Hart, Mark Clements, Nancy Holder, Laura Taylor, Hodge Crabtree, Eileen Alcorn, Howard Hendrix, Shawn Terry, Gerry Williams, Jim Healy, Bill Relling, Bob Holt, Victor Villaseñor, David Brin, Paul Lapolla, Kara Meredith, Myra Westphall, Harold Bloomfield, and Jerry Hannah for all their help, friendship, and support. Heartfelt thanks to Antoinette Kuritz for her belief when I lost mine, and to Barbara Villaseñor for taking up the torch.

More thanks to my brother Mike Pallamary, his family, my sisters Colleen Buckley and Heather D'Agostino and their families for their love, encouragement, and support for my madness. I will always be indebted to all the members of my literary family, the Santa Barbara Writer's Conference, for all their support, inspiration, and friendship—especially Paul Lazarus, Bill Downey, Barnaby Conrad, Mary Conrad, Ray Bradbury, Sid Stebel, Charles (Sparky) Schulz, Monte Schulz, Charles Champlin,

Shelley Lowenkopf, Phyllis Gebauer, Tony Gibbs, Abe Polsky, Bill Wilkins, John Daniel, Fred Klein, Susan Gulbransen, Peri Longo, Joan Bowden, Marilee Zdenek, Anita Kornfeld, Jan Curran, and Frances Halpern.

And a special thanks to Amy Ray and Emily Saliers, The Indigo Girls, whose honesty and passion carried me through the darkness. World Falls.